Wrought by Fire

Wrought by Fire

Book One of:

The Arcadian Complex

Paul James Keyes

ISBN 978-0-9862101-0-5

Published in the United States by Odysseus Publishing.
OdysseusPublishing.com

Cover artwork by Cameron McCool.
Internal artwork and design by Paul James Keyes.

This is a work of fiction. Names, characters, places, and
incidents either are the product of the author's imagination or
are used fictitiously. Any resemblance to actual persons, living
or dead, events, or locales is entirely coincidental.

Visit us at ArcadianComplex.com or like the series at
Facebook.com/ArcadianComplex to become an honorary
Arcadian!

"Any sufficiently advanced technology
is indistinguishable from magic"
-Arthur C. Clarke

Table of Contents

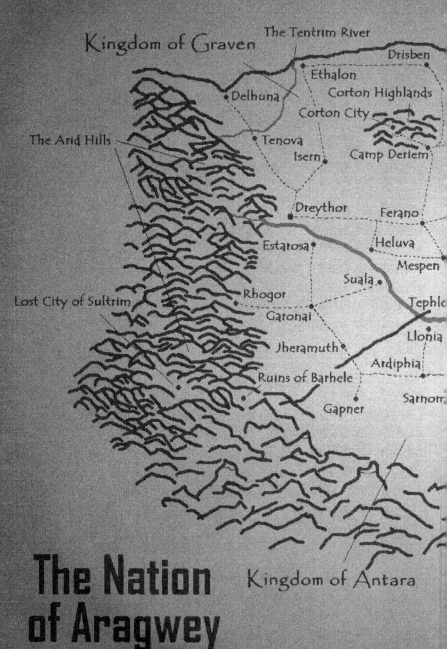

The Northern Sea

Kingdom of Graven

The Tentrim River

Drisben

Ethalon

Corton Highlands

Delhuna

Corton City

The Arid Hills

Tenova

Isern

Camp Deriem

Dreythor

Ferano

Estarosa

Heluva

Mespen

Suala

Rhogor

Garonai

Tephlo

Lost City of Sultrim

Llonia

Jheramuth

Ardiphia

Ruins of Barhele

Sarnom

Gapner

The Nation
of Aragwey

Kingdom of Antara

CHAPTER
1

Enslaved

Clutching her knees tightly to her stomach, the young woman sobbed. She became as small as possible, but it did little to relieve the discomfort of her cramped cage. She could neither escape the sting in her flesh, nor the overwhelming sense of dread that had settled deep within her bones. She carefully shifted her tender backside against the meshing of chicken wire and iron rods of the cage wall. There was no reprieve for her battered muscles.

Her weeping grew stronger as the carriage bumped down the remote country road. Hope of ever again seeing home waned faster with every passing league. Condensation from her breath filled the lightless back compartment of the carriage – every inhale an arduous task in the wet heat. It was truly a test of her resolve to continue living – three days since Salvine Welin was taken.

The darkness of the compartment was nearly absolute, but she could still make out eight or nine other wire cages surrounding her. Apart from a yellow dog located in the cage two over, all the rest were empty. Salvine's whimpers roused the canine. The dog's eyes opened, reflecting as two green dots in the diffused light that entered through the narrow cracks in the carriage's side boards. It picked its head up, instantly growling in Salvine's direction.

Salvine clamped her dirt-stained fingers over her mouth as another bout of uncontrollable sobs wracked her body. She knew what would happen if she enticed the dog to start barking again. The greasy-haired Antaran man driving the carriage wasn't much of a talker, but he did enjoy using his wicked riding crop on Salvine whenever any noise escaped the back compartment, regardless of whether she or the dog had been responsible for the commotion. She saw from her captor's twisted smile that he drew a sick pleasure from her suffering. He had pulled her from her cage and whipped her mercilessly until her skin was so raw and blistered that she felt like one giant welt. The man only ceased the beating after Salvine completely cried herself out and collapsed down into a motionless lump on the ground for several minutes.

The sting was endless, her sense of time shattered by her imprisonment. Within the confines of her cage, minutes passed like hours, making every waking moment drag by as if she were underwater with only a shallow breath as company. She was a stone, trapped beneath the surface of a pond. Her body wriggled with panic as the pressure in her lungs swelled almost beyond what she could endure.

She stared into the shine of the dog's emotionless eyes. "Easy boy, I'm not going to hurt you," she whispered into the darkness, hoping to calm the animal. The dog tensed up at her words. It would rip her throat out given half a chance. Silent tears streaked Salvine's cheeks. She dared not make another sound until the dog grew bored and laid its head back down between its paws.

She should have never trusted Maswald Baltren – if that had even been the man's real name. The young peddler from out of town had intrigued her. Something about his dark eyes and suave tongue put a flutter in her stomach, blinding her to his true intentions. Not for a moment did she suspect the hint of danger in his smile was not the exciting kind, but rather the type that would land her in a cage in the back of a carriage. Maswald sold her for a measly handful of silver marks – barely enough to buy a night at the inn and a decent meal. He never once looked back as the greasy man stuffed her in the cramped cage, already too far out from the edge of Darrenfield for anyone to hear her cries as the carriage rolled away.

Home was a distant memory in the slowly ticking misery that was now her captive life. She wanted to believe that her family would find and rescue her, but she knew the chances of that happening were dwindling fast as the days since her abduction multiplied. With nowhere else to turn, Salvine clutched her hands together against her chest and prayed to the great Goddess, Mast, for an end to her torment.

Dangling from a thin silver bracelet on Salvine's left wrist, the charm Javic Elensol had given her the week before brushed up against her bare skin. She had nearly forgotten she was wearing it. The metal was cool to the touch, but did little to diminish the heat that had soaked her blouse in sweat. She hoped the charm would bring her good luck. It depicted an ancient bird that had long ago gone extinct – a white dove with elegant wings spread wide; once a symbol of peace and love.

She rubbed the flat edge of the charm between her forefinger and thumb and imagined herself somewhere far away. She pretended the heat was a warm breeze blowing off the Gulf of Nerim; her tiny cage a lounge chair atop a balcony attached to one of the grand, sprawling castles that lined those shores. She sat with Javic, such a sweet boy, as the other lords and ladies of the house came up to dine before the sunset, watching from behind their parapets as the waves of jade lapped against the white stone shore. She had never been to the Gulf of Nerim, but her grandmother had spoken fondly of her years there before she passed.

Only recently had Salvine's thoughts of Javic turned romantic in nature. He wasn't her usual type – quiet, but kind; strong, but gentle – she typically went for men more like Maswald Baltren who had that certain flair of excitement about them, but she was starting to rethink her taste. She had been friends with the Elensol boy ever since her family moved to Darrenfield four years ago when she was thirteen.

Back then Javic was just a scrawny twelve-year-old kid, too shy to step out from behind his grandfather's mare as they welcomed her family to town. Javic changed much in the last four years. He was still shy, but he wasn't a little boy anymore. Javic managed to work up the courage to give Salvine the beautiful charm that now dangled from her wrist. Oh how she regretted denying him the kiss he attempted to plant on her lips at the conclusion of their last visit together. He caught her off-guard. Salvine needed a little time to think things through before making that sort of leap with her longtime friend. She had plenty of time to think now, locked away in her cage – if only it were possible to turn back the clock.

The carriage slowed as the terrain became bumpier. The wires drove themselves deeper into Salvine's flesh, drawing her back to the present as she readjusted her position. The scent of spoiled meat started to seep through the floorboards as they went on. The retched odor wafted across her body and up her nose.

She struggled to place the smell.

It fanned the flames of fear in her heart.

The carriage lurched to a stop. The horses whinnied in a nervous chatter as her captor climbed down from his seat and walked around to unlock the back of the carriage. Even the dog, usually excited for a chance to step out and stretch its limbs, cowered against the back of its cage as the door swung open and the stink of rot fully permeated the compartment.

After being in the dark for so long, the intense glow of outside placed white spots on Salvine's vision. She couldn't tell where her tears ended and the watering of her eyes from the brightness began. The greasy man held his crop in his left hand – an ever present threat while he unlocked the front of Salvine's cage.

He didn't give her a chance to crawl out.

Reaching in with his free arm, he grabbed a handful of her tangled locks.

Salvine yelped as a sickening tug brought her across the threshold of the cage. Most of the hair the man had gripped onto was torn free from her scalp. She fell from the back of the carriage, landing jarringly on her knees and forearms against the rocky surface below. Her whole head felt like it was on fire. Her scalp was bleeding freely. The sticky heat flowed over her ears, mixing with sweat as it dripped down the back of her neck in thick globs. Salvine dropped her face to the ground, staying completely still. She prepared herself for the beating that was surely imminent.

The greasy man grimaced slightly as he shook the detached clump of hair from his fingers. "Get up," he commanded whilst wiping his grimy palms on his already discolored trousers. "We're late."

Salvine's agony prevented her from finding her feet, but after only a moment she felt the man's arms grip her around the waist and hoist her upright.

"I said get a move on!" He gave her a sharp shove towards the front of the carriage.

Salvine barely managed to stay on her feet. She continued forward, placing one foot in front of the other in carefully measured steps, nearly falling each time. "Where are you taking me?" she dared ask.

There was a moment of silence followed by a solid knock against her skull, just behind her left ear. Salvine flinched. It only hurt for a second. She paused, glancing back in confusion. The Antaran man's face held an infuriating grin.

The asshole actually flicked me!

Her eyes sharpened into a glare. He gave her another shove. Salvine barely stumbled this time, the blood in her legs finally beginning to circulate after being stagnant for so long in the cage. The Antaran man chuckled audibly, amused by her irritation.

As bright as it had appeared to be outside when the carriage door was first opened, now that her eyes were adjusted it was obvious that the first stages of dusk had already settled in across the clear sky. The smell of rotting flesh strengthened as they stepped off the main road and onto a narrow trail, overgrown with roots and thorny brush. The deathly scent at her front terrified her more than the man at her back.

After walking for several minutes, the reek became undeniably pungent. It hung in the air like a thick sludge. Salvine didn't know what could cause such a stench, but that did not stop her imagination from dredging up possibilities.

A mass grave, ripe and fermenting in the sun?

Will that be my fate – to join a mound of flesh as it putrefies and slowly returns to the earth?

Salvine gagged at the mental image of gravel-hoppers and legged-worms crawling across her decomposing face. Stomach bile bubbled angrily against the base of her esophagus in an attempt to escape. Her insides were already empty. She hadn't been given a bite to eat during her time in the cage, leaving her head spinning from starvation.

She was so distracted by her churning belly that she almost didn't notice the motionless figure standing amongst the trees off to the left of the trail. It was too large to be a man, but it stood upright on two legs, hairless and naked, its wrinkled manhood fully exposed between its tree-trunk-thick legs. Its body was covered in bulging tumors atop dense, gnarled muscles – a frozen statue of pulsating flesh – truly a beast of nightmarish proportions. It followed her movement between the foliage with its black, beady eyes, never blinking. There was nothing human about the way it watched her. Waves of dread replaced Salvine's nausea as she looked upon the unnatural creature.

I've lost my mind....

She wondered briefly if perhaps the lack of food was causing her to see things that did not really exist. She rubbed her eyes and shook her head, but still the monster remained, standing tall like a stone sentinel in the fading light. Other than its eyes, too small on its deformed face, and its undulating tumors, the creature's only movement came in the form of a slow wiggle in its curved claws – long enough to rival a bear's.

"Keep movin'," said her captor, prodding her on a course that took her uncomfortably close to the savage beast.

To Salvine's added horror, she soon realized the monster was not the only one of its kind. Up ahead, more creatures lined the path – some obscured by the trees, others out in the open, all standing as perfectly still as the first beast. Only their eyes moved, following Salvine with unwavering concentration as if she were a steak dinner about to be delivered to their plates.

"Meister Creany," said a man's voice from up ahead in the brush, "what do you bring me on this fine evening?"

For the first time, Salvine's captor was hesitant to move forward. He took a deep breath before urging Salvine once more in the direction of the speaker. "A girl, Your Greatness," he said once he had found his voice. "A young one, just like you asked."

Together, Salvine and her captor, Creany, stepped out of the brush and into a makeshift camp. A narrow tent stood between two trees and a small fire smoldered in the hollowed-out pit of a stump. An older man with graying hair sat by the fire – he was the only person in the clearing. The man crossed his legs casually as he sat back farther atop a massive chunk of limestone he was using as a chair.

"Just one?" the gray man asked, not hiding any of his disappointment. His eyes seemed to glow yellow in the light from the campfire. He glanced over at Salvine before returning his attention to her captor. "And so skinny…. You should have been able to get at least five more by now."

Creany sneered at the older man. "It's gettin' harder to find the young ones," he said. "The people are growin' wary of strangers – they think it's the gypsies that be takin' um…."

The older man didn't respond. He continued to stare at Creany in the dim light until the silence became uncomfortable.

Creany folded first. "I'll have more for you next time," he said, looking away from the older man's intense stare. "Headed north tonight – better pickin's nearer the coast I 'spect."

"By next time it will already be too late," said the gray man. "The one I'm searching for will appear somewhere in this region in exactly two days' time. I need more Whunes immediately in order to conduct my search."

Creany simply shrugged. "I got what I got," he said. "Ain't nothin' can change that. You gunna pay me for this one or no? I want to get a move on before it gets dark."

The gray man's eyes flashed yellow again – this time Salvine wasn't sure the firelight had anything to do with the color change. "Payment?" he asked, uncrossing his legs and climbing to his feet. "Why yes, I believe I've got exactly what you deserve right here."

Salvine noted the shift in the older man's tone, though Creany still appeared blissfully unaware of the danger that was growing before him. The gray man pushed back the wide sleeves of his cloak, exposing the bone-white flesh of his hands. He extended his narrow fingers out one at a time, flexing them back slightly in turn. He was a coiled snake, readying a strike.

Meister Creany's eyes went wide, finally sensing the older man's nefarious intentions. He glanced over at Salvine, a momentary expression of dumbfounded horror spreading across his face as he realized his life was already forfeit. Before Creany could utter a word, the gray man lifted a pale hand and gestured towards him with a swatting motion. Creany's head whipped to the side, though there had been no physical contact – ten wide paces still separated the two men. With another gesture from the older man, Creany fell to his knees.

"Please, Wilgoblikan!" he cried out. "Don't!"

"Don't? You dare give me an order?"

"I'm sorry!" said Creany. "Please, Wilgoblikan, I didn't mean—"

"You disappoint me," interrupted the gray man, "but fear not, I will make you useful to me once more."

Salvine's breath caught in her chest as she watched the exchange in confused horror. She began to back away from Creany as the older man, Wilgoblikan, extended his other hand out from under his black, tattered cloak.

Creany slumped over onto the ground and started to convulse, a gurgling scream escaping from his throat. The guttural noise pierced the quiet evening, growing louder and louder until the greasy man's vocal chords tore from the strain. He continued to expend air from his lungs, but the sound turned into a raspy hiss.

Salvine stood in petrified silence, not knowing what to do as her former captor began to transform into… *something else*.

His skin was glowing like the embers of the fire – the light seemed to escape from his pores as he thrashed from side to side. His arms and torso bulged outward. His skin tore open as it expanded, but then instantly mended itself again before his blood had a chance to seep out. His clothing grew tight and then shredded along the seams as the inner pressure became too great for the fabric to withstand.

Creany, already a hefty man to begin with, swelled up to over twice his original size, tumors and muscles poking out seemingly at random all across his body. His veins pulsated frantically beneath his lumpy skin, forming black lines that started at his heart and quickly spread to his extremities. His head drooped like an overripe pumpkin, bulging out faster to the sides than it did upward. A short snout began to protrude from his jaw while his teeth multiplied and elongated into points – just like the monsters Salvine had seen on her walk from the carriage. His torn vocal chords had transformed as well, allowing a low howl to erupt from his throat in a pitch that was no longer in a range meant for humans.

By the time his fingers began to form into claws, Salvine was already running back through the forest towards the carriage. The other monsters that had lined the path on her approach with Creany were nowhere to be seen. She kept her eyes forward, not daring to check behind her. Thorns tore at her ankles as she crashed through the brush with complete abandonment. Her heart felt like it was going to explode from beating too fast, but she pushed onwards. Her life depended on maintaining a quick pace.

Creany's howls grew distant and eventually ceased. The silence was somehow even more terrifying than the animalistic wails. Her pulse pounded against her eardrums. She gasped for more air to power her straining legs. Ahead of her, about thirty-five paces, Salvine spotted the road. It was a straightaway from here. She risked a brief glance backwards. To her extreme relief, there was no motion behind her. So far as she could tell, she was not being followed, but she did not let that slow her strides. Only when her legs began to give out did she allow her aching muscles to ease up.

She reached the rocky dirt road at a jog and began to scour the area for the carriage. It was nowhere to be seen. Looking behind her again, she realized that the trailhead was narrower and more concealed than before when Creany had first guided her onto it. In her rushed panic she had accidentally diverged onto a different pathway! The horses and carriage were probably just out of sight in one direction or the other down the winding road. There was no way of telling which direction.

She was wasting too much time. Salvine turned left and started running again. It was a completely random choice. The sky had dimmed since she first tumbled from the carriage, making it difficult to see very far up the road. She imagined going around the next curve and seeing the horses, patiently waiting for their master to return. After running for several minutes she was still yet to see any sign of the carriage. She must have chosen the wrong direction.

Her run tapered back into a jog, and then finally into a walk, her legs too tired to keep going. She stopped altogether and looked back behind her.

A dark figure stepped out from the trees. Wilgoblikan. He was only a hundred paces back! Beneath his menacing hood, his yellow eyes were already locked onto hers. He emerged fully from the brush on the side of the road, his gaze never once leaving her face. His long strides made him appear to glide as he steadily closed the gap.

Salvine turned and ran, fighting the burn in her legs with every ounce of determination she had left. Knowing how close Wilgoblikan was, she couldn't stop herself from peering back. Although he never seemed to increase his pace, Salvine found that he was closing on her between every one of her stolen glances. Suddenly, there was a gloriously wonderful sound. A horse whinnied up ahead in the distance.

It's close! Just a little bit farther up the road!

The confirmation that she was on the right track reinvigorated her body, giving her legs the extra little boost of energy they needed to continue on. She bumbled down the road, unsteady but managing, still clinging to the hope of escape… she had to escape, or else she would never get to tell Javic Elensol her true feelings.

I do want to kiss him!

It can't end here. Not like this! Not when I still have so many regrets.

Wilgoblikan was only about fifty paces back now, half of her lead already eaten up. If she could manage to reach the carriage before he caught her, she was certain she could ride away faster than he could pursue on foot! The carriage appeared in the dying light, the horses waiting right where

Meister Creany stopped them. Salvine felt a giddiness in her chest that counteracted her exhaustion.

I made it! After three long days of torture and dread, I'm nearly free! She could hardly believe it!

Time seemed to slow down as several monsters burst from the tree line, instantly slamming into the side of the nearest horse. The pair of horses, hooked side by side, went down together. Their momentum, combined with that of the monsters, flipped the entire carriage over onto its side. The beasts instantly tore into the screaming horses. Vicious teeth and claws pulled out strands of tendon and shredded organs as the horses thrashed violently in their final terrible moments.

Salvine's hope was shattered. She dropped to her knees, her body finally giving in to fatigue. She had nowhere to go. The horses fell silent, the last pulses of life draining from the gaping wounds in their sides. Only the grunts of the monsters and the gnashing of teeth remained as the teardrops began to roll down Salvine's cheeks.

"Impressive, aren't they?" came a voice from behind her.

Salvine pivoted around to face the man who had created the abominations. Wilgoblikan was already standing right above her. They had both come a long distance in a very short amount of time. There was no sign of the exhaustion Salvine was experiencing reflected in the man's wrinkled face. While Salvine was panting for air, Wilgoblikan appeared as if he had only just now stood up from his seat in the clearing.

Salvine tried to scoot away from the awful man. He gestured towards her, clenching his slender fingers into a tight fist. A pinch started in Salvine's gut, and then extended out to her every joint and muscle. She was frozen in place. It was as if she were encased in stone. Every muscle cramped at once, holding her rigid. She strained against the invisible bonds, but even as sweat flowed from her temples, she could not break free. Her muscles soon fell to fatigue. Salvine's shoulders drooped in defeat.

"Good girl," Wilgoblikan said, reaching out and stroking her chin with the back of his hand. "Are you ready?" he asked, his mouth curling into an amused grin.

Salvine stared up into the face of evil. "You're a monster!" she said.

Wilgoblikan winked a yellow eye.

"I…" said Salvine, "I don't want to die…."

Wilgoblikan held her face with both hands now. He had a surprisingly soft touch; his fingers wiping the moisture of her tears from her cheekbones before sliding down her delicate neck and lingering over her collarbone. "You're young," he said. "The young almost always survive. You're not going to die. You'll just be… stronger… better." He stared deeply into her eyes while continuing to caress her pretty face.

Wilgoblikan's expression did not change as Salvine felt her body begin to tear apart. She had never experienced anything so excruciating in her entire life. Her whole existence melted away. Her figure oozed – expanding, tearing, growing. Every nerve screamed as if she had been engulfed by flames. Her muscles contracted all at once yet again as her body stretched outward despite their protest. Wilgoblikan released her face, but continued his terrible work. Her head suddenly felt too heavy and nodded down towards her chest. She was becoming one of his disgusting monsters. She watched as the tumorous growths began to form across her arms and quickly expanding torso. All of her clothing fell away in tatters just as her fingers elongated and sharpened into bony claws.

* * *

The water lapped against Salvine's feet. She curled her toes in the sand. The cooling sensation of the waves wiped away the memory of all that had come before. A slight wind brought the scent of salt and the sound of distant singing to her ears from somewhere across the water. The song grew louder as her head drifted back and forth with her shifting equilibrium.

Her vision was too blurry to focus on anything. She knew something wasn't right, but her scattered mind started to release the thought almost before she had a chance to grasp onto it. She was in the Gulf of Nerim, and her grandmother was in the distance, hanging some fresh laundry out to dry in the breeze. Her grandmother smiled at her, eyes flashing yellow as she beckoned Salvine over.

Yellow? An image of the terrible man with his yellow eyes tore its way back into Salvine's mind.

"No!" she yelled out to no one in particular, refusing to give in to the fantasy world that surrounded her. "This isn't real!"

She tried to wake up. In response, the sand instantly turned to rocks beneath her, their sharp ridges cutting into the flats of her feet. She tried to step backwards, but the water thickened into a sticky slime, refusing to release its grasp on her ankles as the sting of the jagged rocks grew harsher still. A cold wind whipped around her, bombarding her with blast after relentless blast of course beach sand. The granules slowly ground away at her exposed flesh.

"Salvine!" called Javic. His joyful voice cut through the howling gusts like a ray of sunlight across the morning sky.

The sludge around Salvine's feet loosened just enough for her to turn and face him.

As Javic drew near, his smile quickly faded. He slowed his approach. Concern entered his eyes as he scanned them back and forth across Salvine's body. He stopped just in front of her. His eyes narrowed into a guarded expression.

What is he staring at?

Javic's worry gave way to a sneer that was unnatural to his face. "You're a monster!" he shouted, recoiling. "I could never love a hideous beast like you!"

The words cut deeper than a sword.

The elements resurged around Salvine. The singing in the air shifted, the tones becoming dissonant and climbing in pitch like the wind during a raging storm. The melody turned into screams – her own screams, she realized – echoing out from some distant place as the wind ripped at her deformed body. Tumors suddenly bubbled to the surface of her skin – angry pustules bursting from the ever increasing internal pressure. They spewed their vile discharge across her body until every bit of her was slick with the black secretions.

She had changed.

I truly am *a monster....*

Javic's face twisted with hatred as he lashed out with both fists. Salvine fell back. The sludgy water was beginning to boil, slowly dissolving her goopy flesh like acid. Javic forced his palms against her face, pressing her down beneath the surface of the paralyzing tide.

He only saw a monster.

The pressure of Javic sitting on her chest forced the breath from her lungs.

She gasped for more air.

The waves lapped over the top of her nose, sending stinging water down her throat instead. The burning currents surged within her, consuming her from the inside out.

Even without air, she did not drown.

This was her new prison, she realized, one from which there would be no escape.

* * *

The shell of what was once Salvine bit down hard on her tongue, drawing blood as her jaw and teeth turned into the muzzle of a beast. The metallic taste was soothing in her mouth. It excited her in ways she could not understand. Her whole body tingled with the raw energy as the blood coated the inside of her mouth and dribbled down into her stomach. She wanted more – fresh blood; to tear out something's throat and feel its life drain into her. Just thinking about killing made her insides quiver.

"Go on," said her master. "Join your brethren." Wilgoblikan sensed her insatiable need.

She did not hesitate; dropping down to all fours and bounding towards the overturned carriage. Her vision was more vivid than ever before. The dim environment looked as clear as it would have on the sunniest of days. She could smell the yellow dog before she could see it, still trapped within its overturned cage. Wilgoblikan had commanded her brothers and sisters to leave it for her. With one swipe of her massive arm she tore the backdoor right off its hinges. With the next strike, the chicken wire turned to scrap, releasing the frightened animal. It wanted to run, but she would not let it get away. It knew it was cornered now and bit at her hand as she grasped onto its snout. The dog's teeth sank into her flesh, but she felt no pain. She applied pressure with her palm, pinning the dog's head against the shattered wall of the carriage. She straddled the defenseless animal between her thighs – gaining complete control.

With one claw, she poked at its side, feeling the warmth of its insides spilling out. The dog screamed and flailed in vain beneath her massive weight. She could not resist the magnetic pull of its suffering. The excitement pushed her into a frenzy! Craning her neck down, she exposed her jagged teeth and slowly bit into the softest part of the dog's underbelly. The fur and flesh combined in her mouth. Warm juices flowed down her chin. It was the most delightful of sensations. For an instant, she was completely satiated, but then the dog succumbed to its wound and expired beneath her. The craving to kill returned in full force, flooding every fiber of her being like a rushing river.

Wilgoblikan was standing beside her again. She looked up at him in frustration; her eyes begging him for another kill.

Don't worry, he projected the words into her mind, his voice booming within her skull though no words were actually spoken. A slight twinkle appeared in his expression. "There will be much more to come," he said out load, "very soon."

CHAPTER

2

Fuel for the Fire

Riding to escape burden, Javic Elensol had no destination planned. Out onto the winding pathways that laced through the forest and surrounding farmlands of Darrenfield, Javic pushed onwards – away from his ill grandfather. His horse, Olli, led the way. In his mind, her legs were his legs. Her heartbeat was one with his. The rhythmic thumping of her hooves against the dry ground kicked up a large cloud of dust behind them as Javic crouched low in his saddle and increased their pace up to a fast gallop. He lost himself in the moment. The wind rushed over his body, sending his curly hair flying straight back. Moving quickly was the only way to feel a breeze anymore, ever since the wind had stopped.

It was autumn now, though the summer heat had not yet started to dissipate. The trees still knew the season despite the lingering weather; the leaves had already begun to change countless shades of red and orange. Not many of them had fallen yet, for a stale calm had settled over the hills and valleys that make up Darrenfield as if the earth itself were holding its breath.

The lack of wind was the least of the local weather problems, though, for there hadn't been any rain in the past sixty-eight days either. A dry spell every now and then was an ordinary occurrence, but this had escalated into something much more serious. Plant life was beginning to show signs of the drought and even the needles of the evergreen trees were starting to look more brown than green. The dry soil was beginning to crack, the taste of rain a distant memory faded in time by the drawl of the summer's heat. All of the locals were praying to Mast that no wild fires would break out; the dead vegetation would provide ample fuel for the flames and many homes would surely be lost in the blaze. Prudent farmers had cut away as much dead brush as they could. No one wanted to be caught off-guard.

Looking up into the late afternoon sky, Javic noticed the moon was already at the highest point of its trajectory – straight above him in the dimming light. If he wanted to have dinner prepared on time he needed to start heading back now. He tugged halfheartedly at Olli's reins, slowing the mare's pace. For the past month, Javic had been under constant pressure to fulfill responsibilities that usually rested upon his grandfather, Elric. Sixteen-year-old Javic had to bring in the meager autumn harvest unaided, and now, because of his grandfather's illness, he was forced to act as a caretaker as well.

Elric had been bedridden for three weeks, becoming worse with every passing day. To Javic, it felt like it had been much longer than that. He had never seen his grandfather sick before. He knew he needed to return to the farm and take care of his grandfather, but he was reluctant to turn back. He clenched his fists tightly around Olli's tanned leather reins. He had gone on the ride to clear his mind, but the nagging fear that Elric might not recover proved impossible to suppress. He loved his grandfather dearly; he was the only family Javic had left.

Javic was still growing into his post-pubescent body, anyone who had known his father, Bartan, would have said he looked just like him. Growing up, his mostly round features and hazel eyes had helped him blend in with the rest of the townsfolk when viewed from a distance. Up close, however, a bump on the ridge of his nose, passed down from his mother's side of the family, marked him as different. As a young boy, he had been informed that such a nose was a common feature amongst outlanders, and thus it had quickly become a source of shame for Javic. His nose brought him endless ridicule from the other children of Darrenfield. He could not seek comfort from his parents, as they had died when he was still an infant. He did not remember them except through stories told by his grandfather.

As Javic began to steer Olli in a gradual loop that would lead him back to the farmhouse, he prayed to Mast for his grandfather's recovery, feeling the prayer wash over him with the purest of conviction. He hoped Mast would listen to him now, even if this was the only prayer she ever answered in his entire life. He had never had much faith in religion before – he hadn't had a need for it until now – but at this point, he would take anything he could get. Moisture began to build up in his eyes as the warm air whipped against them. He squeezed them shut and felt the sting of emotion. Droplets seeped into his lashes.

Taking care of his grandfather would have been easier if Salvine Welin had stopped by with their food and medicine this week as promised. Javic wasn't sure what to make of her absence – the workings of the fairer gender had always been a mystery to him, but Salvine had never left him hanging like this before. With Javic's daily duties keeping him in almost constant motion around the farm, riding all the way into town was a luxury for which he hadn't the time to spare.

Yesterday, when Salvine missed her visit, a nervous pit started to form in Javic's gut. *I knew I shouldn't have tried to kiss her... shouldn't have given her that damned dove charm either... not so soon, anyway. I scared her away – made things too serious, too fast.*

There was nothing he could do now to take back his impulsive actions. The twisted fluttering he felt in his stomach whenever he was in her presence told him to push forward, to try to take their friendship to the next level, but clearly his instincts were off. She smiled at him when he presented the bracelet to her last week, but the spark Javic felt must have been one-sided. With a second day passing since she missed her visit, she was yet to return to the Elensol Farm. How stupid Javic was for thinking a girl like Salvine would ever want to be with a simple farm boy like him. He brushed away his tears with the back of his hand, focusing his thoughts outward instead.

A static charge began to build in the air. It was subtle at first. The hairs on the back of his neck stood up. He felt tingling all across his skin. Invisible energy built up in the atmosphere like lightening about to strike.

Crack! Crack!

Javic could see no storm clouds. After a brief moment of bewilderment, every hair on his head suddenly lifted up and pointed out sideways, due west, towards the tree line.

A ruckus of wing flaps and frightened birdcalls arose from the treetops as bright lights flashed. A flock of roosting starlings launched their feathered bodies deftly into the sky as the disturbance grew stronger. A few reluctant birds remained behind in the upper foliage, darting from branch to branch in a state of desperate confusion. They squawked angrily as their nesting ground shook in a deep rumble.

Javic sat up straight in his saddle. He quickly reined Olli to a stop. She pranced around despairingly, eyes rolling, her mane drawn sideways by the mysterious energy as well. The odd lights in the trees became almost blindingly bright for a moment. Javic shielded his face with his forearm. The image of the edge of the forest, cast in negative, projected itself on the backs of Javic's eyelids with vertical blotches of purple and green that lingered next to where the trunks of trees had blocked out some of the brilliance of the flash. But then, just as suddenly as it had grown, the intense aura waned. It retreated down to an ominous glow, emanating from over the ridge that marked the start of the old Belford Quarry.

The sounds and flashes, now greatly diminished, continued on for a few moments before ceasing. Javic had no idea what had just happened. His curiosity drew him in to the old quarry. His back remained tense as he held Olli's reins tight in his hands. He was prepared to drive her into a full gallop if the disturbance returned or its cause turned out to be dangerous. He began to cross the creek bed that ran along the edge of the Elensol property.

Many of the smaller rivers and streams that spider-webbed across Darrenfield had long since dried up with the drought, along with the irrigation systems the local farmers had built off of them. Just beyond the creek stretched the old Belford Quarry, an extensive pit carved deep into the limestone. It hadn't been used at all since the end of the Cleansing, some ninety-five years previous.

Looking at the quarry now, it could hardly be recognized as such. Young fir trees grew in the thick soil that had blown overtop the stone throughout the years since the war's end and the quarry's abandonment. Only the jagged rocks that jutted out amongst the young vegetation and the wooden boards lying around haphazardly, mostly rotted through and covered by dirt, marked it as a quarry. The boards had once been used to brace the earth across various sections of the excavation site.

Javic doubted that anyone other than himself had visited the location in at least thirty years. Regardless, he knew *something* had produced those lights and sounds and he was determined to discover what, even if that meant searching every crevice and loose rock in the quarry.

He dismounted from Olli, looped her reins around a tree branch, and then cautiously approached the ridge that overlooked the quarry, staying as quiet as he possibly could. Despite his determination, the strange lights and sounds had left him as jumpy as a jackrabbit. The closer he got, the more he began to doubt his decision to investigate. Part of him wanted to turn back around, hop into Olli's saddle and ride home as if nothing strange had happened at all; to just go back where he knew it was safe, where nothing odd ever happened and there were never any surprises.

Where Salvine didn't love him... where his grandfather lay near death on a bed in the tiny farmhouse that had been Javic's whole life....

His hands were shaking slightly.

He could feel his blood pumping as he reached the edge of the quarry.

He tried to steady his breath, but every rustling leaf made him feel as if his heart were skipping beats. He became overly aware of his breathing as he peered down from the ridge, scanning the rock-filled valley below for any sign of what might have caused the commotion. At first glance he didn't see anything out of the ordinary, but as he crept closer, he noticed just a short distance away what looked to be a young man about twenty years in age, motionless, on his back beneath the top half of a fallen fir tree. The tree was only a sapling, not large enough to have harmed him, though it had camouflaged him quite well. The bottom half of the tree was nowhere to be seen.

The man was clothed very peculiarly, wearing a black jacket that looked much sleeker than any clothing Javic had ever seen before. His pants were of a glossy-black material with a thin, white stripe running down the length of each pant leg. Its shine was akin to silk, but it looked far too heavy to be so. Turning his attention away from the man's attire, Javic wondered if the tiny tree splitting in half could have possibly produced the loud cracking noises he had heard, but he resolved that the tree was too small, and besides, he had heard a series of cracks, not just one. Moreover, that didn't explain the lights he had witnessed.

As Javic moved down the embankment, he observed that the top half of the tree he had seen from a distance had been sliced to an unnaturally smooth surface, rather than the break he had been expecting to find. The closer he got to the man, the more oddities he began to notice. The ground beneath the man was glassy smooth and rounded out. It looked as if the hand of Mast herself had reached down from the heavens and scooped out a spherical chunk of rock and soil and then just plopped the man down in the middle of it. There was no dirt under where he rested; the pocket dug deep into the stone that had been beneath the soil. This extraordinarily smooth area was completely surrounded by dirt that went down a forearm's length deep before it met with the stony surface below.

Javic moved over the man and bent down low. The man's face was clean shaven. He had light-brown hair that was cut close, not overtop his ears at all. He was not very muscular, though not lanky either; the build of a person who had never worked a day of manual labor in his life. His smooth hands attested to this as well.

Suddenly the man's eyes shot open. Javic jumped back in surprise. The man's pupils shrank from their dilated state as he took in the failing afternoon sunlight, then contracted even more as he lifted his head and focused on Javic, who was just standing there gaping at him. The man's eyes did not look angry, actually appearing quite kind. Signs of worry began to show on his face.

Javic was the first to come to his senses. "Who are you?" he asked meekly, his voice full of wonder and quivering slightly. It was like one of his grandfather's stories suddenly brought to life before his very eyes.

"I..." the man paused for a moment. Concern flecked his cloudy-blue eyes brighter than the pigment. "I don't know," he said, now looking even more confused than before.

CHAPTER

3

Flesh and Stone

"Who are you?" a stranger asked.

Specks of light flashed – tiny stray synapses firing off in random directions like a swarm of firebugs shook up in a jar. The buzzing was abominable, teeth rattling and grinding away. It felt like his bone marrow had turned to magma, oozing slowly from the hollows of his skeleton and into each of his joints and limbs. Every nerve in his body was singed by a flash of heat, like a meteor igniting the atmosphere in an arc of fire, rained down from the heavens by some angry god. From the corners of his eyes, ghostly forms skimmed across the surface, echoes of a forgotten time preserved by his senses, overloaded and broken; now just a shimmer remained, stretched thin across countless millennia.

What the hell is happening to me?

"I…" his breath came back to him like ice in his lungs. He felt as if his ribcage might explode as the membrane around the inner walls of his chest expanded in a desperate gasp, followed by a wheezing sputter as the gas escaped in exhale. And then another gasp, and another. His mouth was dry as leather, but the discomfort began to ease as the juices gradually started flowing again. "I don't know."

His heart began to race as panic flooded through his entire body.

Why can't I remember?

All he could hear was the blood in his ears; his heartbeat pounding against the inside of his skull like a maelstrom at the base of a waterfall, churning just below the surface. The pressure rumbled painfully behind his eyes, as if the blood intended to escape through the softer tissue. His whole body ached. He felt a cool, hard surface beneath him. It curved around to the back of his neck, aiming his chin down towards his clavicle. The smell of dirt filled the air, particles of dust catching in his nostrils as he began to breathe through his nose.

The pressure in his head was subsiding, his heartbeat slowing down to a more reasonable pace as his deep breaths steadied his body. A bit of dirt and rock crumbled down around him, sliding along the smooth surface behind his back and coming to a rest against his right pant leg. Looking up, the brightness of the sky was too much for his retinas to handle. His eyelids felt as if they were laden with rust. He fluttered them spastically as he adjusted to the light.

The boy came into focus, curly haired and tanned. His jaw hung slightly askew as he stood staring down at him. "Where did you come from?" the boy asked, frowning.

He searched his mind, trying to remember how he had gotten here, wherever he was, but nothing came to him. He couldn't remember anything at all. He bit down lightly on his lip, mentally grasping for the answer, but nothing was there. Images of flames flickered across his brain, surrounding him, melting his skin and charring his bones. A silent scream reverberated against his spine, it didn't feel like his own cry, but there was no way to know for sure. It was only in his head, but it felt as real as anything.

"I don't know that either," he said. It was as if his mind were an hourglass with every last grain already fallen through the bottleneck, and he stood at the bottom, trying desperately to force it to flow in reverse.

The top part of a fir tree rested across his torso. He pushed it off to his side and stood up, his legs tingling awkwardly as blood rushed to fill his lower extremities. He was standing in the middle of a small clearing, cradled between a spattering of young trees like the one that had been on top of him. Rocks peeked out from amongst the vegetation and a number of old wooden boards were spread out erratically, rotted through and half buried in the darkly colored soil. His eyes traced up an embankment to a vast forest full of evergreen trees.

"What do you mean you don't know?" the boy asked incredulously.

He grimaced. There was nothing to elaborate on. He glanced up into the sky again; it was not nearly as bright as it had seemed when he first opened his eyes. It appeared to be late evening. The cloudless sky was deep blue with sunlight streaming sideways across the atmosphere from just above the distant foothills, low against the horizon. Above him, through a gap in the spotty foliage, the moon hung full in the sky. It seemed almost too large as it stared back down on him, as if at any moment it might fall from its perch and grind him back into the earth. "What is this place?" he asked the boy.

Ignoring the inquiry, the boy cocked his head to the side and narrowed his eyes. "So you really don't know who you are?" he asked more sympathetically this time. The boy ran his fingers through his hair nervously and then slowly gestured down towards his feet. "How did you do that? And what *is* that?" Wonder gripped his voice. He sounded more confused than frightened.

Beneath his feet was an unnaturally smooth, concave indentation that ran deep into the limestone. Its exposed and clean state formed a stark contrast with the dirt that covered most everything else in the valley. He climbed out of the depression and took a few steps towards the boy.

Matching his movement in reverse, the boy stepped backwards, maintaining the distance between them. The boy's uneasy stare demanded answers.

He put his face in his hands. "My head hurts," he said. "I really don't know. I'm having trouble remembering... things...." He made eye contact with the boy for a second, but quickly looked away.

The silence returned. The boy continued to stare at him. Besides a slight breeze rustling in the branches near the treetops, the hush did not break until a shrill birdcall sounded in the distance, finally bringing the boy back to his senses. "Well, in that case," said the boy while hesitantly walking forward and sticking out his arm, fist open, in a handshaking gesture, "I'm Javic." The boy still looked nervous, but now had a hopeful expression on his face.

A slight amount of relief washed over him. Javic's softening put him at ease. He took Javic's hand in his own and shook it, though not entirely without hesitation. He still knew what a handshake was, so his mind couldn't be completely empty – the realization was somewhat comforting. He knew how to speak, and how to move his legs. He recognized the scent of pine needles in the air; knew the radiance of the sun on his face. Every breath he took was a refreshing reminder that he was still alive, although he wasn't sure why that simple fact felt so exhilarating.

Javic smiled. "And I guess since you don't know your own name I'll just call you Belford for now. That's the name of the quarry we're standing in."

Javic seemed friendly enough, maybe even too much so, but Belford – he liked the sound of that – wasn't in the mood for making friends. His eyes began to fog over as the silent scream echoed through his body once more, causing him to shiver despite the afternoon heat. The memory of searing pain prickled across his nerve endings, fluttering momentarily at his core before rippling outwards. It was only a minor tremor; an aftershock of sorts.

"Are you alright?" asked Javic.

Belford recoiled from the sound of his voice. He focused back on Javic, who was beginning to look worried again. "Yeah, I'm okay," Belford reassured him. "Let's get out of here."

Javic nodded in agreement. "I suppose I should take you back to the farm. It will be getting dark soon. We can head into town tomorrow if you want. You would have had to pass through there if you came from the north. Someone is bound to recognize you."

The two of them made their way up the embankment together, stepping lightly over the jagged rocks that protruded along their path.

Upon reaching the top, Javic swore under his breath, "Oh hell, Olli must have pulled herself free!" Though Belford did not know who Olli was, he could judge by Javic's tone that her freedom was a very bad thing indeed. "I hope she can find her way home by herself." Concern lingered in his voice. "There's no way we can make it back by nightfall." He sighed audibly. "We better start walking."

The sun began to set behind the hills and the sky darkened more and more. Time dragged by as they made their way towards the farm. They conversed throughout most of the journey, though Javic did the majority of the talking. Belford replied when he could but mostly stuck to asking questions.

"Where are we?" he asked once Javic finally finished talking about the best way to keep deer and other wild animals out of corn patches.

Javic gestured around at the air, pointing at nothing in particular. "We're right in the middle of Darrenfield."

Belford scrunched his face, thinking hard about the name, but it did not sound familiar at all.

"In the Kingdom of Taris..." Javic added, raising an eyebrow.

Belford frowned slightly.

"Don't worry, nobody else has heard of Darrenfield either. It's just a bunch of cows and farmland. You showing up is probably the most exciting thing that has ever happened here." His tone was lighthearted, but he was watching Belford even more closely now, peering at him out of the corner of his eye as they walked.

Worry tugged at the corners of Belford's mouth. He did not recognize either name. He tried to mask his concern. "I can believe that," he said wryly. "Anyone who can get that excited about corn couldn't possibly have led an exciting life."

"You're telling me," Javic said dryly.

It was another few minutes before either of them said anything more to one another. Javic's thoughts seemed to be elsewhere. He kept his eyes forward as he walked, staring off into the distance.

"So what does a farm boy do for fun around here anyway?" Belford asked, trying to clear away the awkwardness.

Javic turned his head, staring at Belford with a blank expression as if trying to judge whether or not Belford's question had been sincere. "I hunt, sometimes," said Javic, "quail and rabbit, mostly."

"Oh, yeah?" Belford asked. "You a good shot?"

Javic nodded. "I'm pretty good," he said. "You have to hit them with your first arrow, or else you might as well sew bells on your tunic for how fast they disappear."

Archery, thought Belford, *how antiquated.* "I don't suppose many animals would want to give you a second chance after a miss."

Javic's eyes immediately clouded over again.

Belford wasn't sure what he had said wrong this time. "You okay?" he asked.

Javic shook his head. "It's nothing," he said. "Just a girl." Javic's cheeks reddened slightly at the admission. "I messed things up, and I'm not sure if she's going to give me a second chance either."

Belford grimaced. "I'm sorry," he said. "Keep your chin up, kid. There's plenty of fish in the sea."

"What does that have to do with anything?" Javic asked. "The Northern Sea is over fifty leagues from here."

Belford narrowed his eyes, wondering if Javic was screwing with him, but there was no hint of sarcasm in his words.

"And the Sea is mostly barren now," Javic continued. "I hear there are ample fish in the Minthune River, though."

"It's an expression," said Belford. "It means there are lots of other women out there."

Javic nodded with a slow comprehension. "Not like Salvine," he said, almost under his breath. "You talk weird," he added. "You must be an outlander."

Belford wasn't sure what to say about that. Maybe Javic was right; Javic's mannerisms seemed a little strange to Belford as well.

"My mother was an outlander, too," Javic continued, "from the Eastern Territories. I never met her, though. Never met any outlander before. Strangers don't come around here much."

The conversation grew lighter after that, happily distracting Belford from the darkness inside his head. The discomfort of their earlier banter dissipated as Belford grew more accustom to the way the farm boy spoke. Javic was a very literal person, but he was soon picking up on Belford's sarcasm as the conversation went on.

Over the course of the next three hours Javic told him all about his simple life on the farm. *How dreadful,* thought Belford. *Such back breaking labor, and for what?* Javic had to do practically everything by hand – tilling, planting, weeding, harvesting – and by the end of a season had barely enough produce to show for it to scrape by until the next harvest. *Why would anyone work so hard for such little gain?*

"If you don't get grit under your fingernails, you haven't been working hard enough," said Javic. "That's what my grandfather always says."

Belford shrugged. He glanced down at his own nails. They were all chewed too short to hide anything beneath them.

When they finally emerged from the forest, Belford's legs were burning, the exertion clear on his face. He was breathing harder than Javic as well. Javic looked as if he could continue on marching all night long without rest. Belford supposed that was one benefit to a laborious lifestyle. Ahead of them a farmhouse was revealed by the light from the moon. The door stood open and a dark form rested on the ground in front of it, barely visible in the moonlight. Belford could not make out what it was from this distance. However, he was able to identify a horse standing next to the dark shape, its long neck craned down as it nuzzled the unknown object.

"Oh, good," said Javic in a sigh of relief. "Looks like Olli made it back."

The object that the horse was standing over started to move and Javic suddenly began to sprint towards the farmhouse. Belford pushed himself, jogging behind Javic. He was unsure of what to make of the situation. As he got closer, Belford realized that the dark shape he had seen from a distance was actually a person lying on the ground.

"Grandfather!" Javic cried out as he reached the motionless man's side. "Help me pick him up!" he shouted as Belford caught up with him. "Get his arm." Together they hoisted the old man up and carried him into the house.

The farmhouse was small. They maneuvered the old man through the entrance area, which was the largest room; doubling as both a kitchen and sitting area. A room to the left appeared to be Javic's bedroom. Belford could see a desk containing a few books and a framed photograph through the open doorway. It was through the only other door that they carried the old man. They shuffled past a standing stove, and then moved sideways through the doorframe before laying the old man on the bed held within.

The room was dark. Belford started to feel along the wall for a switch, but then Javic lit a candle. Belford put his hands in his pockets. It was a stark room. Other than the bed, there was only a dresser, a wooden chair, and a large reddish-brown mahogany trunk inside. Belford's eyes lingered over the trunk as Javic busied himself covering the aged man's forehead with a moist cloth.

The trunk was intricately carved. It held many illustrations, one of which depicted a man in heavy armor using a spear to battle a large misshapen creature. The other relief designs displayed equally unfamiliar feats of heroism. There were no visible hinges to the trunk, but there was a keyhole top and center on the front panel. Belford wondered what could possibly be inside the extravagant lockbox.

The old man had begun sweating profusely and was now taking extremely shallow breaths. *What a mess,* thought Belford. His limp body was sprawled out on top of the bed sheets. He was completely devoid of energy, unable to lift his arms from his sides. He was a pathetic sight, almost ethereal in his pallor. The old man was hardly conscious as Javic tended to him. Gazing upon Javic and his grandfather, Belford's heart began to fill with a deep shame. He felt as if he were spying on them, like he was an invisible observer to their intimate moment. The love in Javic's expression made Belford's eyes shy away. Javic looked to be even more pained than his grandfather. Belford flinched as the old man started coughing violently, howling after each outburst. His screams filled the room as Javic tried to settle him down.

Oh, no....

Belford could feel his heartbeat in his throat.

Not again....

He hunched to the floor as a wave of nausea suddenly overtook him. The old man's cries set off another aftershock, more powerful this time. His mind exploded with a thousand ghostly screams that threatened to pull him apart. The fire was all around him again, and everywhere he looked, naked corpses, blackened by flames, were staring up at him with unrelenting eyes. Their vacant expressions seemed to gaze endlessly into his soul with a smoldering malice. He could see himself reflected in those dark eyes. There was no escaping their judgment. Their mangled bodies were twisted unnaturally on top of one another, frozen in place wherever their lives had been snuffed out. The scent of death dripped from the air as the flames licked at his cheeks and plume after plume of acrid smoke shot waves of sulfur high into the orange sky. Belford's stomach retched, but there was nothing inside to expel. His breath caught in his throat. He felt as if he were gasping again, a slow asphyxiation seizing his heart as he tried to steady his breath; in and out, in and out.

Leave me alone! Leave me alone!

Javic glanced up at Belford, taking his eyes off of his grandfather for the first time since entering the farm house. Belford wasn't sure if Javic's concerned expression was more for his grandfather, or for him. He watched Belford with narrowed eyes for a long moment until his grandfather gave another sputtering cough that pulled Javic's attention back downward.

Belford could still feel the eyes of the dead watching him, but the images began to fade from his vision, the room untwisting, solidifying back into its correct shape. After a few more moments the screaming winded down to a soft buzz. It remained barely present in the back of his mind, only a distant whimper.

Belford looked over at Javic. He had tears silently running down both of his cheeks as he attempted to ease his grandfather's discomfort. "Why were you out of bed?" Javic cried, staring down at his grandfather with a furrowed brow.

"I was worried about you when Olli came back alone," rasped the old man. Speaking made him cough harder. The coughing and pained wails continued on for another minute before he finally finished hacking up a large amount of yellow and green mucus onto the front of his shirt. His breath was labored. His exhales sounded in a wheeze. Belford noticed a purplish-blue tint starting to appear in the old man's lips and fingernails.

Javic cleaned the mucus off of his grandfather, dabbing lightly with the cloth. With each bout of coughing, Javic's demeanor darkened further and further until it was clear he couldn't take it any longer: "Hang in there, Grandfather," he said. "I'm going to get help from town." Javic turned to Belford. "I need to go, now. He needs a doctor or he might not make it through the night." Javic's voice quivered as he spoke.

Belford looked over at the old man thoughtfully and then back at Javic. "Can I come with you?" he asked. He didn't want to be left behind in the tiny farmhouse with only his ghosts and the old man's screams to keep him company. "I don't think there is anything I can do for him here."

Javic hesitated for a moment. "Fine, just don't slow me down," he said; a fierce intensity steadied his voice despite the tears welling up in his eyes and silently streaming down his cheeks. "Maybe someone will recognize you and take you off my hands," he grumbled before rushing out to prepare the horses for the trip.

Javic quickly saddled up another horse, Amit, he called her, and then rounded up Olli – she had been wandering around the farmyard aimlessly. Belford had a difficult time getting into Amit's saddle, but once he was up, the horse followed behind Javic without needing to be directed. The motion of the animal's stride felt awkward to Belford. He could barely keep up with Javic's quick pace. Javic pushed the animals much faster than was safe for night travel. They rode in the darkness for a half-hour with nothing but sheer luck preventing the horses from breaking their legs on the uneven terrain. Finally, they raced down the last hill that led into the town of Darrenfield.

A low burning campfire on the outskirts of town drew Belford's attention. He felt eyes watching him before he spotted the man – a dark silhouette sitting off to one side of the flames. The man drew his hood over his head as they rode past. Belford glanced over his shoulder, but already the man had slipped back into the shadows. When they reached the edge of the town square, Belford looked behind him again. The dim fire was entirely gone – doused out – replaced by a thin tendril of while smoke, twisting up into the night sky like an uncoiling viper.

CHAPTER

4

Watchers

The village was mostly dark at this hour. Only the occasional cottage cast a faint glow of lantern light through its narrow windows as Belford rode along behind Javic. The moon was the only substantial source of light upon the dirt street. The road was the town's main drag, but there were no light posts. No street signs. No electricity. The sleepy town felt foreign to Belford's senses. Thatched roofs and rough lumber made up each of the small structures that were clustered along the town square.

Up ahead, Javic reined in his horse outside a cottage near the center of town. He dismounted quickly and banged on the wooden door with his fist. There was no answer. He waited a moment before knocking a few more times. Again, there was no sign that anybody was home. Letting out an exasperated cry, Javic hopped back onto Olli. They galloped towards the edge of town to a small inn they had passed on their way to the cottage. Arriving first, Javic dismounted and sprinted in through the front door. Belford was left to secure both horses' reins to a wooden hitching post. He twisted the leather loops into a pair of awkward knots.

From down the road, someone intentionally cleared their throat, alerting Belford that he was not alone. Glancing up, Belford recognized the approaching figure as the man they had passed at the campfire on their way into town. If not for the soft light of the full moon, his cloaked figure would have been completely invisible. Belford's back tensed as the stranger walked up to him. He stopped an arm's reach away and drew his hood back.

"Hello there," the man said with a friendly tone. He smiled, but it did not extend beyond his mouth. He was a stocky fellow with a full beard trimmed to a point and fairly short black, curly hair. The man's cheeks were slightly gaunt, but his face lit up as he took in Belford's appearance. "The name's Maswald Baltren," he said, extending his hand.

Belford accepted the handshake tentatively. The man's skin was clammy. Belford subtly wiped his palm on his pants once the man released his grip.

"Where did you get those clothes?" he asked.

Belford narrowed his eyes.

Maswald smiled again. Coupled with his intense stare, the expression was unnerving. "There's no need to be defensive," he said, "I only wish to know where I could procure some for myself."

Belford wasn't sure what to make of him. His gaze made Belford's skin feel grimy. Something about him just didn't sit right.

When Belford didn't answer, Maswald returned to his questioning: "Are you staying on a farm?" he asked, eying the pair of horses at Belford's side.

Belford said nothing. He could feel his face starting to get hot. His skin itched all over.

"Which one?" Maswald asked. "You can tell me."

Belford stepped back, his legs wobbling beneath him as he stumbled over towards the inn's entrance. Maswald's eyes were like black orbs; the eyes of the dead, unblinking.

Not this shit again....

The door to the inn was smoldering around its edges. He had to lean against the hitching post to keep his balance as more hot blood rushed to his head. The ground seemed to drop away as vertigo clutched his insides and his stomach turned over in a cast-iron knot. His face was shining with sweat as Maswald took a step towards him.

To Belford's surprise, he walked past without a word and vanished into the dark night.

The encounter left Belford shaken. He wasn't sure why, but Maswald's departure, though a significant relief, made him uneasy as well. If only he could remember his past – anything at all – who he was... what was going on... where he had come from.... An answer to any one of those questions would have helped calm his nerves. Everything felt wrong in this place. The constant sense that he was being watched by both the living and the dead put him on edge.

He couldn't help but dwell on the ominous feeling as he double checked the hold of the horses' reins. He gave them each one final tug before entering the inn. Inside, Belford could see Javic conversing hurriedly with a sleepy-eyed innkeeper; his tone half pleading and half demanding as he asked the innkeeper if he knew where the doctor was. The droopy-eyed man had a day's worth of stubble on his chin and shoulder-length, brown hair tied back with a string into a ponytail. He was frowning as Javic explained their situation. The innkeeper roused a stable boy from his room and sent him to retrieve the doctor from a tavern he had apparently taken to drinking at until late into the nights.

"While I've got you here," said the innkeeper, "Arietta Welin stopped by the other day. She ain't at all too pleased with Salvine running off with you. Fair warning: You might want to have Salvine check back in at home before Arietta decides to sick the Hanton boys on the both of you. You know that woman can be quite the mother hen when it comes to her babies."

Javic looked confused. "What are you talking about?" he asked. "I haven't seen Salvine in over a week…. She hasn't been home?"

The innkeeper narrowed his eyes as he gauged Javic's earnestness. "Not for five days," he said. "Everyone assumed she was with you, what with that bracelet you gave her and all. She was flashing that thing all over town as if a dowry were soon to follow."

Javic's cheeks flushed with blood. "I honestly haven't seen her," he said.

The innkeeper didn't look convinced. He shrugged, then disappeared back behind his counter.

Unaware of the curiosity his arrival had earned, Javic began to pace back and forth, his unfocused eyes directed beyond the floorboards.

Around the common room, all eyes turned towards Belford as he made his way across the inn. He overheard some of the guests mumbling to one another about "the young man with the strange clothing." All the unwanted attention made him wish he had changed his clothes while he was back at the farmhouse.

Javic looked up questioningly from his pacing when Belford approached, but looked away again after seeing he wasn't the doctor.

They didn't have to wait much longer, though. The stable boy and a man carrying a large leather bag came charging in through the front door.

"What's so important that you need me at this hour?" asked the doctor, his speech slightly slurred. He walked over to Javic and Belford before placing his bag on the ground between his feet. The stable boy sauntered past, back to his room, giving them a sideways glance as he went by.

"My grandfather is very sick. We need to go back to the farm. We can make it in half an hour if we hurry," said Javic.

"Hold on, now. Why don't you tell me a little bit about what's wrong with Elric before I go wasting my whole night running around."

Javic looked infuriated. "What's wrong? What's wrong?! He's dying, for Mast's sake!" His voice was full of indignation. The doctor motioned for him to continue. "Fine... um, he has a bad fever, and when we left him he was hardly conscious, breathing shallowly and screaming in pain each time he coughed!"

Belford suddenly had a realization – he knew what was wrong with the old man. "Your grandfather has a collapsed lung," said Belford. "He coughed a bunch of yellowish-green snot out all over himself, and his lips and nails were already starting to turn a bluish tint, which is a sign of cyanosis caused by insufficient levels of oxygen in the bloodstream, both of which are signs of a collapsed lung... it's the only thing that makes sense." He wasn't sure why he hadn't seen it earlier; the diagnosis was so obvious. By the look of horror on Javic's face, maybe he shouldn't have said anything, but it was too late now. Both Javic and the doctor were staring at him; the doctor had a curious look in his eyes.

"Cyanosis? What could a boy like you know about that? Where did you even hear that word?" the doctor asked.

Belford merely shrugged; he wasn't sure where the knowledge had come from. It just popped into his brain.

The doctor turned his halfway glazed-over expression back towards Javic. "Well anyway, if what he says is true, that definitely sounds like a collapsed lung, and that means there is absolutely nothing I can do to help him. He's probably dead already. People don't last long with collapsed lungs, you know. If it was a minor collapse it will heal by itself over time, otherwise...." The doctor trailed off. Javic turned away and held his head in his hands. The doctor took the lull as opportunity to slip away. He began to stumble back towards the inn's door.

"Wait! You can't just leave, he needs help!" Javic sounded on the verge of tears. It was a wonder he had held together this long.

The doctor stopped and reached into his leather bag. He pulled out a small vial filled with a fine, brown powder. "You can give him this for the pain. It's an herb – it's strong. Just put it in some tea. There's nothing else I can do for him." He placed the vial on a table before departing.

Javic broke down completely. He crumpled to the floor and cried. His tears carved pathways down his cheeks. Belford stood in silence a few feet away from him, unsure what to do as Javic wept into the sleeve of his shirt as if it were a tissue. The display was awkward to watch. Belford was overly aware of all the people silently watching them from across the common room.

He tried to coax Javic up. "Come on, we should get that herb to your grandfather. He could still heal by himself over time." He tried to sound more optimistic than he really felt, but failed. Javic continued to weep. Belford sighed. "Don't listen to that idiot – he's a shitty doctor – probably self-medicating too."

Javic glared up at him with a look of disgust. "What the hell do you know?"

Belford immediately recognized his mistake: The doctor may have been terrible at his job, but he was all this town had – all Javic had. He put his palms out submissively, easing off from his critical opinion. "Come on," he said, "I'm sorry. Let's just go. There's nothing else for us to do here." He glanced across the crowd of onlookers once more, most silently scowling. "Let's go back and see your grandfather again. At least that way he won't have to die alone." The brutal honesty of the statement felt far too harsh as it passed through Belford's lips, but again it was too late to take it back.

He was worried for a moment that Javic might lash out at him for his tactlessness, but after a few more unrestrained sobs,

Javic's breath began to steady. He wiped his eyes with his hands and got back on his feet, taking a moment to compose himself physically as he straightened his jacket. The anger had completely drained from his face, replaced by the utter hopelessness of a lost child. He nodded to Belford, seemingly resigned in his new task of riding home to see his grandfather one last time. His face had become flush and his eyes were quite puffy, but he was no longer crying. Together they walked out of the inn, Javic grabbing the herb as they passed by. Belford untied the horses' reins from the post and they both mounted and rode out of town in silence.

The quiet stretched on throughout the entire ride back to the farm. As soon as they arrived, Javic hopped down from Olli and ran inside, leaving Belford behind to secure the horses again. He took his time before going into the farmhouse. "How is he?" Belford asked once he was inside.

"Alive. I'm going to go get some water for the tea. Could you light the stove while I'm gone?" Javic gestured to the standing stove as he grabbed a tea kettle and glided past Belford. "There are some matches on the counter over there, in the tin," he pointed to them. "I'll be right back, Grandfather," he called out to the old man. "Belford here is going to keep you company for a moment while I prepare your medicine," he said before disappearing out the door.

Belford quickly lit the stove, and then went into Javic's grandfather's room – Elric, the doctor had called him. His eyelids pealed back at the sound of Belford's approach and a look of recognition quickly settled across his wrinkled brow. Belford frowned, prompting a grimace from Elric in return. "Have you come to kill me?" Elric asked softly, his raspy voice rumbling up from deep down in his throat.

"Kill you?" replied Belford. "Why would you think that?"

Elric coughed vigorously, the exertion causing him to wince in pain. "Then you must have come from Ethan," his frown deepened slightly. "I'm afraid that I have retired. I am no longer in fighting condition, as you can see. Do tell me, though, what word does my Lord send after so many years of silence?"

Belford was very confused; he wondered if the old man had lost his mind. "I'm sorry, but I don't know what you're talking about."

Javic reentered the house with the filled teapot before Belford could question Elric. "Don't worry, Grandfather; I have your medicine right here. It will only be a moment now." Elric didn't respond; he had already fallen back into a fevered delirium.

After heating the water and giving Elric the pain relieving tea, Javic and Belford sat with him in his room. The herb helped calm Elric as Javic began to tell stories, weaving a bright tale about a prince in an imaginary, far off land that seemed as greatly removed from the dusty, agricultural bowl of Darrenfield as Javic could imagine. An hour or so went by and they all became tired. Elric's condition deteriorated further and further and he drifted in and out of consciousness as the night progressed. After resting his eyes for a while, Javic reluctantly drifted off to sleep, his legs curled up beneath him on his wooden chair.

By now Elric was completely unconscious. His whole face glistened with a cold sweat that shined brightly in the flickering candle light. Belford decided it was time for him to go to bed as well. Slowly standing up, he walked over to the bedside. Sadness welled up inside of him at the sight of Elric's emaciated body. He couldn't help but feel guilty for having delayed Javic's return earlier that night. If Javic had never met him, maybe Elric would be fine right now. Maybe he would be recovering from his sickness instead of dying from a collapsed lung.

"I'm sorry," he whispered, kneeling by the bed and gripping one of Elric's hands tight between his own. He let out a sigh of remorse: Remorse for being alive; his mere existence was about to be responsible for Elric's death. With a rush of emotion, he wished he could fix everything; longed for it to be possible.

Belford's hands suddenly began to glow; a soft-blue color emanating from them. The glow spread into Elric's hand and then went up his arm, quickly enveloping his entire body. Belford's eyes grew wide; electric pins-and-needles flowed through his core and out his fingertips. He stared at Elric, full of awe as the soft-blue light brightened more and more, and was eventually joined by a periodic green pulsation that rippled up his limb and into his torso. Elric gasped, taking a large breath of air deep into his lungs. The pulsations began to slow. Soon, only the soft-blue glow remained, until that too started to fade away.

As the last traces of the strange lights vanished into the night, Elric opened his eyes and stared up into Belford's face. It only lasted for a moment, and then they were closed again and he was unconscious once more. His breathing was now steady and both sides of his chest were rising and falling evenly with each breath. Belford stepped back, away from the bedside, a combination of amazement and alarm gripping his insides. *What did I just do? How did I even do it?* His mind was racing. He was frightened by his power. *Did I actually heal the old man?* It had all been so beautiful; so unreal. *Am I a doctor?* The thought resonated with him – a glimmer of a memory trying to claw its way out of the darkness.

Belford smiled to himself as he rolled the title of Doctor across his tongue. It felt right. A sense of pride accompanied the thought. He knew he had worked hard to attain his goals, though he had no specific memories of his studies. He ruminated on it for a moment, but nothing more came back to him. Still, he now knew a portion of his identity, and that gave him hope that the rest of his memories might resurface as well.

Emotionally drained, he once again became aware of his physical exhaustion. He could not recall the last time he had slept, or, for that matter, having ever slept. He stumbled into

Javic's room and flopped onto the bed. His mind became unfocused as he stared up at the ceiling and breathed out a sigh.

The relief was short lived.

The haunting eyes of the dead lurked above him in the blurry shadows, watching him from just out of sight, high on the walls. He did his best to ignore their vacant stares as he drifted off into a deep, dream-filled slumber.

CHAPTER

5

The Looming Storm

Belford stood up against a wall in the middle of a long narrow hallway. The bright lights that normally illuminated the linoleum-tiled floors and paneled walls were mostly burnt out. The few that remained lit flickered sporadically as a deep and violent rumble shook the entire building. Belford looked up and down the hallway, but there was no one in sight. He was all alone.

A harsh whisper sounded in Belford's left ear: "RUN." He jumped in surprise at the sound of the voice. He spun around, but there was no one there. His heart began to race, his pulse pounding in his eardrums. "RUN, NOW," came the voice again, this time louder and from his right side.

He obeyed, stumbling on and on with each nearby explosion rocking the building down to its very foundation. He sprinted past the evenly spaced metallic doors, all closed, that ran the length of the hallway on either side. The hallway began to warp and stretch in front of him, growing longer with every advancing step, but he did not slow his stride. One of the doors on his left stood open. He pivoted himself by placing his left hand on the doorframe, allowing him to swing inside at full speed, then slammed the door shut behind him all in one motion.

Belford braced himself against the closed door as he attempted to catch his breath. He was standing in a conference room. A narrow rectangular table with six low-backed chairs on each of its longer sides took up most of the floor space in front of him. At the head of the table was a thirteenth, more elaborate seat. The modern style of the furniture corresponded well with the angular architecture of the rest of the room. An old style analog clock rested high and center on the far wall of the room. It showed the time to be exactly midnight to the second. None of the hands appeared to be moving though, so the actual time was anyone's guess. He recognized the room. He had been here before, but he could not recall when.

The rumblings finally ceased, the sounds of distant explosions no longer resonating through the walls. The soft hum of the ventilation system circulating stale air throughout the building remained as the only audible noise. Belford turned around to go back out into the hallway, but as he stepped through the doorway the whole world shifted around him in a bright blur of lights and sounds.

The bright lights lingered in his vision for a moment, disorienting him as he tried to take in his new surroundings. The lights faded into spots of color before finally disappearing completely. He found himself now standing in the middle of a grassy field, the sun shining down on him from high above in a cloudless sky. Sparrows chirped noisily at one another from atop a group of red pines growing nearby. In the distance, Belford could see a skyline of tall buildings reflecting the sun's light as they stretched high above the ground and deep into the heavens. He could tell it must be busy over there in the city, but here, in the middle of his oasis, time seemed to stand still.

A colorful butterfly fluttered up to him and circled around for a moment before passing by. Turning his head to watch it fly past he realized for the first time that he was not alone. About twenty feet away from him was a young woman, sitting on one side of a plain wooden bench at the edge of the clearing. He recognized her, but could not place a name with her face. His heart ached from just one look. She was the most beautiful girl he had ever seen.

She was wearing a modest plain gray sweatshirt overtop a more formfitting black uniform that matched Belford's. Her soft skin radiated in the sunlight with a stunning beauty that pulled at his insides, gripping just above his navel and twisting into knots. Her auburn hair, held back with a pin behind her left ear, hung down a little bit below her shoulders. It flowed in reddish-brown waves down the back of her neck to where the slight breeze streaming across the grassy park gently lifted it up and blew it out to one side. She smiled at him; her large green eyes glistening as they welcomed him over.

She spoke; he knew she said something sweet, but he could not hear the words. Her full, pink lips were mesmerizing, warming him all the way down to his core. He walked towards her and found that he was clasping a small bundle of wild flowers tightly between his fingers. He handed them to her as he bent in for a kiss. Caressing the side of her face with his right hand, their tongues met in a passionate greeting.

He closed his eyes, letting his other senses take over, but the world began to shift around him once more. He was being shaken; abruptly roused by a pair of callous hands. He wished fervently for the dream to continue.

"Belford... come on, wake up!" said a voice.

Belford groaned and swung his arm with all the strength he could muster in a feeble attempt to push the shaking hands away from him. "I'm busy," he murmured.

"You're not going to believe this!" said Javic, his voice brimming with enthusiasm. "Grandfather is completely better, his lungs are fixed, his cough is gone – everything! It's a miracle!"

Belford opened his eyes for a moment, and then quickly shut them again as the bright sunlight streaming in through the window completely saturated his vision, temporarily blinding him. He tried again. This time he only opened them to a squint. He could see Javic's happy face beaming down on him with a smile that spread all the way across, ear to ear.

Sitting up in bed, Belford rubbed his eyes with both hands as he fought back the strong pull of exhaustion that threatened to drag him back down into the pillow. "That's great," he said as he finally comprehended what Javic had said. Recollection of the previous night began to flood back to him. He swung his legs over the side of the bed and pulled down the thick blanket that had been covering him throughout the night. He was still completely dressed with the exception of his shoes which were on the floor next to the nightstand. He slipped them on and followed Javic out of the room.

"Grandfather wants to talk to you," said Javic in a somewhat quizzical tone, speaking more quietly than before.

Belford grimaced. If Elric remembered anything from the night before, Belford knew there would be a lot of questions coming his way. He didn't have any answers. He followed Javic into Elric's room anyway. Elric was still in bed, exactly where Belford had left him.

"He's awake now, Grandfather," said Javic.

"Thank you," said Elric. "Could you make some breakfast while I discuss some things with our guest?"

"…sure," said Javic. He gave Belford one last sideways glance as he went back into the kitchen area, closing the door to the bedroom behind him.

Elric gestured for Belford to have a seat on a wooden chair that had been pulled up to the bedside, then waited a few moments until he could hear the sounds of Javic preparing breakfast in the other room. "You say you have come from neither Ethan nor Garrett, yet you are clearly a trained Ver'ati;

only a wizard could have healed me so effectively with the Power. That's no simple feat. Plus, I have only seen clothing like yours once before."

Belford began to slowly shake his head back and forth; he wanted to explain everything, but couldn't think of anything to say; nothing that would be sufficient enough of an explanation anyway.

"Don't try to deny it; no one ever forgets the overwhelming feeling of the Power flowing through his skin. You have the Gift of the Arcanum. Now, where did you come from?"

Belford sighed; he had asked himself that very same question more than a few times since first opening his eyes the previous evening. Belford began to recite everything he had already told Javic, "I don't know who I am; I don't remember anything; I don't know where I'm from; I sure as hell don't know where I got my clothes," he began to sound more and more exasperated as he went on. "I don't have any idea what a *Ver'ati* is, or know anything about this *Power* you speak of. I don't know how I did whatever it was I did last night. I wish I knew, believe me; I want to know what's going on here more than anyone."

Elric remained silent for a few moments after Belford had finished his tirade, but just as Elric opened his mouth to speak Belford started up again.

"I'm sure you have a lot of questions for me, but understand this: I have the same questions as you, and even more on top of those." Now he was done. Belford felt much calmer now that he had spoken his mind.

"Well..." Elric began, "I guess I will just have to ask you questions that you do know the answers to then."

Belford lowered his face into his hands, letting out another frustrated sigh.

Ignoring this, Elric went on, his tone even more serious than before, "I know you and Javic went into town last night. Did anybody see you while you were there?"

The seriousness and genuine concern in Elric's voice worried Belford as he thought back over all of the people who had seen him. "Pretty much the entire inn... the stable boy... innkeeper... and the doctor of course."

"This is very bad," Elric began to explain. "You look so out of place that even if they didn't realize you were Ver'ati they might still spread the story through their gossip."

"Umm," said Belford, "there was this one guy outside the inn who questioned me about my clothes and where I was staying."

Elric's mouth quickly turned into a frown, his glower darkening more and more after each word.

"I didn't tell him anything though, and then he just walked away.... It seemed a bit strange."

Elric's face had become noticeably more pale while Belford was speaking. They sat in silence for a moment, staring at one another.

Javic knocked on the door. "Breakfast is ready."

The interruption brought Elric back to reality. "We must leave at once," he said springing up from his bed and pulling a small key out from inside of his belt pouch. Belford opened the door for Javic as Elric rushed over to the mahogany trunk that rested at the foot of his bed.

Javic walked in carrying a tray of food – three cups, a teapot, six slices of toast, some meat and an assortment of cheeses. "What do you mean we're leaving?" he asked, looking for a place to set the tray down.

"We are in grave danger," said Elric as he got down on his knees and pushed the small key into the keyhole on the front of the trunk. A soft click sounded as he turned the key. The hinges of the trunk creaked and groaned as Elric swung the lid back, revealing its contents.

Javic placed the tray down on the nightstand and Belford grabbed a piece of toast before they both took a couple of steps closer to Elric, attempting to get a better look at the inside of the trunk. Elric reached in and pulled out a battered old sword. He held it up in the air, examining the blade closely in the light. Elric pushed the sword back into its sheath then placed it beside him on the floor before reaching back into the trunk. Belford and Javic shared a quick glance before looking back at Elric to see what he would pull out next. Out came a sack that jingled with metal on metal – clearly a coin purse, and it was stuffed completely full to the brim.

Belford grabbed another piece of toast.

Next, Elric pulled a thick dark-leather tunic with matching leggings out from the bottom of the trunk. Both pieces had traces of battle scarring across their surfaces and could have definitely used a bit of polish. They weren't much to look at, but they appeared sturdy enough.

Elric then pulled out another set of armor, less scarred than the last, which he handed to Javic. "These were your father's. I never meant for you to have to wear them, but there is no other choice now. Go gather as much food and as many supplies as you can. Oh, and get Belford to change his clothes as well. He shouldn't be seen in *those* anymore. Hurry!"

"Grandfather!" exclaimed Javic, trying to settle Elric down.

"There's no time, boy!" said Elric. "We must hurry!"

"There's something else I need to tell you," said Javic. "It's about Salvine…."

Elric slowed his preparations just enough to give Javic an impatient look.

"She's gone missing," said Javic. "No one's seen her in the last five days."

Elric really did take pause now. His eyes shifted slightly, becoming distant for a moment. Suddenly he refocused on Javic. "Things may be even worse than I suspected. We really must leave at once," he said.

"What about Salvine?" asked Javic. "We have to go look for her!"

"I'm sorry," said Elric. "Belford healed me last night. His presence here endangers the whole town. If Salvine's absence is not innocent, it's already too late. It will soon be too late for us as well if we do not leave *now*! I can explain more on the road, but we mustn't delay any longer."

"I don't understand," said Javic.

"There will be no answers here!" Elric was shouting now. It seemed to be more out of fear than anger. "If we stay, nothing but death awaits us!"

The words sent a chill down Belford's spine.

Elric did not allow his grandson a rebuttal. He pushed past Javic and immediately went outside to ready the horses.

Javic's eyes were like daggers as he glanced over at Belford, clearly blaming him for their predicament.

Maybe I am responsible for everything bad that's happening.

He felt the unseen eyes of the dead glaring at him from out of the corners of the room.

Javic quickly slipped into his father's old armor. Once the chest piece was strapped in place, Javic led Belford back over to his room and began digging through the dresser drawers. He tossed various articles of clothing onto the bed. "Here, put on these normal clothes while I get everything together," he said. The harsh tone in his voice did not go unnoticed as he chucked a final shirt unceremoniously onto his unmade bed. Javic grabbed four empty bags out of the bottom of his dresser and stepped out into the kitchen. He set a frantic pace, overturning several kitchen drawers into the open mouths of the bags.

After closing the door to Javic's room, Belford began to undress. He started with his jacket. It was made from a thinner material than the coat that Javic had given him, but despite its slenderness it had been quite effective at keeping him warm. The material was very good at holding in heat and yet it breathed – not causing him to become overheated while he was wearing it inside the farm house. He regretted having to leave it behind – his clothes were his only possessions after all – but if that was the price of obscurity, he supposed the loss was worth it.

Taking off his matching black undershirt, Belford was surprised to find a tattoo on each of his upper biceps. On his right arm, the letters *CB* were drawn in a small, bold lettering with black ink. It was his other tattoo that interested him though. Quite different from the plain ink letters on his right arm, the graphic on his left was no ordinary marking. It consisted of a triangular figure surrounded by four small circles. The graphic was more like a part of his skin – a branding of sorts – than the ink of a normal tattoo. Belford could feel a small bump under his skin as he ran his fingers through the middle of the central triangle figure.

Javic knocked at the door.

Belford quickly put on his new shirt, hiding his tattoos. "What is it?" he asked.

Javic entered and started pulling clothing out of his dresser drawers. "Just have to grab a few more sets," he said. "You should hurry up. Grandfather is almost done getting the horses ready." He finished grabbing what he needed and went back into the kitchen, closing the door behind him.

Pulling his sleeve up, Belford fingered the bump in the middle of the tattoo once more. *What does it mean?* He thought about showing it to Elric, but that would have to come later; there were more important matters to attend to right now. He let the sleeve drop and went back to changing into the "normal," less conspicuous, clothing.

He was actually quite glad to be getting rid of his pants. The material made an irritating swooshing noise every time he took a step. Looking at the rough trousers set aside by Javic, he decided to keep his underwear on. Chafing himself raw was his only other choice. It was an unpleasant thought. Lastly, he looked at the shoes placed out before him. They were much too small for his feet. There was no choice, he would wear his own shoes; a decision which he was perfectly happy with. His shoes fit him nicely and were extremely comfortable to walk around in.

Sneakers... the word lingered across his mind as he caressed the padded tongue of the athletic footwear.

As Belford stepped out of the room, Javic immediately handed him two of the bundles he had gathered. The bags were stuffed completely full with everything Javic was able to get his hands on during his haste. In just five minutes, Javic had packed nearly everything in sight. They hurried out of the house and jogged over to the stables where Elric was just finishing saddling the last of the three horses they were to ride.

"Oh wait, I almost forgot my bow," said Javic, putting down his bags and running back towards the farm house.

Elric, now in his armor and with his sword and scabbard hooked to his belt, no longer looked like the rundown old farmer from the night before. The fire of life shined brightly in his eyes, as if a spirit of vigor had been cast deep inside of him, suddenly and fully restoring a lost vitality that had been absent from him for a very long time. He began to attach Javic's bundles onto Olli's saddle.

"So, why do you need that armor anyway?" asked Belford.

"No time for that now, boy," responded Elric, not looking up from what he was doing.

"If you need armor, doesn't that mean that I should have some too?"

Elric let out a grave chuckle as he finished tying on the second bundle. "I would give you some if I had anymore. I promise I'll get you a set just as soon as I can. Now hand me those bags."

Belford complied with the request, handing Elric one bag, then the other. Elric secured one onto either side of Amit's saddle, balancing the weight. They finished just as Javic made it back from the farm house with his recurve bow and a quiver of arrows strung across his shoulder.

"Do I get any weapons?" asked Belford. "I mean, you've got a sword, and you have a bow."

"Here," said Javic, handing him a tiny belt knife. "Don't hurt yourself."

"Ha ha, very funny. I don't think I could hurt a fly with this."

"Probably not, flies are pretty fast. Maybe we can find you a stick or something when we get into the woods."

Belford sighed. He probably would have hurt himself with anything larger than the belt knife, but that didn't stop him from wanting something more impressive.

Elric disappeared back into the farmhouse, doing one final sweep for any forgotten supplies as Belford and Javic climbed onto their mounts. Getting into Amit's saddle was harder than it had been the night before. Each time Belford attempted to swing his leg up and over her back, his poorly fitting, heavy pants would cause him to fail and fall back down. The dark-brown mare whinnied and began to prance around as Belford managed to get himself into an awkward position with his stomach overtop the saddle.

"Easy there, Amit," said Javic, steadying her with a pat on the nose. Belford was only able to slide into the mount with Javic's help.

"Time to ride, boys," said Elric, back from the house. He hopped spryly onto his horse and walked it past them.

"When are we coming back?" asked Javic.

Elric pointedly ignored the question.

"I still don't even really know where we are right now," said Belford.

Javic looked thoughtful for a moment. "That's true. At least I have a place to come back to."

CHAPTER

6

Slaughter

Wilgoblikan peered out from behind the trees at the edge of a clearing, his attention immediately drawn to a farm house that now stood before him at the clearing's center. The humble home, built in an older style than most in the region, was easily the most pathetic of the nine dwellings he had visited in the past few hours.

One of his Snatchers, Maswald Baltren, had failed miserably in his duties. Wilgoblikan was not pleased. Instead of discovering his target's exact whereabouts, or at least killing him when he had the chance, he managed to alert him of his dire situation and let him slip away unhindered. After receiving Maswald's report, Wilgoblikan traveled swiftly in an attempt to reach Darrenfield before moon-down.

He began to laugh to himself as he reminisced over Maswald's screams for mercy – how quickly the cries for forgiveness had become unintelligible wails, hardly distinguishable from those of a tortured animal dying slowly in a fire. The Snatcher's howls did not stop Wilgoblikan: No, on the contrary, they only fueled him on as he twisted the useless fool into his first Whune of the full moon.

Although stupid, Whunes made superb soldiers; their only downfall was their short lifespan – well, that, and of course their unfortunate odor. Their fierce fighting capabilities and inability to feel pain made them the perfect tool in many situations. And that was what they were to Wilgoblikan: Tools, just like any other. The fact that they were so easy to renew made their one-year-long existence only a minor annoyance. Besides, he did enjoy turning people into Whunes, and to him, this greatly offset any inconveniences. He took great pleasure in hearing peoples' pain-filled wails throughout the transformation process, so much so, in fact, that he purposefully made the transition even more excruciating than already physically necessary.

Such an ignorant corner of the world this was; to think that people would actually run *towards* the sound of the screams instead of cowering beneath their beds where they belonged. It had been so very nice of them to save him the trouble of tracking them all down. He was able to augment his ranks of Whunes within just a few moments of arriving in Darrenfield. Unfortunately, it had not been fast enough. The moon set, and he had not yet found his target.

The moon vanished while he was still at the third farm out from Darrenfield, causing the next five visits to be somewhat messier than the first three. Without the moon, Wilgoblikan was left devoid of his Power and unable to create more Whunes. With the moon down, the existing Whunes were now allowed to partake in a slaughter unlike any seen in Darrenfield since the end of the Cleansing, nearly a century ago. The older Goblikans still spoke fondly of the war – the glorious carnage still fresh in their memories after all this time. It had been too long since the Whunes walked openly throughout the lands of

Aragwey, but their time would come again, and soon; they would leave their ravaging marks upon this land once more.

At the last farm, the Whunes smashed through the doors with their great axes and dragged out all they found within for Wilgoblikan's inspection. A middle-aged couple, Tammy and Obe Milston, along with their three children – Wilgoblikan didn't bother to learn the young ones' names. They were still asleep in their beds when the Whunes forced their entrance. None matched his target's description, and so the Whunes commenced with what they enjoyed most: Maiming and killing.

The father died instantly as he was hacked to pieces by the Whunes' merciless axes. The others were not so lucky: First losing limbs or simply being eaten alive whilst their remaining family members were forced to watch in horror. Of course, none were spared.

Later, stories of bandits or wild animals would start to spread as people began to feel the absence of the dead. But by then, he would be long gone. Wilgoblikan paid little attention to the slaughter. It wasn't as much fun when he didn't get to inflict the pain personally. Without the Power, killing was so messy. All the blood would have soiled his clothing. The stickiness had a way of making him feel so… uncivilized.

Refocusing on the matter at hand, Wilgoblikan lifted his arm and pointed towards the small farm at the center of the clearing. And that was all it took. At his command, the Whunes descended from the woods like a swarm of locusts, destroying all in their path. Some smashed their way inside the farmhouse while others simply lumbered towards the various cattle that had been roaming the fenced in portion of the pasture. The Whunes began to consume the cows, fur and all, lacerating their insides as the beasts desperately tried to cling to life, writhing around on the ground in the vain hope of escape; but there was nowhere to run.

The Whunes that had entered the farmhouse came back out empty-handed and quickly joined their brethren in the

slaughter of the farm animals. Wilgoblikan approached the
farm now; he would conduct his own search. It did not take
long. Lying in a pile on the floor of one of the rooms, he found
his target's clothing. There was no doubt about it: He was the
one they were searching for. Fleeing would only delay the
inevitable. He would find him, and when he did, he would kill
him. The longer he made him search, the more painful he
pledged to make his death, and the more innocent people
would join him in his grave. He commanded his Whunes to
torch the farm – just for the pleasure of watching it burn – then
began his pursuit. He had been looking forward to this hunt for
a long time now; a very long time indeed.

* * *

Orange flames crept up the wooden slats of the farmhouse,
licking the siding black as they climbed ever higher. As soon
as the fire reached the thatched roof, a dense cloud of black
smoke erupted from the structure. It went up quickly. Most of
the Whunes were enjoying the show – dancing around the
flames and howling into the morning air with glee. The sight
of the destructive force was enough to temporarily satiate their
need for violence. It was the closest they got to fulfillment
without actually taking a life. Only during the exact moment
of a kill was a Whune ever truly at peace.

As the farm burned, a slight twinge of regret clawed its way
into the mind of one of the Whunes. She sat low on her
haunches, wrapped in a confused silence over the pinch that
was forming in her gut. It was an unfamiliar feeling – Whunes
were not meant to experience such emotions, but something
about this particular farmhouse sparked a sensation within her
that was more primal than even her lust for destruction and
bloodletting.

An image of a boy tore its way through her thoughts – jaw
held tight with reservation; hazel eyes, unfocused and sad
beneath a mop of curly, brown hair. His face stirred raw

emotion within her. The loss of the farm would devastate him. Picturing the hurt in his eyes sent a tidal wave of guilt coursing down her curved spine. She yelped out as the unpleasant sensation consumed her – physical ailments could do her no harm, but this mental anguish was something else entirely!

She scratched at the sides of her head with her claws, trying desperately to tear the image of the boy straight out of her skull. As her skin peeled up and black blood dribbled down her temples, her method actually seemed to be working. The boy's face began to fade, sliding back into obscurity and out of her conscious mind.

Soon, distracted by the flames, she began to forget the strange occurrence altogether. Whunes did not dwell on the past. The only time that mattered was the present moment. The crackling flames consumed the farmhouse, rendering it into a dense pile of embers and ash. She joined her fellow Whunes, prancing around the edges of the charred structure until her master commanded them onwards.

CHAPTER

7

A Time for Luck

Stale tranquility stretched on throughout what was proving to be yet another windless day amidst the sparse undergrowth of the forest. The wilted shrubbery drooped low against the dry soil of the forest floor as if in testament to the drought's hold over the lands of Aragwey. The calmness of the morning was accentuated by the lingering smell of pine needles filling the motionless air around the trees, the stillness broken only by the wings of the morning birds hustling about their daily activities. Even the birds seemed less than exuberant about the midsummer's heat continuing on through another month of autumn.

It was slightly cooler under the canopy, where branches blocked out the direct light from the sun, than it was out on the main road. There, the shade was often broken by rays of sunlight shining down onto the faces of the three travelers. Fortunately, the lack of humidity in the air made the heat at least somewhat tolerable. The path they rode on was wide enough for four horses to walk abreast, but they had chosen to ride in single file.

Javic watched as Belford leaned forward in his saddle, laying his face down onto the back of Amit's neck. He quickly sat up again, wrinkling his nose at the scent. Looking up ahead, Javic could see the path beginning to open up into a small clearing. The gap in the trees exposed a grouping of large boulders that looked like a convenient place to take a rest. Elric thought so too. He led them up to the rocks and they all dismounted and began to stretch out their legs.

Although they had only been riding for a few hours, it was clear by the way Belford was walking that his legs were already stiff as boards. This was no surprise to Javic. Early on, he observed Belford using all of his might clenching his knees against Amit's saddle. To Belford's credit, he at least partially heeded Javic's advice by loosening up his grip with his hands; he was more relaxed than the night before on their ride to town.

Although Amit was the tamest horse Javic had ever owned, Belford still insisted she was plotting to throw him off. Javic informed him that horses don't plot, but he would not be dissuaded. Javic wondered what would happen if Belford ever tried to ride a horse with a little more spirit. Imagining Belford on Olli was amusing. He surely would end up doubled over in the saddle with his eyes squeezed tightly shut, holding on for dear life. Javic smiled to himself at the thought, but a moment later his concern for Salvine forced the corners of his mouth back down into what had become their default position.

Elric offered Javic and Belford pieces of dried meat from his saddlebag. Belford accepted eagerly and began gnawing at the jerky as he walked over to the boulders in the center of the clearing. Javic didn't have an appetite, but he took a piece as well, placing it in his shirt pocket for later.

As worried as Javic should have been for his own safety, his thoughts had room only for Salvine. *Missing for five days....*

*Nobody bothered searching for her because everyone assumed
she was with me.... This is beyond terrible!*

Elric's declaration that it was "already too late" for Salvine
didn't make Javic feel any better. His original assumption –
that Salvine missed her visit on purpose as a rejection of his
romantic advances – was all wrong. Something bad must have
happened to her. Javic could feel it in his bones. He couldn't
hold back any longer. He needed the explanation his
grandfather had promised him. "How do you know we're in
danger?" he asked. "And what do you mean 'it's too late' for
Salvine?"

Elric looked uneasy. Javic watched as his grandfather let the
fingers of his right hand run idly across the old wedding band
that hung loose on a chain around his neck. It belonged to
Javic's father, Bartan, before his death. The ring had resided
against his grandfather's chest for many years now. Though
they never spoke of it, Javic noticed his grandfather caress the
ring whenever the subject of his father came up in
conversation. Javic wasn't sure why Elric's fingers went there
now. Elric seemed lost in thought for a moment. With a
vacant stare on his face, he began to speak. "Let me tell you a
story," he said, glancing back and forth across both Javic and
Belford.

Javic sighed. Elric's stories were always filled with great
deeds of valor and heroism that were normally reserved for
fairytales and myths. As a child, Javic had often longed for the
stories to be true, daydreaming about being a great hero
himself. He realized now, though, that many of the events that
his grandfather spoke of were simply too outrageous to have
ever really happened.

Elric grimaced slightly at Javic before taking a deep breath.
"Back nearly twenty years ago, just four years before you were
born, Javic, after your father and I had already been recruited
into the Ver'konus, Lord Ethan's resistance group, we were
assigned to a guard detail and had been sworn to protect a pair
of young sisters by the names of Meldreth and Kali."

Despite Javic's concerns, he couldn't help but smile at the mention of Kali, his mother. Elric rarely spoke of either of Javic's parents, and although Javic was naturally curious about them, he had learned to carefully avoid bringing up the subject with his grandfather. The last time he questioned Elric about his parents, Elric started crying. It made Javic very uncomfortable to see his grandfather in such distress. Because of this, most of what he knew about his father had come from talking to the other residents of Darrenfield – those who were old enough to remember his father when he was just a boy. No one in Darrenfield had ever met his mother, though, so he knew very little about her beyond her name.

"This assignment wasn't until after your grandmother passed away, mind you, and as you might imagine, your father and I were both furious with King Garrett, for it was he who was responsible for her death." Elric's eyes unfocused slightly, he seemed to be staring right through Javic now. When Elric talked about Javic's grandmother, Teresa, he always became angry and sad at the same time. His voice faltered a little as he continued on with his story, "When your father found out about Lord Ethan's resistance he joined the fight against Garrett without a moment of hesitation, and I was right there by his side. It's fortunate that we did join, for if we hadn't, your parents would never have met."

Javic perked up. He had always wondered how his father, born a simple farm boy like himself, had ended up with an outlander for a bride.

"Your mother was a very beautiful young lady – Kali Genavil, she used to be called back then. She was only nineteen years old, but she was brilliant for her age. She had long dark-brown hair and it was quite wavy – not so much curly like yours. You got that from your father.

"King Garrett sent out search parties all over the countryside, hell-bent on finding your mother and her sister. He launched quite an exciting chase for us. Every day, we would move closer towards the coast, dodging patrols as we rode farther and farther away from the great city of Tavallon. We were headed east towards the harbor town known as Salenport. Lord Ethan promised a Phandolian merchant vessel would be waiting for our arrival there. He was to have it manned by a loyal crew and sailed there under the pretense of trading, but really they were on a mission to smuggle us all the way around to the other side of Aragwey, far from Garrett's search parties.

"For a time, it seemed as if your mother and her older sister were the ones protecting us rather than the other way around. They had great power, as did your grandmother before she died. I've told you before how King Garrett is a powerful wizard. People say he is one of the greatest, actually, though not if you measure greatness in kindness, for he surely doesn't have much of that. Garrett despises anyone who can use the Power like he can, though I would bet it is fear that drives him to hunt down people with the Gift. When he finds them, he has them killed like rabid animals. People like your grandmother." Elric said the last part very coldly, frowning now. "Garrett has been doing this for nearly a century, ever since he first rose to power. That's why he had your grandmother killed, and that's why he was chasing after Kali and Meldreth.

"You would think King Garrett would be quite an old man after ruling for one hundred years, but people say he makes himself younger every few decades by use of the Power. Others insist he just gets replaced each time he's old enough to be knocked from the throne with any ease.

"Anyway, when your grandmother first started showing signs of the Gift, we couldn't help but be excited. The things she could do... miraculous things... she made all of our lives better. We hadn't known much about the dangers of King Garrett at the time, but we decided to keep Teresa's abilities a secret anyway, and were successful for a number of years. Unfortunately, one day, someone from town must have spied upon her using her powers. Overnight, rumors began to spread across the village. It wasn't long before assassins showed up at our farm and murdered her while your father and I were away purchasing supplies for the upcoming harvest. That's why we joined up with Lord Ethan: Partially out of revenge, but mostly to stop Garrett from doing the same to anyone else.

"With your mother and Meldreth being able to use the Power, they hardly needed strong-arms like your father and I to protect them. We watched them incinerate more than a few assassins in fiery explosions during our time together. They could rip people into tiny pieces, a flurry of blood and guts, if they wanted to. However, they could only use their powers when the moon was up, strongest when it was high in the sky, and so they needed our swords to protect them during the rest of the day. That's one of the drawbacks with the Power – I learned that much from your grandmother – and it must have been true, for I never once saw the girls use their powers when the moon was down, not even the day we were ambushed just shy of reaching Salenport Harbor.

"It was late in the afternoon, the moon not yet visible above the horizon, when a group of Kovani assassins dropped from the trees and attacked us. They must have heard our approach and climbed into the branches above our path, hiding until we were right below them. It was a bloody struggle. The other three men in our party were killed, but somehow we still managed to take down all eight of our attackers. Kali even killed one of them herself, using only a dagger. We pushed the horses as fast as they would go for the remaining few leagues into Salenport. Our mounts nearly gave out during the last five hundred paces, but we finally made it to the harbor just as the sun was setting.

"As we walked the horses through the town towards the docks, I noticed that something was amiss. You see, normally in busy port towns, such as Salenport, men continue working long after the sun goes down, but that night nobody was in the streets. All of the houses and stores were dark. Neither man nor beast broke the palpable silence as we cautiously approached the docks. Our horses' steps echoed off of the high walls of the Port Authority building as we made our way through the final square before the waterfront. We reached the harbor, but there seemed to be no one there either. Dismounting, we led our horses up to the piers.

"Just then, off in the distance, a darkly dressed man noticed us and ran away down an alleyway. We wanted to ask him what had happened there; he could have been a frightened survivor of whatever dark magic had stripped the town of its inhabitants. Leaving our horses behind – as they were too tired to put up a chase – we lumbered after the man. He turned down one alleyway and then the next, at times darting out of sight; we followed the sound of his footsteps ahead of us in the darkness, though the directions the man had taken were difficult to determine. Echoes often play tricks on the ear. We rounded a final corner and found ourselves at a dead end. The man was nowhere to be seen, and we couldn't hear his footsteps any longer.

"As we turned around to retrace our path, a group of large, hideous monsters rushed in at us. No two were exactly alike, but they all had massive limbs as thick as tree trunks and bulging features, like a patchwork of filthy lambskins sewn together and stuffed full to the point of tearing. Their eyes, too small on their enormous faces, bulged from their heads. The scent of spoiled meat and bile filled the air, wafting from their bodies in wave after nauseating wave. I had just enough time to draw my sword and swing at the nearest creature before it turned to dust right in front of my very eyes, my sword swinging through nothing but air. In my state of surprise, I inhaled some of the powder that had just been part of the monster. Coughing uncontrollably, I attempted to expel the filth from my lungs.

"These creatures, called Whunes, are the twisted soldiers of King Garrett's dark army. And unfortunately for me, another Whune rushed forward to take the place of the first before I'd even finished coughing. It proceeded to knock me off my feet, then hefted a large black axe made from some sort of peculiar metal above its oddly shaped head. Its face twisted into a grotesquely un-human expression as it bore down on me with its axe. I thought I was surely going to die. But just before the axe could dig into my flesh, that creature too, axe and all, vanished into dust.

"It had been the girls who saved our lives. I hate to think what would have happened had the moon not emerged before the Whunes attacked. We ran back towards the docks as more horrible monsters leaped out at us through the darkness. They came out of buildings that appeared empty the first time we passed them in pursuit of the stranger. They sprang out to meet us from every alleyway that merged in with our own. The girls kept destroying them, one after another, before they could harm us. At one point, we all had to duck a large axe that was thrown our way. It surely would have beheaded us had we remained standing. One of the axes struck a wall right by my arm, nearly taking it off. We never did learn what happened to the people of Salenport; we never saw any bodies, but surely they had not escaped the Whunes.

"When we finally made it back to the docks, we selected the fastest vessel a crew of four could successfully sail, brought our horses onboard and left Salenport behind in the darkness. We traveled past a few ports before turning the boat to meet the shore.

"After that, it was just the simple matter of selling the boat we took from Salenport to get the money necessary for hiring a larger vessel with an experienced crew to take us to our final destination. It was on that trip that your parents fell deeply in love."

As fascinating – and clearly embellished – as Elric's story was, Javic had heard enough. "What's the point of all this?" he asked. "What does any of this have to do with why we had to leave?

"Look!" exclaimed Belford, pointing back in the direction they had just come from. Elric and Javic both turned their heads to where Belford was pointing. Shading their eyes from the sun they could just barely make out through the morning haze what appeared to be a thick cloud of black smoke streaming up above the treetops in the distance.

Elric's eyes were stone cold. "Fire."

Javic's heart jumped into his throat. "Is it... our farm?" he barely managed to speak out, the implications too horrid to bear.

"I don't doubt it," said Elric, a tone of sadness apparent in his voice. "We better assume the worst."

"You were right..." Javic whispered. He had ridden to this point many times before. He knew precisely where the farm was. He couldn't even begin to think about it; he had spent his entire life on the farm with his grandfather, it was everything he knew, everything he loved. *It can't just be gone!*

"The worst?" asked Belford.

Elric nodded. "That whoever did this is trying to find you, and that they're heading our way." Elric turned away from the smoke. "We need to get off the main road." He walked his horse off the path, into the trees to the left of the clearing. "Come on boys, break time is over. There's an old hunting trail to the east of here. It winds down through the hills. I think it's probably our best chance of escape."

Belford grumbled to himself as he began the long struggle of trying to get back into his saddle. It took him several tries, but he managed without Javic's help. After he was back up, he attempted to eat his jerky and ride at the same time, but nearly fell off as Amit veered slightly to the left. He put the meat away in his shirt pocket and returned to holding onto his reins with both hands.

Javic rode along in a dazed silence. His grandfather hadn't answered any of his questions, and seeing the smoke in the distance piled many new questions on top of the existing ones. *Where will we go? What will we do if the farm is really gone?* He had always assumed he would live there forever and be a farmer like his grandfather. With no home to return to after this was all over, it no longer felt the short interlude he had been anticipating. This would be his reality now: On the run with nowhere to call home, like some sort of vagabond gypsy or refugee. *But who are we even running from? What does Salvine's disappearance have to do with any of this?*

Zigzagging through the trees was going to be quite a bit more time consuming than riding on the path had been. That, coupled with the threat of pursuit, made Javic anxious.

Belford, on the other hand, did not seem as concerned about the whole situation as he ought to be. "So, how long before we get to wherever we're going?" he asked.

Elric turned around in his saddle and looked at Belford before answering. "After we reach the hunting trail," he gestured ahead of them, "we have another full day's ride before we get to our first stop: A border city called Felington."

Belford looked thoughtful for a moment, but then shook his head. "That name doesn't sound familiar. Not that that's a surprise."

"I've got a map with me. How about I show it to you the next time we stop – see if you can remember anything?" Elric asked.

"That sounds good," said Belford.

Javic barely heard their exchange; he was surrounded by a chorus of his own despondent thoughts. *What if I never see Salvine again? How is running away supposed to help me find answers?*

The autumn harvest festival was coming up in just a few short weeks, and Javic had been planning on asking Salvine to attend with him. Now he would never get the chance. Javic had planned out exactly how he was going to ask her – played out every scenario over and over again in his head. None of the futures Javic had envisioned for himself would ever happen now. He would never win her heart; never get to kiss her and tell her how long he had wanted to hold her in his arms.

"What's the point of going there, though? To Felington, I mean," asked Belford.

"I hope to find someone there that can lead us to the Ver'konus – to Ethan," said Elric.

Javic hadn't really been paying much attention to Belford and his grandfather's conversation up until this point. But now, with the mention of Ethan – *could the 'Lord Ethan' from his stories really exist?* – Javic suddenly burst into the conversation, "Wait, wait, wait. Lord Ethan is real?" Skepticism was clear in his voice.

"Of course he's real." Elric looked surprised that Javic would even ask such a thing. "I must have told you at least a hundred different stories about him while you were growing up. Did you think I just made them all up?"

Javic's face went red – that was exactly what he had assumed.

Belford chimed in: "You said he was the leader of some resistance, but who exactly is this 'Lord Ethan'?" he asked.

"He formed the Ver'konus," said Elric, "but to me he's just an old friend – a man I used to work with."

"Just a man!" Javic exclaimed. "He's a wizard! And not just any ordinary wizard, he's Ver'ati, and an extremely powerful one! And he rescues people from King Garrett, people who can use the Power!"

Belford looked confused. "There's that word again… could somebody please tell me what *Ver'ati* means? I feel like we're not even speaking English anymore."

It was Elric's turn to look confused. "What's *English*?" he asked. "We're speaking Aragwian – though the word *Ver'ati* is of the old tongue."

Belford rubbed his hand across his temple, as if trying to massage away a headache. "I don't know… the word just popped into my brain… I thought it was right."

Elric gave a grim chuckle. "Well, anyway, to answer your question: Ver'ati are wizards trained by the Arcanum; it means *Hand of God* in the ancient tongue. They can use the Power – magic – and yes Javic, Ethan is a wizard and so is King Garrett for that matter. But wizard or not, Ethan is still a man, and with his fair share of faults and vices just like any other. I would say King Garrett, on the other hand, has more than his fair share."

The murder of Javic's grandmother and his grandfather's subsequent attempts at revenge floated back into his mind.

Elric seemed to be thinking about those events as well, but he did not waste time reminiscing. He glanced back at Belford again before continuing, "As I said before, Belford, King Garrett hunts down and murders anyone who can use the Power. Many years ago Ethan organized a resistance against Garrett's expanding rule, the Ver'konus – *Hand of Man* – they are called. Now he rescues people with the Gift and trains them to fight alongside him."

Thinking back through what his grandfather had just said, a couple of thing still didn't quite add up. "If all of this is true, what are we going to Lord Ethan for? What does he have to do with us?"

Elric turned to Javic. "Because, don't you see: I told you Belford healed me last night. He can use the Power; I suspect he is Ver'ati – he has too much talent to be untrained – though without his memory, it is impossible to say for sure. Regardless, he is a wizard, and that makes the people chasing us most likely Garrett's men, sent to kill him. Only Ethan can protect us now if that is the case." A pinch of horror latched onto Javic's chest, constricting tightly. Elric flashed him a little smile intended as reassurance. "Do try to keep your spirits up; I've gotten out of worse situations. Well… not much worse, but worse none-the-less."

Javic was speechless. He turned to Belford, expecting him to dispute the claim that he was a wizard, but he only diverted his eyes, his silence confirming it as true. Javic didn't know how to feel. It was just too much information to take in all at once. He could only imagine how Belford must be feeling: One man wanted him dead – a king no less! – and another wanted to save him and train him to fight for the Ver'konus. Even for Javic, it was almost too much to handle. A daze of bewilderment danced through his mind as he tried to comprehend it all. "That means you must have been casting some sort of spell when I found you yesterday. There were all kinds of lights and sounds!"

"That's not really how it works," said Elric.

"You know how it works?" Javic asked, even more amazed.

Elric nodded. "Your grandmother told me many things about the Power before she died, and I learned much during my years in the Ver'konus. What you saw could have very well been magic, and most likely was, but wizards have no spells or rituals like those practiced by medicine-men or the self-proclaimed mystics of Antara. Those sorts of things are reserved for religious practices. Using the Power is more of a discipline than anything else. I'd tell you more about it, but I don't want Belford trying anything stupid and getting us all killed."

"What sort of things can I do with the Power?" asked a wide-eyed Belford, clearly intrigued.

"Like I said, I don't want you trying anything stupid." Elric smiled. "It would be best if you didn't think too hard about it until your memory returns. There are many dangers one should be aware of before using the Power."

Javic and Belford shared a quick glance. The initial shock of the situation was only just beginning to wear off, but already a cloud of apprehension was settling around them.

Belford had more questions. "How common are wizards?"

Elric answered matter-of-factly, "Not all that common, actually. You probably won't find any out in the open in the whole kingdom of Taris – uh, that's where we are now," he added, "King Garrett holds much influence over these lands; King Vouldric, our own king, has been little more than a puppet of Garrett's will for many years now. In Garrett's own kingdom – Kovehn, as it is called – it's not even legal to speak of the Power, let alone use it. These days, when people learn they have the Gift, they usually try to flee to Phandrol before anyone else recognizes them for what they are. That's where the Ver'konus is, operating with aid and support from the

Queen of Phandrol herself. So that is where we are ultimately headed. Ethan's contact in Felington should know the fastest and safest route to get us there."

"Who is this *contact* you keep speaking of anyway?" asked Belford.

Elric shrugged. "I really don't know. We can only hope that Ethan still has a contact in Felington. If indeed he does, and provided that things haven't changed too much since I left the Ver'konus, I know a secret code for asking him to reveal himself to us."

Belford looked troubled. "But what if he isn't there or doesn't reveal himself?"

"We move on. We need to put as much distance between ourselves and our pursuers as we possibly can in the next few days."

Belford nodded in acceptance, satisfied in his queries for the time being. Javic, on the other hand, had so many things jumping around inside of his head that he simply didn't know where to start. "And what about Salvine...?" he finally managed to ask.

Elric slumped slightly in his saddle, clearly not wanting to answer the question. The silence stretched on for another moment before he finally spoke. "The mission your father and I went on to rescue your mother and her sister... you see, we were sent to them because of the other missing children. When Garrett's minions are about, the youth are always the first to go missing. I don't claim to know their fates, but those they take are never heard from again."

Javic suddenly felt as if his heart had crumbled to ash beneath his flesh. It still beat, but with a hollow thud as all his blood turned to ice within his veins. If it was true, Salvine was really gone, and Javic would never get to know what they could have been. There were no answers – not back in Darrenfield, not anywhere. Part of him wished he hadn't gone into town the night before. That way he would have left Darrenfield thinking that Salvine simply did not love him back.

The pain in his chest did not subside. There was nothing he could do to numb this kind of hurt.

Salvine was gone forever. He reserved himself in silence as he mourned. He could still picture her radiant smile and the way her golden curls bounced from side to side as he presented her with the dove charm bracelet the week before. Her gray eyes lit up brighter than he had ever seen, sparklingly like gemstones in the sunlight as he said the final goodbye he would ever speak to her.

If only I had known what was about to happen. I could have stopped her from leaving. Made her stay with me where I could have kept her safe.

It was a fruitless line of thought. He knew there was no going back, but that did not stop his hollowed out heart from yearning all the more for the impossible. Javic could not stop the tears from falling as he moved onwards through the parched forest – away from the burnt remains of the only place he had ever called home.

CHAPTER

8

Mark of Kings

Javic did his best to put everything his grandfather had told him out of his mind as they continued towards the hunting trail. They rode for almost two hours without talking. The off-road journey was difficult to traverse compared to a path across open country. The jagged limbs of the trees slumped ominously towards them, thrusting withered branches precariously into their path as they rode by. This was a particularly troubling trend as far as Elric was concerned. He worried that the continuous stream of snagged branches would be enough for anyone who knew what they were looking for to easily follow their trail, defeating the purpose of abandoning the main road in the first place. They quickly learned that no amount of caution would completely conceal their trail, and so decided to focus all of their energies on traveling with as much haste as possible.

Javic tried to pretend he was just out on an ordinary ride, but thoughts of Salvine kept creeping back in. He found himself replaying their final conversation over and over again in his head.

"What's this?" she had asked him as he slid the thin silver chain out of his pocket and clasped it around her wrist.

"It's for good luck," he said.

Salvine held the dangling dove charm up to her eyes, inspecting it from every angle. It was made of Tarisian silver, the purist silver in all of Aragwey. Its flawless surface reflected her face back to her. "You know, giving a girl a gift like this might make her think you have certain *intentions*."

Javic felt his cheeks flush. "It's not like that… it's just—"

"Do you?" she asked, her eyes flashing with amusement as Javic squirmed. "Do you have *intentions* for me, Javic Elensol?" Salvine smiled brightly, her gray eyes sparkling.

Javic knew she was just teasing him, but he really did have intentions. It felt like Salvine was looking right through him. His only choice was to return the banter if he was to have any hope of coming out of the situation with his dignity still intact. "If you don't like it, I'm sure I can find somebody else to take it off my hands," he said, tongue-in-cheek.

"Now, now," said Salvine, "I didn't say that. I can unburden you of this charm if you really need the help. It is quite heavy on my wrist, though." Salvine feigned as if the thin charm was dragging her whole arm down with a massive weight.

Javic caught her wrist in his open palm as she made it fall to her side. He reached out with his other hand and swept aside a golden lock of hair that had fallen across her face. He began to lean in. He had no idea what had come over him, but his heart was beating out of his chest as he pursed his lips and went in for the kiss.

At the last moment, Salvine shifted her head to the side, and Javic's lips brushed up against her cheek instead. He felt his face growing hot once more as embarrassment seeped from his every pore. Salvine didn't say anything; she too had a slight tinge of red visible in her cheeks. Javic ran his hand through his own hair. He wanted to shrink into the ground and never come back out.

"Next week, then?" said Salvine. She quickly jumped onto her mare. Her posture was stiff as she stared out ahead with a wide-eyed expression.

Javic mumbled some kind of answer as Salvine began to ride north, back towards town. "Bye," Javic managed to speak out finally, before Salvine had moved out of earshot. She looked back and gave a little wave before kicking her mare into a full gallop.

Javic nervously anticipated her return all week, but when she did not come, he had given up hope of her sharing his feelings. Now, though, he knew her absence was not of her own choice. He continued to replay the conversation, trying to envision a scenario in which she would have stayed with him instead of riding back into town, but his imagination failed him. Salvine always rode away; always gave the same little wave as she pushed her mare to move faster away from Javic and his botched kiss. Maybe if he hadn't tried to kiss her at all, her actions would have been slightly different. Maybe she would have stayed for a few minutes longer, or joined him for supper, changing the entire trajectory of her week so that she did not have to disappear.

Javic's worries and what-if's formed a pit in his abdomen. He latched onto the solid feeling and used it to compartmentalize his emotions for Salvine. He pressed them together like a lump of coal and forced them into the dense structure in his gut where he would not have to feel them so heavily. They remained as pressure, ever present, but somewhat subdued on the inside.

Elric had no idea of the inner turmoil that plagued Javic over the loss of Salvine. He was already sick in bed by the time their relationship began to blossom. As far as Elric knew, Salvine was just a longtime friend to Javic, nothing more. Javic wasn't sure what Salvine was to him either, really, but he pressed all of that inside as well. It was all in the past now. Nothing would come of it. He didn't want Belford or his grandfather to know how badly he hurt. He felt it would be embarrassing, somehow. Putting on a straight face, he masked his pain as the group pushed forward along the hunting trail.

Elric increased their riding pace to a slow trot. He dared not drive the horses any faster. He wanted them to be able to maintain the pace throughout the rest of the day; any faster and the animals would be required to stop every couple leagues to recuperate. Elric did not wish to waste even a single moment. He pressed on until around noon before stopping to let the horses eat their feed and drink some water from a nearby stream. While the horses rested, Elric prepared a small midday meal that consisted primarily of more dried meat and a block of cheese left over from their uneaten breakfast.

As he had promised earlier, Elric produced a small map from his saddlebag and handed it over to Belford to have a look. Elric then proceeded to take a mental inventory of all the supplies that Javic hastily packed earlier that morning. He opened the first bag and began digging through it.

Belford, map in hand, wandered to one side of the trail before lifting the parchment up to his eyes. He closely examined the words and glyphs on the finely detailed drawing, at times holding it right up against his nose.

Javic walked around behind him to get a view of it from over his shoulder. "You're holding it upside-down," he said.

Belford yanked the map away from his face. He was looking flustered but did not say anything. Holding the map the right way around, Belford once again began to scrutinize its markings, but after only a few moments he pulled it back down to his side in exasperation. "I can't read a single word on here. I don't even know how to pronounce any of these letters!"

Javic raised one eyebrow. "A wizard *and* illiterate? Now that's a strange combination."

Belford sighed and handed the map to Javic. "Why don't you make yourself useful and start pointing out some places on here for me?"

They walked over to a fallen tree on the left side of the trail and sat down. Javic unfolded the map the rest of the way. "Alright, well we are somewhere around here, southeast of Darrenfield."

Belford nodded along. "Does that make this Felington?" He pointed at the closest dot south of Darrenfield.

"Yes, it does," answered Javic.

"Then that means we're only about a fourth of the way there," Belford sighed with disappointment, then rubbed his sore backside with dreaded anticipation of the next leg of their journey.

Javic moved on, ignoring Belford's complaint. "This city up here on the coast is Saldrone – it's the capital of Taris, which encompasses this whole region here," he traced a circle around the kingdom with his fingertip. "As you can see, Felington sits right on the corner of the borders between Taris, Kovehn, and Graven; it's officially part of Taris though. I went to Felington once a couple of years ago with Grandfather. It's a very... diverse city. Anyway, I've never traveled beyond Felington before, but way down here in the south, past the Minthune River, is Phandrol."

Before Javic could continue, Elric strode over with a frown on his face. Javic glanced up from the map.

"You didn't do a very good job packing," said Elric. "You brought enough dried meat to last us until we get to Felington, at least, but all of the other food is useless since we don't have any pots or matches to start a cooking fire."

Javic's face reddened slightly. Elric wasn't usually so reproachful. They gathered their horses. Javic rubbed Olli's nose before reattaching his now lightened saddlebag to her side, and Elric disposed of the extra provisions into a patch of particularly thick underbrush. There was no use in weighing down the horses any further than they needed to, but they still couldn't afford for anyone else to find the supplies either. If their pursuers discovered the provisions it would only confirm that they were on the right track. Elric chose the leafiest bush he could find and tossed the lot of it deep into the middle where it would be least likely to attract notice.

They continued riding southeast throughout the remainder of the daylight hours. The trail weaved through an unchanging landscape of hills and fir trees until, finally, the path began to curve back around on itself into an increasingly northern trajectory. This signaled that it was now time for them to depart from the trail and start heading directly south towards the city of Felington. With daylight beginning to fail, it was nearly time to make camp for the night. They continued on until dusk, getting as far away as they could from the hunting trail before settling down in a small clearing for the night.

Hungry and exhausted, Elric pulled out some more dried meat for them to eat for dinner.

"Oh great, more jerky..." said Belford. "This stuff makes my teeth feel loose."

Javic's face reddened again. He was still getting used to Belford's sarcasm, but it was clear he was displeased with Javic's packing job as well. He put his hand into one of his shirt pockets and discovered what felt to be a small tin box. He didn't remember putting anything there. He wrapped his fingers around the box and withdrew his hand. It was the box of matches from the kitchen.

Elric noticed the tin, but didn't comment.

Belford saw it as well. He rolled his eyes, shaking his head slightly as he chuckled softly to himself. He reached over and patted Javic on the shoulder.

I guess I didn't do such a bad job packing after all.

Despite now having the capability of making fire, they continued to sit in the cool night air as they finished their meal. Even if they hadn't thrown out their other provisions, a small cook fire might have given away their location. None of them were willing to risk detection for a little warmth. Garrett's men would surely keep watch throughout the night for any sign of smoke.

After dinner, as they were preparing to get some rest, Belford began removing his shirt and looked over at Elric. "I have something here that I've been meaning to ask you about."

Javic moved closer to see what Belford was referring to.

Belford undid the last button of his outer shirt and slipped it off his shoulders, and then began to pull his undershirt over the top of his head. "This," he said as he revealed a tattoo like branding on his left arm.

Elric moved his head closer to Belford's arm to get a better view in the moonlight. Before Javic could even make out what it was that he was looking at, Elric gasped in surprise. He reached out to touch the marking for a moment before pulling his hand back and placing it over his now gaping mouth.

"What is it?" Javic asked, feeling a chill run up his spine.

Elric did not answer straight away. Instead he continued to stare at the branding. His mind seemed to be in another place entirely. Suddenly he snapped back to his senses and looked straight into Belford's eyes. "It looks authentic. I just wish I could be sure." He spoke more to himself than to anybody else.

Javic had no idea what he was talking about, and so repeated his question.

Elric heard him this time. "It appears to be the *Mark of Kings*. We are in even greater danger than I thought."

"Why? What does it mean?" asked Belford apprehensively.

"It is a very ancient marking. The triangles represent the four elements: Fire, earth, air, and water. That's not what has me worried though, but rather what the symbols represent when put together in this arrangement."

Javic realized he was holding his breath. He forced himself to start breathing again, but neither he nor Belford dared speak while Elric still had more to say.

"As far as I know, the first person to bear this mark was a man named John Graven. That was a thousand years ago.

Legend says he was the first and most powerful wizard to ever walk the lands of Aragwey." Elric removed his diary from his saddlebag and frantically began flipping through the pages. He continued talking as he scanned through. "Before John's time, Aragwey was little more than a multitude of warring tribes. He used his vast Power to unite all of Aragwey under one rule and brought civilization to the land like none before him. After he passed away, peace lasted for only one more generation before the whole nation broke down into civil unrest."

Javic wondered where all of this was going, he had heard many stories of John Graven before; the Father of Civilization, the Harbinger of Power, and the Peacebringer were just a few of his many nicknames.

"John had one son, Jacob, and he too was a wizard. With skillful leadership Jacob managed to prolong the period of peace that his father had instilled during his reign. However, Jacob had twelve children of his own, and after Jacob died those twelve children began to fight over who would succeed their father. After much argument, Aragwey was eventually broken up into twelve separate kingdoms. The oldest son formed the largest kingdom, to which he gave the family name: Graven. The kingdom of Graven is the only one of those original twelve kingdoms to still exist to this day, though its borders have changed substantially since those times.

"The second person to bear the Mark of Kings was a woman named Emily Fox. She rose to power a little more than three hundred years after John Graven's time. She, like John, could wield vast amounts of the Power. She too attempted to unite all of Aragwey under one rule, but found that people were resistant to the idea of a female ruler. Though she never did manage to rule all of Aragwey before her death, she was able to bring peace to the lands again, the likes of which hadn't been seen since before the formation of the twelve kingdoms. She began a tradition of queens ruling Phandrol that continues to this day with Queen Havorie Elveres.

"Again, three hundred years went by before the mark made its return. It was another woman of great Power. Her name was Hannah Davis and she claimed that the mark was a sign indicating that she was the legitimate ruler of all of Aragwey. The existing queen of Phandrol at the time stepped down from power and allowed Hannah to rule over her kingdom, but the other rulers of Aragwey blatantly refused to bow down to her. None were more resistant to her reign than the rulers of Graven. The kings of Graven have always been descendants of John Graven, and as such feel that, they, if anyone, should be the all-powerful rulers of Aragwey. In the end, neither Hannah Davis nor any of the kings of Graven ever got their wish. Hannah spent the remainder of her days as just another queen of Phandrol and nothing more.

"Another three hundred years passed – this was just one hundred years ago – and another person with the mark emerged: Garrett Rames. That is to say, King Garrett. He wanted to become the next John Graven and set his mind on taking over all of Aragwey. I do not pretend to know what sort of fate rippled forth to brand these people with the Mark of Kings. What I do know, however, is that after Garrett emerged, something changed. The three-hundred-year intervals that had always separated the appearances of the mark ceased to hold.

"In my lifetime, I have seen this mark with my own eyes once before. It was about twenty years ago, when I first joined the Ver'konus, and the mark was on Ethan himself." Elric held up his diary, opened to an old sketch of a glyph:

It matched Belford's branding down to the last detail. "If it wasn't for Ethan, Garrett would probably rule all of Aragwey by now," said Elric. "Forty years ago, Ethan used his mark to gather followers, forming his resistance group, the Ver'konus.

It was the first time that two marks ever coexisted. Now, seeing the mark on you, I really don't know what to think. If King Garrett knows that you bear the mark... there is no telling to what lengths he would go. The more marks that coexist, the less legitimate Garrett's claim to the throne becomes and the more likely it is that Ethan and the Queen of Phandrol will be able to rally the support they need to overthrow Garrett's reign once and for all."

No one spoke. No one even dared move. Javic didn't even know what to think. He didn't know what all of this meant for them; he only knew that this was big. Really big.

"Couldn't the mark be faked?" asked Belford wistfully. The silence was broken, but the tension still held tight.

"Maybe, but I can't tell you anything more with any certainty. We must get to Ethan as quickly as possible. We leave at first light. I suggest you both sleep while you can."

Javic lay down on his bedroll with his hands behind his head and stared up towards the darkening sky. He was feeling quite small. *What did I get myself into by going on that ride to the quarry?* Despite his body's exhaustion, his mind was now stuck in a continuous state of anticipation. Thoughts racing, he continued to stare up at the sky as more and more stars began to flicker into view. Every once in a while, he would glance over at Belford to see the moonlight still gleaming off of his open eyes as well.

How does Grandfather expect us to sleep after news like that?

CHAPTER

9

Into Oblivion

Belford peered out over the edge of oblivion. He was searching for something, though he did not know what. Just half a step separated him from the nothingness that stretched out before him. He didn't dare move; his legs were rooted firmly to a stone ledge. He could sense a vast open space, but there was nothing to see beyond the ledge. Glancing over the side, he was immediately struck by a wave of vertigo that rippled through his body. He barely managed to keep his footing. Below, the smooth stone precipice stretched endlessly downward, its infinite depths masked in darkness. Glancing to his left and then to his right, Belford could see the ledge curving ever so slightly inwards before it vanished beyond his vision. Perhaps it surrounded the vastness of the abyss. He couldn't be sure.

Going around the void was out of the question – that path would prove to be as long and desolate as it was useless. He couldn't turn back either. What he sought now resided within the chasm.

I don't want to go in there....

But he knew he must. The very thought of it caused fear's icy hands to grip hold of his chest. He tried to force his legs to move, but they would not budge. Instead, he simply leaned forward, allowing the weight of his body to do the work for him as he tumbled down, over the edge of the cliff.

As if falling through water, Belford glided through the bleakness with unexpected ease. If it was not for the cliff face whizzing by behind him, there would have been little to indicate that he was falling at all. He did not feel the butterflies that usually fluttered in one's stomach when plummeting a sufficient distance, nor, as far as he could discern, was there any amount of wind blowing upon his face or body. A slow motion sensation stretched on as the cliff face began to fade from view, replaced instead by a swirl of bright lights and colors which streamed about, churning all around him. He no longer felt like he was falling as the swirls gradually solidified into vague shapes, like patterns cast by the headlights of a car through the branches of a tree. They sharpened further and further until they hardened into actual objects.

Belford found that he was suddenly standing within a very white room. The floor, walls, and ceiling were all lined with white linoleum tile. It was some sort of laboratory. Glancing around, he found that he was not alone. Technicians dressed in white lab coats labored diligently at various workstations across the room. Although Belford remembered that he was a doctor, his instincts told him that this was not his lab. Here, he was a patient. Huddled together around him stood ten other people, all of which Belford felt he somehow knew. They were all candidates for something, though he could not recall anything more about why they were there. The lot of them seemed to be waiting for their turns to go into a curtained area in the corner of the lab.

Just as Belford finished taking in his surroundings, a short man with a kempt beard and thick glasses drew back the curtain and stepped out of the cordoned-off area. He wiped his hands up and down the front of his white lab coat, seemingly out of habit, straightening out nonexistent wrinkles in an attempt to appear professional in front of the onlookers. The doctor's face shifted, blurring into indistinguishable features as Belford tried to focus on him. The effort made his head spin.

And then there she was – the girl from the park.

Belford's heart fluttered as she emerged from behind the curtain, shifting his attention away from the doctor. She was the most beautiful thing he'd ever laid eyes on. Her large green eyes scanned across the gathered crowd while she rubbed a sore spot on her left arm. Her eyes met with Belford's for a moment and she flashed him a quick smile before joining the rest of the candidates.

Looking back over at the blurry doctor, Belford saw that he was motioning him forward, towards the curtain. He rubbed his eyes before approaching somewhat apprehensively. He took a deep breath before stepping through the opening in the curtain. On a table sat a briefcase, left open to display a number of syringes filled with a strange, clear liquid. Against the wall sat an examination bench. Belford walked up to it and took a seat as the doctor closed the curtain behind them.

The doctor grabbed one of the syringes out of the case and walked over to Belford. He already had his left bicep exposed in anticipation of the injection. The doctor quickly plunged the clear liquid into Belford's arm. It did not hurt much; only a quick pinch.

Belford began to get up, but the doctor placed his arm across his chest, stopping him mid-rise, and pushed him back down onto the examination bench. The doctor raised a large evil-looking syringe into the air. Sneering maliciously, he thrust the huge needle deep into Belford's arm. A red-hot, searing sensation ripped through his flesh. The pain radiated outward mercilessly from the point of the injection, intensifying with every passing second.

The world began to spin, the bland colors of the room melting together into indistinguishable blobs. The whole room flew apart, spiraling like the inside of a clothes dryer – buckets of paint tumbling through the air. The pain subsided as the blotches of color swirled into something new.

The sickening spinning spell did not last long. Everything settled, the shapes once again falling into place. Belford found himself immersed in darkness. This time, it was not the nothingness of the void, but the darkness of night that surrounded him. Standing close to him on his left side were several people who he now knew to be his friends. He was not sure why he had not recognized them as friends before; they were seven of his fellow candidates from the laboratory – the beautiful girl included. Their names were right on the tip of his tongue, tantalizingly out of reach. They all stood in front of the entrance to a wide eight-story building at the edge of a large grassy park. It was too dark to see all of this, but he knew it to be true.

One of Belford's friends, a skinny girl slightly younger than himself by the look of her, began to create a transparent energy shield out of thin air. Initially forming as a wall in front of them, it steadily curved across the whole group, molding into a dome above their heads. As this shielding dome moved into position, it disturbed the air. The girl's shoulder-length, mousy-brown hair blew wildly around her face as the wind rushed to escape the confines of the bubble.

A bright, blue glow radiated outwards from the energy bubble as it fixed itself to the ground around them. The girl's eyes, illuminated by this unnatural light, blazed as she redoubled her efforts to hold the shield in place. Her hardened features held an underlying fear as she focused everything she had on her task. The intensity of her expression belied her otherwise youthful appearance. The light quickly faded away, casting them all into darkness once more, leaving only the slight refraction of the moonlight as it traveled through the barrier to mark the dome's position. Others joined in now, concentrating on maintaining the shield.

Looking closer at the people that surrounded him, Belford noticed several serious injuries. One woman was covered in small lacerations and bruises – someone had violently beaten her – while a bald man with strange facial tattoos had a severely shattered ankle. Belford did what came naturally to him as he healed their wounds with his thoughts.

There was a loud popping noise in the distance. Belford quickly turned his head. Still in the distance, but closing fast, he could see something large and on fire hurtling towards them through the open air of the park. Reflexes uselessly brought Belford's arms up to protect his head. Without the dome shield surrounding the group, there was no question they would have been killed. The flaming object impacted the top portion of the dome, sounding in a low-pitched thud as it compressed the shield before ricocheting off and smashing into the side of the building behind them. The ensuing explosion lit up the air with a light so bright that Belford was forced to close his eyes. The shield rippled violently, threatening to falter. The force of the shockwave reverberated all across its surface, resonating in a low hum.

Another popping noise reached Belford's ears as a second fiery mass was created and simultaneously launched towards them. Even before it reached the shield, Belford heard another pop, and then another, as more projectiles were formed. The first object from this barrage reached the energy dome with such massive velocity that its impact broke the shield down completely.

Thinking quickly in the few seconds before the rest of the barrage found its mark, Belford willed a thick wall of stone up out of the ground between his friends and the incoming fireballs. The rock wall was immediately struck by the remainder of the volley. Chunks of rock shot back at them, but the others managed to reform the shield in time to block these bits of debris with ease.

During all of the commotion, no one – neither the unseen attackers nor his friends – noticed the large streaks of light streaming down out of the eastern sky towards them. The first streak collided with a skyscraper in the middle of the city across the park, instantly vaporizing the building and creating the largest explosion Belford had ever witnessed. He only looked upon it for a second before squeezing his eyes shut tight. His face burned from the sheer radiance of the blast. He could still see the lingering image of the devastation on the backs of his eyelids – seared into his retinas. Another streak impacted before the first flash dissipated. Explosion after explosion wracked the city as more streaks of light descended upon it, the ground trembling violently with every impact.

Belford turned away.

The world was unhinged; broken at its seams. The sky burned in reflection of the pale glow beneath. Embers whipped up by the winds continued to dance, spreading the fires everywhere. Beyond the soot and smoke, where once great nations had resided, glassy plains were all that remained, stretching from one coastline to another in a frozen sea of molten death. The earth was being wiped clean; all its wrinkles smoothed away, meticulously erased. There was nowhere to hide, for it was truly the end of the world.

The explosions stopped, but the ground still shook softly as one by one the remaining skyscrapers began to collapse into piles of rubble. Debris clouds consumed the horizon with phantom structures – seemingly dense, but expanding rapidly in every direction.

Once the ghostly images faded from Belford's overwhelmed vision, he looked up into the sky, just in time to see one last streak coming right towards him.

He awoke with a start – someone's hand was over his mouth. He let out a muffled yell before realizing what was going on.

Elric was kneeling over him, one finger pressed to his lips in a "be silent" gesture, his other hand pressed firmly over Belford's mouth. As soon as Belford met his eyes he removed his hand and then silently got up and moved over to where Javic was sleeping. Elric roused Javic in the same manner – one hand over the mouth to stifle the cry of surprise and a finger to his own lips to signal silence.

After Javic was up, Elric quietly unsheathed his sword and slinked out of sight into the stillness of the dark night. Belford looked over questioningly at Javic. Javic shrugged. Neither dared make a noise. Not far off, Belford began to hear something in the brush. Leaves were being rustled and occasionally a snapping twig or stick could be heard. Something was coming their way, and by the sound of it, it was a very large something.

Belford and Javic sat in wide-eyed silence as whatever it was got closer and closer to their clearing. Belford's heart started pounding in his chest and his breath quickened. Belford was sure Javic could hear his heart beating, it had become so very loud.

Some sort of huge creature emerged at the edge of the clearing. It was a good arm's length taller than an average man and extremely bulky. It had a slightly curved back, making it look hunched over even while standing at its tallest, and jagged claws, each at least two inches long. Its skin was blotchy with shades of pink and brown – dirt stains – all across its mostly hairless body. Massive muscles bulged out all over its shoulders and arms like tumorous growths. Despite already having claws, it also carried a large double-sided axe, which it held hefted up by both arms, ready to strike at a moment's notice. It was hunting, and Belford was pretty sure he knew who it was looking for. The monstrous fiend turned its head back and forth, scanning the area with its beady eyes. It hadn't noticed them yet. They had not moved a single muscle since hearing its approach.

The monster came closer. Belford thought for a moment that it might pass right by without noticing a thing.

One of the horses stirred.

The creature's head swung towards the sound and immediately spotted Belford and Javic lying down directly in front of their mounts.

With a grunt, the creature charged.

Javic and Belford both jumped to their feet to run, but before they could do more than stand up, Elric rushed into the clearing and sliced the creature through the neck from behind with his sword. Its head was not completely severed, though, and the monster managed to let out a gurgled squeal before succumbing to its wound.

The damage was done. The sound had alerted two more creatures. The monsters lumbered noisily into the clearing and rushed at Elric. The first one to reach Elric swung its great axe straight down towards him, attempting to split him in two, lengthwise. Elric lunged towards the creature's left side, dodging the attack and landing a blow of his own in the same moment. He brought his sword across in a slashing motion through the fiend's belly, disemboweling it instantly. One motion flowed into the next as Elric skirted around behind the monster and swung once more, completely decapitating it before the other creature could reach him.

As Elric began dueling with the beast, yet another monster stumbled into the clearing from the side nearest Belford. Elric had not yet noticed its presence, but even if he had, there would not have been enough time for him to stop it from reaching Javic and Belford. It ran at them, axe already held high above its grotesquely malformed head.

With no time to react, Belford shut his eyes and put his hands up over his face. There was a *poof* and Belford could feel a sand-like substance envelope his body in a cloud of dust. Belford lowered his arms and opened his eyes. A massive amount of gray powder now covered everything in sight. Both he and Javic were coated from head to toe, while the monster was nowhere to be seen. Javic was rubbing his eyes furiously – they'd been open when the cloud of dust struck him in the face.

"You used the Power!" said Javic.

Belford looked back over at Elric – the last monster was already impaled on his sword. The creature collapsed into a heap. Elric turned around and rushed over to them. One look at the gray dust covering their bodies was all it took for him to realize what must have transpired. "Nice job, Belford!" he said.

They quickly gathered all of their belongings. Some of it was difficult to locate now that everything was covered by monster ash, but soon they were jumping onto their disgruntled horses and proceeding south as quickly as the forested terrain would allow.

"It won't be long before those scouts are missed," said Elric. "We will be seeing more Whunes before long."

Belford shivered at the thought. "What *are* they?" he asked.

"Garrett's monstrosities."

Elric needn't say more. He'd confirmed all of Belford's greatest fears: King Garrett wanted him dead and he'd pulled out these heavy hitters to get the job done. If only he could figure out exactly how he had used the Power, they might yet be able to escape unscathed. Unfortunately, all he could remember about obliterating the creature was a feeling of utter panic as his heart jumped into his throat.

He had fully expected to die.

The disgusting smell of the creatures still lingered in Belford's nose as the sky began to lighten – night swiftly turning into dawn. Elric took the rear, allowing Javic to lead the way. He expected any attack to come from behind, constantly looking back over his shoulder into the forested wilderness for any sign of pursuit. The woods seemed to stare back at them with a silent animosity as their horses' hooves beat hard against the dry soil. The forest, most alive during the early morning hours, was ominously quiet. Not a chirp of a bird nor the buzz of an insect sounded as they carried onwards through the tangle of branches.

The sky became just bright enough to ruin their night vision without providing enough light to actually see. Shadows formed, playing tricks on Belford's eyes, making him see enemies where none existed. The world was as colorless and dull as the sooty ash that still lined his hair and clothing. The trees began to thin out, allowing them to increase their speed as they weaved past the fallen logs and rocks that littered the forest floor.

"Let's stop for a moment so I can get a compass heading," said Elric. "We need to keep going straight south until we reach the river."

They all stopped as Elric dismounted and began rummaging through the bags attached to his horse's saddle. He withdrew his compass and opened it, being careful to hold it completely level as the needle rotated in its display. Elric pointed to indicate the correct path – slightly left of the direction they had been heading. He put the compass away in his pocket and remounted his horse.

Behind them in the distance came a snarling cry. Belford's head spun around just in time to see a group of Whunes rush into view, bounding towards them rapidly through the trees.

"Ride!" yelled Elric.

They did not hesitate and neither did their horses – sprinting as swiftly as possible, they dodged between trees and leapt deftly over obstacles that threatened to block their escape.

The Whunes ran quicker than their large frames suggested possible as they steadily closed the distance to their prey.

"Can you destroy them like you did the other?" Elric shouted up to Belford who was riding in front of him.

"I'm not sure how I did it," responded Belford truthfully. The same panic he experienced before was rising inside of him now, but nothing magical seemed to be happening this time. Belford glanced back for a moment at their pursuers. He counted six Whunes, all closing the gap behind them.

Their horses jumped another log. Belford clung desperately to his saddle horn with both hands. He copied Javic's posture, leaning low in his seat.

Suddenly Javic reined Olli back, allowing Belford to take the lead. Javic pulled up his bow as Belford overtook him. There was already an arrow notched by the time he was adjacent to Elric. He turned around in his saddle, taking careful aim as he drew back the string. He let it loose. The shot soared through the air before taking the lead Whune right in the neck. It never even saw it coming as it collapsed to the ground. The Whune directly behind was unable to stop in time and ran full speed into its downed brethren, toppling over and smashing its face roughly into the hard ground. The rest of the Whunes jumped over their fallen comrades, and continued to close the gap.

Notching another arrow, Javic took aim at the next Whune in line. The arrow sunk deep into the creature's shoulder, but it did not slow in its stride for even a moment. The next arrow, however, pierced it in the head, killing it instantly. Arrow after arrow left Javic's bow, rarely missing their targets and dispatching the next two Whunes quickly.

All but one Whune now lay dead or dying, but this last one had closed the gap. Less than ten paces separated Javic from the monster. As Javic drew back his bow once more the Whune clumsily hurled its huge axe at him. It was an act of desperation, but the axe managed to strike Javic – his bow blocked the deadly blade, but the handle smashed into his arm, knocking him from his saddle.

Elric leapt from his horse, unsheathing his sword as he fell through the air. He moved with such great haste that he seemed almost a blur as he struck the oncoming Whune down with his sword. It all happened so fast that Belford didn't even notice that Elric was off his mount until after it was all over. Despite the creature's bulk and claws, with no weapon, the Whune was left nearly defenseless against the long reach of Elric's sword. Elric moved quickly and without hesitation as he executed the monster in a flash of steel.

Miraculously, Javic had avoided the blade of the axe, and although he now had many tender spots, he would receive little more than bruises from both the hit and his fall from Olli. His recurve bow, on the other hand, was a little bit worse for wear, taking the brunt of the flying axe's hit. Although the bow itself was not broken, its string had snapped in two and would need to be replaced before the bow could be used again. Elric helped Javic back to his feet, embracing him briefly before they both remounted their horses.

Hours passed uneventfully as they rode south through the wilderness. Belford was still trying to figure out how he had turned the earlier monster into dust when the roar of water ahead in the distance stole his attention. The sound of the rushing river grew louder until finally they could see the bank through the trees. When they reached the water's edge, they turned west and followed it up stream in search of a shallow stretch through which to cross.

Elric instructed them to ride just within the slow moving water on the edge of the riverbank so they could travel without leaving tracks. When they finally reached a crossable section of the river, Javic and Belford both took a moment to wash some of the remaining ash from their hair before leading their horses across to the south bank. The water felt like ice as it dripped down Belford's spine. It carried the gray soot downstream in an expanding cloud of murkiness. The grime darkened as the water touched it, but it came off quickly without much hassle. He scrubbed it from his skin and out from under his fingernails.

"Let's continue west along the river," said Elric. "They might be able to pick up our tracks if we abandon the water too soon."

They pushed on, heading farther and farther out of their way, clinging to the safety of the water's edge. Belford's mind drifted back and forth between the Whunes and the Power. Looking down into the river, the reflection of a large rounded boulder caught his eye. Its outline shimmered as the morning sun met with the clear running water. It abruptly reminded him of the dome of blue light he'd seen in his dream.

Everything was so different inside his dream world; so far removed from the waking world. Some of the things he'd witnessed were truly frightening: Explosions so incredibly massive that they couldn't possibly be real – he hoped they couldn't be real anyway.

How much of my dreams are pure fabrications and how much are actual memories leaking back into my conscious mind?

Strangely, the odd scenes, though often frightening, had given him hope: Hope that his memories would one day return in their entirety. Regardless of the nightmares, there were some things that he longed to remember; some *one* he longed to remember.

How could I have forgotten her? All I can remember about her is her face, so how can I feel so strongly for her?

He knew how she made him feel, he just wished he had the memories to support his feelings. He had known she was worth remembering ever since his first dream, back on the Elensol farm. Even if it meant suffering through more nightmares every night for the rest of his life, she was worth remembering.

Hours slipped by, the sun rising high before Elric decided it was finally time to leave the river behind and head straight for Felington. They ate for the first time that day – more dried meat from Javic's saddlebag – but did so while on the move. Felington lay southeast of their position, across rugged terrain. They continued on, riding up and down rolling hills as the afternoon slid slowly into evening.

Suddenly the trees opened up to reveal a wide road. Elric informed them that it was part of the same road system they had abandoned the day before when they left to travel along the hunting trail. Finding the road meant they could not be far from Felington.

They traveled eastward along the road at a fast canter. It wasn't long before they came across a farm. Vast fields of crops stretched out on either side of the road. Belford wasn't sure what was being grown, but he didn't really care either. He simply enjoyed looking down the long rows of produce as they whizzed past. The geometric symmetry of their organization was comforting to him. It meant they were finally out of the wilderness and back into the structured world in which he felt more at ease.

After passing several more empty farmhouses, Elric's posture began to stiffen. "We should have seen somebody by now," he said. "These crops don't harvest themselves."

They still hadn't seen any sign of life when the outer wall of the city of Felington rolled into view. The city stood at the end of a long pathway branching out to the left of the main road. They began up the path, being cautious as they approached; they did not want to ride headlong into an ambush. As they got closer to the city, Belford could see that the entrance gate was shut and that there were a great number of people walking about on top of the outer wall. Some were pointing in their direction; many held longbows at the ready. The main gate opened slightly, permitting three men on horseback, each wearing a full suit of armor, to ride through.

The horsemen rode forward, two of them falling back into escort positions, protecting the third man's flanks. Each horseman wore a red tabard depicting, in gold, a symbol of a knight on a prancing stallion. Now that they were closer, Belford noticed that this insignia was the same as the ones drawn on the banners and flags that stood in various places across the city's outer wall.

"Halt," called the lead rider as he approached Elric. Belford and the Elensols stopped their horses immediately. "What is your business here?"

"We seek refuge for the night," said Elric. He hesitated, then reluctantly continued, "...and we were attacked by Whunes earlier today. You might want to inform your captain that there may be more around."

"I am the captain of the guard. And we already know of the Whunes," the guardsman said gravely. "The city is under siege from the north and our countrymen have taken refuge behind our walls. I do not believe that there is need for worry just yet, however, as our archers have been successful in keeping the Whunes at bay." There was more than a hint of pride in his voice. "We have held them back within the tree line for many hours now. The city will be on lockdown tonight as a precaution – no one will be allowed in or out between sundown and sunup."

Elric appeared to be contemplating whether or not he should even bother to ask for entry into Felington. The urge to ride away from the city at a full gallop must have been rising: A city under siege would be a dangerous place to be trapped. Belford's rumbling stomach made up his mind for him, but for Elric it was perhaps the knowledge that without help from Ethan's contact, they would likely never make it out of Taris alive, let alone all the way to Phandrol. "May we enter your city?"

The guard captain nodded. "I shall escort you in." He gestured for them to ride forth into Felington.

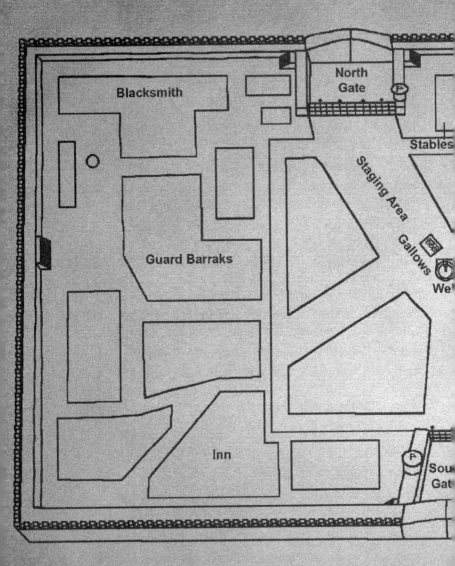

The City of Felington

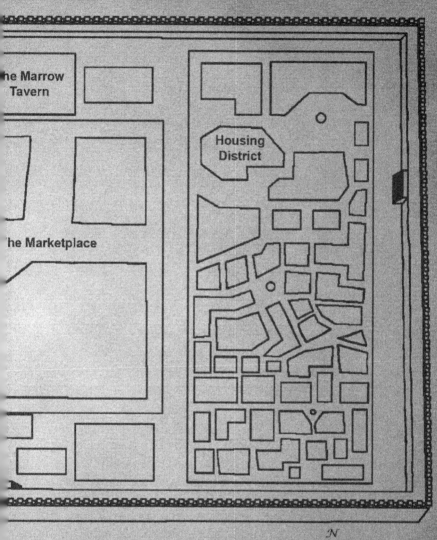

The Marrow
Tavern

Housing
District

he Marketplace

CHAPTER

10

The Marrow Tavern

As the ground changed from compressed dirt to cobblestone, the dull pounding of horse hooves became solid thuds, echoing back and forth between the high walls of the city's narrow entrance courtyard. Javic moved with the rest of the procession, passing through the thick outer door before approaching a closed inner gate, crisscrossed with metal bars. Four men stationed high above on the wall began to rotate a large wooden crank. The chains attached to the outer door instantly became taut, slowly shifting the blockade back into its closed position. Once the outer shell was shut, the men returned to their watch stations along the outer wall.

They were now trapped within the courtyard. After several minutes the inner gate still remained closed. The guard captain lowered his eyebrows into a deep frown. Nobody spoke as the moments ticked by. Without warning, the inner gate finally gave a deep groan and began its rise; the pulley system clicking loudly with each rotation.

"We haven't had to lower the gates in years," the guard captain explained offhandedly.

Metal spikes on the bottom of the gate appeared out from holes in the ground. As the gate was hoisted higher, the spikes began to look like jagged teeth; the archway like a giant mouth yearning for a meal. They rode forward. Javic passed through the threshold quickly; he did not wish to be devoured by those sharp teeth should the chains holding the gate aloft break at an inopportune moment.

After they were all clear, an order was given and the gate was released. It fell swiftly shut, producing a deafeningly loud clang as it hit the ground.

The guard captain sighed as he dismounted from his horse. He handed his reins to one of his escorts. "They forgot to hold the crank in place again," he said, shaking his head as he turned towards the gate house. He strode off with a clear air of authority in his steps.

The crash of the gate unsettled Javic's nerves. He couldn't help but feel that they had barely avoided death once again. He shivered at the thought of being impaled by one of those falling spikes.

The guards left them to go their own way. Elric led Belford and Javic down the main road through the Merchant Quarters. Many people were about, but no one was trying to buy or sell anything. Merchants and patrons alike stood together in clusters, speaking in hushed whispers. The city folk cast weary glances over their shoulders at Elric, Javic, and Belford as they rode past.

A twinge shot through Javic's left arm. It was badly bruised from the attack that morning that knocked him from Olli's saddle; his arm had been throbbing ever since. Whenever he thought about the pain, he inevitably thought about the Whunes, and thinking about them only made him ache for Salvine.

What did those horrible creatures do to you?
A terrible thought went through Javic's mind:
Fresh meat.
He prayed he was wrong – that the monsters hadn't used her for food – or at least that she had died without suffering.

He bit down hard on his lower lip in an attempt to ebb the flow of tears before they even broke free. He could feel the all-too-familiar sting in the corners of his eyes. Tears would do him little good right now. He pushed the pain from his mind, refusing to acknowledge it openly, and tried to turn his attention towards the city around him instead.

The streets were far from clean, but that was hardly anything new. Javic remembered the stink of the city from the last time his grandfather had brought him here. There were far too many people together in one place; the air had gone sour. The pigsty back on the farm smelled like daffodils in comparison. From Javic's experience, people were far less cleanly than animals.

Felington had been built around its Merchant Quarters. There were constantly people coming and going. The open-air stands and many in-house shops of the Felington marketplace held a little something for everyone. A motley assortment of trinkets, trifles, and ornaments lined the displays of the many stands. Pottery, garments, jewelry, and plenty of crude antiquities were put on exhibit for the day's negotiations. Felington's location as a crossroads between three kingdoms made for a wide array of goods.

Now, as the hours until nightfall dwindled, and with the threat of attack from the Whunes, nearly all of the booths and shops had shut down early for the night. Even the most determined of merchants had already begun the process of closing. A shoddy sign marked simply, *Fruit*, hung from an overturned wooden pushcart. It had been abandoned by its owner sometime in the hours previous. Apples were spilled out all across the ground. No one was watching, so Javic saw little harm in snatching up one of the plumper ones for himself.

He dusted it off on his shirt before taking a bite. It was nice to finally eat something other than dried meat. Belford grabbed one as well.

As they approached the center of the city, they came upon a large group of people gathered within a staging area near the public well. With a gallows as a backdrop, a youthful man in his late twenties was attempting to address the crowd. Holding his helmet under his left arm, he wore a suit of light armor which gleamed brilliantly despite the waning sunlight. His blond hair was trimmed short – a sign that usually suggested one's blood to be of noble decent. His educated accent also attested to that likelihood.

"...and we must ride forth hence!" he said. "The vile slime that dares desecrate your homesteads must not see us tremble within our boots. I am certain that the tides will turn in our favor against these foul beasts, but if not, we needn't fear our own destruction. The honor of battling such Mast-less heathens as these will surely carry us dignified into the next life. Now," said the young noble, "who is with me!?" He unsheathed a sword from his side and pointed it up into the sky in a dramatic gesture. A large opal, clearly visible in its hilt, seemed almost to glow.

The people in the crowd, mostly scrappily clad merchants and farmers, were not as enthusiastic in their response to the young man. They murmured to one another, clearly not as pleased with the prospect of dying for honor as their nobler counterpart seemed to be.

"The guards are doing just fine keeping the creatures at bay," shouted one man.

"You're mad!" came the voice of another.

More yelling erupted throughout the crowd. Insults flew as the mob became united against the man. At one point, from behind Javic, an apple was thrown. It glanced off of the nobleman's breastplate, and although it caused no physical damage, it appeared to have been a hurtful blow to his pride. Javic turned around and looked at Belford. He would have appeared innocent enough if not for the lack of an apple in his hand.

The nobleman looked disheartened, but refused to give up on his quest for honor. He frowned at the crowd as he descended the steps of the gallows. The crowd dispersed around him; they had already lost interest in the would-be hero. He approached a young lady who was watching him fretfully. Neatly dressed in a brown and green riding dress, she stood in silence as he drew near. Concern lingered in her large round eyes, but she kept them all the while locked onto his. She fidgeted with her free-flowing, brown hair while waiting for him to speak.

"Ready my steed, my dear Mallory," he said simply. "If none shall ride with me, I shall face this menace alone." Though he seemed without fear, his voice held a slight note of remorse.

The girl whimpered at his words. Javic felt pity for the girl. He could tell that she cared very deeply for the man. Being that his demise was almost a certainty, the whole thing was painful to watch.

A passing guardsman had also stopped to watch the scene unfold, but now butted into the conversation before the girl, Mallory, could obey the man's command by retrieving his horse.

"Sir," said the guardsman, placing out his hand for the nobleman to shake.

The nobleman grabbed the guardsman's hand and shook it firmly. "What is it, good sir?"

"May I ask the name of the man who dares to take on an entire battalion of Whunes by himself?"

"Of course, but first I must question your judgment of *battalion*, are there really so many of them?" He had narrowed his eyes at the guardsman's word choice.

"I'm afraid so. By modest account, there are at least eighty."

The nobleman turned slightly pale, but immediately shook the words off with his steadfast resolution. "Arlin. Arlin

Calary is my name," he said, answering the guardsman's question.

"I'm afraid, Arlin, that I have some bad news for you, though perhaps not so bad for your lady."

Mallory raised her eyes at this. She had been on the verge of tears, but now expressed a combination of confusion and hope.

"By order of the captain of the guard, none may depart the city until first light tomorrow morn."

Mallory's face lit up at the news, though she attempted to hide her true feelings. Arlin appeared a little relieved as well, though he was quick to replace this with signs of discontent at the lack of control he held over his own destiny.

"Thank you for this news," said Arlin to the guardsman. "I suppose I shall have to wait until tomorrow." The guardsman nodded. He placed a consoling hand on Arlin's shoulder momentarily before walking away.

Javic could hardly believe his ears. *Eighty! Eighty Whunes!?*

They had been lucky to survive against the few that had attacked them earlier. The average man was no match for the brute force of one of those creatures. The thought of so many gave Javic a sick feeling within his stomach. He could still smell the stink of their flesh on his clothes – a hundred times worse than sour air of the marketplace.

"Come on boys," said Elric, riding past Javic and Belford and leading them on down the road between the gallows and the well.

Javic shot one last glance towards Arlin and Mallory before taking a left turn down another street lined with shop buildings. They continued until the end of the block, where a final row of buildings stood against the northern wall of the city. They approached a rickety, old building. A faded sign above the doorway read *Marrow Tavern*, and a buzz of conversations could be heard coming out from within its thin walls. The three travelers dismounted and handed their reins over to a stable boy who came up to greet them. He took Olli and Amit first, but quickly returned for Elric's horse once he had taken care of the other two. Elric handed the boy a dull coin from out of his satchel and, in turn, the boy gave Elric a stub of pulp-paper with their horses' stall numbers written across it. They proceeded into the shabby tavern.

Javic had to take a moment to allow his eyes to adjust to the dreary atmosphere of the bar. The muggy heat of the room made the abundant pipe-smoke lingering in the air feel thick and repressive to his senses – a bitter contrast to the mostly fresh air they had just come in from. He coughed slightly as he walked forward. A large amount of sooty filth was caked onto the only window in the barroom, resulting in very little natural light filtering in from outside. Lanterns placed along the bar and across various tables around the room illuminated the tavern's many patrons with an eerie, orange glow. No one paid any attention to the newcomers as Elric led the way across the room to an empty table that stood against the far wall.

"Now what?" asked Javic as they all took their seats around the small table.

Elric glanced around at the adjacent tables, making sure nobody was listening. "To contact the Ver'konus," he began in a hushed whisper, "I must recite an old poem for the whole tavern to hear and hope that the right person recognizes it as a secret code."

Javic looked across the room at what had to be the most unfriendly crowd he had ever seen. The patrons were almost entirely men of the burly variety. Many sat alone with their faces buried in large mugs of grog, while others were massed together in groups of three or four, chatting adamantly with one another. One group of nine men around a large table in the far corner of the room erupted periodically in a mixture of loud cheers and angry groans every time a handful of dice was thrown across the tabletop. Coins exchanged hands with every toss and the barmaid was running a nonstop flow of alcohol back and forth between the bar and the gamblers. They did not look like the type of men who took kindly to unwarranted interruptions, nor like the sort of folk who understood the finer points of poetry.

"A poem?" asked Javic.

Elric recognized the problem as well. "Yes," he sighed. He was clearly hesitant to proceed with the necessary recital. "It is entitled 'The Moon,' and it's the last poem from a collection that was written a very long time ago." Elric pulled out a piece of folded parchment from his shirt pocket. It was tinted pale brown by time and had a discolored stain across its back side. Elric was careful not to tear the paper as he unfolded it. The areas around its creases were worn thin with age. "Many centuries have passed since the original was inked and its authorship has been long forgotten in time." Elric looked around once more, making sure that they were still unobserved. He leaned in close and continued, even more quietly than before, "Lord Ethan himself penned me this copy many years ago. He claims the poem to be a prophecy foreseeing the downfall of King Garrett. He even fashioned his emblem after the poem's title: A white circle; the full moon. It has since become the unofficial flag of the Ver'konus – a white circle on black cloth. The resistance has no official flag mind you; they are technically just a branch of the Phandolian military, along with random Aragwian nationalists and other supporters. The Ver'konus began using the poem as a means to secretly reveal loyalties and bring allies together many years ago, though it is only supposed to be used during times of emergency. You know the old saying, 'You can always find a friend when the moon is high?' Well, let's just say Ethan really took it to heart."

"I think our current situation may apply as an emergency," said Belford, dryly.

"Indeed," said Elric as he began to rise from his chair. The barmaid silently approached him from behind and placed a hand on his shoulder, pushing him back down into his seat.

"No need to come seek me out," she said. Despite her boisterous attitude she was not a large woman, in fact, she was actually quite dainty. The men, even when drunk, treated her with an air of respect. She was a pretty woman, which made this respect even more noticeable. Her piercing, steel-blue eyes held a clear warning within their stare: Any unwarranted advances would not be a wise use of time. She had raven-black hair that ran down over both shoulders and rested atop her breasts. She wore a starched white apron overtop her dress. There was not a single stain or marking of food or drink across the apron's pallid surface.

Javic guessed her age to be somewhere in the early thirties, but this estimate was based on a combination of factors – her composure, which pointed to the wisdom of age, and her complexion, which was still smooth and youthful looking – and so the accuracy of his guess was difficult to determine. She smelled of flowers. How anybody could smell of flowers within a dirty hole like the Marrow Tavern, Javic had no idea, but somehow the barmaid managed to pull it off. Her mix of authority and girlishness was confusing to Javic, but he decided to smile at her anyway. She did not return the smile.

"What can I get you gentlemen?" she asked. Her tone was not unfriendly, but neither was it warm.

Javic got the feeling that it would be best if they ordered something.

"Whatever food you have on hand would be wonderful," said Elric.

The barmaid's eyes lingered over Belford. His short hair and youth made him stand out amongst the more rugged patrons. She turned away as he returned her gaze. She gave a curt nod and left as quickly as she appeared.

Javic, Elric, and Belford all sat in silence for a long moment.

"The poem?" asked Javic, reminding his grandfather of what they came here to do.

The time for hesitation was over. Elric stood up with great determination, cleared his throat, and spoke out loudly for the entire tavern to hear. "Excuse me everyone. May I have your attention?" The tavern grew silent. He began reciting the poem:

She traveled forth alone to call the man before his time,

The mighty King who sat in wait, sipping from his stein.

The land so thick of wither wrought a ghost to trifle all,

But no lethargic horde could waste or catch his trembled call:

"Your hands are quick and nimble" said the Fire to the Moon,

"But no one Mast can hold such luck" he chimed in fretful tune.

The Moon spoke not – the crackles chilled – for time was on her side,

And the King once wrought by fire to the fire did subside.

The crowd remained uncomfortably silent as he finished. Everybody was staring at Elric, confused by what was going on and what they had just heard. Slowly, people began to decide that he was either drunk or mad. The gamblers were the first to return to their business, and with the sound of the dice rolling, the rest of the patrons were quick to return to their booze and conversations.

Elric sat down again. They all waited to see who would present themselves. Javic looked around the tavern to see if anybody was still watching. As he scanned across the crowd, he accidentally caught the eye of an old man that was sitting at one of the tables adjacent to theirs. The man had wispy, white hair and dark spots on his pale skin. His cheeks were sunken in, making the outline of his face look like a skull. He looked up at Javic and smiled, revealing a mouth full of disgusting teeth; the ones that were not missing were stained yellowish-brown and crooked. Javic grimaced at the old man. The man stopped smiling and returned to his grog.

It was as if nothing had happened; as if the poem had never even been recited. Elric was frowning as he looked around the tavern. "Wait here boys. I'm going to go listen to the tavern gossip and gather some news while we wait. Maybe the contact hasn't arrived yet."

"What if the code or location has changed since you were in the Ver'konus?" asked Belford.

"I don't know. Let's not worry about that, at least not until after I have tried reciting the poem once more." Elric reached into his coin purse and then handed some money to Javic. "Pay the barmaid with these when she gets back with our food," he said. Elric stood up again and walked over to the bar. He tried to start up a conversation with the bartender, who just so happened to be the largest man in the room, but the massive bearded man didn't seem to be in a very chatty mood. The dirty mugs he was wiping down were quite large, but they looked minuscule in comparison to his massive hands.

Javic turned his attention to Belford, who had started spinning an apple around on the table. Seeing the fruit, Javic immediately felt foolish for having assumed that Belford had thrown his apple at the nobleman, Arlin, in the square. Belford didn't have a mean bone in his body.

"Did you hear what that guard said outside?" Javic asked. "He said there are more than eighty Whunes waiting in the forest around the city...."

Belford had a distant expression on his face as he spun the apple around and around. "I can't turn this apple into dust," he said, glancing up across the table at Javic.

"Huh?"

"I can't figure out how I did it, and it almost got us all killed."

"What are you talking about?" asked Javic. "You saved our lives! It's not your fault you couldn't do it again—"

"But why can't I do it? It's just so frustrating. I keep replaying it over and over again in my head, but no matter how closely I try to duplicate what I did, nothing happens. If I could just figure it out again, I could probably get rid of the rest of the Whunes and we would all be safe." Belford spun the apple around once more but it hit a notch in the wood and rolled right off the edge of the table. "It just won't *die*."

"Well," said Javic, "for starters, the moon isn't up yet. You can only use the Power when the moon's up. There's no use straining yourself until then. I'm sure it will all come back to you eventually."

"I wish I could be so sure," said Belford.

The old skull-faced man got up from his table and walked over to Javic. He was holding the fallen apple in his hands. He placed the fruit down on their table, but did not leave. He continued to stand there, staring at Javic.

Javic returned his stare. "What?" he asked, a hint of irritation in his voice.

The man held out his upturned palm.

"You want money?" Javic laughed, shocked at his audacity. "What for?"

"Wizard," whispered the old man, his eyes flashing at Belford as he grinned his filthy smile.

What did he overhear? Did we give ourselves away?

"Wizard," he said again, a little more loudly.

"Alright, alright. Take what I have, but if you say one word—" Javic left the threat unspoken as he handed over the money Elric left him for their meals.

The man snatched the apple up as well and shuffled back over to his table. He put the apple in his pocket and began sipping from his mug once more.

Javic and Belford only had time to look at one another before the barmaid arrived at their table carrying three plates of food which she began to place in front of them. Javic looked over at the bar, searching for his grandfather, but he was not there. He scanned his eyes around the rest of the room. Elric was nowhere to be seen. "Um... my grandfather has the money for this, but I don't know where he's gone."

The barmaid began to pick the plates back up, but Belford was already eating.

"Hold up," he pleaded, grabbing one of the barmaid's wrists. "He'll be back soon."

The barmaid shot him an icy look and he let go of her arm immediately.

She stood there for a moment holding all three plates, but ultimately decided to put them back down on the table, though not without warning: "Don't you dare try to leave without paying for these or I'll have Thorin break every bone in your body. Thorin—" she yelled over to the barman, "keep an eye on these two."

Thorin put down the mug he was wiping and lifted up a huge cudgel that was resting against the edge of the bar. He pointed it at Javic and Belford in a threatening manner before returning to his business.

Javic gulped.

"That man is freaking huge," whispered Belford.

"I think he could rip us in half," said Javic.

"So could that lady!"

"Yeesh!" They both chuckled gravely and proceeded to stuff their faces.

Javic kept one eye on the skull-faced man while he attempted to fill the hollow pit he felt in his stomach with the gravy-thick mound of mush that the barmaid had left in front of him. The old man sat humming to himself, rocking slowly back and forth in his chair. He muttered something inaudible, then stood up and walked straight out of the bar. There was nothing they could do; the man was clearly crazy, but they could not follow him from the tavern without first paying for their meals.

Where is Grandfather? No sooner had Javic thought this than Elric sauntered in through the front door of the tavern.

"I was at the latrines," said Elric, preempting their questions as he stepped back up to the table. "And I've got some interesting news."

"Us first," said Javic. He quickly explained the situation, but Elric did not look concerned.

"No one listens to drunkards," he said offhandedly. "But what I wish to tell you about is a rumor that has been going around town. The word is that the king of Taris has been assassinated – King Vouldric is dead!"

It was very odd news to Javic. Elric had always said that King Vouldric was just a puppet ruler, left in power by Garrett because it was more convenient to leave him there than it was to replace him. "But why would Garrett have him killed now?"

Elric shrugged. "People are saying that Garrett plans to officially invade Taris – that the Whunes are merely the first wave of his attack." He paused for a moment, shaking his head slightly. "That is what people are saying, but that does not make it true. If Garrett wanted to invade the kingdom, he would simply march an army to Saldrone. Felington is too far out of the way for a political struggle. The people of Felington are not Vouldric's men; they do not care to whom they pay their taxes. No, do not fool yourselves: It is no coincidence that the Whunes have pursued us here. Now," said Elric, "it is starting to get late. I must try to contact Ethan's proxy once more."

Elric got up again, excused himself in front of the crowd, and began to repeat the poem. This time, however, he was met by more than silence. In particular, it was the men who had been gambling that became the most rowdy. Elric spoke no more than the first line of the poem before they began to shout out angry words and insults from across the bar.

Continuing to the end of the poem was enough to infuriate one man. He started to approach Elric, but Thorin – the barkeep – reached Elric first. He was holding his cudgel in one of his absurdly large hands, and it took no more than his presence to make the drunken gambler stand down from his advance.

Thorin turned to Elric. "If you know what's good for you, you'll get out of here right now." He spoke sternly, his deep voice rumbling up out of his chest.

Elric threw some coins down on the table and he, Belford, and Javic all hastily made their way towards the exit. Before they could reach the doors, a short young guard in a red tabard burst in. He was winded from a run and his cheeks were rosy from the cool evening air outside.

"What is it, Milo?" asked the barmaid.

"It's the creatures, ma'am. They're advancing on the city!"

CHAPTER

11

The Fight for Felington

A sudden urgency filled the tavern. Chairs were overturned as men pushed and stumbled their way out of the bar. Javic shuffled past the barmaid and cherry-faced guardsman while following Elric and Belford to the exit. He overheard the tail end of the barmaid's conversation as he walked past. "…close enough?" she was saying.

"No, not yet, but soon," responded Milo. "I've come straight here, just as you asked, but I really must be returning to my post."

"Very well," said the barmaid. "But first, I need to know one thing. Would it be possible for me to get up on the wall?"

"On the wall? Out of the question. Only the City Watch is allowed on the wall." Milo shook his head apologetically. "I'm afraid I cannot help you with that one, Shiara."

"That's alright, Milo. You have done well."

Milo exited the tavern after Javic and took off running towards the northern entrance of the city. A sea of red-tabard-wearing guardsmen had amassed there in front of the gate. Most of the City Watch was already present, clustered together in a clumsy formation, though a few men still scurried about delivering messages. Off-duty guards were being roused from the nearby barracks. Everyone was readying themselves to defend the city.

The tavern patrons were directed south towards the city center by a young guardsman on crowd control duty. People whose homes were within the city walls were being asked to return to them; the City Watch wanted the streets clear. All of the travelers and people who had been uprooted from their homes and farms during the initial Whune attacks were being sequestered into a large crowd within the staging area at the center of the city.

Elric, Javic, and Belford ended up along the outer edge of the crowd, right next to a very disgruntled Arlin Calary.

"Let me do something," he cried out to one of the guardsmen. "I can aid you. I'm already in my armor and Mast knows I can wield this sword with dexterity." He unsheathed his sword with a flourish of his wrist.

"Put that away, sir. Just sit tight while the City Watch does its job," said the young guardsman.

Javic watched as the nobleman returned his sword to its scabbard and glowered at the guardsman. Arlin muttered something under his breath which Javic could not make out. "Why are you so eager to fight?" Javic asked him.

Arlin's eyes widened in surprise, he hadn't realized anybody was watching him. "Oh…" he cocked his head sideways at Javic and narrowed his eyes in careful consideration of his words. "…for justice," he answered. He did not elaborate. His face settled with a distant expression; evidently lost in thought.

Javic nodded slowly, unsure what to make of Arlin's response. He was surely brave, but he was also a fool. He had the love of a beautiful girl, Mallory, and yet seemed completely oblivious to it. He was willing to throw everything away.

And for what? Justice? What does that even mean?

Javic would have done anything to have Salvine at his side, both of them alive and well. He would never risk losing that gift if he had it. Arlin was too obsessed with confronting the Whunes. It was difficult for Javic not to tell him exactly what he thought of his stupidity. Instead, he decided to remind Arlin of what he could lose: "What will your lady do without you once the Whunes hack you down and tear your limbs off?" he asked with a straight face.

Arlin laughed and shook his head. "Do not worry about us, boy," he said, returning the condescension in his tone. "Sometimes there are things worth fighting for that are more important than oneself. Besides, it is the beasts that should be wary of me. They won't know what hit them." Arlin turned away from Javic, clearly finished with the conversation. He addressed the guardsman once more, "I cannot stand idly by while the fighting ensues. There is no honor in repose. I must fight!"

A man with gray streaks in his fading hair agreed with Arlin's sentiment. "We need to do something," he said.

"There's no need to panic, just sit tight while the City Watch does its job," repeated the young guardsman. Most of the guards around the crowd were young, but this one appeared to be the youngest. He could not have been more than fourteen years old and he was so scrawny that his tabard hung across his shoulders awkwardly, loosely flapping in the wind and nearly touching the ground. The guardsmen who had been left to watch over the crowd must have been apprentices – all of the older men were already positioned near the north wall.

Javic could hear the shouts of the officers as the bowmen began releasing volley upon volley of arrows into the dimming sky from behind their battlements. Fire pits alongside the wall were ablaze with flames, and pots of boiling goo – tar, based on the acrid smell wafting through the streets – were being prepared in case the attackers reached the wall. The scent reminded Javic of the time he and his grandfather assisted Aston McGrutto, Darrenfield's roofer, clean out his tar-smoldering oven – tar-shingle roofs were a growing trend in the area. The air had been so saturated with sticky particles that the tar literally stuck to Javic's teeth for days after finishing the job.

Although the guardsmen were readying themselves for a fight, it did not look like close combat would be necessary. By the cries of the officers, the Whunes were dropping quickly to the far reaching longbows atop the wall. From what Javic could gather, every Whune that abandoned the safety of the tree line was soon pincushioned with dozens of arrows. It took a few hits, but eventually their bodies would give out and they would collapse into bloody heaps of muscle within the grassy expanse that lay between city and forest. The Whunes did not approach in an organized manner; instead, one or two at a time, they would stagger out of the trees and walk carelessly towards their demise.

Javic spied Mallory making her way towards Arlin around the edge of the civilian crowd. She was dragging an ornery-looking horse behind her. Every step was a battle for Mallory as she tugged at the horse's reins. The horse would only oblige her with two or three unhindered steps at a time before coming to a halt. She had to pour all of her effort into getting the horse to move after each pause.

The horse wore armor plating along its body in strategic locations – its head and neck were covered, as well as the upper portion of its legs. The plating matched Arlin's in appearance and style so closely that it must have been crafted by the same hand – it was so reflective that the metal appeared completely black as the horse passed through shadows, then suddenly ignited into a brilliant orange as the light from the firepots gleamed off its surfaces. The staging area was well lit by at least a dozen of these firepots.

As Javic watched Mallory approach, there was a sudden change in the tint of the light. The shadows softened and the landscape seemed to flow with milk. The moon peeked up over the crest of a distant hill. Javic shivered as a shout from one of the officers reached his ears:

"HOLD YOUR FIRE!" came the cry. "There is a man in the killing field!"

The civilian crowd grew silent as everybody tried to listen to the discussion taking place between the officers. The bowmen lowered their longbows and there was a moment where nothing could be heard apart from the wind whistling through the alleyways between the buildings.

"He approaches alongside the Whunes!" exclaimed an officer.

"RESUME FIRE!" shouted the captain of the guard from his position at the head of the formation. He was dressed similarly to the rest of the guardsmen, except that he wore a large feathery plume that stuck out of the top of his helmet. The plume was meant to distinguish him from the rest of the guardsmen, and it did its job well, as even from a distance, Javic was able to tell exactly where the captain was at all times. The captain paced back and forth in front of his guardsmen. They had tightened their formation and now held position obediently in front of the inner gate.

The bowmen lifted their bows at the captain's command and fired a volley of arrows into the sky, but before they had released a second volley, shouting erupted all along the top of the wall. There were too many voices all garbled together for Javic to make out what any one individual was saying, but it was clear from the tone of the uproar that something had caused much fear among the bowmen.

The captain of the guard sent a messenger sprinting towards the officers stationed at the south gate. As the runner got closer to the civilian crowd, Javic realized that it was Milo, the guardsman who delivered the news of the Whunes' approach to the Marrow Tavern. He stopped momentarily and exchanged a

few words with one of the young guardsmen along the edge of
the civilian crowd before continuing towards the south gate.

The guard he spoke to ran over to the guard nearest Javic.
"My brother says all of the Whunes are approaching in
formation around a man... and that the man's using the Power
to stop the arrows!" The young guard's voice trembled slightly
as he spoke. His eyes were wide with fear. He had spoken too
loudly; most of the crowd heard Milo's news.

The edges of the crowd bulged as panic spread through the
civilians like wildfire. The young guardsmen whose job it was
to prevent this exact occurrence stood by helplessly as the
crowd fled in all directions. Javic was shoved from behind as
everyone surged forward. He lost his footing and tumbled to
the ground, sending shockwaves through his injured arm. The
wind was knocked out of him as a dozen feet quickly trampled
over his body. Thinking swiftly, Javic pulled his arms in to
protect his head and began to roll in the direction of the nearby
line of shops. He found a wall and stayed pressed up against it
until the majority of the crowd finished rumbling by. Standing
up, he was relieved to find himself relatively unscathed. He
looked around for Belford and his grandfather, but they were
nowhere to be seen.

Javic decided to climb onto one of the shops' second-floor
balconies to get a better view. He jumped up and grabbed hold
of the edge of the balcony then crawled under the railing.
From there, he was able to see a little better, but he was still
unable to locate the others, so he decided to climb higher. The
roof was easily accessible from the balcony – standing on top
of the railing gave him half the height he needed, and he was
able to pull himself up the rest of the way without any trouble
at all. Once on the roof, he spotted Belford and his grandfather
at the opposite side of the staging area. Javic waved to them.
It took a moment for Belford to notice, but once he did he
waved back and pointed out Javic to Elric.

Javic was actually quite high up. He found that, from his
vantage point, he could see all the way over the wall and onto

the hill on which the battle was taking place. A man, unremarkable in appearance, stood at the center of a large grouping of Whunes as they slowly made their way towards the gate. Javic was horrified to note that there were far more than eighty Whunes surrounding the man. The number was closer to double by Javic's estimate. The man wore a black cloak with a hood drawn up over his head, partially obscuring his face. Javic was unable to make out any other details from this distance.

A volley of arrows rained down towards the Whunes, but as they got closer, the hooded man simply flicked his wrist and the arrows deflected away harmlessly as if they were struck by a giant, invisible flyswatter. A few arrows made it through along the outer perimeter of the advancing Whunes. The remaining creatures crowded in closer towards the man for protection.

Just as Javic was about to climb down from the roof, he noticed a curious sight: An oversized guardsman in a too-small tabard was ascending the steps towards the battlements at the top of the wall. He held a massive cudgel in his right hand; it was obvious to Javic that the man was Thorin, the barkeep from the Marrow Tavern. The barkeep looked about cautiously as he reached the top of the wall, and then gestured for a tiny guardsman at the base of the steps to follow him up. Javic knew that there were no females within the City Watch, and this fact made the barmaid's long-haired and full-busted attempt at portraying a guardsman only that much more comical.

It didn't look like anybody else had noticed the mock guardsmen yet, or perhaps they had but simply didn't want to question Thorin's hulking appearance. As the barmaid, Shiara, reached the top of the wall she took position alongside the officer who had been ordering the arrow volleys. She spoke to him and he ordered the bowmen to fire on her mark. The arrows soared. Just as the hooded man waved his hand to deflect the arrows, Shiara waved hers as well. Half of the arrows changed their trajectory, but the other half stayed the course and penetrated deep into the cluster of Whunes. Approximately twenty of the creatures collapsed dead on the spot.

The hooded man seemed surprised by the resistance. He pulled his hood back, revealing a pale face and graying hair. He scanned his eyes back and forth along the wall, searching for his adversary.

Shiara continued to direct volley upon volley of arrows into the ranks of Whunes. Their numbers quickly dwindled to less than half of what they had been at the start.

Without warning, the battlement that Shiara was standing in front of shattered into bits of gravel. She was sent flying backwards from the concussive shock. With surprising swiftness, Thorin reached out and snatched her out of the air. The officer that had been standing beside her was not as lucky; he smashed into the ground with a sickening thud, landing a full twenty paces back from the wall. Several more battlements exploded, sending a number of bowmen falling to their deaths.

With an enormous blast, the outer door of the north entrance splintered into nothing. The Whunes had reached the city. The shockwave from the explosion rattled the shingles on the rooftops. Startled screams rang out across the city. Javic decided he had overstayed his welcome on the rooftop. He lay down onto his stomach and swung his legs over the edge, then dropped down to the second-floor balcony. Suddenly, from the direction of the wall, came the most horrible sound that Javic had ever heard. He looked towards the mayhem.

A quickly expanding pool of molten metal now sat where the inner gate once hung. The pool had already engulfed a dozen or so guardsmen at the front of the formation. The sound Javic was hearing was the cries of those guardsmen as they were consumed by fire; their bodies melting into what had previously been the inner gate.

A few hasty Whunes rushed forward, taking no more than three steps into the puddle before they too burst into flames and suffered the same fate as the unfortunate guardsmen. The rest of the Whunes held back. Their lumpy, ragdoll-like heads and beady eyes shifted back and forth across the guardsmen's broken formation. The flickering flames of the burning corpses cast an orange glow that illuminated the tumorous growths and bulging limbs of the surviving Whunes. The clawed fingers of the fearsome beasts gripped their dark battleaxes tightly. The pool of molten metal suddenly made a loud hiss as it hardened into a smooth, silvery surface. A second later, the Whunes were already swarming through the opening.

Javic hopped over the edge of the balcony. Elric and Belford were waiting for him on the ground when he landed. He quickly told them of the Whunes within the walls, and about the barmaid using the Power.

"Where is she now?" asked Elric.

"The last time I saw her, she was just east of the gates," said Javic.

"You boys will be safest with her," said Elric. "Go around behind the Marrow Tavern. I will meet you there when the fighting is finished."

Javic knew better than to argue with his grandfather. He and Belford broke into a run and skirted the edge of the battle that was now beginning to spill into the staging area. As they rounded a corner and passed the Marrow Tavern, Javic spotted Thorin carrying Shiara away from the direction of the fighting. He held her in one arm, still carrying his cudgel in the other – prepared for anything that might come his way. As they got closer, Javic could see that Shiara's eyes were closed and that she was bleeding profusely out of a wide spattering of small wounds that covered her face and chest.

Belford ran up to Thorin and put a hand on his shoulder. Thorin turned, ready to attack, but Belford put his hand up. "I think I might be able to help," he said. Belford had Thorin lay

Shiara down onto the ground. He crouched over her and placed both of his hands, palms down, onto her stomach.

Javic watched in awe as Belford's hands began to glow pale blue. Shiara was glowing as well. Soft-green ripples flowed through her body. Bits of bloodied rock rose out of her wounds and tumbled to the ground. The gashes sealed up, leaving no trace that they had ever existed apart from the holes left behind in her clothing. There was still a little bit of residual blood caked onto her face, but most of the blood that had leaked out had disappeared entirely, used up somehow by the healing process.

"Shiara!" exclaimed Thorin as the barmaid opened her eyes. She was too weak to stand, so Thorin propped her up against the wall.

Shiara's eyes glazed over with moisture as she looked up at Thorin. "Stop worrying over me," she said. "You need to go turn the tide of this battle."

Thorin's face hardened into an emotionless mask. He gave a curt nod before looking over at Belford. "You, Wizard," he said. "Protect her with your life." Thorin did not wait for a reply. He stood up and rushed towards the fighting. He reached the front shortly – the battle was expanding quickly into the streets. Using his cudgel, he smashed in the side of one Whune's head, not even pausing before ramming it into the jaw of another.

Javic's eyes darted across the fray of combat, searching for his grandfather. Finally he spotted him. Elric was standing back to back with Arlin Calary, fending off Whunes from every direction. Neither Mallory nor Arlin's horse were anywhere to be seen. Arlin appeared to be quite light on his feet. He dodged sideways with a somersault and was back up with a slash before the Whune he was fighting even had a chance to react.

Ten paces away from Arlin stood the captain of the guard, made obvious by his plume. Javic could see now why the man had been made captain. He cut down one Whune after another, his sword constantly moving and his feet flowing from one stance to the next so smoothly that it looked like a dance.

Then Javic saw the man in the hood.

He sauntered in nondescriptly, no weapon in hand, glanced about the battle, then gestured towards the captain of the guard with his right hand. Javic's heart sank as the captain crumbled into nothing and blew away in the wind, plume and all. He hadn't even seen it coming. The hooded man turned to the next nearest guardsman and disintegrated him as well. He turned to Thorin, who by this point was starting to smash a path through the Whunes towards him. The man made his killing gesture towards Thorin, but nothing happened. He gestured again – same result. The man scowled. He glanced to the Whunes and eight or nine swarmed over Thorin all at once.

With Thorin distracted, the hooded leader of the Whunes went back to disintegrating guardsmen. He killed several more before turning towards Elric.

Panic spread throughout Javic's body as he watched what was sure to be his grandfather's final moment.

Elric spun around and saw the man staring at him. A look of horror sprang onto Elric's face as he stumbled backwards over the corpse of a Whune. Elric was on the ground now, staring up at the hooded man. They looked at one another for a long moment, neither moving. It was unlike Elric to give up, but that was what he appeared to be doing. He did not attempt to fight back, or even to rise.

Javic wasn't sure what was delaying the hooded man's attack. The hesitation demonstrated by both men was perplexing, but Javic didn't waste any more time analyzing the situation. He lunged for the corpse of a bowman who had fallen from the wall and snatched up the dead man's longbow. He grabbed an arrow and sent it flying.

The arrow struck the hooded man square in the back. He crumpled forward slightly, but did not fall to the ground. The man cried out and all of the nearby Whunes immediately surrounded him, protecting him from further attack with their bodies. They retreated in a huddled mass while the rest of the Whunes – of which there were maybe twenty left – continued to fight to their deaths.

Thorin, Arlin, and the remaining guardsmen made short work of the Whunes that stayed behind, but Elric seemed to be in shock. He stared in the direction of the retreating man until long after he had already vanished from his line of sight.

CHAPTER

12

Flicker

Whipped up into a pink froth, blood and saliva dripped from her mouth. She snapped at the guardsman's throat, but his chainmail hood blocked her teeth from sinking in. He was squirming desperately under the pressure of her massive forearm. She pushed even harder, relishing in the sound of his cracking ribs.

Snap. Snap. Crunch.

For a moment, everything was drowned out by the man's screams, until all of his breath was expelled from his lungs and he had none left to pass through his vocal chords. She smashed her forearm into his body again and again, pressing him viciously against the cobblestone of the square. She did not stop until his lungs were thoroughly crushed, never to fill with air again.

Another guardsman was at her back, sword shaking in an outstretched hand. She spied him over her shoulder and sent a horse-kick straight into his stomach. He was sent sprawling backwards onto the ground in a heap.

She was on him in an instant.

This new guardsman was young. Ill-prepared. He had his red tabard draped over a plain cloth tunic. There was no chainmail protecting his vital organs. She snapped at his throat, this time meeting no resistance. Her teeth severed his arteries cleanly. His cries quickly turned into gurgles as she tore out the rest of his throat with a second chomp. Warm blood filled her mouth, delighting her senses.

The young guardsman turned pale as a crimson puddle expanded around him. Life left his eyes. She gnawed at the chunk of flesh in her mouth, savoring its chewy texture as she turned her attention towards her next plaything.

Fear got the best of the next guardsman. As soon as her gaze passed over him, he spun on his heels to flee. Another Whune struck him in the side of the head with its axe.

She'd nearly forgotten about her own weapon. It lay beneath the guardsman with the crushed lungs. She bent to retrieve it. The axe was important to her – a gift from her master. Before her fingertips reached the handle, she felt a sharp tug behind her navel. Her breath caught in her lungs. It was as if an invisible hook had implanted itself in her belly.

She was being drawn forward, away from the fray of the battle by the call of her master. There was panic in Wilgoblikan's mental command. He was injured. Desperate. She could sense his pain – fire exploding from her spine as if the arrow in Wilgoblikan's backside had struck her instead.

Every other thought abandoned her. She stopped what she was doing, deserting her prized axe where it lay. She moved with every bit of haste she could muster to reach her master's side before any more harm could befall him. The scent of blood was thick in the air as she joined with her brethren, forming a fleshy wall around Wilgoblikan. Anyone who came for her master would have to go through her first!

That was when she spotted the boy in the distance: Longbow in his hands, hazel eyes sharp and focused beneath his curly hair. He was staring beyond her, to her master at her back.

Something stirred within her. Unwanted emotions rippled beneath the surface, tugging at her insides like dozens of tiny hands clawing for scraps of food. She knew the boy – a part of her did, anyway. It didn't make any sense.

He was the one responsible for injuring her master. All of her instincts told her to hate him, to destroy him if she ever got the chance, and yet, another part of her was screaming out the exact opposite.

The cries were faint at first, but grew stronger the longer she stared at him.

Javic!

That's Javic!

That's my Javic!

The words shook her, tearing their way through her mind. Her feet stumbled over themselves as the message drilled its way deep into her core. She could feel its reverberations in her bones.

She feared the voice. Whunes did not typically experience fear, but she was frightened by the implications of her slipping sanity. She did not want to lose control. She needed to protect her master! He was relying on her now more than ever. With much difficulty, she forced herself to look away from the boy. He was trouble. His piercing eyes had started all of this.

Together, with her brethren, she carried Wilgoblikan through the bloodied streets, out of the city, and back into the silent forest. To her great vexation, even with the boy far behind her, the voice did not entirely fade.

CHAPTER

13

The Lies That Bind Us

The city wall did not make a comfortable headrest. One of the stone blocks bulged out a little farther than the rest and poked right into the back of Belford's neck. He flopped his arms down to his sides, too tired to adjust his position. The barmaid sat to his left, and although she was no longer lucid, she was still trying to speak. It came across as mumbled nonsense, much like a person talking in her sleep.

Although Belford continued to refer to her as the barmaid in his mind, his opinion of the lady changed vastly the moment he learned she could use the Power. She was Ver'ati – a wizard, just like him – the world bent to her will, prostrate at her feet. And yet, she seemed so fragile. She was fighting back sleep, and from the looks of it she was losing the battle. Her eyelids were closed more often than not and her head bobbed over every few seconds. She uttered one last mumbled phrase before sliding down the wall. Only her neck remained propped up.   She stopped fighting the inevitable.   Snores began emanating from her nose almost immediately, and they were actually quite loud, considering her petite size.

Belford lifted his left arm.   He intended to move her into a position that was less restrictive on her nasal passages, but raising his arm used nearly all of his remaining strength.   The healing process had taken a lot more out of them both than he had anticipated.   He let his arm fall back to his side and contemplated lying down on the ground, but even that would take too much effort.

Dwelling on his discomfort, Belford glanced over his shoulder at the wall.   It seemed to wiggle a bit, and then it began to give in under the pressure of his back.   He was sinking into the wall, or it was molding around him, he wasn't sure which.

"Stop that!" cried Javic's familiar voice.   "You'll bring the whole wall down on top of us!"

Belford hadn't even realized that Javic was there.   Hands grabbed onto the front of Belford's shirt and yanked him forward.   The impression of his head and back remained in the stone despite its return to a rigid state.

"Sit tight," said Javic.   "I have to go help Grandfather. Thorin is here to look after you."

Belford felt himself being lifted into the air.   He cracked his eyes open and saw that he was being carried under one arm by the massive bartender.

Thorin crouched down and picked up Shiara with his other arm; she was still fast asleep.   They began to move away from the wall.   Thorin carried them between the stables and the Marrow Tavern before heading into the street.   He stopped abruptly.

"This doesn't look good," he said.

Belford opened his eyes again.   At the entrance to the Marrow Tavern were three guardsmen standing next to the old skull-faced drunkard who had accused him of being a wizard. Never mind that the man was right, it had still been very rude.

The man opened his mouth into what would have been a toothy grin if most of his teeth were not missing from his head. He pointed at Belford and laughed.

"Wizard!" he shouted. "Wizard! Wizard! Wizard!" He chanted the word over and over again; it seemed to amuse him. He cackled even harder now, as if he had just finished telling a raunchy joke.

Thorin placed Belford back on the ground as two of the guardsmen began to approach him. They stopped a few paces short of Thorin, remaining out of his reach. Both men gripped their sword hilts tightly, but they did not unsheathe their weapons. One of the men spoke. "By order of the captain of the Guard, you must leave the city immediately."

"The captain of the guard is dead," responded Thorin. He eyed the guardsmen, daring them to make a move.

"The new captain of the guard," said the third guardsman who had hung back. He gestured towards himself. He spoke confidently, but Belford could see fear in his eyes.

"It makes no difference," said Thorin, "we will not be leaving the city until Shiara is fully recovered."

A small crowd was beginning to amass around them, drawn in by the loud voices.

"It's their fault the Whunes came!" shouted the skull-faced man.

"Hang them!" cried someone else.

A man lunged out from the crowd and rushed at Thorin in an attempt to pry Shiara out from under his arm. Thorin punched him square in the face, sending him straight to the ground, blood gushing from both nostrils.

"Without them, the Whunes would have killed us all," said Arlin Calary, appearing along the edge of the crowd.

"We are staying until morning," said Thorin. He spoke calmly and with more authority than the new captain of the guard could ever hope to muster. Nobody else dared to argue against him.

Thorin picked up Belford again and continued walking towards the Marrow Tavern's entrance. The guards had no choice but to step aside as Thorin walked through the doorway.

Belford thought he could hear the faint sounds of music playing somewhere off in the distance. He closed his eyes, unable to fight back his eyelids any longer. The music grew louder as he drifted off to sleep.

From out of the darkness, a glowing figure began to emerge – the girl from his dreams.

You again!

This time she had a golden aura surrounding her. As Belford stared into her lightly freckled face, a room began to form around them.

They were seated inside a tiny tea house. Six circular tables filled out the floor space, each matched by two round-backed, wooden chairs. There were no other people in the room. Dozens of colorful saucer plates adorned the walls, each decorated with its own unique picture or design.

The golden aura became a stream of sunlight shining in through a nearby window. It silhouetted the girl, making her glow around the edges. She sipped from a teacup and smiled at Belford; not a care in the world. Belford reached for his own cup, but it was empty. And so was the teapot. He frowned.

"Who are you?" he asked.

The girl giggled, then took another sip from her cup. "Don't you recognize me?"

"I do," said Belford. "But I just can't remember."

"Sure you can," she leaned across the table and touched Belford's arm, "it's all inside you. Maybe you just need a little reminder; a marker to help you find your way back to the path."

"What reminder? Why can't you just tell me?"

"Drink this." But it wasn't the girl that spoke; it was Thorin's gravelly voice, coming from somewhere else.

Belford began to choke as a lukewarm and slightly granular liquid poured into his mouth. He sputtered and coughed, spitting up onto the front of his shirt.

"Come on now. Don't get it everywhere," said Thorin. He continued to tip the liquid into Belford's mouth until Belford snatched the cup out of his hand.

Belford was completely awake now. He had been close to figuring out something important about his past. If only he had been allowed to continue sleeping! But at least he did learn two things: The girl assured him his memories were still somewhere inside his mind, and that he would be able to get them back, eventually. Belford didn't think the girl would lie to him, because that would be tantamount to lying to himself; the whole experience had just taken place inside of his own head after all. Still, Belford wished the fog would clear itself away faster. She was so damn beautiful.... All Belford knew for sure about his past was that, with her, he had been happy.

Belford eyeballed the cup of brown muck that Thorin had been trying to shovel down his throat. "What *is* this?" he asked. "It's disgusting!"

"Oh, it's not that bad, really – my own special brew; a little bit of this, a little bit of that. It's packed full of protein."

Belford scraped his fingernails across his tongue, trying to rid himself of the terrible flavor.

"It really gets the blood pumping in the morning," said Thorin.

Shiara was also awake now. She was sitting in a chair by the fireplace. "Don't worry, I can't stand the stuff either." She tossed a chunk of dried meat over to Belford. "Here," she said. "You'll need to get your energy back. That was a pretty stupid thing you did back there, you know. Using your own energy like that... you could have gotten us both killed."

Belford grumbled about having to eat dried meat again.

"Who taught you that technique, anyway?" she asked.

Belford shrugged. "Nobody. I just... I just did it, I guess."
He nibbled at the corner of the jerky. Better to let her think
him untrained than attempt to explain his memory loss.

Shiara and Thorin shared a quick look. She opened her
mouth to speak just as the front door of the tavern burst open.
Javic and Elric came inside. Javic was supporting most of his
grandfather's weight as he walked him over to a chair. Javic
was breathing harder than normal, but it was Elric that drew
Belford's attention. His face was sweating profusely, and his
eyes were strangely vacant.

"What happened?" asked Belford.

"I don't know," said Javic. "He just sort of freaked out when
that man..." his voice trailed off as Elric started to come back
to his senses.

Elric turned his head and looked around the room. "I need a
drink," he said.

"Get him some water," ordered Javic.

"No, no," said Elric, "bring me a shot of the hardest liquor
you've got."

Javic looked baffled. "What's going on, Grandfather?"

Elric shook his head. Whatever it was, Elric was either
incapable or unwilling to talk about it.

"Here you go," said Thorin, "I brought the bottle."

Elric took a swig of the amber liquid straight from the bottle,
and then placed it down hard on the table.

"Who was that man?" asked Javic, staring at his grandfather.
"Why didn't you fight back? And why didn't he kill you?"

It was Shiara who answered him. "There is little a non-
wizard could have done to fight against such a foe," she said.
"It's not so much a question of *who* he was, though, as it is a
question of *what*."

Javic cocked his head to the side.

"That man is not really a man at all," she said. "He is a
Whune."

"But that doesn't make any sense," said Belford. "We know
what Whunes look like. They're enormous."

"That is one type of Whune," Shiara corrected him. "But that man was a Whune as well. A Whune is simply any creature that has been Compelled with the Power. If I am not mistaken, he was a Goblikan Whune. A dark wizard; Compelled by King Garrett himself."

"Wilgoblikan," said Elric under his breath.

"Hrrm? Yes, a Goblikan," said Shiara. "They are the highest amongst the Whunes, enslaved minds; Garrett's only trusted subjects."

Belford looked at Javic, but all of his attention was focused towards Shiara. Nobody else realized what Elric had actually said. Belford's ears were not playing tricks on him – he distinctly heard Elric's whisper.

Wilgoblikan – that's a name, not a title.

Elric grabbed hold of a chain that lay around his neck. He pulled it out from under his tunic and began to absently fiddle with the golden ring dangling at the bottom. Elric stared over at Belford for a moment. Belford wasn't sure what to make of the look.

"It's a good thing you shot that – what did you call it? A goblin thing? – with an arrow, Javic," Elric said. "I really thought that was the end for a moment there." Elric was hiding something. He knew much more than he was letting on.

Belford decided not to call Elric out on his dishonesty – at least not yet – but there was definitely going to be some explaining for Elric to do the next time they were alone.

"From the sound of it, you truly are lucky. Mercy is not among the traits granted to the Whunes," said Shiara. "Now, who are you people and what are you doing here?"

Elric looked slightly taken aback.

"Not to be rude," said Shiara, "but you people just so happen to show up using a contact code that hasn't been in use for well over a decade on the same day a Goblikan Whune leads a siege on the city with creatures that haven't been seen this far west since Garrett first took the throne a century ago."

"I cannot blame you for being suspicious," said Elric. "I was once in the Ver'konus myself, but I left after my grandson, Javic, was born," he gestured towards Javic. "My name is Elric Elensol, and I believe that the Whunes have pursued us here because of this young man, Belford. He is a wizard, like yourself." Elric looked smug; he seemed to think that he had just enlightened Shiara with new information.

"She already knows I'm a wizard," said Belford.

"Oh," said Elric, frowning. "Well, anyway, we have come here in hopes that you can lead us safely to Phandrol."

"I have never seen so much effort put into trying to kill a single, pathetic, untrained wizard," said Shiara. "Normally I would just tell you all to go away, but seeing as everybody in this damned city now knows I'm Ver'ati, I have no choice but to return to Phandrol myself for reassignment."

There was an awkward silence. Belford was starting to think they might be better off without her. If this was how she was going to act after he just finished saving her life, he didn't want to see her on a normal day.

"Well," said Thorin, "my name is Thorin McGowlin, and this is Shiara Nighfield."

Everybody exchanged pleasantries with Thorin. No one tried to shake Shiara's hand. She sat silently, glaring suspiciously across the room at Belford. Her eyes were sharp as daggers.

"Nighfield?" asked Elric. "Of the Nighfield house, the lowest of the thirteen ruling houses of Erotos?"

Shiara's eyes narrowed farther.

Thorin answered for her. "Shiara would have been royalty if Queen Hannah Davis's grandson, Sir Geoffrey Davis-Nighfield, hadn't been estranged from the family for killing one of his brothers in a duel four hundred years ago."

"The Nighfield lineage is one of the oldest and most prestigious lines of wizards that still exist to this day," Shiara said defensively. "*Lowest* house or not, the Mark of Kings is in my bloodline."

Javic, Belford, and Elric all exchanged silent looks at the mention of the Mark of Kings.

Belford decided to change the subject. "So, are you two a couple?" he asked.

"That's none of your business," said Shiara.

Shiara may have been attractive, but she sure was prickly.

It was just an innocent question....

"Be nice," said Thorin, "the kid did save your life." He turned back towards Belford. "But no, we aren't together. I'm just her guardian, keeping her safe when the moon's down."

Thorin and Shiara began to argue about whether or not her life had actually needed saving. They eventually settled on the decision that it had, but also concluded that Belford had been reckless, nearly getting them both killed by using energy from unsustainable sources during the healing process.

Belford began to notice a curious scent. It was difficult to distinguish exactly what it was over the pipe-smoke that still filled the air within the tavern, but he knew something about the odor of the room had changed. He interrupted the conversation, "Does anyone else... smell burning?"

Shiara pointed towards the fireplace, which was ablaze with flames.

"Not that," said Belford, "something else." Turning towards the entrance, he saw an unmistakable glow shining between the gaps around the doorframe.

"I guess they really were serious about wanting us to leave," said Thorin.

"I'll take care of this," said Shiara. She gestured towards the door. All at once, it ripped free of its hinges and flew backwards into the street. Flames crawled through the opening as Shiara leapt out of the tavern. A mob had formed outside, and they were piling debris against the side of the tavern and setting it ablaze. The mob scattered as Shiara used the Power to throw a flaming applecart away from the side of the tavern and into the center of the street. She was too late; the fire had already spread from the debris onto the tavern itself. "Thorin," she called through the doorway, "what's the best way to put out a large fire?"

The tavern walls groaned and there was a loud snap from somewhere within the ceiling. Belford decided that it was time to evacuate the tavern. Everyone else agreed. When they got outside, they saw that the flames had already engulfed the entire south side of the tavern and were now beginning to spread onto the thatched roof.

"How do we stop it?" Belford asked.

"Fire is tricky," said Shiara. "It's like a life force; volatile by nature and full of raw energy. To kill it, you must take away its source of food, which in this case is both the tavern and the air around it."

"So we should make a vacuum around the tavern to keep the oxygen away from the flames?" asked Belford.

"Impossible," said Shiara, "that's not how the Power works. Oxygen is all around us; the Power could push it away, but more would immediately take its place. You would just be fanning it. Don't you know anything?"

Belford thought about the energy dome he had seen in his dream, but he was hesitant to mention it. Nobody else had any ideas though, so he felt he had to say something. "What about... a bubble of energy, like a shield to keep the oxygen away from the flames?"

"A 'bubble of energy?' That makes even less sense than your last idea," said Shiara. "To manipulate something with the Power you must know its composition and the exact steps required to modify that structure into something new. An energy bubble would require a constantly changing structure as well as vast knowledge of the properties of physics and energy. Although..." she paused for a moment, "that does give me an idea." Shiara stared hard at the side of the flaming tavern. Suddenly the fire started to give off a huge amount of black smoke.

"What are you doing?" asked Belford.

Shiara didn't respond immediately. Black smoke filled the air, almost completely blocking the tavern from view. "I'm trying a new approach," she said. "Rather than taking the fuel away from the fire, I am transforming the fire's energy into something new. If I can dissipate enough energy, the fire should go out on its own."

She continued creating the smoke until everybody began coughing; she then swung her arms around in a wild gesture, using the Power to push some of the smoke filled air away from the group. As the air cleared, her extinguishing method appeared to have worked. The whole wall of the tavern was thoroughly charred, but the flames appeared to be gone. Shiara clapped her hands together. "Not bad if I do say so myself."

There was a loud crash as part of the roof caved in.

Shiara sighed.

"You should have just made it rain," said Thorin.

Shiara did not respond.

The mob had completely dispersed by now. They must have been fearful that Shiara would retaliate against them, and from the look on her face, they were right to be afraid.

Thorin placed a consoling hand on her shoulder, but she shrugged it off and began moving at a brisk pace towards a guardsman standing at the corner of the stables with his back to them.

"Shiara, no!" pleaded Thorin, trotting along behind her as she approached the guardsman. "Don't do anything to him."

"Don't be silly," she snapped. "It's just Milo. He waved me over."

The guardsman stepped into the stables. Shiara and the rest of the group followed him in. The air buzzed with flies, attracted by the heavy stench of manure.

"I'm really sorry, Shiara," said Milo. "It's Aberdine – he's the interim captain now – he ordered us not to interfere with the mob. He really wants you out of this city, and fast."

Shiara grimaced slightly and clenched her fists at her sides.

"He knows that you were only helping," Milo continued. "It's just politics. The only way he can make a grab at controlling the city permanently is if he gets enough people rallied behind him, and for that he needs somebody to point the finger at for the attack; somebody he can take an active stance against."

"Where is Aberdine?" asked Shiara.

"I know he is a bit of a fisheater, Shiara, but if you injure or kill him, it will just prove him right in the eyes of the populace," said Milo.

Belford wondered momentarily at the term 'fisheater.' It was clearly derogatory, but he got the distinct impression that it was a racial term as well.

"He tried to burn me alive!" said Shiara. "And you expect me to do nothing?" Her eyes flashed with fury.

"He has friends who are all equally as ambitious as he, and they won't hesitate to use anything you do to Aberdine to gain more followers," said Milo. "But no, I don't expect you to do nothing: I have a plan – a way to insure that no one from Aberdine's circle will have the support of the populace."

"What's that?" asked Shiara.

"It's simple, really," said Milo, "all you have to do is make the people feel safe again. First, reform the gates, then announce that you will pursue the dark wizard who was responsible for the attack."

"Well, that sounds great and all, but there's just a couple of little problems with that plan," said Shiara. "Ignoring the fact that I have no clue where he's run off to, if I actually did manage to find him, he would still be too strong for me. I couldn't even stop him from entering the city; I wouldn't survive a face-to-face encounter."

"All I said was that you make an announcement, not that you actually pursue the man. As long as nobody sees either of you again, no one will be the wiser."

Shiara raised an eyebrow. "How do you know the wizard won't attack the city again as soon as I'm gone?" she asked.

Milo, too, raised an eyebrow. "Will he come back after you're gone?" He looked as if he already knew the answer.

"Probably not," Shiara half mumbled her response. "But he was not here because of me," she added.

"I do not doubt you, Shiara" he said. "You saved my brother's life, and for that I will always be in your debt, but I also know that you have an awful propensity for attracting trouble." Milo glanced over at Belford.

"Alright," said Shiara, "I will do it." Shiara followed Milo out of the stables. Thorin stayed behind with Belford and the Elensols.

Belford couldn't hold his breath any longer. He had no choice but to let out the air he had been holding in ever since he first entered the stinky stables. The air was beyond ripe. He gagged at the thought of where all the little particles entering his nostrils had once been. Nobody else seemed to take any notice of the smell.

"We keep a wagon over on the other side of the tavern," said Thorin. "If you bring the packhorses there while I gather supplies we might be able to get out of here a little faster."

Elric nodded.

"Our horses are down in the last two stalls," Thorin said as he left the stables. He turned down the opposite direction from the way Shiara and Milo had gone. Elric watched him walk away.

"You can't tell me that this smell doesn't bother you," said Belford.

"What smell?" asked Javic. He had already opened the gate to one of the packhorse's stalls and was beginning to lead it out into the walkway.

"Boys," Elric said as soon as Thorin was safely out of ear shot, "we've got to get our stories straight."

"What do you mean?" asked Javic.

"I believe Shiara is already suspicious. We are not to mention anything about the Mark of Kings to either her or Thorin. It is vital that we keep that between us until we have reached Lord Ethan. Also, to avoid unnecessary questions, let's try to keep it quiet that Belford doesn't remember who he is. If anyone asks, just say you two are cousins."

That seemed reasonable to Belford.

"Now," said Elric, "if you don't mind, Javic, I would like to have a quick word alone with Belford. Take the packhorses over to the wagon. We will meet you there."

Javic sent Belford a quick look and mouthed the words "we'll talk later" as he retrieved the second packhorse from the end stall.

Elric waited until Javic was completely out of sight, then turned towards Belford, but it was Belford who spoke first: "What happened with you and that Goblikan Whune?" he asked.

"It's not something that I want Javic to know about," said Elric. His hand went to the chain around his neck. "I used to know that man, a long time ago." Elric paused, taking a deep breath. "I didn't want to say anything because I never thought it would come up, but I just ask that you keep what I am about to tell you to yourself."

"Of course," said Belford. "You've kept my secrets. But why keep it from Javic?"

"I have learned in the past that some things are better left unspoken," said Elric. "When Teresa, my wife, was murdered, our son, Bartan, was just a little younger than Javic is now. I lied before – it wasn't really a random assassin that killed Teresa. It was her brother, Wil, who ended her life. King Garrett twisted Wil into the Goblikan you saw today and sent him to stamp out his family's bloodline so that there would be no chance of the Gift being passed down to future generations. He hadn't been in Teresa's life for many years and so didn't know of Bartan's existence, or else he surely would have come for him as well. Bartan didn't inherit his mother's abilities, but that wouldn't have mattered to the monster in his uncle's flesh. After Teresa's death, when Bartan asked me what happened, I told him the truth. We were both inconsolable with rage at

what Garrett and Wil had done.   And even after years of
fighting in the Ver'konus, Bartan's thirst for revenge never
diminished. I don't want to condemn Javic to the same fate."
A silent tear ran down Elric's cheek. "When Javic was just a
baby, his mother, Kali, and her sister were sent on a mission to
assassinate Garrett. Wil captured them both. Bartan mounted
a rescue attempt, but when he arrived, Wil was ready. He
killed them all... Wilgoblikan murdered Javic's parents."

Belford didn't know what to say.

Elric's eyes were flooded with tears now. He wiped his face
with his sleeve. "Promise me you won't tell him," he said.

"You have my word," Belford replied.

CHAPTER

14

A Long Road Ahead

Shiara's speech was inspiring. At least half of the city showed up for her announcement. Javic really had to hand it to her – she knew how to please a crowd. A few men even tried to join the pursuit of the murderous wizard, but Shiara, of course, turned down the offers. Arlin Calary was amongst those men. He wasn't dissuaded by Shiara's description of the perils they were about to face, and it wasn't until Shiara insulted him by calling him a "liability to the team" that he finally backed down. Arlin left the crowd in a huff.

If Shiara had actually intended on following through with her promise of exacting revenge against the dark wizard, she would have been able to use all the help she could get, but seeing as the plan was actually to get as far away from the Whune as possible, any outsiders in the group would have quickly learned of the ruse and called her on it.

After winning over the crowd, Shiara slipped in a few snide comments about the interim captain. Her steel-blue eyes shined with glee as the crowd booed at the mention of his name. It looked like Aberdine wouldn't be given the title of captain after his interim period.

Before Shiara's speech, Elric went off to join Thorin in his search for supplies. They needed to track down various shop owners and convince them to open their stores in what was now the middle of the night. Javic doubted there were many people who would refuse Thorin, but simply finding the owners was easier said than done.

Belford and Javic had stayed behind at the wagon. As soon as they were alone, Javic questioned Belford about what his grandfather said to him at the stables. Belford made up something about Elric helping him bolster his cover story, but Javic knew he was lying – Javic would have been allowed to listen in if that was all they had discussed. He couldn't think of any reason whatsoever for his grandfather to need to talk to Belford without him present. The whole thing was beginning to make Javic angry. He had always been very close with his grandfather, and he just couldn't figure out why Elric had chosen now to start hiding things from him.

Javic pressed Belford for the truth, but Belford insisted that they hadn't discussed anything else. Belford flashed Javic a thin smile – perhaps to try to assure him of his honesty, but it did not look genuine. Javic gave up on trying to make Belford talk. He walked away in disgust, but not before lashing out with one last comment over his shoulder.

"I thought we were friends," he said. Javic headed off towards the crowd gathering in the staging area for Shiara's announcement. He immediately regretted his words, but at the same time, he genuinely had been hurt by Belford's dishonesty. He knew it was childish, but he wanted to punish Belford for keeping secrets from him.

What have I done to lose their trust?

When the speech was over, Javic cheered with the rest of the crowd as Shiara approached what was left of the northern gates. Javic was glad most of the bodies had already carted off somewhere out of sight, but the street was not entirely clear yet. The ground, still gray in places where the ash of unfortunate souls lay undisturbed, would not soon forget the horror of the Whunes. Guardsmen had labored diligently into the night, attempting to move the slain beasts into a large heap just outside the wall. With the last of the Whunes added to the pile, it had recently been set ablaze. A dense cloud of smoke marked its position from anywhere in the city. Burning the Whunes released their foul odor, amplifying the potency of their stench tenfold. The guardsmen who were dragging the corpses to the fire wrapped handkerchiefs and other random cloths across their mouths and noses, but even then, it was not uncommon to see a man off to the side, retching out the contents of his stomach.

The inner gate was still lying in a flat, melted sheet that spread across the entire entrance to the city. Guardsmen had a difficult time dragging the Whune corpses across its surface. It was as slick as ice and there was no way of getting around it. The metal reflected the moonlight like a flawless mirror, except where the charred remains of Whunes and guardsmen alike had broken its flow. At this point, it was nearly impossible to tell which bodies belonged to men and which to monsters, as none really resembled people. In some places, the metal had frozen with waves and ripples running across its surface as a result of an individual thrashing about at the moment the pool hardened into a solid; they were now merely blemishes on an all but immaculate surface. Some of the crowd wept at the sight of the disfigured bodies. More than a few had loved ones within the pool, burnt beyond recognition.

Shiara told everyone to stand clear of the metal. She used the Power to reform the gate. It did not glow red hot like before when the Goblikan had been using it as a weapon; it merely streamed together, like a glacier flowing quickly in reverse. It appeared to remain solid, and yet was viscous at the same time; a pool of liquid silver rising straight up against gravity. The gate was not exactly the same as before. Rather than a wall of plain bars crisscrossing the opening, there was now a memorial to the dead added about two-thirds of the way up in fancy lettering:

"Ashes Return to the Earth, From Sacrifice Comes Salvation."

Shiara reformed the outer door as well. She had to use some of the material from the fortifications on top of the wall – half of the wood that made up the original door was nowhere to be found. Bits of wood were probably blown over halfway to the tree line by the sheer force of the blast that ripped it apart. The magnitude of the explosion could still be seen by the shards of wood that had embedded themselves into the stone wall. They protruded like knives stuck into a block of chilled butter.

When Shiara finished, Javic watched as she swept the hair from her face. A number of people walked over and thanked her. She smiled, only slightly, but it was enough to make dimples appear in her cheeks. It was the first time that Javic had ever seen her with any expression other than a scowl. She really was quite pretty, especially when she smiled; it softened her face. Javic wasn't sure why she didn't smile more often, since it suited her so well.

Elric approached Javic from behind and tapped him on the shoulder. He had a long thin bundle under his left arm and various other items draped across his shoulders. "I got this for you," he said with a smile, holding out a bowstring in his right hand.

Javic didn't know what Elric was so happy about all of a sudden, all full of smiles. It would take more than a little gift to make Javic forget that he was keeping secrets from him. He took the bowstring without a word and turned his back on his grandfather. Elric followed him as he headed for the wagon.

When they arrived, Belford was lying across the driver's bench, fast asleep. Elric shook his leg and he sat up with a start, looking around wildly.

"Again? Really!?" he said. "Why won't anybody around here let me sleep?"

"I'm sorry," said Elric. "I just wanted to give you this, seeing as I promised it to you and all." He handed Belford the bundle he had been carrying under his arm.

Belford unfolded the cloth from around the package and pulled out a set of thick-hide armor. It had a much more sophisticated style than the armor that Elric and Javic were wearing. Metal rivets were studded all across the surface of the tunic and leggings, and adjustable straps for the shoulder pads hung down on the sides. It had an oaken-color finish that shined as if a thin layer of water were flowing across its surface.

Elric rapped his knuckles on the center of the chest piece; it made a solid thud. "Pretty nice, huh? Gravish Armor – I found a man who has these imported all the way from Dreythor. This was his best piece; it's made in the same genuine style and quality as what the Gravish Imperial Archers wear!"

Javic couldn't believe his eyes. He felt as if he was being replaced. First, Elric had taken Belford into his confidence, and now he was giving him what must have been a monumentally expensive gift.

That tunic alone must be worth several seasons of crops.

Shiara and Thorin showed up behind him, each with an armful of bags full of various supplies. Shiara placed the bags into the back of the wagon while Thorin attached the large packhorses to the front.

Elric suggested to Belford that he ride in the wagon with Shiara and Thorin, but he was quite insistent on riding Amit instead. At first, Belford's sudden change in attitude towards horses seemed a bit odd to Javic, but then he realized that it was only because he didn't want to be anywhere near Shiara, not that he was any more comfortable around the animals. She did tend to say insulting things about Belford whenever they were around each other, but then again, Shiara's insults were not limited to Belford; she was like that with everybody. Belford just took it more personally than anyone else.

Javic offered to assist Shiara in loading her bags into the back of the wagon. She refused the help.

"Thank you, though," she said. "At least one of you boys isn't a useless sack of potatoes."

Being angry at Belford, Javic laughed at the comment. He almost thought he saw a tiny smile crack Shiara's lips again as well.

Javic ended up riding within the wagon alongside Shiara and Thorin. Elric rode out front with Olli at his side. Belford was right behind him, trying to stay as far away from Shiara and the wagon as possible.

The sun was just starting to rise as they passed through the northern gates like a parade procession. Javic was surprised to see that a lot of people were still awake and in the streets at this hour; they lined up on either side of the road and cheered for Shiara to show no mercy when she captured the evil wizard. Javic was beginning to feel guilty for the deception, but he supposed that this was a far better send off than being chased out of town by an angry mob, the way Aberdine would have preferred.

Once out of the city, it was time to decide exactly how they were going to get to Phandrol. Thorin stopped the wagon and Elric fell back to discuss their choices. As they talked, the gray of dawn began to give way to a dense blue that quickly filtered away the remaining stars until only a few were faintly visible. A cool breeze blew through the wagon as Javic breathed in the crisp morning air. It felt like a shock to his lungs; invigoratingly fresh. It was the first sign – now months overdue – that summer was finally coming to a close.

Javic listened as Shiara explained their options. They could follow the road they were on north to Saldrone, where they might be able to chart a vessel to take them around the coast and up the Minthune river to Phandrol; or they could loop around and pass Felington again before heading west on the road into Graven; or, the most direct path, they could head east into Kovehn.

Shiara explained that the problem with going north was that if the rumors of King Vouldric's death were true, there was no telling what condition the capital city would be in when they reached it. Garrett would no doubt be planning an invasion now that the kingdom's hierarchy was in disarray. One of the first steps of an invasion would be to cut off sea trade to and from Taris. If a Kovani blockade was in place, there would be no hope of making it out of Taris by sea.

Option number two, heading east and then south through Kovehn, was the most direct path to Phandrol, but Garrett's influence would undoubtedly be the most prominent there within his own kingdom. The only thing they knew for certain about the Goblikan wizard was that he came from Garrett; they could not predict what dangers they would face if they chose to go through Kovehn, for it would surely be the path of which the Whune was most familiar, giving the enemy just one more advantage over them.

The only option that remained was an extremely long and arduous route, leading west straight into the heart of Graven. The Gravish people were not known for their hospitality, but at this point it didn't look like there was much of a choice left in the matter. Their number one priority had to be moving away from the enemy. They turned the wagon around and headed off-road to the west and then south to bypass Felington before starting back down the road that Belford and the Elensols had originally come in on.

Shiara fell asleep leaning against Javic. Her breathing became deep and regular. Her breath was warm against Javic's neck and he couldn't help but notice how soft her hair felt on his skin. Javic had the sudden urge to lean his head over onto hers, but at the same time, he had never been more aware of

Thorin's presence. Thorin was sitting just opposite Shiara, and Javic wasn't sure what he would think of such an action.

Thorin glanced over at him.

Javic gave him a small nervous smile.

Thorin chuckled softly. "Just push her off if she's bothering you," he said. "She probably won't even wake up."

But Javic didn't want to push her off. He knew that Shiara was too old for him, but he was enjoying the closeness. Immediately, a pang of guilt hit him in the gut.

What would Salvine think?

It had only been a whirlwind three days since he learned of her abduction, and already he was thinking about the touch of another woman. He wished it was Salvine in his lap instead – he longed to hold her like this.

Salvine's dead, whispered a sad voice in the back of his mind, *the dark wizard fed her to his Whunes.* No other explanation came to him. The Whunes were not the type to take prisoners. Javic closed his eyes to stop the tears from rolling out. He hoped Thorin wouldn't notice. With his eyes closed and the soft bumps of the wagon rocking him back and forth, it did not take long for exhaustion to kick in and pull him off to sleep, just as the sun began its rise.

When he awoke, the sun was high in the sky, and Shiara's head was resting fully in his lap. She stirred slightly as Javic shifted his position. He was feeling a bit stiff and was not at all comfortable with the situation. He tried to move her head off of him, but she woke up as soon as he touched her. Shiara sat up with a yawn. Javic blushed as he thought about the futility of his own feelings. He hid his red face, turning away from Shiara and Thorin.

On a deeper level, Javic knew he was only yearning for Salvine – it was not really Shiara that he wanted at all. Salvine was gone to him forever. He let out a slow exhale as he wiped the remnants of sleep from his eyes and did his best to push the tragic thoughts from his mind.

Looking out ahead of the wagon, Javic realized that Belford was no longer riding Amit. Olli and Amit were now strapped together in front of the packhorses and were helping pull the wagon along. Olli nipped at her sister's neck; Amit's ears went back a little as she shook her head from side to side. The larger packhorses ignored the entire exchange, continuing to walk at a steady pace. Elric was still riding out in front of the wagon. Only Belford was nowhere to be seen.

Javic looked over his shoulder into the back of the wagon and saw that Belford was lying there, asleep. He was curled up on his side, hugging a large burlap sack against his chest. Shiara turned to see what Javic was looking at and immediately began to laugh, her dimples becoming visible again.

"What's so funny?" Javic asked her.

Shiara pointed at the sack that Belford was holding. "Potatoes," she said.

Javic began to laugh as well. Belford really did resemble them now, looking extra lumpy and brown with his new armor on.

Time passed slowly while Belford slept. He did so for another hour, occasionally kicking or mumbling a word or two. When he awoke, he sat up, smacking his lips together. He frowned, apparently displeased to find himself so close to Shiara. After shaking off his sleepiness, Belford moved forward so that he was now sitting directly behind Javic and Shiara on a large wooden crate that doubled as a bench seat. He reached his hand up to tap Shiara on the back, hesitated, then pulled away without touching her.

Javic nudged Shiara with his elbow and gestured behind him with a nod of his head. She turned around in her seat and looked at Belford.

"What?" she asked sternly.

Belford swallowed with a gulp. "I was wondering if you would teach me how to use the Power."

Shiara just laughed. "No," she said, turning her back on him. "Charity case," she mumbled under her breath.

After a minute, Shiara peeked back around at Belford. He was staring down at his feet. She looked him over with a long contemplative gaze before giving a slight shake of her head and smiling briefly to herself. She exhaled, almost in a sigh. Exhausted, Shiara readjusted her arm along the top of the bench, her wrist brushing against Javic's shoulder. The touch sent another wave of guilt through him.

Stop enjoying this… stop enjoying this… stop enjoying this….
Even the slightest accidental caress as the wagon bumped along was enough to send tingling sparks flowing across his skin. He wondered if Salvine, were she still alive, would have been jealous or just angry to see Shiara cozying up to him.

Belford remained in his gloomy mood. Leaning against the side of the wagon, he stayed silent for most of the day, though no one else spoke much either. Javic passed the time looking out at the countryside as it rolled by. As they got farther away from Felington, they came across fewer farms until they eventually stopped seeing any altogether. They passed by a short stone wall which ran perpendicular to the road. It seemed to stretch on forever off into the distance. The terrain became rockier, and the road began weaving around to avoid the foothills. It had taken all day, but they were finally getting close to the border of Graven.

Javic zoned out, staring into the trees on the right side of the road. He hadn't seen anything interesting for a number of hours now. Suddenly, through the branches, he thought he spotted something that he knew he couldn't possibly have seen: It looked like Belford, half hidden by the leaves, standing absolutely still among the trees. Javic looked into the back of the wagon to confirm that Belford was still sitting behind him. Belford sat twirling his belt knife around in his fingertips. Javic stared back into the trees. He did not see anything at first, and began to think that he had imagined it, but then there he was again – this time farther ahead… too far ahead – it most certainly wasn't the same person.

"Stay calm," Thorin said quietly. His posture stiffened in his seat. "We are surrounded by archers."

Javic widened his eyes.

"It's not an ambush," said Thorin. "They are wearing Imperial uniforms."

Javic wasn't so convinced. "They are wearing the same armor as Belford," he whispered, "and if we were able to get our hands on a set, doesn't that mean that other people – like bandits – could do the same?"

"I guess we are about to find out," said Thorin. As the path curved, a man on horseback became visible. He was blocking the way ahead. The man's armor was exactly the same as Belford's, except that his tunic bore a blue double-slash mark across the left breast and he had on a steel helmet with a thick nose guard protecting his face. The man dismounted from his horse. Elric did the same.

"Everybody out," said the man, looking towards the wagon.

As Thorin stepped down, two more men dressed in identical uniforms emerged from the trees.

The first man appeared to be their leader. "Line up over there," he said, pointing to the side of the road.

The other men climbed up into the back of the wagon and began searching through their supplies.

Shiara and Javic hopped down. Belford came out last. When the man saw Belford, his eyes narrowed. "Impersonating a soldier is a serious crime," he said with a sneer, "punishable by death."

Belford's face went pale.

"Lucky for you there aren't any rank markings on here," he said as he looked Belford's armor over closely. "Without rank markings it isn't technically considered Impersonation. But there are others who wouldn't be as forgiving as I am."

Belford looked like he was about to sink into the ground.

"State your business here," said the man.

Thorin answered. "We mean to travel through your kingdom, south to Antara."

The men searching the wagon came back out empty-handed. Their leader turned towards them and they shook their heads.

"Well, I have good news and bad news," he said. "The good news is you're not trafficking anything, so I don't have to have you all arrested. The bad news is our borders are closed for the foreseeable future.   None may enter without proof of citizenship. So turn around now and don't come back."

Shiara's scowl hardened, she was not used to people treating her with such little respect. She lifted a finger and pointed it directly into the man's face. "This is absurd," she practically shouted at him. "What is the meaning of this?"

The man opened his mouth, intending on telling her to calm down, but he seemed to think better of it. One of the other men responded instead, "Kovani soldiers have been sneaking across the border disguised as civilians. They burnt Hurspen and Benmoth to the ground. High King Nemos has ordered all of the borders shut, indefinitely." And with that, the men directed them back into their wagon and stood by, watching silently as they made their way back around the bend.

"So what are we going to do now?" asked Javic. "Wait until nightfall and sneak through?"

"With five horses and a wagon? I don't think so." Shiara's temper was right on the edge of boiling over. "Closing down the entire border....   What kind of an idiot must this King Nemos be? You know, I'm pretty sure Graven doesn't even grow enough food to sustain itself – they import from Taris."

"So we fight our way across?" asked Belford.

Shiara rolled her eyes. "Look around," she said gesturing towards the woods. "I have counted at least thirty men pathetically attempting to hide within the brush. There must be an entire company stationed here."

"So we don't fight our way across, then?" Belford said with an eye roll. He was pushing his luck now.

"Do you still want to learn how to use the Power?" Shiara snapped. "Because if you do, I suggest you stop asking such stupid questions. All you do is whine, complain, and talk back, and I won't have any of that from a student of mine. Garrett has many eyes and we will all need to be on our toes when we are in Kovehn."

Belford opened his mouth for a retort, but smartly closed it again a moment later without speaking. Despite Shiara's insults, Belford was actually getting what he wanted – a Ver'ati at least slightly willing to train him in the Power.

Javic, for one, was excited that he would be able to witness more of the Power firsthand. In his mind, he imagined what it must have been like for his mother when she first began her Ver'ati training; summoning up orbs of fire to launch at her enemies, or whatever it was wizards did with the Power. He wondered what she would say to him if she could see him now – on his very own dangerous adventure. And this was just the beginning. Even if they weren't traveling through Graven, there was still a very long road ahead.

Javic noticed a pensive look in Shiara's eyes as they continued back down the path towards Felington. It was the same distant expression that had befallen his grandfather several days ago upon seeing smoke rising from their farm. Shiara's life in Felington was over. She'd been uprooted just as surely as the Elensols. Although their path into Kovehn would take them past Felington again, Shiara would never be able to return to the city she once called home. Not now that the people there knew she was a wizard. There was nothing ahead but the uncertainty of the road.

CHAPTER

15

Flames of White

The wagon had been blue, once. Years of weather had chipped and curled away its paint, leaving behind only the tired remains of its once dignified self. It must have belonged to somebody else before Shiara and Thorin got ahold of it, for it didn't seem possible to Belford that they alone could have been responsible for wearing it down into its current condition. The canvas that stretched across its top was patched many times over, and its color – faded to a dirty beige – was darker on one side than the other. Looking up towards the top, it became sun bleached, giving it the appearance of a pale membrane stretched thin across the rotting carcass of a beached whale; the inner bracings of the wagon, arched like a barrel, evoked the image of a giant ribbed skeleton. The canvas seemed on the verge of tearing from the tension it was under.

Sitting cross-legged on the ground against one of the wagon's wooden-spoked wheels, Belford's chest became tight as he inhaled a deep breath. The pressure to absorb all of Shiara's teachings was great. He was glad for her instruction – the intricacies of the Power were vast and challenging – but Shiara's methods were not forgiving to his body. More often than not, he received singed fingertips from poorly managed energy exchanges. By the end of each session, his muscles always ached from straining himself in all the wrong ways.

Elric and Thorin started preparing dinner around a small cooking fire, but the food could not possibly come fast enough for Belford. The smells of the herbs and seasonings had already worked up anticipation in his stomach; it rumbled loudly, drowning out his thoughts as he looked up into the sky. Belford was eager for dinner, but nervous for the moon to rise. The continuation of his training was set to commence the moment he could reach the Power again.

Despite his misgivings, Belford still had high hopes that relearning how to use the Power might help unlock the mysteries of his past. So far, nothing new had developed in that regard. Although he'd slept several times since his last dream of the girl with the auburn hair, none of his dreams were anywhere near as vivid or as easy to recall as the ones he experienced the first two nights after waking up in the quarry near the Elensol farm.

Fragmented images haunted his thoughts with a constant sense of loss looming in every direction. The recesses of his mind were impenetrable fathoms; in his dreams, he felt as though he were fumbling around in the dark – everything beyond his fingertips a complete mystery – and he was afraid to venture forward into the unknown for fear of what he might discover.

When dinner was ready, he made himself eat slowly. Focusing on the food helped keep his mind grounded in the present, away from his disparaging dreams.

Javic was still refusing to talk to him most of the time, but there was nothing he could do about that. He'd given his word to Elric that he wouldn't reveal the truth about Wilgoblikan to

Javic. Belford just wished Elric wouldn't have pulled him into the middle of the drama in the first place.

During the day, while traveling, Javic and Shiara spent most of their time making fun of Belford. One of them would get into a teasing mood and the other would feed off of the malicious energy, reflecting the sentiment back and forth, until finally their joint presence became unbearable. Whenever they got that way, Belford tried to stay as far away from the both of them as possible, although the confined space of the wagon made that a difficult task. When the moon came up, Belford had to put everything aside so that he could make the most of his training.

During their first session, Shiara lectured Belford about energy transfer and mass conservation for nearly four hours straight. It was extremely technical and boring to Belford, but Javic seemed to lap up every word of it. There were far too many side effects and complications to worry about as far as Belford was concerned. He found it all to be quite overwhelming. The next two sessions had been equally as technical with Shiara walking him through the process of extracting energy from various sources in the environment. She did not, however, show him how to dissipate the energy safely when he was done. His fingers throbbed at the memory of the scorching heat. Parts of his fingerprints were beginning to char away. He hoped tonight would be different.

After dinner, when the moon finally rose, Shiara called Belford over to the side of the campfire to start their next session. She was holding a small rock conspicuously in the palm of her hand. Belford sat down opposite her and stretched out his legs in front of him. Javic joined them in silence; his curiosity was unyielding when it came to learning about the Power. Belford estimated that Javic had asked Shiara more questions about the various processes than even he himself had. The rapidity at which Javic and Shiara were becoming friends astonished Belford – he was still under the impression that Shiara's frigid exterior only held an even colder interior.

Just how Javic managed to crack her frosty armor was a mystery to Belford.

"Tonight, I will be showing you how to move things," said Shiara. "It's pretty straight forward, really." She held the small rock out in front of her, balancing it between her thumb and forefinger as if it were a fragile egg. She tossed it into the air with a flick of her wrist and traced its trajectory with her eyes.

As it reached the top of its arc it suddenly lurched sideways with uncanny acceleration. It collided with a tree in the distance, producing a devastating crack. Part of the trunk splintered away as the rock ricocheted. It came to rest somewhere beyond the edge of camp.

"The key is to concentrate," she said. "You have to feel the outcome deep inside of you before you can ever hope to make it a reality."

Belford began to look around on the ground for another rock to launch. He chose one about the size of his fist.

"Oh, and one more thing," said Shiara. "What we are doing here is focusing bursts of kinetic energy on objects. We are not attempting to make things levitate – that would require a sustained use of the Power, which is impossible – attempting to do so could have dire consequences."

Belford cocked one eyebrow. "Like what?" he asked.

"Death, mostly," Shiara said nonchalantly. "You might want to start with something a little bit smaller," she added with a sneer. "The bigger the object, the more difficult it will be to move. It takes much practice and a lot of concentration to move larger objects, and even then, your innate level of ability will put restraints on the amount of energy you can summon up from your surroundings." Shiara liked to remind Belford of her lack of confidence in his abilities as often as possible.

Belford decided to ignore her advice – it was a matter of pride. He held the rock in his palm and looked at it closely. There was a large dark spot on one side. He kept his eyes locked onto the spot as he threw the stone into the air. Belford concentrated on the intended result – to launch the rock as far and as fast as he possibly could. After reaching the peak of its trajectory, the rock fell straight back down to the ground with nothing more than a thump to mark its landing in the dirt. Belford's face began to redden. He could sense Shiara's smug expression without even having to turn around.

"Try to *really* feel it," she said. "You have to want it to happen."

Belford picked the rock back up and held it in his palm. He envisioned the result just like before, but he began to notice something ever so subtly different this time: Emotions were beginning to flow through him. He didn't realize what was happening at first. The wall that held back his feelings was thick, but light was starting to pierce through, small cracks rupturing all along the surface. His emotions seeped into his conscious mind. The frustration he felt from being alienated by Javic; the confusion of his half-empty mind; his eternal fear of the unknown. It all began to sweep through his body like water crashing through a crumbling dam.

Leaks became torrents under the pressure, tearing down the remainder of the wall at an alarming rate. He didn't want to embarrass himself by failing again. Hopeless pangs of desire surged from his heart as images of the girl from his dreams – still familiar though they were becoming increasingly distant – flashed across his mind.

It was too much to hold in.

With a rush of energy, he refocused the emotion outward towards the rock. The stone soared off into the night above the treetops and vanished into the darkness. It had a cathartic effect on Belford, as if he had just cried out at the top of his lungs. He let out a slight sigh of relief at having not failed a second time, likely defying Shiara's expectations.

Belford listened for the thud that would indicate the rock's landing.

The noise never came.

"That was odd," said Shiara. "It must have landed in some soft soil or something." She stood staring off in the direction of the projectile for a moment longer, then turned her eyes towards the ground, searching for a new rock. "I've got an idea," she said as she scooped up another chunk of stone. She placed it on the ground in an empty patch of dirt directly in front of her. "Before you launch your rock, but after you have thrown it into the air, I want you to make it start releasing energy so that we will be able to see it in the dark." She gestured towards the rock in front of her and it instantly began to glow red hot like a coal in a fire. "Simply focus on making it give off energy, and it should do so." She gestured at the rock again and it cooled down. The rapid temperature change caused it to crack, sheering in half. Its surface appearance was altered; it now held a glossy-black sheen instead of the dull gray comprising the rest of the landscape.

Belford mentally prepared himself to use the Power again. He decided to practice first on a stationary stone. He stared at a nearby rock and focused his mind on having it release a flow of energy. As soon as he felt impassioned, all it took was his gaze and his will of intent and it instantly obliged. He stopped the combustion with another thought before picking out a second rock for the real challenge.

It was slightly larger than the first one he launched, but Belford still felt confident. He tossed the stone into the air and immediately focused on having it release energy. Before the rock even reached the peak of its arc it burst into flames, giving off a surprising amount of heat; the flames burned white hot, almost causing Belford to lose sight of the stone in the brightness. Belford squinted through the flames, scarcely able to maintain the crucial eye-lock on his target. He shifted his intentions to the second part of his task, and the fiery stone shot off into the night sky. The rock zoomed over the trees, passing above the crest of a distant hill before its glow became insufficient for it to be seen any longer. It vanished silently once again into the distance.

At first, nobody moved or even made a sound. Belford turned around to find that everybody was staring at him. Shiara was shocked – her expression a combination of bewilderment mixed with a hint of fear. Elric looked worried. He kept switching his gaze back and forth between Shiara and Thorin as if expecting one of them to make a sudden move. Javic's face, on the other hand, was an endless grin – he immediately began scurrying around the camp in search for a larger rock. Only Thorin's expression was unreadable. Thorin's eyes seemed to bore right into Belford as if he were capable of seeing something beneath the surface.

Belford began scratching his arm nervously, but stopped abruptly when he realized where he was rubbing: The little bump under the skin of his bicep – the center of the Mark of Kings.

Javic stumbled over to him carrying a huge stone, approximately the size of his head. He passed it over to Belford, but Belford was barely even able to lift it up. He didn't have the strength to throw it into the air high enough to safely ignite and launch it over the trees. Thorin stepped up and took the stone from Belford's arms. Belford couldn't tell what the hulk of a man was thinking at first, his face still a mask of stone, but as soon as Thorin began counting down from five, Belford realized Javic wasn't the only one who wanted to see how much more he was capable of doing.

As Thorin reached zero, he heaved the rock into the air. It reached an impressive height before Belford set it on fire and sent it flying above the treetops. This time, as the rock went over the distant ridge, something caught Belford's eye. The white light emitted by the flames reflected off of something on the ground as it zoomed overhead. Though it only lasted for an instant, Belford was sure there was something on the crest of the hill. After the rock cleared the ridge, it smashed into the ground with a heavy thud.

"Did you guys see that?" he asked.

"Of course we did!" exclaimed Javic. "That was amazing!"

"Not that," said Belford, dismissing the praise with a wave of his hand. "There's something on the ridge." Belford pointed in the direction of where he saw the reflection.

"Don't point. You don't want to tip them off," said Thorin. He snatched up his cudgel from where it was propped up against the side of the wagon and calmly walked off beyond the edge of the campfire's illumination.

Belford furrowed his brow. "Who's up there?" he asked.

"Just pretend like everything's normal," said Shiara, ignoring Belford's question.

"Whunes?" asked Javic.

"Maybe," said Shiara, "though if it is, I don't know why they haven't attacked yet."

The feeling of being watched was always uncomfortable for Belford. He couldn't help but imagine the corpses again – the ones he had hallucinated back in Darrenfield and on the Elensol farm, naked and crumpled in heaps, staring up at him with their black eyes, devoid of human expression. He was grateful that the waking nightmares had mostly ceased. Every now and then, he would still catch a glimpse of something from out of the corner of his eye and it would send shivers down his spine, but the visions had become hollow now, like smoke drifting across water.

The eerie landscape, somewhat visible in the moonlight, all but vanished as a cloud began to pass over the moon; the moon was still nearly full in its cycle, but the cloud enveloped it entirely, dimming the sky. A milky halo appeared around the edges of the cloud as it lit up from behind. It drifted effortlessly along, its form appearing to take the shape of a giant bird – a colossal phoenix soaring through the night sky, ablaze with flames of white. Shiara was still talking, but Belford did not hear a word of it. As the cloud withdrew from the moon, the countryside lit up again. The moonlight seemed to shine even brighter than before, causing everything to cast a second shadow distinct from the one generated by the campfire.

"You're not even listening to me, are you?" Shiara buried her face into her hands and let out an exasperated sigh.

Belford looked up, unsure of what to say; he truly hadn't been listening.

Shiara threw her hands into the air. "Without first having a solid understanding of the basics you will just end up killing yourself. All it takes is one little mistake...." Shiara shook her head slightly from side to side, causing her tear-shaped earrings to bounce around in circles. The dangling jewels were crafted from some kind of orange and red composite, shining brightly with iridescence as light from the fire struck their smooth surfaces. "There's something very peculiar about you."

The breeze picked up. Belford took a seat on the ground nearest the campfire, hoping the flames would cut the chill of the wind. The radiance of the fire flickered softly over his face as he closed his eyes. All of the lingering images from his dreams began to flood back into his mind as he sat in silence: The meadow-filled park, cradled by humanity; the arcs of fire streaming across the night sky, descending all around with explosions so bright they blinded everyone foolish enough to gaze upon their faux-daylight; the girl – the image that pained him the most – her elegant features, her sweet smile, her warmth.

In his dreams, everything was so different from the waking world. Maybe it was all fake; maybe he had simply slipped and hit his head that day at the quarry and his dreams were nothing more than a symptom of brain trauma. Of course, there was the Mark of Kings on his arm as well as his knack for flinging large rocks ridiculously long distances which still needed to be factored into the equation. His dreams had to be real; they just had to. If he couldn't trust in that, there was nothing else left. The aching feeling he experienced every time she popped into his mind was far too intense for her to be a mere figment of his imagination.

"We're being followed," said Thorin.

Belford opened his eyes. He hadn't noticed Thorin's arrival back at the campsite. Thorin sure could be light on his feet when he wanted to be.

"Whoever they are, they were already gone when I reached the ridge," Thorin said, "but from their tracks, it appears there are only two of them, riding on horseback – definitely not Whunes anyway. I'll keep watch tonight, but I doubt we are in any immediate danger."

With everyone's minds put somewhat at ease, it was time for the nightly preparations of the camp to commence. The supplies in the back of the wagon had to be brought outside and placed onto the ground in order to make room for Javic and Belford to sleep in their stead. They'd been sharing that spot for the last couple nights now. Javic rolled around in his sleep a lot, which tended to wake Belford. Belford didn't really mind the frequent interruptions anymore, though. His sleep was always filled with nightmares.

Shiara had been spending each night stretched out across the driver's bench of the wagon. It was the most comfortable position available because of its ample padding. Belford's back was terribly sore from sleeping on the hard wood of the wagon bed night after night. He couldn't really complain though – he was still better off than Thorin and Elric, who were stuck sleeping outside on the lumpy ground. Even so, Belford's soreness had solidified feelings of jealousy within him for Shiara's comparative comfort. He was beginning to suspect his back pain might be responsible for his tumultuous dreams. As the hours slid by, Belford tossed and turned alongside Javic.

Belford's lower back began to spasm again. He sat up in the darkness and tried to massage the area with his knuckles but found the bothersome spot to be slightly out of reach. Seemingly on cue, Javic rolled over onto his stomach in a diagonal position, managing to take up the entire floor space of the wagon. Rather than push him back over, Belford silently climbed over him and stepped out of the wagon altogether.

Elric was fast asleep by the campfire and Thorin was seated beside him. As Belford approached the fire, he started to feel an odd, static sensation flowing across the surface of his skin. The hair on the back of his arms began to rise as he got closer. Upon noticing Belford's confused expression, Thorin pointed upwards.

About halfway between the ground and the treetops a number of rocks, pebbles and other bits of debris hung weightless in the air. The stones drifted around slowly on the air currents as if gravity had ceased to exist. Effortless and without sound, they rotated about, bumping into one another periodically as they glided above the campsite.

"Are you doing this?" Belford asked in astonishment. "How is this even possible? Shiara said levitation couldn't be done."

"Spectacular, isn't it?" responded Thorin as he turned his gaze back up towards the aerial display. "No, I am not doing this," he said. "Shiara spoke the truth: Levitation is impossible, for wizards anyway."

The hairs on Belford's head were standing up now as well. He wasn't sure exactly what Thorin meant. Levitation was clearly happening, so if a wizard wasn't responsible, who was?

"You look worried," said Thorin, "but there is no need to be. This is just an Echo – a sort of reverberation, or memory, if you will."

"A memory?" asked Belford. "Of what?"

Thorin bumped a rock with his fingertip as it floated within his reach. It spun off into the distance. "When vast amounts of the Power are used in one location, sometimes it creates a vortex of energy, and then strange things can start to happen," Thorin shrugged. "Some say it is proof of the existence of Mast, but no one really knows for sure what causes it."

"Mast?" asked Belford.

Thorin narrowed his eyes slightly. "Earth's living spirit," he said. "Everyone knows who Mast is."

Belford froze in place, his mind racing to come up with some excuse for his ignorance, but before he could think of anything, Thorin spoke again.

"I think it is about time for you to come clean," he said. "You are obviously not from around here, I could tell that much from your shoes the moment I first saw you."

Belford couldn't find any words, but his expression said enough.

"It just doesn't add up," continued Thorin. "The attention you have attracted from the Whunes, the things you don't know, the things you *do* know, and now with your ability to use such great amounts of the Power that you can create an Echo all by yourself... I have only seen an Echo once before outside of Erotos, and that was after quite a large battle in which both sides utilized the Power."

"I... I..." Belford couldn't think of a suitable lie. Thorin's eyes were digging down into him; there was nothing else to do but tell the truth. "I have no memory," he said finally. Belford's shoulders slumped down slightly in defeat.

Thorin just continued to stare at him as if expecting more.

"It's the truth," Belford insisted. "I don't remember anything before a few days ago." He looked Thorin in the eyes and hoped that his omission of the Mark of Kings from his explanation wouldn't make him look guilty. He still wanted to keep that little piece of information to as few people as possible.

Thorin stared at him a little longer. Belford held the gaze. "Alright," said Thorin.

"Alright?" Belford was taken aback by Thorin's casual acceptance of his story.

"You can't tell me what you don't know," Thorin said with a smile, "and besides, if Whunes want you dead, that's already enough of a reason for me to keep you alive."

"Well," said Belford, "I guess they've done one good thing for me then, haven't they?"

"I wouldn't go around praising them just yet," said Thorin. "If you want to know the true soul of a wizard, you need only look at the ways in which he chooses to harness the Power. The Goblikan used Combustion to tear people apart, and pure energy to consume everything in his path. All wizards are physically capable of these feats by virtue of their connection to the Power, but only somebody with a propensity for darkness and violence in their heart could possibly gather the necessary conviction within themselves to strike out in such a way. All Goblikans have been twisted to suppress the human instincts that stop us from committing such evils upon one another."

Belford's thoughts immediately jumped to the Whune that had attacked him and Javic in the forest during the first night of their journey. He had turned it to dust without so much as a thought, purely on instinct – Combustion, Thorin called it – he still wasn't sure how he'd done it. *What other dark tendencies might be lingering inside of me,* he wondered, *hidden away by my forgotten past?*

"You should go back to bed now," said Thorin. "We have a long day of travel ahead of us tomorrow if we want to reach Bronam by sundown."

Belford nodded in acceptance of this dismissal, and then started back towards the wagon. He was looking forward to getting to Bronam; their arrival there would mean sleeping in a real bed again, at least for one night.

"Watch your head," said Thorin.

A floating rock collided with the side of Belford's head. A lump immediately started to form. Trying to look on the positive side of things, Belford figured that the headache would at least help draw his attention away from his back pain. He climbed into the wagon and reached down to push Javic back over to his own side. As soon as his finger made contact, a strong static surge zapped through his hand and into the sleeping boy's body. Javic grunted and rolled over without any further effort from Belford. He hoped it signaled a change in his luck.

After more tossing and turning, he finally drifted off to sleep. He dreamt of a phoenix gliding across the sky, at times even becoming the phoenix himself, gazing out from its eyes at an endless landscape of clouds that churned and billowed below, effortlessly – like a living sea of tenuous pillars, if only they were solid, but of course they were not. As he descended into their wispy froth, even his wings vanished from sight. He lost all orientation and, try as he might, he could not rise again from out of the fog.

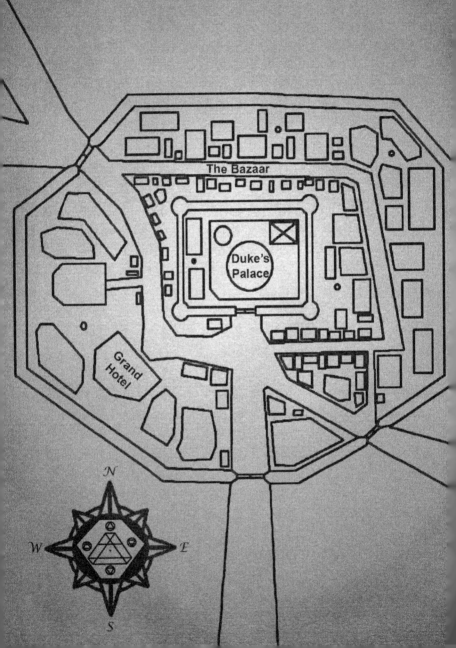

The City of Bronam

CHAPTER

16

The Stone and the Butterfly

By morning, the Echo had dissipated. Belford was the last to wake. His body shuddered uncontrollably as he stretched his arms out above his head. He let out a particularly airy yawn before joining the rest of the group, already in the process of eating breakfast. Fine dew had settled over the land making the various patches of grass shimmer and flash whenever the morning light caught their blades. A dark layer of grime had accumulated over Belford's hands and under his fingernails from the days of not washing, so he crouched down beside one of the grassy patches and ran his fingers through the greenery to claim its moisture.

The droplets turned black as he rubbed them around on his hands. His skin itched as he thought about the filth covering the rest of his body. Nobody else was feeling the weight of the journey quite as heavily as Belford. The tangy aroma of dried sweat mingled with the various body odors of the travelers and dust kicked up by the horses' hooves to form a concoction so fetid it turned Belford's stomach. The dust, which tended to accumulate along the road, had a sandy quality to it that made it particularly difficult for the travelers to breathe while it was thick in the air. Belford's shoes, damp with dew, collected a fine layer of the dust as he walked over to the remnants of the campfire to eat his morning meal.

A small portion of what could only be described as of gray mush lay before him, scraped together into a pile at the bottom of a pot that had been left in the center of the burnt out ashes of the campfire. The pot had been allowed to cool, and the mush had congealed into a mostly solid glob. Despite its unappetizing appearance, Belford's stomach began to rumble loudly at the sight of it. Seeing no utensils around, Belford looked to Javic for a spoon. Javic ignored him, walking away without a word. The silence was starting to weigh on Belford. Elric gave Belford a concerned grimace as he handed him a spoon to use. There would never be a good time for Javic to learn the truth about Wilgoblikan. Belford wished Elric would just tell Javic already. Maybe then they could go back to being friends.

Belford took a seat on the log Thorin dragged out of the brush the night before and shoveled a large scoop of the mush into his mouth. As expected, it was flavorless. The texture alone was enough to make him gag. It coated his throat with a slimy film as he swallowed it in one large gulp. Belford continued eating, though with less enthusiasm than he started the meal with. He wondered if something so bland could possibly contain enough nutrients to sustain him until midday.

Elric and Thorin loaded the wagon as Belford finished up the meal. Belford caught Shiara looking at him from beside the horses. It was an incredulous stare, but she turned away as soon as their eyes met. This was unusual for Shiara – her glares usually lasted until long after the other person had already turned away in discomfort. Perhaps Thorin had spoken to her about his confession the previous night regarding a certain lack of memory, or maybe it was simply his awe inspiring display of rock launching that was affecting her demeanor – either way, Belford was receiving extra attention from Shiara, and that could only lead to more awkwardness and discomfort for him in the future. He was not pleased.

Despite his misgivings, the day went along smoothly with little awkward conversation. Every once in a while, Belford would notice Javic looking at him out of the corner of his eye with a sort of yearning expression, as if he wanted to say something but couldn't find the right words to bring to his tongue. Javic looked lost at times, his mind clearly drifting. The wagon didn't stop for lunch; instead the travelers snacked while on the go.

As the sun began to set over the western horizon, they cleared a bend in the road and found the walls of the great city of Bronam just ahead of them. And it truly was a great city, being easily twice the size of Felington. A large towering dome could be seen looming from behind the walls at the center of the city. The dome topped a large structure which Thorin explained was part of the palace the Duke of Bronam had commissioned some years previous. The dome was only half covered in a golden alloy. It hadn't been finished yet due to a lack of available funding for such a lavish project.

Given the perpetual economic and social instability that plagued this region, it wasn't at all surprising that it would be left unfinished. It wasn't the only structure awaiting a long-overdue completion either: A smaller dome and another half-finished tower stood beside the main dome. The scaffolding set around the outside of these structures seemed to have become a permanent feature of the skyline.

Not long ago, Bronam used to sit right on the border between Graven and Kovehn – just on the Kovani side of the division – but due to the recent expansionary efforts of King Garrett, the Gravish border now resided at a substantial three-and-a-half days' march to the west of the city's location. Town after town had been sacked by Kovani troops as they pushed farther and farther into Gravish territory. Being the only city left unburned in a large radius made Bronam a popular place to be, at least for the moment.

On top of the steadily increasing refugee population, the city was also tasked with hosting the official garrison point of the entire western division of the Kovani military. The city, however, was not as crowded as one might expect under the circumstances, as rather than staying within the city limits, most of the troops stationed in the region were spending their days in the ever-advancing tent cities that marked the dynamic border between Graven and Kovehn. Thorin didn't think the troops could advance much farther before the supply lines would overreach their effectiveness. The logistics were simply unsustainable. Belford merely nodded along to Thorin's assessment of the region, pretending to understand what he was talking about so as not to look stupid.

"Even mentioning the Power is punishable by *what* in Kovehn?" Shiara quizzed him.

"Death," said Belford. He had only been reminded a dozen times since leaving Felington.

"Good," said Shiara. "While we are here, there is not to be any mention of the Power. Hell, I don't even want you to think about the Power, just in case that should tempt you to use it and get us all executed by the state."

Given their experiences in Felington, Belford expected there to be quite a fuss getting into Bronam, but surprisingly, this time they were able to ride right through the already open gates without receiving so much as a passing glance from any of the officials at the wall. Once inside, Belford quickly saw why the security was so lax within the military city: A second wall separated the palace and other official buildings from the rest of the city. Patrols ran non-stop, both on top of the inner wall and around its base.

The streets were wide and muddled with people on horseback. The smell of manure was thick in the air. Belford wrinkled his nose at first, but his sense of smell was soon exhausted. The wagon carried them down the main road past a line of tiny single-stand shops that ran along the left-hand side of the street against the base of the inner wall. Peddlers were offering all sorts of goods: Pieces of jewelry, pottery, clothing, and raw cloth. Even some fruits, vegetables, and various cooked food items were available. Everything was held up to them by the heavy-browed merchants as the wagon rolled past. On the right side of the road, a row of military garrisons was followed by a tavern and a wide block of stables.

The wagon pulled up alongside one building, it was the largest of all they had passed; it stood three stories tall and had balconies coming off of each room on the third floor. It was an inn unlike any Belford had seen yet – a grand hotel – clearly catering to the more affluent patrons of Bronam. He hoped they could get one of the fancy rooms on the top floor.

Shiara, Javic, and Belford all exited the wagon and made their way inside while Thorin and Elric took the horses over to the nearby stables. A jolly man with plump cheeks greeted Shiara as she entered through the doorway.

"We need sleeping accommodations – one night for five," said Shiara. She paused and looked at Belford before adding, "And access to a bathing chamber."

"Just one night?" the man frowned. "That will be fifteen silver marks."

"I have gold bullion," said Shiara.

The man disappeared without a word into a storeroom located behind and to the left of the counter and retrieved a scale. Shiara handed him a large golden coin which was surprisingly dull in appearance. He took a handful of little weights out from his shirt's front pocket and used them to balance the scale. After some quick calculations on a piece of parchment paper, he handed Shiara back eight smaller silver marks as change. Shiara wasn't pleased with the exchange rate, but she held her tongue. The man handed her a key for a room on the second floor, thoroughly dashing Belford's hopes of having a balcony from which to look out over the city. The man then directed the group to the bathing rooms – on the first floor, all the way towards the back of the hotel.

"You should go bathe first," Javic said to Belford. "You smell really bad."

Belford couldn't argue with Javic's assessment. The road had not been kind to him. Shiara and Javic headed up to the room while Belford went to check out the bathing rooms by himself. Inside the bathing area, he found ten separate rooms branching off from the main hall. He tried to open the first door, but it was locked. He moved to the second door, tried that one, but was met with the same result. After trying three more random doors, he finally found a vacant chamber. It was the last door at the far end of the corridor. Inside was a large, solid-brass bathtub with a crude system of pipes attached to its side. One pipe led to a large basin with a built-in coal heating stove which was already ablaze with fire. Another pipe stuck straight into the back wall through a damp hole. The hole was too large, leaving empty space between the pipe and wall where one could look into the crawlspace beyond if they so wished; it was surprisingly poor craftsmanship considering the air of wealth exhibited throughout the rest of the hotel.

Both pipes had pump levers attached to their nozzles where they connected to the bathtub, leaving Belford to do the work of getting the water into the tub himself – one tedious pump at a time. He imagined that the third-floor patrons were granted access to a separate set of bathing chambers – ones with fine, tiled tubs and natural light throughout, where attendants would see to their every need and bring them endless refreshments. Belford sighed. He supposed the important thing was just being able to get the filth off.

He started with the water from the heating basin first, one push sending a short blast of the near-boiling water into the tub. He reached down to test the temperature and burned the tips of his fingers as the steaming water flowed over them and out through the drain at the bottom of the tub. Belford scanned the rest of the chamber while blowing on his scalded fingertips.

He found a drain plug sitting on a stool in the corner of the room. Next to the stool sat a pumice stone, a cup full of some thick soap-like liquid, and a spongy scrub brush with a long wooden handle.

Belford grabbed the plug and inserted it into the drain before trying to fill the tub again. This time, he started with the water from the wall pipe. It was ice cold. He added one pump of the hot water – the mixture was too hot now. So he added another cold pump – too cold this time, but better. After experimenting back and forth a couple times, he finally found a comfortable mixture at four pumps cold to three pumps hot and then went about filling the rest of the tub with that ratio.

Before the tub was filled, he decided to add some of the liquid soap from the cup beside the stool. It immediately began foaming into a thick froth of bubbles as the bursts of water stirred it about. The air in the chamber quickly filled with the rich scent of lavender as the bubbles multiplied. Once the tub was filled, Belford began to undress, laying down his tunic and leggings first and then the rest of his clothing on top of the corner stool.

Belford submerged himself in the bubble bath, every muscle in his body relaxing as the heat soaked its way into his skin. He hadn't realized how tense he was until that moment as all of his muscles began to release their grips. As his shoulders finally relaxed for the first time in days, he felt as if a weight were lifted from them.

His mind started wandering; he didn't really want to dwell on the silent feud that Javic had started, so instead his thoughts strayed to his usual preoccupation: The girl with the auburn hair. The one dream in particular that he'd been replaying through his mind over and over again in recent days was the one where she spoke to him in the tea house. It really stuck with him for some reason; perhaps because Thorin woke him up right in the middle of it.

Lifting a handful of bubbles out from the rest, Belford blew on them, sending a few drifting about on the subtle air currents that filled the room. What exactly had she said to him in that dream? *It's all inside of you.* The words began floating back to him. *You just need a little reminder; a marker to help you find your way back to the path.* But what marker? She had been touching his arm when she said that, he remembered, so his thoughts had immediately gone to the Mark of Kings – that seemed like the logical choice anyhow – but wasn't he already following that path? It had sent him towards Ethan and the kingdom of Phandrol. But that was a literal path... could his dream really have been so straight forward? He was beginning to have doubts.

He prodded the bump at the center of the mark again; it was like a cyst – solid and smooth. It was right where the painful injection was given to him in that other, more sinister dream. He wondered what it might be. He contemplated cutting the bump out, but that would be a messy procedure and he would surely ruin the Mark of Kings in the process. He hadn't decided yet if that would be a good thing or a bad thing. Elric believed the mark might be of some use to Ethan in destabilizing King Garrett's rule, so Belford didn't want to rush into anything prematurely, regardless of whether or not he wanted the mark. It was still possible that the bump actually was just a cyst after all.

Belford picked up another handful of froth from the tub. A particularly large bubble was sitting at the top of the pile. He tried to pop it with his index finger, but his digit sank in – the surface tension remaining sealed around his fingertip. Images of the energy dome from his dream suddenly streamed back to him with a flood of realization. Shiara told him that a bubble of energy would be impossible to create because it would require a complicated and sustained use of the Power to maintain. And since sustaining the Power could lead to death, Belford had shied away from trying to recreate what he had seen in his dream. But there was a flaw in Shiara's argument: Nobody was maintaining the soap bubbles. The tension at the surface of the bubble was enough to keep it in existence. It was made up of three layers, a thin layer of water sandwiched between two layers of soap molecules. He wasn't sure exactly how he knew that, but everything just made sense to him as he looked at the bubbles in his hands.

In a way, though, Shiara was still correct: A pure bubble of energy would repel itself and disperse immediately; the negatively charged particles would have to be forced together unnaturally, which would only be possible with a sustained use of the Power – but if those same negative particles were all aligned facing inwards towards some type of bonding agent, like the water in a soap bubble, then the bubble could be made stable. It would maintain itself automatically! Belford found the idea too good to pass up without trying it.

Although Belford hadn't been outside recently and didn't know whether or not the moon had already begun its rise over the eastern horizon, he decided to start preparing himself mentally to use the Power anyway. He thought of the girl – he couldn't help feeling impassioned whenever she was in his thoughts, and that was exactly the state of mind that he needed to summon in order to access the Power.

He molded his passion around his intentions: Layering two fields of energy around *something*... he knew what it was – fundamentally anyway – but it had no name. It was just a kind of polymer, a synthetic compound; the blueprints of which he pulled out from some barely conscious part of his mind. He didn't know how it had gotten into his head in the first place, but there it was. The compound was specifically tailored to bond with the negative energy layers that he simultaneously placed along either side of the material. The bath water cooled substantially as Belford redirected the heat towards the creation of the energy layers.

A perfect sphere the size of an orange appeared – it sat glowing blue in the palm of his hand for a moment before settling into a clear state as soon as he finished adding the second energy layer. It was nearly weightless and barely visible. Belford held it up in front of his eye and found that the light refracted as it traveled through the orb, warping the contours of his hand as he waved it back and forth behind it. He tried to crush it between his fingers, but it resisted the pressure. He tried smashing it against the side of the tub, nearly dropping it in the process, but it wouldn't give in. He threw it towards the tiled wall, but the air was enough to slow it down with its friction. The orb barely made it to the wall. It was too light. It harmlessly rebounded and rolled across the floor, stopping out of reach.

Belford made another orb, this time with just the polymer compound, leaving off the energy layers. It immediately collapsed under its own weight, melting into a pile of goo that ran through his fingers. Belford wiped his hand off on the side of the tub and looked over to where the first orb had come to a rest. It too was starting to lose its shape now. He would have to be careful when using this new material. Without continuously feeding it energy it would soon weaken and become useless.

If he was able to get the hang of drawing energy from his surroundings rather than from his own body – which Shiara had informed him was very dangerous, since he needed that energy to live – he thought he would be able to utilize this shielding material very nicely. He already knew what Shiara would have told him if she had seen this display: He should have used energy out of the floor or walls, taking only a little bit from any one area instead of from the bath water he was sitting in. Belford was beginning to shiver already. He reached over to pump some more hot water into the tub.

As he extended out his right arm to operate the pump he noticed, again, the little tattoo drawn on his bicep. He hadn't really paid any attention to it the first time he discovered it, since he found the Mark of Kings at the same time. The smaller tattoo of the letters *CB* simply fell by the wayside. He hadn't thought about the plain tattoo since that moment, but now it came crashing down on him – it was so obvious: The Mark of Kings wasn't the only marker on his skin!

"CB," he said to himself. *CB, CB, CB*, over and over again he repeated the letters in his head. He closed his eyes and thought of the girl.

What does she want me to discover? What are these letters supposed to mean?

She seemed so confident that he would be able to remember. He felt in his gut that he was close. It was all just right there. The way she smiled at him, her eyes so knowing....

He bit down on his lower lip until it turned white, nearly drawing blood. He closed his eyes even harder now, trying to imagine the girl down to every last detail. Her auburn hair; her large green eyes; her bright complexion; that smile, that beautiful smile; her dimpled cheeks; her lips; chin; soft breasts – he could rest his head there for days; he went all the way down to her long legs with her graceful feet and slender toes. Claire truly was the most beautiful girl he had ever seen. *Claire! Claire! Claire Birch! That was it! Finally!*

He stood up, intending on drying himself off, and without even meaning to, he used the Power to pull the water off of his skin. In that moment, he felt like he could do anything. He looked at his underwear and it flew right up off the stool, soaring through the air and into his awaiting hands. He put it on, then did the same with his pants. He looked at his belt buckle, it was made from a zinc alloy; on a whim he turned it to pure gold. He picked up the pumice stone sitting by the stool and turned that to gold as well. He remembered the golden coin that Shiara had paid the man at the front desk and decided to try to form a couple of his own. Bright, blue light filled the room as the golden stone dripped and melted into a puddle and then started to reform into three separate coins. Just as the light reached the height of its display, Belford noticed that the door to the bathing chamber had been opened.

Belford lost his concentration in his surprise, and the lights immediately ceased as the gold solidified, only halfway transformed into coins. Standing in the doorway was a girl – Belford's heart nearly stopped as he took in her reddish-brown hair and green eyes. "Claire?" he whispered. He felt silly immediately after saying it; it wasn't her at all – just another girl with similar features. She was younger than the girl he knew, and unlike his Claire, whose face was an image of perfection as far as Belford was concerned, this girl had a slightly hooked nose; although really that was the only thing marring her appearance in his opinion.

The girl's eyes darted over Belford wildly. Her mouth hung open in shock whilst her legs stayed rooted firmly to the floor with fear. She focused on Belford's left arm, her eyes growing even wider, transfixed by the Mark of Kings.

Belford quickly realized what she was looking at and scrambled to pull his shirt on over his head. He didn't know what he would do if she ran away or called for help. So far she was still stunned, but Shiara's warnings were beginning to buzz around in his head: If he were discovered as being a wizard here in Bronam, he would be executed; there would be no trial, no appeal.

He could grab her now, he figured, and probably knock her out or even kill her with little struggle – he could even change her body into something else with the Power. Before Belford finished the fleeting thought, he already felt ashamed that the morbid idea had crossed his mind. He knew he could never do it – she was just like Claire; innocent, beautiful, somebody's daughter, lover... well maybe not a lover yet, she was still fairly young, but one day she certainly would be. He couldn't take that away from her. Not now, not ever.

She must have seen the brief look of sadness that passed over his face, for she suddenly came to her senses. Rather than running away or screaming, which were the only two options that Belford had imagined her taking, she instead looked back and forth down the hallway, and then entered fully into the bathing chamber, making sure to close – and lock – the door behind her.

Belford mentally rebuked himself for being so careless as to forget to lock the door when he first entered the room.

As the girl got closer, Belford realized she really wasn't that much younger than Claire after all; she was at least sixteen, maybe even seventeen years old.

"You're Ver'ati!" she exclaimed, her eyes lit up with excitement. "I've never met a real wizard before."

Belford didn't know what to say; he was still half afraid she might suddenly change her mind and decide to run away and turn him in to the authorities. There was no indication that she had ever even considered doing such a thing though, so Belford tried to stop himself from panicking. He needed to think clearly now. Belford decided he needed to take back control of the situation, but just as he was contemplating how he might achieve such a position, the girl started talking again.

"And you have the…" she began in a normal voice, but then switched over to a whisper, "the Mark of Kings," she finished. "I know that's what it is. I've seen it before in one of my father's books."

In his nervousness, Belford had forgotten to swallow his saliva. He did so now, in a big gulp, which only added to the look of guilt that was already plastered across his face.

"Don't worry, I won't tell anybody." It was as if she were reading his mind. "I wouldn't want to be responsible for the soldiers cutting off your head." She giggled then grimaced cutely. "So what's your name, anyway?" she asked.

"B-Belford," he said, his voice sounding odd as he stumbled over the name Javic had given him.

"That's a strange name… Belford," she said it back to him as if trying it on. "My name's Kara. Kara Delaway."

"Nice to meet you, Kara" said Belford, trying to return a bit of normalcy to the conversation. He nervously extended his hand for her to shake.

Kara looked at it hesitantly. "You're not going to turn me into a toad or something are you?"

Belford laughed. "No, that's not how it works," he said. "I wouldn't need to touch you to do that anyway."

Kara frowned, but then reached out and grasped his hand. She had a surprisingly firm handshake for such a small girl. "You have the Mark of Kings," she said, "so that makes you an enemy of the state… or the rightful ruler of all of Aragwey."

"So I've been told," said Belford. "Those two things aren't really mutually exclusive though."

Kara's eyes lit up again. "Do something with the Power," she said. "I've never seen it used before!"

It was Belford's turn to hesitate now. He knew he wasn't supposed to be using the Power while in Bronam, but it hardly seemed like it could get him into any more trouble than he was in already. *If anything*, he tried to convince himself, *it would be stupid not to do whatever the girl with my fate in her hands wants me to do.* Belford motioned for Kara to stand back from the failed gold coin transmutation and began summoning up the emotion he would need in order to do his work. The half-made coins began giving off blue light again as they melted together into one big puddle.

Kara gasped slightly. "It's so beautiful," she said in awe.

The gold elongated, forming a thin looping strip. It turned into a necklace with a round pendant attached at its end. Belford focused on the first thing that came to mind; he began morphing the pendant's shape into an ornate golden butterfly. It was quite delicate work – far finer and more precisely detailed than any human hand could have possibly crafted without the use of a microscope or machinery. He let the gold set, taking on the shape permanently. Belford reached down and picked up the necklace, then leaned in towards Kara to drape it over her head. The sweet scent of lavender filled Belford's nostrils as he got close. He was careful not to get the chain tangled up in her soft hair as he placed it down around her neck. She was absolutely ecstatic.

"There you go," said Belford, looking straight into Kara's eyes. She really did remind him a lot of Claire.

Kara blushed and diverted her eyes away from his. "I'm sorry I walked in on you like that," she said. "I was just going to take a bath and the door wasn't locked or anything. I left my stuff here earlier while the water was warming," she paused for a moment. "Hey, where's my pumice stone anyway?"

Belford smiled. "You're wearing it."

Kara's hand rose up to her neck and she caressed one of the wings of the butterfly necklace. "I like it better this way," she said. "Thank you."

"Anytime," said Belford. "Just don't tell anyone…."

"I told you not to worry," said Kara, and before Belford could say anything else, she hugged him.

CHAPTER

17

Days Past

Shiara was humming a tune as she sat down on the edge of the bed and began brushing her fingers through her long dark hair. She pulled a clip out of her pocket and pinned her hair back behind her left ear. After rummaging through her bag for a fresh shirt to replace her dirty riding dress, she glanced over at Javic momentarily. Javic averted his eyes before Shiara needed to ask. She began undressing behind him.

Javic took a seat in a cushy armchair over in the room's sitting area. In front of him was a small fireplace with a hanging brass teakettle and a wonky, old bookshelf that leaned crooked against the wall. The shelves contained several tattered leather-bound books, left behind by some previous tenant – scientific journals based on the handwritten scrawl across their spines. Other than the sitting area, the room only contained two double beds and an extra cot that had been brought up by a servant boy about Javic's age shortly after he and Shiara arrived.

Movement caught Javic's eyes – the curved surface of the shiny teakettle captured Shiara's reflection and sent a distorted version of her back at Javic. His eyes lingered over the reflection for a moment before he realized what he was doing. He diverted his gaze immediately. Naturally, he was curious about the female form, but he didn't dare sneak a peek.

He felt insecure whenever he was around Shiara, partly because of her strong personality, but mostly due to his lack of experience with women in general. He had never been with a girl before; he only ever had eyes for Salvine. Darrenfield was a small community with few children Javic's age, and even fewer that he actually got along with. He was never very good at making friends. Growing up, his peers all just made fun of him for his outlander nose.

When he was younger, though, Javic did manage to befriend a boy by the name of Harvey McGrutto, the roofer's son. They spent quite a bit of time together one summer when Elric offered to help out the boy's father, Aston, after Harvey's mother died unexpectedly from an illness. The family was grieving, so the Elensols aided Mr. McGrutto with his workload and household chores until he got back on his feet.

Javic and Harvey spent a lot of time playing make-believe games all across town. Sometimes they climbed trees together, just to see who could get the highest, or raced to the old creek and back. It had been one of the most fun summers of Javic's young life, but Harvey and Javic drifted apart soon after.

A few years later, when Javic was twelve, he saw Salvine for the first time. She belonged to a large immigrant family that had just moved to the area. Salvine's family was from Kovehn originally – they came to Darrenfield in the wake of rising violence in Kovehn caused by the famine there. The food shortages in the Gestrcho region had been a problem for years, but it finally reached its tipping point. The Torus Desert was literally swallowing up whole farming communities, and no one was able to do anything about it. Salvine's hometown was amongst those eventually blotted off the map. It was just the changing times, Javic guessed. That's what people always said anyway.

The first time Javic saw Salvine, he was too nervous to talk to her. He hid behind his grandfather's horse as they welcomed her family to town. Salvine wasn't shy at all, though. She went right up to him and introduced herself. Javic was sure he had turned as red as a beet. He could still remember the feeling of the heat in his face, the way it burned through his cheeks as if he'd been standing on his head for an hour straight. He may as well have swallowed his tongue for how many words he managed during that first exchange. Even so, he had to count his blessings: Despite his awkwardness, the prettiest girl he'd ever seen ended up asking him to give her a tour around town.

Salvine's eyes were light gray, and that, along with her blonde hair, made her stand out among the sea of dark-haired, dark-eyed farmers that made up the rest of Darrenfield. Rather than being ridiculed the way Javic was for having the outlander bump on his nose, Salvine was seen as exotic. Every boy wanted to be with her.

That year, Javic was impatient for the autumn harvest festival to arrive. He made plans with Salvine to see her again and was counting down the days until its commencement. On Festival Day, while looking for her in the crowd gathered at the center of town, Javic came across Harvey. The boy told Javic that Salvine was waiting for him down by the old creek – that he would show him where she was – but when they arrived at the water, Harvey and a few of the older boys from town beat Javic with sticks until he was heavily bruised and bloodied. They then ran off, leaving him crying in the dirt. Javic didn't understand why they'd done it – how anyone could be so cruel.

He didn't want anyone to see him in this demeaned state, so he dragged himself back to the edge of town and tried to wait out the festivities while he tended to his wounds. The thing he still remembered most vividly about that day, besides the feelings of betrayal and shame, was the metallic taste of his own blood as it trickled across his tongue and coated the back of his throat.

He never found Salvine. Later, he discovered that Harvey had asked her out, but that she turned him down. Even so, Javic missed his chance: By the next time he saw her, Salvine was already seeing somebody else. Javic never spent much time around girls after that, preferring instead the company of his grandfather, or of the horses and other animals on the farm. He remained friends with Salvine, always maintaining the lingering hope that he might one day win her heart. Sadly, for as long as he'd known her, Salvine was always dating one boy or another. He'd never gotten the chance to tell her how he truly felt – until recently, that is.

This isn't how things were supposed to turn out.

Salvine had been plucked from Javic's life, and although he knew he would never see her again, a part of him still refused to believe it. When he closed his eyes, he could picture her smiling face, alive and well, riding up to the farm on her next visit to see how he and his grandfather were faring with the autumn harvest. He could hear her sly banter, teasing him over his slow progress with the fields, and then she would offer to stew him up some rabbit while he finished his work. They would sit down together like a real couple and talk until late into the night. Eventually the fire would cool, and it would be time to go to bed. But they wouldn't sleep. Instead, Javic would kiss her, and this time she wouldn't turn away. She would tilt her chin up as Javic caressed her neck with his fingertips and he would feel the thumping of her heart, beating faster and faster within her chest, right alongside his.

Javic forced himself to let go of the fantasy. He was just torturing himself. Knowing Salvine was forever gone made it too painful to continue. He didn't know if he would ever find another girl that could make him feel the way Salvine had.

"Done," said Shiara.

Javic turned back around. Shiara's new top did not leave much to the imagination. It was low-cut, dipping down to expose enough cleavage to make Javic blush. She had put on a dark-blue skirt as well. The color complemented her eyes, making them stand out even more than usual. Her hairclip had been knocked askew, but she straightened it now, directing every soft strand of her raven-black hair back into place. She was a beautiful woman; any man would be fortunate to have her as his other half.

What if Salvine was my other half?

He hadn't gotten a chance to find out.

No one can ever replace her. How can I ever move on?

Javic let out a heavy sigh.

Shiara glanced up at the sound. "Missing home?" she asked.

Javic shrugged. He didn't really feel like sharing his sorrows.

Shiara gave a sympathetic smile. "Just try not to think about it," she said. "You'll love Phandrol – trust me. The capital, Erotos, is like no other city in all of Aragwey. People come from all over just to experience its wealth of culture... lots of girls your age too." She gave a little wink.

Javic's face reddened.

"It's really easy to meet people there. You'll have plenty of fun," she said. "I envy you – to be young and free in the Glowing City – all the years I was in Erotos, I was tied down by the Ver'ati training academy." She pursed her lips slightly. "It's hard to find time for a relationship when you're studying all the time. Harder still after graduating – especially if you're assigned a long-term deep-undercover position doing important work like pretending to be a lowly barmaid in a faraway land with only drunkards to interact with. Did I mention my bloodline is descended from the Mark of Kings?"

Javic frowned. "How did that happen? Why did they send you to Felington?"

Shiara waved her hand dismissively. "Pissed off the wrong guy," she said. "It was Thorin's fault, really." She took a seat on the edge of the bed again. "We met in Phandrol, Thorin and I, at the academy. I had just been raised to Ver'ati, still finishing up my schooling, and he was in the process of getting kicked out of officer training," she began laughing. "He tells the story differently than I do, but don't you believe a word of it," she said. "He probably could have passed his evaluations, but, you see, Thorin used to have a bit of a temper back then: He punched General Guther Aldune – that's the master of the academy – he punched him square in the face for something he said. Aldune deserved it, but anyway, the general fights back, and he starts going a bit over the top, using the Power to try to drown Thorin in the fountain outside the exam hall – that's probably the only reason Thorin didn't get a tribunal; they thought he'd already received enough punishment."

Javic could hardly believe his ears. It didn't sound at all like the laidback Thorin he'd gotten to know.

"After Aldune sealed Thorin in the fountain I went over to see if he was still alive. Sure enough, he was trying to punch his way out through the fountain's stone wall, still completely submerged. He couldn't get out of the top after what Aldune did to it, but Thorin managed to make it almost halfway through the side by the time I got there – using the Power on his own body to make himself stronger. He was running out of air by then, so I—"

"Wait, wait, wait," interrupted Javic, "Thorin is a wizard?!"

"Of course," said Shiara, "just not a very strong one." She laughed again. "He has a very low innate ability, so he can only affect his own body or things that are in his immediate vicinity. That's actually what he and Aldune had been arguing about." Shiara looked thoughtful for a moment. "You see, officers are generally supposed to be strong in the Power. They train for years and are the top of their class. Thorin wanted to go career and was managing to pass all of his courses with high marks despite his disadvantage, but Aldune still refused to promote him."

"What are you two talking about?" asked Thorin. He and Elric were just entering the room, finally arriving after dropping the horses off at the stables and readying the wagon with fresh supplies for the next leg of their journey.

"Just the story of how you pissed off Guther Aldune and got us sent halfway across the nation to manage a shitty tavern," said Shiara.

"Oh," said Thorin, "you mean when I broke out of that watery death-chamber and ravished you with my glistening muscles?"

"Yes," said Shiara, "only wasn't it I that broke you out of there? And before you say it, I did *not* fall into the fountain, I was only wet because I leaned up against you while resuscitating you."

Thorin shook his head. "Nah, I'm pretty sure it happened the other way around."

"Are you sure you two aren't a couple?" asked Javic.

"Me and this big oaf?" asked Shiara. "If it wasn't for my compassion rescuing his insubordinate ass, I probably would have made Major by now."

Thorin stuck his tongue out at her as he threw his bags over into the corner of the room.

"Should have let him drown…" said Shiara.

Over the next couple hours, once Belford returned from his bath looking and smelling like a new man, everybody else took turns going down to clean up as well. That night, despite memories of Salvine still tormenting Javic's mind, he managed to have a decent night's sleep – his best since leaving home. He awoke feeling somewhat refreshed; ready to hit the road again. He convinced himself that the farther he got from Darrenfield, the easier it would be to forget about the things he had lost. Maybe he would enjoy Erotos, as Shiara suggested, after all.

CHAPTER

18

The Taste of Copper

Belford was surprisingly talkative in the morning. His cheerful attitude quickly rubbed off on the rest of the group. Everyone was happier now that they were clean, but Belford really had an added glow about him. Javic still wasn't talking to Belford in light of the secrets he was keeping from him with his grandfather, but the silence was becoming harder and harder to maintain. Only his stubbornness was holding him back now.

Thorin and Elric were going over travel plans on Elric's tattered map while Belford watched in interest. The next resupplying stop would be at the city of Rasile on the southwestern border of Kovehn. It was a three-day ride from Bronam. After that stop, they would finally be leaving Kovehn for good.

They bid farewell to Bronam after breakfast, riding away as the central dome, with its partially gold-plated roof, shined beautifully in the morning light. It was like a second sun rising up from the middle of the city. Javic was thankful there hadn't been any incidents during their brief stay in Bronam. With all of the anti-wizard military presence within the city, he had just kind of expected Belford to mess up somehow and get all of them in trouble.

The whole rest of the day went by without a hitch as well. The weather was hot, but comfortable, and the wagon ride was quiet and relaxing. That night, they found a soft field of grass and all decided to sleep out under the stars. During their second day on the road since Bronam, the wagon didn't come to a stop until late in the afternoon. When it did, Javic could hear running water somewhere off beyond the tree line.

"That's the last source of clean water before Rasile," said Thorin. "We should refill at the creek before moving on."

Everyone stepped out of the wagon, stretching their cramped legs before starting the short hike to the waterside. Elric stayed with the horses as everyone else departed from the road. Javic grabbed his canteen and finished off the last few swigs so that it was ready to refill. He slung his bow and quiver over his shoulder, just in case he spotted a pheasant worth shooting down by the water. Fresh meat was always a nice find while on the road. A plump pheasant would make a fine meal come supper time. He didn't really look forward to Thorin's cooking – it was quite terrible. Bless his heart though, he did try.

The creek was fast moving and perfectly clear. Javic crouched down beside the water and drank a few deep gulps out of his cupped hands – ice cold – his throat ached as he swallowed it down. He filled his canteen to the brim and sealed the top shut. Everyone else had already finished up and were starting to head back to the wagon when Javic noticed a slight rustling in the bushes across on the other side of the creek.

Javic took his bow from his shoulder and aligned an arrow in anticipation. He crept closer, stepping carefully across the creek. He didn't have to be too quiet here. The sound of the running water was enough to conceal his footsteps. When Javic reached ten paces away from the bush, a scrawny rabbit burst from the leaves and scampered along a narrow trail that led away from the creek. Javic loosed his arrow, but it missed. The rabbit bounded back and forth, narrowly avoiding death. Javic chased after the critter, pulling a second arrow from his quiver as he ran. He followed the rabbit for some distance, but couldn't get a clear shot. It ducked into a copse of heavy brush. There was nothing Javic could do; the critter escaped.

Javic turned around, disappointed. While walking back to retrieve his first arrow, he heard more rustling from somewhere off to his left. He scanned the brush for the culprit. The wind shifted, wafting the heavy scent of death into his nostrils. A bad feeling settled deep in his gut. There was no mistaking it.

Whunes....

Just as the thought filled his mind, a particularly gnarled Whune lunged out of the vegetation.

It had smelled Javic first.

His heart skipped a beat and he nearly fell down as the creature burst towards him. Out of instinct, Javic released the second arrow that he had prepared for the rabbit. It took the Whune in the chest with a solid thud as if hitting a tree trunk. The monster howled, but it did not stop its chase. Javic put his bow over his shoulder as he turned to run. He didn't look back, focusing on speed as he sprinted towards the creek. He prayed for the safety of the wagon, waiting on the other side of the water.

"Whunes!" Javic shouted at the top of his lungs as he rounded what he hoped was the last line of bushes before the creek. On the other side of the brush, Javic was faced with a horrible surprise: Three more Whunes were down by the creek bed, and he'd alerted them to his presence with his yell.

The three Whunes at the creek were already moving towards him, their eyes and axes focused with deadly intent. He heard a snarl from behind him. It was the injured Whune. Javic dove sideways as the Whune swung its axe at him with devastating force. It would have cleaved him clean in half had he not moved aside in time. The axe dug into the thick clay that ran beneath the soil near the creek. It sunk down so deep that the Whune couldn't pull it back out, though it tried several times. Javic took the distraction as an opportunity to scramble away.

The Whune gave up trying to free its axe and began to pursue Javic once more. The other three Whunes were getting close now as well, but their attention was suddenly pulled away by an eruption of shouting from the other side of the creek. It was Elric and Thorin, weapons brandished, descending the far bank as quickly as they could. The other three Whunes turned towards the new opponents and released a battle call. Thorin echoed it back, kicking up a spray of water as he bounded through the creek. Elric was right on his heels. Thorin shouted for Javic to run as he collided with the first Whune, decking the creature onto its back in the soil.

The Whune pursuing Javic was too quick; he could not get away. It knocked Javic to the ground with its meaty arms and was immediately on top of him before Javic could scramble away again. The Whune began to pummel Javic's face and body with its fists, showing no mercy. Javic felt the sting of the creature's claws across his face. Blood gushed from his nose and forehead. He started to taste the familiar, coppery flow as it dripped down the back of his throat. It was a warm trickle amidst the stinging pain.

Trying not to blackout, Javic grabbed the only thing his fingers could find: The arrow sticking out of the Whune's chest. He pulled it free with a sharp tug and used it to stab the Whune over and over again as quickly as he could. The Whune's fists only rained down more viciously in response. Javic tried to cover his face with his left arm, but felt a sickening snap as the Whune smashed down on the limb. Pain filled his whole body and the corners of his vision began to go dark. He was overcome by a wave of nausea, nearly making him vomit. As the Whune swiped low once more, Javic made one last stab with the arrow out of desperation, aiming for the creature's face. The Whune flailed its arms around wildly and squealed.

Javic had put out one of its eyes.

It didn't seem to be in pain so much as it was simply disoriented by the blow; perhaps it was a little stunned as well by the fierce resistance that Javic was managing. Regardless, Javic wasted no time getting back to his feet.

While he was on the ground, more Whunes had joined the fight against Thorin and Elric. It was now five on two, but both Thorin and his grandfather were still holding their own. The original three Whunes that started the fight were already dead, their putrid carcasses polluting the creek bed with their molasses-thick blood.

Javic's whole body, especially his head and left arm, was pounding painfully with each beat of his fluttering heart. He stumbled along as quickly as he could, moving away from the fighting. His adrenaline kicking in, he began to shake uncontrollably as the hormone pulsed through his veins. Javic glanced behind him. Although he had gained some ground, the Whune was moving after him again. It tore the arrow from its eye and threw it away. Javic dodged through the trees, wiping the blood from his face to prevent it from obscuring his vision.

Javic's legs were beginning to give out; he stumbled twice, nearly collapsing entirely the second time. He looked back again. The Whune was closing on him fast. It pushed on, completely unhindered by the loss of its eye. Javic knew what was required of him. He couldn't give up. He knew the consequences of that. He couldn't just lie down and take it. There would be no crawling off to lick his wounds. There was no use in crying, or of being afraid, or calling for help. He thought of little Harvey McGrutto – just another bully with a stick. This was one race Javic needed to win.

Spotting a suitable tree, Javic began to climb. His hands were bleeding from the Whune's claws, and he couldn't put any weight on his left arm, but he just kept reaching for branch after branch, pulling himself up higher and higher, desperately clinging with his knees and fingertips, using all his remaining strength. The Whune grabbed at his foot, but Javic kicked free and continued to climb higher still.

The Whune tried to follow him up, but the branches snapped under its weight, so it grabbed hold of the trunk instead and shook it with all of its might in an attempt to knock Javic loose.

Javic had one trick left.

His bow was still over his shoulder. Although he lost many of the arrows out of his quiver when he was first knocked to the ground earlier, five remained.

Looping his legs around the tree trunk so as not to fall from the Whune's shaking, Javic notched one of the remaining arrows in his bow and, as painful as it was with his broken arm, he began to draw the bowstring tight. He fired straight down onto the Whune, hitting it in the shoulder, only missing its head because of the motion of the tree. The Whune snarled ravenously, but continued shaking the trunk.

Javic's brow began to bead with sweat as he notched another arrow; the pain was almost too much to bear as he drew the bow tight. He fired again, this time hitting his target. The arrow punctured the top of the monster's skull. The Whune dropped its arms, though it miraculously remained on its feet. It began screeching a bloodcurdling scream; it was fairly high pitch, sounding almost eerily human. A shiver ran down Javic's spine. He shot it once more in the head. The scream stopped as the monster tumbled to the ground in a huddled mass of flesh.

All Javic could do was breathe out a heavy sigh of relief as he hung there sideways in the treetop. He carefully righted himself and was about to climb down when he heard something else approaching. He remained silent in the upper branches just in case it turned out to be another Whune. He hoped desperately for his grandfather to come walking out of the trees, so much so that he entirely forgot about being mad at him for the moment.

What am I really mad about anyway?   Grandfather's just keeping some secret with Belford – maybe it's a private matter of Belford's and has nothing to do with me.

It all seemed so trivial now.

A man sauntered out of the undergrowth. Javic nearly called out to him, assuming it was his grandfather, but then he noticed the frayed, black cloak draped loosely over his shoulders. Fear crept into Javic's heart as he realized who the man must be: The dark wizard – the Goblikan Whune – there was no doubt about it now.

Javic quickly glanced up into the sky, taking note of the moon perched just above the horizon. He might have considered shooting one of his remaining arrows at the dark wizard had the moon not been up, but as things currently stood, the man could turn Javic to dust with a single thought.

The pale-faced man walked by the dead Whune in silence. He took notice of it, but didn't seem to care about its death one way or another. He was hunting. He stopped just beyond the tree Javic was in and looked back and forth along the ground. There were no more tracks for him to follow. He growled under his breath. Javic silently notched another arrow lest the dark wizard should look up into his hiding place, but he began to walk back in the direction he came from instead.

Drawing his cloak back over his graying hair, the man came to a stop at the edge of the last group of trees that Javic could still see from his high vantage point. He raised his arms into the air and roared violently; the whole area began to heat up, rippling with warmth as the leaves on all the nearby trees began to curl around their edges.

The earth was smoldering. The vegetation adjacent to the dark wizard ignited into open flames. Javic could feel the unbearable sting of the heat on his face as the fire quickly grew in intensity. The leaves on the tree he was in began to singe. The smoke started to make Javic choke. He covered his mouth with his shirt and tried not to cough, but he felt as if he were being smothered. The burning forest crackled and groaned as the trees began to burst and split internally and the remaining moisture in their leaves sizzled away. The dark wizard seemed to be impervious to the heat. He lowered his arms and disappeared into the dense smoke without any hesitation.

Javic couldn't take the smoke any longer. He climbed down the tree – the branches burning his palms as he descended in more of a mildly controlled fall than a proper descent. The wind was beginning to pick up now, carrying the smoke and flames away from Javic and back towards the creek. It looked as if a storm would hit soon. Black clouds were darkening the western horizon with the shade of heavy rainfall – the first real rain in months. It was as if nature were responding to the dark wizard's malice by releasing a tempest of its own. Periodic flashes of lightning lit the sky, growing closer by the minute. Javic cradled his broken arm to his stomach and limped off into the approaching gloom.

CHAPTER

19

From the Shadows

The wind cut to the bone. The grain of the petrified wood holding up the old shack nearly buckled under the strength of the gusts. The walls creaked and groaned as stormy howls sounded across the gap where the door had once resided. Unhinged and abandoned to the floor, the door remained behind as a shattered memory of protection; an allusion of better times – but that façade had long since disappeared. Rain dampened the floor as it dripped through holes in the rafters. Leaves and other bits of refuse crawled through the hollow entrance and scraped their ways into the various nooks and corners of the room. No possessions were left; everything worthy of plunder had long since been removed – no shelter remained. All of the walls were bare, and the floor, apart from the rotting door and decaying leaves, was void of content as well.

A boy suddenly stumbled in, soaked and shivering, to find himself cloaked in shadows amidst the ever-increasing darkness of the night. It was Javic, his left arm twisted unnaturally across his body. It had turned black and blue from blood pooling just beneath the surface of his skin. Rain beaded on his brow as his eyes shot across the room in a frantic search for anything that could be used as a sling. Finding nothing of consequence, he threw his bow to the ground and knelt down beside it. He slowly pulled off his leather tunic and undershirt, wincing as each piece slid across his injured arm. He tied the sleeves of his shirt together with his good hand by pinning it against his upper thigh, then looped it around his forearm and the back of his neck.

He was breathing hard; his heart pounding out of his chest. His hair, singed by unnatural heat, smelled strongly of sulfur. The distinctive scent floated up into the rafters. His hair drooped despondently across his forehead where it became matted with dark blood, flowing freely from a precarious head wound located just above his right eye. A combination of blood, sweat, and rain dripped down towards his eyes but he wiped the droplets away with his free hand just before they crested his brow.

In the distance, a pattering of feet could be heard approaching swiftly over the sounds of the weather, although the din was still faint at this time. The footsteps grew louder as their source drew nearer. As soon as Javic noticed the noise he spun around, focusing his eyes on the open entrance. He held his breath, attempting to be completely silent. The footsteps stopped. A figure, poised in the darkness, glided towards the doorway.

Suddenly, a milky glow filled the entrance. It was a dull light, easy on the eyes but still bright enough to see by. The glow silhouetted a man. His elongated shadow cast across the floor of the shack and onto the far wall as he stood facing outwards towards the storm. The light landed uncomfortably close to where Javic was crouched, but he was still guarded by the shadows. He remained motionless.

The man turned now, revealing the source of the luminance – it was a slightly oblong orb sitting in the palm of his hand. The uniform radiance lit up the shack as the man entered. Only a few eerie shadows remained upon the walls.

"Javic?" asked the man with a tone of surprise.

Javic sat up with a sigh of relief. "Belford! I thought you were the dark wizard…."

"Thank god you're alive!" Belford exclaimed.

"Where are the others?" asked Javic.

"No idea, I got separated during the fighting. I was hoping they were with you."

Javic shook his head.

Belford took a seat next to Javic and began to look over his injuries. "Hmm," he said as he looked under the sling, "I think I can fix this." A blue glow enveloped Javic's arm and the tension immediately began to drain from his face. The milky orb that Belford had been using to light the room grew dimmer as he healed Javic's wounds. A soft-green light with a hint of purple pulsed through Belford's hands and down into Javic's injured extremity. The orb's shape began to elongate further, melting away. Belford continued to focus all of his attention on Javic while whatever force was maintaining the orb quickly dissipated. The orb ceased to exist entirely and the remaining light shot outwards in a final flash before disappearing. Nothing remained of the orb but a gooey residue left over from the globe's outer casing.

"What was that?" asked Javic.

"An energy bubble," Belford stated plainly.

Javic narrowed his eyes. "But that doesn't make any sense – Shiara said that couldn't be done."

Belford chuckled softly. "Since when does anything ever make sense around me?" The glow of the Power faded away as Belford finished the healing process, blanketing the room in darkness once more.

"Thanks," said Javic as he began rotating his joints around to check their flexibility. "We should keep heading south towards Rasile," he said. "Grandfather will be expecting us to go there."

"On foot?" asked Belford. "In the dark… and rain?"

"The Whunes are probably close by," said Javic. "They might find us if we wait here."

"Fair enough," said Belford, hopping to his feet.

Javic got up as well, and the two of them stepped out of the shack and disappeared into the night.

Once Mallory was sure they were completely gone, she swung down from where she had been hiding atop the rafters. Her heart was beating quickly at the thought of nearby Whunes. She began to pace across the floor.

Is that why Arlin hasn't returned for me? Have the Whunes gotten him…? No, that's unthinkable. Arlin is too tough.

She forced herself to sit down in order to remain calm and began to pray to Mast for Arlin's safe return.

Mallory bumped something with her foot and it slid with a scrape across the floor. Startled by the sound, she reached down with her left hand and groped around for the item that had made the noise. She grasped onto the object. It was some sort of stick with a cool, smooth surface. She followed the curve of its shape with her fingertips, not realizing what it was she had found until her fingers ran across the string that connected the ends of the object together.

It was Javic's bow.

Suddenly, she heard voices. Already too close, there wasn't enough time to climb back up into the rafters.

Javic and Belford stepped back through the doorway, another orb in Belford's hand lighting their way. They stopped their conversation abruptly when they saw Mallory kneeling on the floor, Javic's bow in hand.

CHAPTER

20

The Touch of Heat

"Gates of Galdren—!" exclaimed Javic. His heart nearly stopped at the sight of the young woman, thinking again that he was seeing the dark wizard. He was becoming too jumpy – starting to act like Belford. With Belford's energy bubble providing just enough light to see through the darkness, they both took a step closer to Mallory.

Her large round eyes were like a cat's, reflecting the soft glow of the orb back with a fierce shine that pierced the darkness of the room. Her long brown hair bounced loosely around her shoulders in wobbly curls that were beginning to frizz out in the damp air. Suddenly Javic realized who it was he was looking at.

"You!" he exclaimed. "You're that lady from Felington. The one who was with that fellow, Arlin, during the Whune siege. You're Mallory, right?"

The lady nodded, looking quite disheveled in her brown and green riding dress. It appeared to be the same dress she was wearing the last time Javic had seen her back in Felington, only now it was a bit worse for wear. Her expression was like that of a scolded child, caught stealing the last sweet out of the jar.

"Mallory Worvon," she said. "Arlin Calary is my liege."

"Well then," said Javic, "how did you end up all the way out here?"

Mallory started pacing back and forth across the cabin floor like a trapped animal. "We've been following you," she said.

Belford looked around the room as if expecting to find more people hiding in the vacant corners. "Where's this Arlin guy?" he asked.

Mallory let out a little whimper and began to bite her fingernails. "I don't know," she said. "We came here to take shelter from the storm, but then we saw smoke to the north and Arlin went out to investigate."

"Yeah, I saw that too," said Belford with a puzzled look on his face. "I wonder what that was about."

The wrath of the dark wizard as the forest ignited into flames flashed across Javic's mind. He reached out and put his hand on Mallory's shoulder, preventing her from continuing her nervous pacing. "We should get going," he said. "The Goblikan is near. If Belford and I found this place, the Whunes certainly will as well."

"Wait a second," said Belford, "it was you and Arlin spying on us from atop that ridge that night when we were launching the rocks, wasn't it?"

"You are truly a powerful Ver'ati," said Mallory, a slight look of awe flashing across her face. Suddenly, her eyes widened. "You can protect Arlin!" she said. "You can go save him and kill the Goblikan once and for all!" Her voice was full of excitement, but also openly desperate and pleading.

Belford looked as if he might actually give in to the suicidal request.

"No, we can't," said Javic before Belford had a chance to respond. "It's too dangerous."

With her hopes dashed, Mallory looked on the verge of tears.

"I know you care about him," said Javic, "but Arlin is a resourceful man. Smart too. I'm sure he'll be fine."

Mallory didn't look convinced.

"He's probably more worried about you, sitting here all alone in the dark, than he is about himself," said Javic. "So what we need to do now is start moving again so that we will still be safe when he finds us."

Mallory's eyes were glistening, but no tears broke free. "I will be strong," she said, "for Arlin."

Belford raised his eyebrows, clearly impressed by how well Javic had handled the situation.

Javic smiled briefly, reveling momentarily in the silent praise. "Excellent," he said. "Now, is your horse around here somewhere?"

Mallory shook her head. "We had to sell Elsa, my mare, back in Bronam in order to afford supplies." She lowered her head and wiped her eyes with the wrinkled sleeve of her riding dress.

Javic couldn't imagine selling Olli – other than Salvine, Olli had been his best friend for years now. Mallory must have been devastated over losing Elsa, and now with Arlin's life in peril... and yet she was still functioning. Javic had found a new respect for Mallory. She really was strong. Still, the fact remained that they had no means of transportation other than their own feet to carry them all the way to Rasile, and although the city would have been just a single day's ride away by horse or wagon, on foot it would take them at least twice as long to make the journey – perhaps longer. It all depended on how rocky the terrain turned out to be.

Grandfather must be worried sick by now.

The rain slowed slightly as Javic, Belford and Mallory cautiously set out from the abandoned cabin. The wind was still in full force, whipping against their faces and tugging at the hems of their clothing every step of the way. Javic ducked his head as burst after burst of cold air smashed against his damp skin. The branches of the trees swayed dangerously low, spilling large chunks of debris to the forest floor as the blustery weather shot through the upper foliage. A long animal howl pierced the night from somewhere off in the distance. It was probably just a coyote, but the sound put Javic on edge.

They found the forest floor to be difficult to navigate in the darkness. All three stumbled and tripped multiple times across rocks and roots and little hidden divots in the dirt. Belford was hesitant to use his energy bubbles to light their path at first because he thought it might give away their location, but Javic told him to do it anyway. He remembered from his grandfather's stories that Whunes could see just as well in the dark as they could by sunlight; if they did come across a Whune during the night, an energy bubble would be their only chance of seeing it as clearly as it could see them.

With the orb lit up, Javic was able to keep an eye on their compass heading, assuring that they continued moving straight southward. Their course took them parallel to the main road, somewhere off to the east of their location. Javic didn't want to risk actually walking along the road, as it was a near certainty that the Whunes would be watching for them there.

After a while, Javic noticed that Mallory was shivering. Her riding dress was soaked all the way through and it clung to her skin tightly. Javic took off his outer shirt and draped it over her shoulders. It wasn't much, as both the shirt and Mallory were already drenched through and through, but at least it was something. Mallory thanked him profusely and drew the shirt snugly around her person like a blanket.

Belford pushed on at the lead. He still looked surprisingly dry; he seemed to be repelling the raindrops away from him with the Power. Javic wished he had the same luxury. Periodically one of Belford's orbs would falter, sending pulses of bright light flashing out like a tiny cosmic explosion. Every time, Belford would curse audibly and the whole group would have to stop for a moment and wait until he had created a new orb before they could start moving again. Javic began to worry about the flashes attracting the Whunes now. They lit up the sky like beacons, but there was simply no way they could travel at any meaningful pace without a light source.

Each time a new bubble was formed, Javic felt a draft of especially chilly air spread outward from its creation point. Rather than giving off warmth like Javic had hoped, the bubbles were sucking massive amounts of energy out of the environment instead. It wasn't just heat energy that the orbs were eating up either: The leaves on nearby trees reacted to Belford's presence as he walked past, discoloring and withering noticeably, their life essence draining away.

All too soon, the moon began to dip over the western horizon, causing Belford's final orb to burn out almost instantaneously as his connection to the Power was severed. As the light went out, the travelers were plunged once again into total darkness. The sun would not rise for at least another hour, and until then, there would be no way for them to continue moving forward. Javic couldn't even see his own hands when he held them out in front of his face. The energy bubbles made such a convenient light source that Javic had forgotten just how dark a moonless night could be. When the moon was up, even when Belford's orbs had failed, there was always a soft glow cast over the landscape to navigate by. Now, left completely in the dark, things were beginning to look more dire than ever.

Feeling completely exhausted from walking throughout most of the night, Javic was beginning to wish they'd created some sort of shelter to protect themselves from the weather before Belford's light went out. As soon as they stopped moving, Javic's body temperature began to drop. The wind and rain became even more unbearable as shivers racked his body. His teeth chattered uncontrollably as he curled up against the trunk of a thick tree nearby. Mallory sat down beside him, shivering as well, and the two of them huddled together in an attempt to preserve body heat.

By the time the sun finally started to rise, Javic could barely feel his arms and legs. He and Mallory were well into the throes of hypothermia. The brunt of the storm had passed, but the ground was still far too damp to start a fire, even with Javic's matches.

"This is all my fault," said Belford. "I should have dried you guys off and started a fire before the moon went down."

Belford was really starting to beat himself up over the blunder. Javic couldn't blame him though – he knew if anyone was at fault, it was himself; he was the one who should have known better. He hadn't thought far enough ahead. He was so focused on moving away from the Whunes that he'd forgotten about the more basic survival requirements. Getting wet in the middle of the night without any means of drying off or making a campfire was certainly not one of Javic's finer moments. He was far more experienced in the wilderness than Belford, so there really was no excuse for him to have made such a large mistake either.

Belford covered Javic and Mallory with his own over-shirt and began searching the area for any semblance of dry tinder to use in starting a fire. The rain had left the forest floor muddy and covered with wet leaves. Looking back in the direction from which they came, Javic could clearly see their tracks. The distressing reality of the situation was that anyone could easily follow their trail. They hadn't exactly been making very quick progress throughout the night either.

Javic wanted to stay awake. He needed to be alert. It was far too dangerous for him to take a nap, but the cold was dragging him down. His eyes became unfocused as he started to nod off. From beside him, Mallory was mumbling somewhat incoherently, drifting in and out of delirium. Javic tried to shake his head, move his fingers, anything to keep his mind working, but the pull of sleep was becoming increasingly appealing.

And then Belford was back at his side, pulling his arm, forcing him to his feet, telling him to stay awake. Belford's voice quivered slightly as he spoke. He sounded frightened in his urgency. Belford was pulling Mallory up as well. Her skin had become pale, chalky white, and damp with dew. Her eyes were strangely vacant and she hardly responded to Belford's touch.

Forcing his unsteady legs to move, Javic tried to walk forward without Belford's support. It was surprisingly difficult, but there was no other choice. Belford had his hands full with Mallory, and Javic didn't want to weigh him down any further.

Mallory was already too far gone to move on her own, so Belford was forced to carry her in his arms. The strain on his face was apparent as he pushed forward, fighting to earn every step that they advanced. Javic tried to keep up, his gait broken as he trailed behind Belford. He was beginning to feel strangely lightheaded, but he just kept putting one foot in front of the other. He glanced down briefly at his arms and was surprised to see that they were the same corpse-white pale color as Mallory's.

Javic wasn't sure how much more his body could take. It was becoming harder and harder to hold out. He wouldn't be able to continue moving his legs much longer. Belford kept telling him that they were almost there, that it was just a little bit farther – just over that dip or just beyond that next stand of trees – but the walk felt like an eternity. The farther he marched, the louder a tiny voice in the back of his mind grew. It was screaming at him now, getting more and more desperate – begging him to give up, to just lie down for a moment and rest his weary eyes.

Javic wanted nothing more than to give in to the voice's urging, but he had the sneaking suspicion that if he did close his eyes, he might not ever open them again. Belford kept leading him forward, one step at a time, until there, in front of him, sat the opening to a narrow cave. Burrowed into the murky hillside and surrounded by a thicket of tall trees, the fissure was protected from the wind and rain. Inside the mouth of the cave was the most beautiful sight Javic had ever seen: Golden flames leapt from a bundle of dry cave moss in Belford's left hand as he lit the clump with one of Javic's final matchsticks. The touch of the cradling warmth radiated new life into Javic's body and limbs as he stumbled in and collapsed to the floor of the cave entrance. Belford used the burning moss as tinder to ignite a pile of dry wood that he had inexplicably managed to gather.

Javic rolled over to face the fire as Belford tended to the flames. Mallory was breathing shallowly, her eyelids shut tight. Javic reached over and caressed her hand gently with his fingertips. Her fingers felt like tiny icicles, her skin seemingly devoid of any heat. Her face was relaxed into an expression of calm bliss, but as soon as Belford moved her closer to the flames, her body began to stir almost at once. Just a twitch of a finger here, a slight shift of a leg there; the warmth of the fire was doing its job. Mallory was smaller than Javic, making her more heavily affected by the cold – Javic just hoped that she had enough fight left in her to survive.

How close did we come to death?

As Belford departed from the cave in search of more dry wood to keep the fire going, Javic's eyes began to tear up. He had been on the edge of giving in to the little voice in the back of his mind – so close to quitting – but when he was there he hadn't experienced any sort of great revelation; his life had not flashed before his eyes; he hadn't felt any sense of calm; or the presence of Mast, or anything else like that. He had just felt terrifying turmoil – a jumble of pain.

He had been all alone; completely and insufferably alone.

The only reason he hadn't given in was because of fear. He was too afraid of the emptiness. It made him feel like a little child again. It was the same as when the gnarled Whune attacked him by the river – once the adrenaline faded, he had felt like nothing more than a defenseless child; frail and pathetic. He hated feeling vulnerable. What good were all of his muscles, all of his wit, all of his dreams and aspirations when the Whunes were so much stronger; when a wizard could destroy every trace of him in an instant; when the cold could tear him down to nothing just as easily as anything else? What meaningful impact could his life possibly have on the world when he was so fragile? If he had died, with Salvine gone, nobody apart from his grandfather would have even missed him. Once his grandfather passed away, there wouldn't be anyone left to mourn him at all.

Javic stared into the flames, feeling the biting touch of heat on his skin. Mallory stirred again; the color beginning to flow back into her round face. Her soft features tightened into a cute frown as her cheeks returned to their usual rosy blush. She had somebody to fight for; a reason for being. Javic could see it on her lightly furrowed brow. She was fighting to survive for Arlin's sake. Turning back to the fire, Javic began to wonder what it was that he was fighting for.

CHAPTER

21

The Scent of Lavender

A solitary buzzard-hawk circled in the northern breeze, its white-tipped wings staying motionless in the air as it slowly spiraled downwards, around and around again, getting closer to some unseen prey. Something had caught the hawk's keen eyes, but the cautious bird seemed reluctant to land.

Belford's thoughts strayed hopelessly towards Arlin. From what he had gleaned from Javic, Arlin had fought valiantly during the battle for Felington, but with a reckless abandon that did not bode well for his continued survival. He walked a fine line between bravery and stupidity; too gutsy for his own good.

The presence of the Whunes in the forest was enough to scare off most animals – they seemed to possess some sort of sixth sense when it came to danger, or perhaps they could simply smell the foul reek of the monsters in the air. The Whunes exuded a decayed musk that seeped incessantly from their pores. If the hawk had spotted a carcass through the foliage, there was a fair chance that Whunes were responsible for the kill. Belford just hoped the hawk's meal wasn't Arlin. He proceeded through the brush even more cautiously than before, keeping his eyes and ears open for any sign of danger.

Just ahead, an outcropping of large boulders produced a slight overhang, sheltering a few sticks and fallen branches from the elements. The torrent of rain that lasted through the night and into the early morning had been swift, but the wind had maintained blowing east throughout the storm. Little, dry pockets remained here and there wherever something large enough to block the flow of the storm had withstood the powerful gusts. A number of trees failed the wind's test during the night, crashing to the ground with sounds reminiscent of the thunder overhead.

Belford walked around the stone outcropping, gathering up every bit of dry wood he could find. His face began to redden slightly as he thought about the horrible position he had led everyone into. He had been so confident and determined since his bath in Bronam; after remembering Claire's name he felt like absolutely nothing could stop him. Without even trying to, he kept the rain and cold off of himself simply by riding the high of rediscovering that link to his past. If only he had been more thoughtful, more aware of the present, he might have noticed Javic and Mallory's tumble towards death's doorstep. They had both come so very close – Mallory in particular.

Without the moon, the exhilarating touch of the Power was gone, leaving Belford feeling completely useless. All he could do now was gather up a sufficient amount of wood to keep the fire burning. He just hoped the warmth would be enough to bring Mallory back from the abyss. His arms full, Belford began following his own muddy footprints back towards the cave.

Out of the trees, a sharp animal squeal pierced the air. The sound was close – just up the path – and it seemed to be full of pain. Belford edged nearer. He realized that if he abandoned the trail now, he might not be able to find his way back to the cave.

The squeal stopped just as abruptly as it started.

The hairs on the back of Belford's arms rose up with goose bumps. The trees began to open up into a small clearing as he moved along. Belford could sense movement now, forward in the brush, but it was low to the ground. He ducked behind the decaying stump of a large old-growth tree and peered cautiously around the side.

Oh, shit....

Whunes – three of them.

They were ahead of him on the trail; each hunkered down on all fours. One could almost mistake them for a group of bears, though the Whunes were mostly hairless. All three were gathered around the dead carcass of some animal – perhaps a coyote, though at this point it was already too mutilated to tell for sure. The Whunes tore at the dead animal's flesh with claws and gnashing teeth like mindless eating machines.

One of the Whunes was slightly smaller than the other two. From Belford's angle he was able to observe that the two larger Whunes were males while the smaller one was a female. It was a new dynamic to the monsters that Belford hadn't really thought about before. The idea of the disgusting creatures actually reproducing was enough to sicken him. He wondered what their tiny hell-spawn offspring would look like – if they would be just as grotesque as the adults.

The male Whunes growled like dogs and swiped at the female with their claws, pushing her back, away from the kill. The female had to settle for the small amount of meat that she had been able to tear off before being pushed away. She held it in her hands, trying to feed it into her cankerous mouth, but she was having difficulty swallowing. Something around the female's neck was stopping her from being able to easily consume the meat. Whatever it was, it was tight, digging into the creatures flesh like a choke collar.

The other two Whunes finished feeding and began sniffing around at the air. Belford's heart pounded as one of the Whunes picked its axe up off the ground and stood upright. It began wandering in the direction of Belford's hiding place. He could feel vibrations from the ungraceful clomp of the Whune's thick feet as it moved across the ground, getting closer and closer. Belford pressed his back firmly against the old stump as the Whune approached on the opposite side. One of the other Whunes snarled suddenly and then all three creatures let off a chorus of howls before bounding off through the trees at a frightening pace.

Belford realized he was holding his breath. He let it out now in a sigh of relief as he stepped out from behind the stump. The Whunes were gone. There was nothing left of their kill other than a streak of blood and a few bones, picked clean and strewn out across the ground. As Belford looked up over the trees at the edge of the clearing, his relief quickly turned to dread: A few wispy tendrils of smoke rose up into the air from the direction of the cave – the Whunes were headed straight for Javic and Mallory!

He dropped the gathered firewood and sprinted after the Whunes. He didn't know what he was going to do when he got to the cave, but he simply couldn't allow the monsters to get there unhindered. He wouldn't be able to use the Power with the moon down, and the only weapon he had was a tiny belt knife at his waist, yet he continued running. Even though he knew he stood no chance against the hulking Whunes, he didn't think he could live with himself if he simply allowed Javic and Mallory to be slaughtered.

He tried to push the idea of defeat out of his head, but it stayed at the forefront of his mind, taunting him as he dodged through the trees. He was breathing hard and his calves were burning as he burst through the final barrier of vegetation before the cave. The Whunes were already there, of course; they could traverse the woods much quicker than any mere human. All three of the monsters were at the entrance of the cave, sniffing around at the nearly burnt out campfire. Mallory and Javic were nowhere to be seen. Belford halted his reckless sprint, but it was too late, the Whunes had already heard him and craned their necks in the direction of the commotion.

All three Whunes put their backs to the campfire now as they leapt towards Belford. They could outrun him easily, but Belford turned to flee anyway. While turning, he saw one of the larger Whunes stumble – taken by surprise with an arrow that streamed out from the dark depths of the cave. The arrow buried itself deep between the monster's thick shoulder blades. The Whune staggered forward, but quickly regained its composure. It turned back towards the cave just in time for a second arrow to strike it right between the eyes. The Whune collapsed, its muscles convulsing uncontrollably as it took its final breaths.

The female Whune stopped running as her larger companion fell twitching to the ground. She turned around and began dashing back towards the cave. No more arrows were released – Javic's supply was exhausted. The second large Whune didn't even notice that the other two were no longer following in its flanks. Axe held high, it continued its charge towards Belford.

Belford bounded through the trees with his arms held out in front of him, trying to stop the low-hanging branches from whipping across his face. Suddenly his foot snagged under a twisted root that had breached the surface of the soil. He landed hard, face first, deeply scratching his palms as they collided with the rocks and dirt to break his fall. He expected to feel the sting of the Whune's axe, white hot as it burrowed deep into his flesh, but the moment stretched on, too long for how short his lead had been. Instead, he heard the Whune grunt and the clash of steel ring out behind him. He jumped to his feet and spun around.

Arlin!

The nimble man swung wildly at the Whune, dodging sideways as the Whune swiped back at him with its axe. The axe collided with a tree, digging deep into the trunk. Arlin kicked the Whune's right arm, forcing it to abandon its weapon. The Whune backhanded Arlin with its other arm, disarming Arlin's sword while knocking him to the ground at the same moment. Arlin scrambled for his sword, but the Whune had already retrieved its own weapon. It swung it down towards Arlin. He rolled to the side, avoiding the chop, and was back on his feet in an instant, dodging deftly left and right. The Whune swung its axe around madly, audibly slicing the air with mighty force.

A scream rang out from within the cave, rattling Arlin's concentration. The Whune clipped Arlin's helmet with its axe, dazing him under the crushing weight of the blow.

Belford's feet were already carrying him towards the cave before he even realized he was moving again. Mallory and Javic needed him. He hoped Arlin would be alright.

Arlin was on the ground a second time, but this time he threw a handful of dirt into the Whune's bulging eyes. Fighting even more desperately than before, Arlin removed his own helmet and began using it as a bludgeon, repeatedly bashing it against the side of the Whune's head before it could regain its eyesight.

Belford entered the cave and quickly found himself blind in the darkness. He fumbled around at his belt, unsheathing his puny knife while his eyes desperately tried to adjust to the dim light. He moved deeper into the cave as soon as he was able to discern some shapes. Another scream echoed against the walls. Belford threw himself into the darkness, knife held out in front of him in a wobbling hand.

He could hear grunting and multiple bodies shuffling across the cave floor just ahead of him. There was hardly room for Belford to stand. The Whune must have been crawling at this point. A body lay crumpled against the wall. Belford knelt down, quickly checking for a heartbeat. It was Javic – he was still alive. Warm blood was trickling from the side of his head. Belford grabbed the box of matches out of Javic's left pocket.

His fingers fumbling about as he pulled out one of only three remaining matchsticks. He struck its head against the rough surface on the outside of the box.

Tsak.

The match sparked, but did not ignite. He struck it again and again in desperation.

Tsak. Tsak. Tsak. Fwoosh.

As the flame ignited, he could see Mallory at the very back of the cave. She was curled up against the wall as far back as she could get. The Whune was scooting closer and closer to her, still holding its axe.

The match went out.

Mallory and the Whune vanished into the darkness.

Belford nearly cursed out loud, but stopped himself. He struck another match as quickly as he could.

Tsak. Tsak. Fwoosh.

The Whune was nearly upon Mallory now; there was no more time to spare. Belford stumbled over something – a quick glance revealed the over-shirt he had blanketed across Mallory earlier, crumpled on the cave floor. Before the matchstick could extinguish itself, Belford scooped up the over-shirt and lit it like a torch. The cloth was burning up fast, but for the moment he could still see. He dropped the shirt to the ground and immediately lunged onto the back of the Whune.

He stabbed into it with his belt knife. He thrust again and again into the creature's flesh, but the blade was simply too short to reach its vital organs. The Whune picked itself up off the ground, smashing Belford hard against the ceiling of the cave. He lost the knife as the monster flung him from its back with a quick jerking motion. The Whune tried to roar, but the choker around its neck caused it to gasp for air instead.

There was nowhere for Belford to go.

The beast held its axe up greedily above Belford's head, preparing to finish him off. He flung his arms up in front of his face – a useless gesture.

With a grunt, Mallory brought a large rock down on the back of the Whune's head. It landed with a solid thud. The creature flopped to the floor, motionless.

Without a word, Mallory quickly scooted past Belford and the fallen Whune, making her way over to Javic's side. She began trying to coax him back to consciousness.

Suddenly, Arlin swept into the cave, sword drawn in one hand, a flaming stick in the other. The light from Belford's shirt had all but gone out by now as the cloth burned through. As Arlin came closer, Belford could see a deep gash running down his left cheek. He was covered in blood from the tip of his sword to the bottom of his boots, but it appeared as though at least most of it was not his own. His helmet was still off and his blond hair had a heavy spattering of blood across it as well. His eyes burned fiercely as he quickly assessed the situation.

Belford noticed a sweet scent in the air as Mallory sprang to her feet and turned towards Arlin.

Javic was awake now, holding the side of his head while he looked around cautiously.

Mallory ran to Arlin's side and hugged him desperately, tears flowing from the corners of her eyes.

"Careful of the flame," said Arlin as he focused on the downed Whune. Arlin pulled away from Mallory and began making his way over to the creature. The front of Mallory's riding dress was smeared with the blood from Arlin's armor.

Looking closer at the Whune beside him on the ground, Belford noticed that it was still breathing. Mallory's blow had only knocked it unconscious.

The sweet smell in the air was becoming stronger. It seemed familiar somehow.

As Arlin came closer, the light from the flames reflected off the object around the Whune's neck.

Lavender, thought Belford, *that's what I'm smelling.*

Arlin raised his sword to run the Whune through.

The object around the creature's neck shimmered again.

"Stop!" shouted Belford, leaping from the ground to block Arlin's attack.

Arlin pulled back in surprise. "What's the meaning of this?" he asked sternly.

Javic and Mallory were looking at Belford in confusion as well.

Belford leaned over the Whune, inspecting the object around its neck. It was some sort of thin chain, digging deep into the Whune's skin. The chain was squeezing so tight that hemorrhaging blisters had formed all around its neck. Its raw flesh was bulging overtop the chain.

"Help me turn it over," demanded Belford.

Arlin handed Mallory his makeshift torch. "We shouldn't waste time," he said. "The foul beast could wake at any moment." Despite his words, Arlin knelt down beside Belford and the two of them began trying to roll the massive creature onto its back.

Belford had some difficulty pulling the Whune's arm under once they got the creature onto its side, but after he did, the Whune flopped all the way over to its back. "Bring the light near," he said as he lowered his face closer to the front of the Whune's neck. Something was attached to the front of the chain, but it was buried deep within the bleeding folds of the Whune's thick skin.

Mallory brought the light closer, hesitantly. She shared a silent look with Arlin, but neither of them argued with Belford's command.

Belford sunk his fingers into the crevice formed by the chain and pulled back the folded flesh. A glimmer of gold flashed out from between the folds. Belford pulled the skin back a little farther. Two tiny golden butterfly wings emerged, ornate, just the way he created them. Belford's hand recoiled.

This is impossible… it can't be… Kara is just a young girl, safe and sound back in Bronam.

Belford reached down again and pulled back one of the Whune's eyelids. The Whune's eye was unfocused; its pupil shrunken to the size of a pinprick. The iris was a deep green; it reflected the light of the torch back to him. There was no mistaking it, the scent of lavender gently floated up Belford's nostrils, even overcoming the telltale stench excreted by the Whunes. It was too horrible to even consider. This was Kara, he knew it for sure now – he could see it in her eyes.

But how could it be Kara?

If Whunes were people, that meant Wilgoblikan must have been turning whole towns of innocent people into these monsters just to hunt him down.

That means we've been slaying people every time we cut down a Whune... that I'm responsible... a murderer....

Belford vomited onto the cave floor, retching over and over again until only bile came up from his otherwise empty stomach. And then nothing was coming out, but he kept going through the motions. His stomach still churned and twisted into knots, his throat tightening, making him feel as though he'd been kicked hard in the chest. His heart physically ached as he dry heaved again and again.

"What's wrong?" Mallory was at his side, patting his back, her eyes wide with concern.

Tears were streaming down Belford's face by the time the heaving subsided. He wiped the vomit from the corners of his mouth with his grimy fingers and then spit a few times to get the bitter taste of bile off his tongue. He looked up, though his eyes remained unfocused, staring towards the far wall of the cave.

"They're people," he hardly managed to whisper. "Whunes are people."

The Whune's arm – Kara's arm – began to twitch.

Javic looked pallid. Belford wasn't sure if it was from the news or simply from the blood loss. Either way, Javic said nothing; he just stared back at Belford with glossy eyes.

"It will wake soon," said Arlin. He held no emotion whatsoever on his face. "I need to kill it, or it will attack us again."

"No!" cried Belford. "Didn't you hear me, Whunes are people... I know her...."

Arlin looked into Belford's eyes. Belford tried to give him his sternest stare through the tears in his lashes.

Arlin sighed. "Alright then," he said. "Help me drag it outside before the light dies out."

Arlin and Belford each took one of Kara's deformed arms and began to pull with all their strength, dragging her towards the entrance of the cave.

"What are you going to do?" asked Mallory.

"I've got some rope in my saddlebag," said Arlin, "though I dare not hold the fiend with such little restraint for long."

Javic didn't move from his position against the cave wall. He appeared to be deep in thought as Belford and Arlin made their way past him with Kara.

Once they reached the mouth of the cave, Arlin ran into the woods to retrieve his steed. The amber light from the remaining coals of the fire Belford built earlier was finally beginning to fade away. When Arlin got back, he dismounted from his horse and pulled a bundle of rope out of his saddlebag. He looped the bundle over his shoulder and helped Belford drag Kara the rest of the way to the nearest tree.

Arlin began stringing the rope around Kara and the tree, around and around again, taking special care to lock down her bulging arms as tightly as possible. It was hard to believe this was the same young girl he had met in Bronam. Apart from her eyes, she was virtually unrecognizable.

Nearby, just beyond the edge of the trees, the corpse of the Whune Arlin had been fighting earlier lay in a bloody mass of crumpled flesh. Its face had been beaten in by Arlin's helmet. The helmet was still lying next to the poor creature's head, covered in blood and chunks of broken cartilage. The Whune's body had been carved up by Arlin's sword as well. Belford forced himself to look even closer at the remains. Around one of its fingers was a thin silver ring, a wedding band, half buried in the flesh of the creature's knuckle.

Belford nearly retched again; he had to turn away.

Arlin finished tying the rope around Kara and walked over to stand beside Belford. "What are we to do now?" he asked. "Whoever this was before, they are no longer human. What do you intend?"

Belford had been staring at Kara, but now he shifted his gaze over to Arlin. The determined look in his eyes was slightly crazed. "I'm going to change her back."

CHAPTER

22

Unseen Eyes

Distant howls tore through the forested valley – her brethren were calling to her. They'd found something. She started in the direction of the cries, eagerly anticipating the taste of her next kill.

I won't let you do it.

The meddling voice shook her concentration for the hundredth time. Ever since she first saw the boy in Felington, it wouldn't leave her alone.

Shut up! I'll do what I want, she snapped back.

Her foot suddenly seized up as she went to place her next step. She tripped, barely catching herself against a nearby tree.

Her temples throbbed with pressure. The battle for her mind was becoming a tedious one. A single moment of lapsed concentration was all it took for the eager presence in the back of her head to take control.

Leave me alone, she thought, *go away!*

I won't let you hurt anyone else! The voice was screaming now.

The resistance angered her. This was her body. She let out a roar of her own and began to beat her fists against the sides of her head. She would pummel the voice into submission! The edges of her vision went fuzzy for a moment after each blow she landed.

Yes! The voice was laughing now, taunting her. *Keep going! Hurt yourself!*

She stopped her physical assault immediate – she was only giving it what it wanted. She changed her approach. The voice was too weak to control her as long as she stayed focused. She pushed through the mental resistance and forced her feet to keep walking in the direction of her brethren. She could see smoke rising into the air; a campfire was nearby.

No!

She ignored the cry. Her scabbed lips formed a smirk. She had bested the intrusive presence. As she went on, it continued to try to trip her. Even with the hindrance, she was still making steady progress towards the thin smoke trail. She could smell the charred particles now. She was close.

The forest opened up into a small clearing at the mouth of a cave. She could hear human voices coming from inside the dark hole. The other Whunes were already dead, their bodies lying motionless in the clearing.

She tried to move forward, but her legs suddenly went stiff, holding her in place within the brush at the edge of the clearing. The voice in her head couldn't have stopped her alone, but another part of her was hesitant to attack as well. She didn't yet know what she was up against. She was concerned she might lose the fight. Normally she would have been able to suppress her worries and serve her master's will, but the annoying voice in her head latched onto the slight hesitation and used it to overpower her.

The voice remained silent. It was concentrating hard on keeping her still. A man in a suit of armor emerged from the mouth of the cave. He was covered in blood. The sweet scent was intoxicating to her senses. He strode off into the forest on the other side of the clearing.

Her legs began to twitch, all of her instincts begging her to pursue the man like a cat to a mouse, but the intrusive presence in her mind was growing bolder and more confident with every second it remained in control. It was able to stop her legs from straying more than a step or two in the man's direction.

The man returned shortly to the clearing, now on horseback. He dismounted and withdrew a bundle of rope from the horse's saddlebag before stepping back into the cave. A moment later he emerged again, this time with another man, a younger one, dragging the body of a Whune between them.

She watched the curious sight unfold. Soon, her eyes were drawn to the younger man's odd footwear. The shoes were just as her master had described. He was the one they were after – the one she'd been created to destroy – she was sure of it!

Her resolve hardened, quickly overpowering everything else. She won the battle of wills, regaining full control of her faculties, but she remained still, held back by her own accord this time. The other three Whunes had been defeated in an ill-fated attack. Her adversaries were not to be underestimated. She couldn't risk a direct assault. No one besides she knew the location of her master's target. If she attacked and failed, the young man would get away, but if she reported his location to Wilgoblikan at once, she and her brethren could sweep down on him in an unstoppable avalanche of destruction.

She crouched down, remaining hidden as the young man unexpectedly drew nearer to her. He was inspecting one of the other Whunes' corpses. The armored man took this time to tie the Whune they'd dragged from the cave to a tree. It was not dead as she originally assumed, merely unconscious – a peculiar course of action for the humans to be taking, keeping a Whune alive.

"What are we to do now?" the armored man asked after he finished securing the unconscious Whune. "Whoever this was before, they are no longer human. What do you intend?"

She listened intently for the younger man's response – the more information she could gather for her master, the better.

"I'm going to change her back," he said quietly.

The armored man frowned at the young man's declaration. Suddenly, he peered out into the forest, straight in her direction – perhaps sensing the unseen eyes spying.

She was still obscured by the brush, but slowly withdrew now, sinking back into the forest in case the armored man decided to investigate further.

She needed to reach her master before their target moved on from the cave. She tried to make haste through the forest, but again, the meddlesome presence worked to confuse her feet, slowing her progress to that of a drunken stumble.

The voice inside her head resonated with the young man's words, emboldened.

Change her back? He can change her back? Is it really possible? I might still have a chance!

The words buzzed around her head like an incessant fly.

CHAPTER

23

The Call of Death

Pain-filled wails echoed out hopelessly. The despair seemed to magnify as the sound entered the hollow of the cave. The dreadful cries carried up well above the canopy of the forest as the creature shook in its bindings. The disturbance sent a flock of nearby roosting magpies soaring skyward in search of safer nesting ground. All else had been silent for quite some time now, with the natural-born creatures all giving the Whune a wide berth. The pure horror in the monster's tones settled harshly on Javic, rattling his very sense of compassion.

The Whune was transforming, albeit slowly, and although Javic normally had a great interest for anything to do with the Power, he just couldn't bring himself to watch this particular procedure. Instead, he sat quietly, easing his battered body just within the mouth of the cave. Beside him sat an equally silent Mallory. They were both doing their best to avoid catching the madness that hung foul in the air around the makeshift camp.

Belford had been obsessing for hours about how to turn the girl back into her old self. Ever since they captured the Whune, he had been pacing back and forth, chattering endlessly about human physiology. At first he tried to explain some of the concepts of his plan to Javic, but it had all gone completely over his head. Belford drew a dozen diagrams in the muddy soil with a stick. It was as if he were trying to solve a complicated puzzle in his mind, only there were far too many pieces for him to keep track of all at once.

By the time the moon came up, Belford claimed to have worked out what he needed to do. Nowhere in his plans had he mentioned the terrible pain he would be inflicting upon the poor girl. The screams were mammoth-sized roars.

"We need to move on – start heading south again," said Arlin.

Belford didn't respond. He wasn't letting anything shake his focus – not even good advice. It was as if he were enchanted by the call of a siren, already past the point of no return, jagged rocks glistening just beneath the surface.

Javic's back tensed up as another howl ripped through the night. This was all getting far too dangerous.

How easily might she break free of her bindings and tear us all apart?

Her cries were so loud they could have roused the dead. Javic worried her wails might call down more monsters upon them. Their luck would run out eventually – it was only a matter of time. Sooner or later, more Whunes would find them. They needed to do as Arlin suggested and put the cave far behind them.

The howls continued. There was so much fear and hatred in her cries. Javic could feel the intensity building in the air as he waited through a moment of eerie calm; it sent chills up and down his spine each time she grew silent. After a while the animalistic sounds restarted. Soon they began to morph, becoming more human-like. It wasn't until the howls became the helpless sobs of a young girl that the horror truly struck home for Javic. It sounded like Belford was killing her. The weeping was almost more than he could bear.

His heart sank. What small amount of doubt remained about Salvine's fate quickly resolved itself. He knew with a terrible certainty why the Goblikan wizard had taken her from him. Becoming a Whune was a far worse fate than anything he had dared imagine for her. Just like the girl tied to the tree outside, Salvine had been used and perverted, her body molded into a vessel of pure destruction and hatred – the truth stung at the corners of Javic's eyes. The dark wizard violated her, consumed all her goodness, and left behind a monster in her flesh. Javic's hands began to shake as fury settled deep into his bones. Salvine hadn't just been taken from him – she was turned into the thing he most detested!

As a particularly bloodcurdling scream imposed itself upon the night, Javic found himself unable to keep to his own thoughts any longer. He turned from the campfire and faced the night in earnest.

Convulsive tremors tore through the girl's naked body. The torment and strain of the procedure was clear in her face. It was a shock to her system. She whimpered and moaned, sobbing uncontrollably between bouts of screaming. It was plain to see she was suffering. Arlin stood behind her, pulling the rope tight against her body. She stayed pinned to the tree as chunks of flesh shed away. The tumors and muscles melted off. Some shrank back within the girl's body while others literally dripped to the ground in revolting piles of gooey flesh.

Belford's face was a mask of concentration. He was sweating profusely, beads of moisture clinging to his brow. All the while, he kept his eyes locked on the girl.

Soon, the transformation was finished. The girl fell completely still. Arlin loosened his grip on the rope and she slumped forward onto the ground. Belford lowered his hands to his side, his whole face drooping with exhaustion as he let out a small sigh of relief.

Javic couldn't help but take in the girl's nude form. His face flushed mildly as he gazed upon her. She appeared to be about his same age, and she was quite pretty. All she had on was a thin necklace with a golden butterfly pendant dangling from it. Her skin was fair with soft-olive undertones and she had a slight amount of freckling about her nose. Her light-brown hair had a mild red tint, though that was only noticeable when the light from the fire reflected directly off its shiny surface. She was slender with curvy hips and long legs.

Under any other circumstance, Javic would have found her beauty mesmerizing, but all of the excitement that should have accompanied seeing a girl naked for the first time in his life was lost. All he could think about was Salvine, alone and afraid as the Goblikan stripped her of her innocence. Javic would have gladly stricken the image of the girl's body from his mind. This wasn't how he wanted to remember his first naked girl. He diverted his eyes from her private areas, but it was too late. The mental image would not fade. He was filled with an overwhelming wave of sadness.

Belford stepped closer to the girl. "Kara," he said softly. "Kara, can you hear me?"

The girl's eyes opened slowly; her head rising to look up at him. Belford smiled meekly. Without any warning, Kara burst forward with startling ferocity, slashing wildly at Belford's face with her fingers as if she still had the pestilent claws of a Whune. Her pupils were dilated, seemingly unaccustomed to even the slightest amount of light. She snapped her teeth loudly as she struggled against the rope still looped across her breasts. She nearly broke free from the binding, but her arms became entangled again as Arlin pulled back hard on the line.

Belford was shaken. Blood trickled down from his right cheek. One of Kara's swipes had landed a glancing scratch against his skin. Belford wiped the back of his hand across the cut, but it only smeared the blood around. He did not heal himself with the Power, though it would have been easy for him to do so.

"Hold her tight," Belford said to Arlin.

"Are you sure you know what you're doing?" Arlin asked, his eyes becoming quite large as he spoke.

Belford ignored him. He moved in close again, this time staying just out of reach of Kara's thrashing hands and feet. He closed his eyes for a moment, breathing deeply as Kara began to emit a low growl from the bottom of her throat. She had the appearance of a human, but there was no humanity present within her sinister, green eyes. Belford's face was still full of compassion. His gaze shifted. He seemed to be staring straight through to the back of Kara's skull. He was using the Power.

A vein in Kara's forehead began to bulge, pulsating rhythmically with the frantic beating of her heart. The muscles under her eyes twitched as scream after scream racked through her body all over again. The cries grew quickly in intensity until they were the most severe yet.

Javic tried to block out the noise by covering his ears, but the piercing cries broke through just as loudly as if he'd done nothing at all. The sound ceased abruptly. Javic looked up, expecting either Belford to be finished meddling with her mind or for the girl to be dead. Instead, Kara's jaw strained wide open – her face still writhing in anguish – only her voice had given out. It was as if she simply forgot how to scream.

As Belford continued, Kara's jaw swung loose. Her eyes rolled up into the back of her head and she began to shake violently, her whole body seizing.

"Belford!" Javic called out. "You're killing her!"

Javic's exclamation seemed to bring Belford back to reality. He ceased his invisible actions immediately and began to openly weep. Large tears dripped from his eyes as he slid forward and cradled Kara's head between his hands.

"Hold on," he cried out to her. His whole body began to glow with the unusual, blue light that always accompanied his healing touch.

Mallory was at Javic's side now, pulling him back, away from the scene – trying to stop him from watching. He allowed himself to be taken.

"Come on!" Belford shouted.

Javic glanced back. Kara was laid out on her back now with Belford on top of her. He was using both hands, pushing down between her breasts, compressing her chest over and over again in desperate thrusts. Javic felt moisture on his cheek; he looked up, expecting to see rain clouds, but the skies were clear. He realized he was beginning to tear up now as well.

With a loud snap, the temperature of the air plummeted to near-freezing levels as a great flash of light burst out of Belford's fingertips like a bolt of lightning. The light blinded Javic, leaving spots of color on his vision as the arc of electric energy surged straight down into Kara's chest. She gasped for air, her back arching up with an intense spasm as the charge coursed through her veins. A strange metallic scent lingered in the air. The spots began to fade from Javic's sight.

Belford moved to Kara's side, supporting her head and neck as she struggled to sit up. Her eyes were wide with fear as her chest heaved up and down.

"Kara?" Belford asked again. "Please look at me." But Kara didn't respond to her name at all, merely continuing to stare dolefully into the surrounding forest, as if she alone could see some invisible terror lurking just within the shadows. She avoided Belford's eyes as she sat in her muted state. It was as if she wasn't even aware of his presence.

"Well," said Arlin, "you put up a valiant effort. There is honor in that, at least."

"No," whispered Belford, "I can fix her." His voice was adamant, although tears were streaming unabated down the sides of his face now. "I just need more time."

Arlin looked up at the moon. Already, its movement was low against the horizon. "We can't waste another day here," he said. "We must proceed south."

Belford nodded reluctantly. "I know," he said. "We're bringing her with us."

At that news, Arlin looked as if he might mount a protest – Kara would certainly slow them down and would very well be a liability to the group – but once again, all it took was one look into Belford's eyes and it was obvious that there would be no argument.

Before the moon went down, Belford used the Power to produce some simple clothing for Kara. It was truly remarkable to watch lumps of dirt and fallen leaves turn into a tightly threaded sheet of ivory cloth. Belford draped the sheet around Kara like a blanket, leaving only her head sticking out the top. He grabbed his knife, intending to use it to cut slits in the fabric where her arms could poke through, but Kara became horribly frightened as he approached her with the blade. She made no noise as she recoiled from the knife, merely curling up into a petrified lump on the ground.

The utter terror on Kara's face was heartrending for Javic to watch. He imagined Salvine in her place, brutalized and broken – unable to escape what had happened to her. To Javic, it seemed like a fate worse than death.

Belford quickly sheathed the knife and knuckled his forehead with his closed fist for a moment in a quick self-rebuke for having been so careless. Kara was incapable of movement; the fear had shut her down, literally paralyzing her entire body. Belford showed Kara his empty hands before crouching down beside her. He began to cradle her in his arms like a newborn baby. He continued to comfort Kara in this way, making soft hushing noises every couple of seconds until she finally calmed down enough to regain control of her motor functions. After helping her to her feet, Belford retied the sheet, this time allowing her arms to stick out over the top of the cloth. It resembled a strapless gown now, the hem at the bottom dangling to just above her bare ankles.

Belford hadn't thought to make shoes for Kara before the moon descended, so Javic scavenged a few bits of leather scrap out of Arlin's saddlebag and began binding the soles of Kara's feet with the rough hide. As long as no one displayed any blades, her expression remained distant with her eyes unfocused and unblinking, as if her mind were vacant of any thought or emotion. She allowed Javic to wrap the leather around her feet without hassle. Her skin was soft to the touch; her tiny toes, dainty and fragile.

As they walked through the trees, a strange sense of nostalgia began to settle over Javic. The atmosphere was becoming heavy; the winds had come and gone with the previous morning's storm. Although the sky remained overcast with a palette of gray, here and there, bits of blue were beginning to peek through. Rays of sunlight pierced through the upper atmosphere like holy arrows – pillars of heavenly light jutting through the cloud cover to ease the dreariness of the land below. It reminded Javic of home – of riding Olli through the woods around Darrenfield without a care in the world. The forest came alive again as birds flew overhead and squirrels rustled about in the brush, jostling over the odd nut or berry. The scent of pine and fresh sap drifted about, sweetening the breeze.

It was a false calm.

In the distance, the exiting black storm clouds drifted slowly to the east in an imposing block of churning coal. The rain hung dense below, like a curtain to some abominable stage. It stretched as far as the eye could see, all across the horizon. Javic knew things could never go back to the way they used to be. A darkness had crept in and tainted his world. So much had been taken from him.

He could no longer look back on the good times without feeling a vast sense of loss – not just for Salvine, though that was a huge part of it, but for his entire life on the farm. He missed his days spent working the crops and taking care of the animals. He missed the simplicity of it all. His greatest fear had once been that Salvine would reject him when she learned of his true feelings for her. Now he would gladly take that rejection one thousand times over if it meant keeping everyone alive and well, safe and at home.

Next to Javic, Belford's expression was etched with tension lines. His puffy eyes told a tale of much sorrow as well. Javic understood why, of course – they were both responsible for killing Whunes. Now that they knew the truth, it was difficult not to imagine the innocent people behind the beasts. Even so, Javic's conscience remained clear: Every Whune he slayed would have killed him had he not ended them first – it was the Goblikan who was truly responsible for murdering those people, not Javic, not Belford. Killing Whunes stopped them from hurting anyone else; it was an act of mercy, freeing them from their terrible fate.

Unfortunately, Belford didn't see things that way; he was punishing himself harshly for crimes he hadn't committed. Javic realized that the dark wizard's actions were beyond their control. Perhaps Belford would realize that too, one day. But for now, Belford was brooding. He would continue to feel the shattering weight of those deaths upon his soul until he was able to admit to himself that he wasn't really in control after all. None of them had ever been in control, not really – not since starting their journey, anyway. Control was merely an illusion. They could only react, nothing more. They did what they had to in order to survive.

After a while, Arlin stopped their march to feed everybody one last meal out of his and Mallory's quickly dwindling stock of provisions. He rationed out the last of the food as Javic double-checked his compass to make sure they were still moving south on a constant heading. As long as they remained on course, they would make it to Rasile by nightfall and wouldn't need to worry about hunting for more food.

Arlin handed Kara a slice of rye bread. She wiggled her nose at it, but did not take a bite. She immediately lost interest, dropping it to the ground as she returned to staring off into the distance at nothing in particular. Belford picked up the bread and brushed the dirt off with his shirt. He began to nibble at it as Arlin passed around sticks of dried jerky.

Javic glanced over at Belford, half expecting him to make a comment about having to eat more dried meat, but Belford's emotions were too frayed to mount a complaint.

Kara picked her head up as Arlin extended the beef to Belford. She sniffed deeply at the air before turning around to face Arlin with a sudden jerk. She snatched the jerky right out of Arlin's hand and crammed the whole thing into her mouth. It was more than she could chew at once, but she somehow managed to choke it all down, throwing her head back like a bird with every swallow.

Arlin frowned disapprovingly as he retrieved another portion of meat for Belford. Kara finished her meal and began looking around for more. Belford handed his new portion over to her without a second thought. She took the offering straightaway, consuming it just as ravenously as the first.

They continued walking at a grueling pace all day until the afternoon turned into evening and the soft breeze began to feel like an icy chill on Javic's skin. As they crossed a small stream, Arlin called for a break. Javic's feet were beginning to ache, so he sat on a rock to rest. Belford crouched down over the stream and drank deeply from the clear water; he was the only one, other than Kara, not carrying a water pouch with him.

Mallory offered to fill Javic's canteen. He accepted with much gratitude. The pause gave him time to remove his boots. He massaged his throbbing heels and dumped out several tiny pebbles that had accumulated in the toe of his left boot.

Arlin soon became antsy to get moving again, but Mallory, Belford, and Javic all wanted to rest for a little while longer. Kara stood by motionless like a statue; she was the only one of the group that looked as if she could continue marching forever without exhaustion. Her gown was damp and sullied with clay and mud from the bed of the stream. She had dragged the bottom of the gown through the silt without a hint of hesitation.

She looked like a serene Earth goddess – a depiction of Mast herself – white robes growing out of the soil; an expression of perfect patience on her creaseless face, both girlish and ancient. She was a force of nature.

As Javic admired her relentless will, he noticed that the leather binding from around her left foot was missing. He approached her and lifted her leg up as if inspecting a horse's hoof for thorns. The bottom of Kara's foot was torn up and already badly blistered. Blood was seeping out from several spots where rocks and sharp sticks had pierced the skin, but Kara didn't seem to be in any pain.

When Belford finished drinking from the stream, he joined Javic in cleaning up Kara's injuries and attaching a new binding around her foot and ankle. Kara's lack of a pain response was disturbing to Javic: Although her Whune aggression appeared to have been tamed by Belford's meddling, there was no telling what permanent damage he might have inflicted on her brain, or what other Whune traits she might still possess.

With darkness quickly approaching, Javic was beginning to worry that they might not make it all the way to Rasile after all. Soon, however, the trees began to thin. Somewhere off in the distance, the sounds of a blacksmithing hammer rang out faintly – one clang after another in even intervals. Javic grinned at Mallory, and she smiled back at him sweetly. As the forest opened into grassland, they could see the main road just off to the east. Arlin, who had been leading the way on horseback, rode out ahead to make sure there weren't any Whunes poised to ambush them in the final stretch before the city. Everybody else remained as inconspicuous as possible just within the tree line as they waited for Arlin to signal that it was safe to continue.

Belford sat down with Kara and removed the binding from her left foot again. He examined her sole thoroughly, borrowing Javic's canteen to clean off the dirt from around her wounds. He fretted awhile over the largest blister; it covered most of her heel. Javic didn't think it was the injuries that Belford was truly concerned about, rather the absence of pain. There was no telling what exactly was damaged inside Kara's head – perhaps she couldn't feel anything at all.

Belford brushed the hair out of her face with the back of his fingers. She still wouldn't make eye contact with him, or anybody else for that matter. She seemed to be mentally detached from the physical world around her. She showed no indication of awareness as Javic walked by right in front of her face. She simply stared through him as if he did not exist.

As they waited for Arlin, Kara began fidgeting. Other than her overreaction to Belford's belt knife and her ravenous eating, it was the first unprovoked movement Javic had seen her make all day. She looked anxious as she teetered back and forth in her seated position. Her eyes were even more unblinking than usual as she shifted her stare slightly, shooting her intense gaze deep into the forest behind them. Without warning, she took in a quick gasp of air and began to shriek at the top of her lungs. The sudden noise made Javic jump. Belford and Mallory were startled as well. Belford tried to quiet her down, but there was nothing he could do to stop her screams.

"Put your hand over her mouth or something," said Mallory as she covered her own ears with her hands, attempting to muffle the racket.

"I would," said Belford, "but I'm afraid she'll bite my fingers!"

Javic thought it to be a legitimate concern.

Kara flailed her arms and scrambled to her feet. Belford was right behind her, grabbing her around the waist as she attempted to run off into the open field that separated them from the road. He dragged her to the ground, nearly disrobing her in the process. She kicked and screamed as she tried to push Belford off. Javic ran over to join the throng of limbs, helping Belford restrain Kara's legs. It took all of his weight and strength to stop her from throwing him off as she thrashed about, struggling more violently than a cornered boar. Her strength seemed about ten times greater than what a young girl should have been capable of producing.

Suddenly Javic heard something moving towards them through the trees. Panic swept through his body.

She's trying to flee for a reason!

She sensed whatever was coming, but they ignorantly disregarded her warning. Now, it was too late to run.

Kara kicked Javic in the side of the head while he was distracted. He loosened his grip and Kara managed to break free, escaping Belford's grasp as well. Javic's head was spinning, disoriented by the blow. He saw a flash of brown moving quickly through the trees; it was large – too large to be human. Neither Belford nor Mallory had noticed the creature over Kara's shrieking, but before Javic could stand up, the beast burst from the trees right behind them. It stopped over Javic and picked him up by the nape of his tunic.

"You alright?" asked Thorin.

Javic wanted to laugh. He felt silly, but relief poured through his veins. Thorin wasn't a monster, though he was awfully large. Javic could have kissed him full on the lips, he was so relieved.

"It's Javic and Belford," Thorin shouted over his shoulder. He put Javic down on his feet and sprinted over to help Belford handle Kara. Belford was back on top of her, but she was still struggling desperately to free herself.

Elric dashed out of the trees, breathing hard. Javic was still in shock. Elric paused for a moment; taking in his grandson's disheveled hair and filthy clothing. He frowned deeply as his eyes fell across the cuts and bruising on the side of Javic's head. Without words, he embraced him warmly with a tight hug.

Javic wrapped his arms around his grandfather, returning the love. Javic felt emotion welling up inside him; his whole body tingled as he melted into his grandfather's arms, feeling Elric's chest heave in and out as he regained his breath. Javic found himself suppressing tears. As the hug continued, he couldn't hold them in any longer and allowed them to flow freely from his eyes.

"We were beginning to fear the worst for you guys," said Thorin as he finished wrangling up Kara. "What's with this one?" He nodded towards Kara – she had fallen silent again, though Javic's ears were still ringing from her wails.

"It's a long story," said Belford. "Where's Shiara?" Surprisingly, he seemed genuinely concerned by her absence as he scanned his eyes back and forth across the trees.

"Oh, she's over in Rasile with the wagon" said Thorin. "We arrived nearly two days ago. Elric and I have been searching for you two ever since."

Just then, Arlin came galloping back. He reined in and dismounted from his horse, greeting Thorin with a friendly nod and giving Elric a quick salute; he brought his closed fist swiftly to his chest in a distinct military gesture. Elric returned the salutation in kind, leaving Javic slightly puzzled by the whole exchange.

After Elric thanked Arlin for watching over the boys, the whole group began their final march into Rasile. Javic yawned audibly. He couldn't wait to rest his head on a soft pillow. His stomach rumbled in protest, but his priorities held steadfast: Sleep first, food later. Javic's eyelids were already beginning to droop as the city came into view.

A vast spiked wall cut across the rolling hills, giving rise to towers with arrow slits cut into their stone. A large building could be seen over the wall; it appeared to be some kind of factory. Plumes of dense smoke rose from a dozen wide chimneys on the building's slanted roof. The billows streamed upwards into the atmosphere, leaving behind the stink of sulfur. The acrid scent invaded Javic's nostrils as they got closer. Belford appeared to be disturbed by the odor as well. A frown appeared on his face as his eyes took on a vaguely distant expression. The clang of blacksmith hammers now mixed with other industrial noises – machines whirring in a constant hum that rattled through the ground. The general bustle of city life filled the air.

Thorin directed them through the crowded streets to a small inn located on the opposite side of town from the industrial district. The roads were long, sloped, and wet. Water flowed constantly down the streets from public wells located at the crest of every hill. The sidewalks stood above the level of the streets, requiring people to hop across large stepping stones at the center of the roads if they wished to bridge the gaps without getting wet. Horses had just enough room to move between the stepping stones, and the carts and wagons they pulled behind them glided along through wheel grooves with ease, guided safely around the stones as well. Carried away by the water, animal dung and other refuse flowed out through grates in the city wall, leaving the streets refreshingly clean.

Each stepping stone was spaced a full pace apart from the next, making it a challenge to get Kara across – she kept stepping down into the water flow. Eventually Belford quit trying to stop her despite the funny looks she was receiving from the locals. She seemed happier in the water. It was a childlike delight, like a little kid splashing through mud puddles. She had no concern for the mess it was making out of her gown.

Upon finding out where they were to be staying, Arlin and Mallory took their horse to a nearby stable while the rest of the group entered the inn. Belford looked nervous as they approached the room in which Shiara was staying. Javic wasn't sure why he was acting so strange at first, but as soon as Shiara greeted them he realized what Belford was dreading.

"I told you to stay at the wagon!" Shiara screamed at Belford. A nasty, dark-blue bruise surrounded her right eye, which she seemed barely capable of opening. The entire right side of her face was horribly swollen. "And what did you do?" she spat venomously, nostrils flaring. "You ran off into the forest like a conch-blowing moron!"

Belford slumped over onto the bed as Shiara continued to berate him.

"Do you know how *this* happened?" she asked, pointing at her own battered face. She continued before Belford had a chance to respond, "I had to stop a Whune from chasing you down – that's how!"

Javic stepped backwards into the hallway where the rest of the party was smartly waiting for Shiara to finish. Javic turned to Thorin, his curiosity getting the better of him. "Why is Shiara's face still so smashed up if that happened days ago? Can't she just heal herself with the Power?"

Thorin responded in a whisper as Shiara's shouts continued to surge out through the closed door. "Healing with the Power is very difficult," he said. "Neither of us really have much talent for Amelioration. If you don't know what you're doing, more harm can come of it than good. Sometimes it's best to let nature run its course."

"What's *Amelioration*?" asked Javic.

Thorin smiled thinly. "I forget sometimes how little you know about the Arcanum. *Amelioration* is a term used by Ver'ati to refer to the discipline of healing. Well, it's broader than that, really; any other permanent body enhancement would fall under that category as well, like altering ones appearance, physical ability or internal workings... you know, like growing gills and such."

Javic could hear the low tones of Belford's voice through the door as he began to speak. He was much quieter than Shiara and his words remained muffled. An intense, blue light shone out around the doorframe. Javic glanced up and down the hall, making sure no strangers were present to witness the display. After the light faded Thorin stuck his head in for a quick moment to make sure everything was alright. While the door was open, Javic got a glimpse of Shiara's face: She was healed, looking like her usual, pretty self, but she was still furious. Thorin closed the door again as the yelling started back up. After another minute Belford spoke again, he seemed to be defending himself now.

"I knew a man that did that once," said Thorin, "grew gills, I mean."

"Oh, yeah?" asked Javic. "How did that work out for him?"

"I'm not sure," said Thorin, shaking his head. "He disappeared early during the rebellion... a lot of people went missing back then, though. He could be dead, or maybe he just swam away...."

On the other side of the door, the heated conversation abruptly ceased. Javic assumed the scolding was complete and started to reach for the door handle, but before his fingers could reach the knob, a clear shout rang out through the wall.

"You did *WHAT?!*" Shiara screamed.

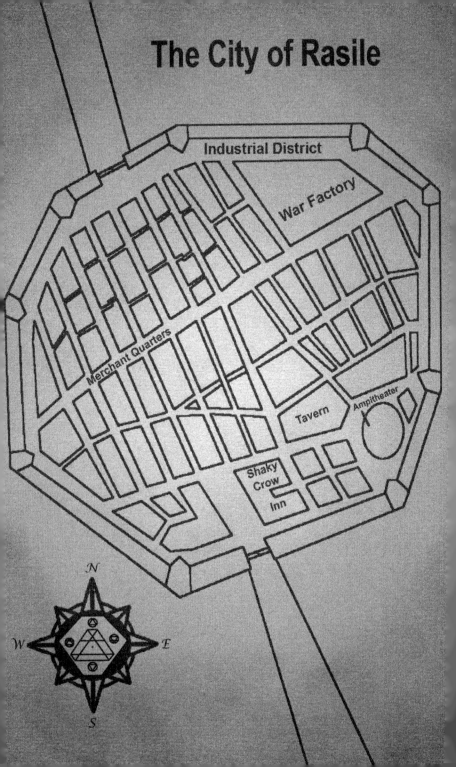

CHAPTER

24

Visions of Arcadia

"Reckless!" Shiara shouted. "You are an irresponsible idiot!"

Shiara stomped to the door and threw it open. She was fuming as she scanned her eyes callously across the group before settling on Kara. She grabbed her by the front of her gown and pulled her into the room before slamming the door shut again.

Belford bit down hard on his lower lip.

"Your meddling has merely prolonged her suffering – nothing more." Shiara looked as if she might strike Belford; she seemed barely capable of holding herself back. "You have sullied whatever memories you have of her! And for what?" she asked. "To drag her along like an invalid? For Mast's sake!"

"You're speaking as if she's already dead!" Belford cried out.

"She might as well be," said Shiara. She lowered her voice slightly, though she maintained a stern frown. "The girl can't be saved," she said. "A person stops being human when they're turned into a Whune. No one has ever come back from that."

Belford narrowed his eyes. "You knew Whunes were people?" he asked incredulously.

Shiara sighed. "Of course I did."

A look of disgust appeared on Belford's face. "Why didn't you tell me?"

"What good would it have done?" Shiara brushed a strand of stray hair off her face before sitting down on the edge of the bed directly across from Belford.

"But...."

"No buts," she said. "The girl you knew isn't in there anymore."

Belford turned towards Kara. She was staring blankly into the corner of the room.

"The best thing for her now would be to end her suffering."

Belford's head snapped back towards Shiara. "What are you saying?" he asked, narrowing his eyes even farther.

Shiara stared back at him, unblinking. "I think you know."

"No," said Belford, "I can't do it. I won't."

"You have to—"

"No!" he cried. "I can save her!"

"But you can't." Shiara put a consoling hand on Belford's shoulder, but he pushed it away instantly.

"Maybe I'm different!" he said stubbornly. "Maybe I *can* save her!" He was nearly shouting now.

Shiara glanced solemnly over at Kara. She hadn't moved since Shiara pulled her into the room. "What makes you think you're so special?" Shiara asked, looking back over at Belford.

Belford's eyes burned with fire. His whole face tightened into an unforgiving glare. There was only one way to prove to Shiara that he was different – but Elric had expressly warned him against showing his mark. Shiara didn't really expect an answer to her question; she was just trying to prove a point. Belford felt hopeless.

"If you won't end this," she said, "I will. I won't let you extend this poor girl's suffering any longer."

As Shiara stood up, Belford jumped to his feet and moved in between her and Kara. There wasn't really anything he could do if Shiara decided to destroy her, but he hoped the gesture would show his resolve.

"Get out of the way," said Shiara.

Belford had no other choice now; he needed more time to fix Kara. In an act of desperation Belford pulled off his shirt, exposing the Mark of Kings on his bicep.

"Put your shirt back on. You're not that attractive, and you're going to make yourself cold," said Shiara.

Her eyes wandered across his body. They froze on the Mark of Kings. She looked back and forth between Belford's face and the mark. Her expression glazed over as Belford put his shirt back on. She moved away from the bed and walked straight out of the room without another word.

Belford wasn't sure if he'd made the right choice, but he couldn't think of any other way to stop Shiara. At least he had more time now. He would figure out how to save Kara, no matter the cost. After Shiara's exit, nobody else entered the room. Belford was left alone to fret over Kara and his worrisome thoughts. After a while, he supposed Shiara and the others must have rented a different room for the night.

Belford led Kara over to one of the beds and had her lay down. He wasn't sure if she was capable of sleep – the Whunes never seemed to rest – but he figured the reclined position would be better for her body than standing in the corner of the room all night. Belford sat down beside her and stroked her hair idly with his fingertips. He had no idea how to proceed at fixing her.

She'll probably just start shrieking again if I use the Power on her anyway.

Instead, he settled for trying to comfort whatever part of her was still human. He didn't believe Shiara – Kara was still in there somewhere; she had to be.

As Belford became absorbed by his thoughts, a hopeful idea popped into his head: Maybe his memories could help him figure out how to fix Kara. He had no idea what sorts of things were locked away inside his mind. He was already capable of instinctively healing most wounds – where he came from, he was a doctor – he knew that much. If the answers really were hidden inside him, he owed it to Kara to figure out what they were.

Belford already knew where to start. He concentrated on his memories of Claire, attempting to stimulate the part of his mind where he thought his past must be locked away. He focused on his emotions the same way he did when he wanted to reach the Power, but instead of diverting the flow outwards, he pointed it back on himself, keeping the mental energy pent up inside. He drew out the feeling, dwelling on every detail of Claire he could remember as he began to paint an image of her in his mind.

The way the sun shone through her hair in the morning, bringing out the soft-caramel highlights in her delicate curls; the sweet fragrance of apricot on her skin, so tantalizingly smooth and touchable; the flirty giggle she let out from time to time whenever a conversation was beginning to get the least bit steamy. More and more details were coming back to him all the while – they were only little things, but each recovered memory felt like another victory.

As exhaustion settled within Belford, he noticed his thoughts drifting. His mind was clouding over, making it harder and harder to concentrate. He tried desperately to stop his thoughts from straying, but concerns for Kara began relentlessly slipping back in despite his efforts. Maybe Shiara was right about Kara. He had no idea what he was doing with her. What Wilgoblikan had done to her mind was still very much a mystery to him – for all he knew, every bit of it could have been corrupted and contaminated beyond repair.

Without meaning to, Belford fell asleep. At first he thought he was still awake – he was aware of his body lying in bed, but when he went to move his arm, he found it unwilling to respond to his commands. His body had fallen into a light slumber, yet his conscious mind still retained a sense of awareness. The feeling of the bed against his back engulfed him, and then faded away as a lucid dream coalesced around him. In the back of his mind, the knowledge that he was asleep remained present, maintaining a constant link to reality.

The slow oscillation of a quiet tower fan sent a periodic gust of crisp air across his skin. Belford shivered. He was standing in the center of a dimly lit room. Just in front of him was a narrow bed, its white sheets and blue comforter neatly made and folded down at the edge, as if awaiting an occupant. A single fluffy pillow rested at the head of the bed. The pillowcase was blue, like the comforter, but due to more frequent washings, it was a slightly lighter shade. The ambient light in the room grew as two light-strips turned on and intensified in brightness. Both strips were concealed within alcove-like compartments that ran the perimeter of the room – one facing up and running along the ceiling, the other downwards near the floor.

A metallic box sitting on the nightstand started to beep. Bright red lights flashed in each of its corners as the beeps became shrill. The side of the box facing away from the bed slid open, revealing a lens and projecting the time on the wall: 9:45am. A hand reached out from under the covers and slapped the top of the box, disabling its sound and display.

Belford would have been surprised by the sudden appearance of a person in the bed, but that wasn't the only change that had taken place in the room. It was as if he were reliving multiple memories of the same room overlapped across his vision. It was difficult to keep track of the constant changes. Every time he looked into a different corner of the room, something would change: A chair shifting slightly; a pile of clothing appearing or disappearing; the mess of take-out containers growing taller, then suddenly vanishing, replaced by a bowl of cereal and then dirty plates and utensils.

Belford tried to concentrate on one memory – the one that seemed most important. He forced the visions to settle. The person in the bed turned away from the alarm clock and returned to sleeping, but the beeping returned, louder this time; 9:52am flashed on the wall. The hand swung back over, hitting the clock again. When the person finally rolled over to look at the time, Belford realized he was observing himself.

He had shorter hair. Belford was quick to notice that neither the Mark of Kings nor the *CB* tattoo were present on his skin. He sat up in bed, yawning widely as he reached for a small device that had appeared next to the alarm clock. He pushed a button on the device and a short tone sounded from speakers hidden in the walls, followed by a pleasant female voice that echoed throughout the room.

"Hello, Doctor Levy," said the voice.

"Display messages," he said.

The projector in the alarm clock flashed on. The far wall of the room lit up, displaying a list of messages.

"You have three new messages," chimed the female voice. "First message, received yesterday at 10:19pm from the Swedish Medical Association: Dear Dr. Aaron Levy, the National Board of Health and Welfare regrets to inform you that your request to join the medical residency internship program at Sahlgrenska University Hospital has been declined—"

He threw his pillow across the room at the wall display, got out of bed and started kicking things around the room. Cursing loudly, he violently knocked a chair onto its side and threw the hand-held device at the headboard of the bed. It bounced off with a clang, but the sturdy gadget remained intact, coming to rest in the middle of the bed.

Belford watched the tantrum unfold with wide eyes. Aaron Levy, as he was apparently named, stomped right towards Belford at one point. Belford shuffled back on the balls of his feet, but Aaron was moving quickly. The dream figure passed right through him like a ghost; it was a creepy sensation. He had to remind himself that he was still sleeping.

"—subpar Swedish language skills are the primary reason for your rejection at this time. For students who have not met our high-eligibility standards, it is recommended that an intensive Swedish study program be completed before reapplying," the voice continued. "A list of links to available Swedish language courses has been included at the end of this—"

"Delete," Aaron said angrily as he snatched the controller back up off the bed.

"Please repeat command," said the female voice.

"Delete!" Aaron shouted.

"Message deleted," it said. "Second message, received yesterday at 10:21pm," it continued on steadily.

Aaron paced back and forth, still distraught as he started getting dressed. He was muttering under his breath as he began to pull a gray sweatshirt over his unwashed hair.

"—you may be a prime candidate for this project. The position will pay fifty-eight thousand euros upon completion at the end of May," said the computer.

Aaron froze with his shirt only halfway on. He turned his attention to what the voice was saying.

"Interviews will be held tomorrow at 10:30am at the Gothenburg Convention Center Expo Hall. We apologize for the late notice, but the position opened up unexpectedly and must be filled immediately for the project to continue on schedule. We look forward to making your acquaintance tomorrow. Sincerely, CIOX Project Manager, Dana Ferris."

Aaron finished pulling his shirt on and looked over at the clock. It was already 9:58am. The interviews were starting in just thirty minutes. He grabbed his pants, struggling to pull them up as he simultaneously slipped into a pair of sneakers left beside the door.

"Third message," said the computer, but Aaron was already out the door and in the hallway.

As the door slammed shut, the memory skipped ahead. The room faded away, leaving Belford in nothingness for a moment, but his mind already knew where to go next.

The convention center was huge, and the expo hall entrance was bustling with people as Aaron ran across the footbridge from the bus station. It was 10:45; Aaron was late. Belford followed closely behind Aaron as he entered the hall and quickly discovered that his lack of punctuality would not be of concern. He was far from the only person who'd been invited to interview for the mysterious project. He joined the end of a long line that looked to contain close to one thousand people by Belford's estimate. The odds of being selected for the position were not in Aaron's favor.

Aaron's hair was still sticking up in the back from how he had slept on it, but surprisingly, he wasn't the most disheveled individual waiting for the interview. Dirty clothes and tattered backpacks abound, half the people in the hall looked like they had just stepped out of a refugee camp. The crowd ranged from men and women no older than Aaron to those who appeared to be in their thirties and forties. A few more individuals arrived after Aaron, but most of them left after seeing the lengthy line.

"Not all these people could possibly be here for just one opening," Aaron said, addressing no one in particular as he sized up the line.

A scrawny blond boy leaning against the wall a few positions ahead of Aaron looked up from a tablet computer that he'd been engrossed in. "Twelve positions, actually," he said. A few more hopefuls within earshot of the boy decided to leave upon hearing the poor odds of actually landing the job.

"But still," said Aaron, "there must be a thousand people here, do they really need to interview so many?"

The boy laughed. "Oh, it gets worse," he said. "This isn't the only city they are scouting – they're looking all over the Union." The line dwindled further as more nearby individuals gave up. "Whatever this job is, it must be dangerous," he continued, "otherwise the pay wouldn't be so high." The boy smiled as more and more people departed. "Did you hear about what happened to the guys who had this gig before us?" he asked loudly.

"No," said Aaron, "only that there was an unexpected opening on the project."

"Exactly," said the boy. "Rumor has it, a series of unfortunate *accidents* befell the first team they assembled – not a single one of them survived." The last person between Aaron and the boy stepped out of line and hastily made his way towards the exit. The boy grinned at Aaron. "The name's Wes Flairity," he said.

"Nice to meet you. I'm Aaron Levy." They shook hands.

"So, where are you from, Aaron?" Wes asked. "All I can tell from your accent is you're not a local."

"You're right, I just moved here last year to finish school," said Aaron, "but I was an army brat before that, so I've lived all over the place. What about you?"

"I'm from here, Stockholm actually, born and raised," said Wes.

The line was starting to move forward now, slowly, but steadily. Belford followed behind as they made their way into a huge lecture hall. Wes and Aaron separated as everyone was handed a brief questionnaire to fill out. It contained simple questions about their gender, age, and ethnicity, as well as queries into the state of their health, education, and past fields of employment. It all felt quite routine – the same questions any job application might ask.

Aaron filled out the survey quickly and was one of the first people to move on to the next part of the interview. He ran his fingers through his hair, trying to force it to stay in place as a tall man led him to a conference room across from the lecture hall. A table, two chairs, and a set of recording equipment was all the sparse room contained. As Aaron sat down, his expression made it was obvious to Belford that the chair was not very comfortable. Had there been a one-way mirror on the wall, the chamber would have felt exactly like a police interrogation room. Aaron placed his questionnaire down on the table and waited for his interviewer to arrive.

After a while, Aaron grew bored and began tinkering around on his phone. Soon after, an older woman in a business suit entered the room and took the seat across from him. He slipped his phone back into his pocket as the woman spent a moment tying her dark hair into a bun. She used her left hand to readjust a pair of thick-rimmed glasses that had slipped down the length of her nose and began flipping through a thick binder full of paperwork with her other hand.

It was strange to see physical copies of anything – nearly everyone operated exclusively in digital these days – but apparently it was what the woman preferred to use. A smudge of blue ink colored the side of her right hand. She produced a pen from out of her bag before settling on one of the pages in the binder. She began writing on the paper without saying a word to Aaron, transferring various pieces of information from his survey.

The woman looked up at Aaron after a minute of examining the paperwork. "Hello," she said with a smile. It was as if she had only just realized he was present. "I am Dr. Gerard," she said, a French accent clear on her tongue. "It says here that you have completed your medical schooling and are looking to start working towards your residency?"

Aaron nodded.

"This is very good," she said. "It's nice to see a young man with such drive." She flipped through a few more pages in her binder. "Your school records indicate that you were near the top of your class with high aptitude in the maths and sciences, but we are looking for people who possess creative skills as well as analytical."

"If you don't mind me asking," said Aaron, "what is it exactly that I am applying for? Nobody around here has told me what this job actually entails."

"Curious, cautious, to the point – very good...." Dr. Gerard jotted down a few quick notes in Aaron's file.

Aaron glanced around the empty room, waiting for her to finish. He was beginning to grow impatient.

"The position is for a test subject," she said, looking up again from her binder. "I cannot tell you anything more specific than that at this time I am afraid, but I can assure you that although it may not sound like a glamorous job, it is quite important work – exciting work."

Aaron looked skeptical. "Is it safe?" he asked.

"Safe..." Dr. Gerard rolled the word slowly over her tongue. "Is anything truly safe? You could be hit by a car while traveling home tonight; or be blown up by a stray rocket; or get struck by lightning!" The doctor's glasses slipped down her nose again. She removed them from her face entirely, placing them in a hard case before depositing them into her bag. "It would fully pay off your student debts," she said. "This is a good opportunity, and frankly, I do not see that you have much of a choice if you wish to follow your dreams."

The woman's eyes shifted up for a moment and Belford imagined that she was staring right into his eyes as she finished her sentence, "follow your dreams." A shiver ran up Belford's spine, but the woman quickly looked away. The eye contact might have been purely coincidental. Belford wasn't sure though; he felt the words had been meant for him somehow; perhaps some part of his subconscious was trying to lead him in the right direction.

Belford skipped forward through the memory, remembering, but not dwelling on the lengthy testing that Aaron was subjected to. Dr. Gerard and a number of medical doctors took blood samples from each applicant before putting them through the company's own version of an aptitude test. They did everything short of running an obstacle course: From essay writing to memorizing sequences of shapes and numbers, the tests seemed to concentrate mainly on determining the mental capacities and problem solving skills of the applicants.

Each of the remaining applicants was placed in front of computer terminals, displaying a series of questions across their screen. The questions spanned many different disciplines, all the way from engineering to geology. There were even a few medical questions thrown into the mix. By the end of the test, Aaron was mentally exhausted. He looked disappointed as he stood up from his terminal. He'd done well on the medical questions, but there were plenty of others he had to leave blank. Many of the questions felt more like random trivia to Aaron than an accurate testing of his knowledge on the various subjects. As he exited the testing hall, he noticed Wes coming out from a different room a few doors down.

Aaron waved to him, but Wes quickly put his index finger over his pursed lips in a silencing gesture. Aaron was confused. Wes walked swiftly towards the exit, ducking under the small observation windows in the doors as he went by. He gestured for Aaron to follow him onto the footbridge and over to the parking lot on the other side. Aaron followed, curiosity clearly biting at his heels. Wes didn't stop until they reached the line of bus stop shelters.

"What's going on?" Aaron asked.

Wes looked back and forth down the road, making sure nobody was close enough to overhear them. He smiled wryly at Aaron. "I hacked their system," he said.

"You did what now?"

Wes laughed. "After I finished my test I wanted to know how well I'd done, so I snuck into an empty room within range of their wireless network and broke through their firewall." Wes held up his little tablet computer. "It was quite simple, really," he said. "The testing data wasn't even very well encrypted. And it's a good thing I did take a look, because a few of the guys in there actually scored very high – much higher than you, anyway." Wes paused for a moment as an old homeless man wearing a pair of faded red trousers ambled slowly past the bus stop with a limp.

Aaron didn't like where this was headed.

"I mean, you were still taking the test when I was hacked into the system, but it was clear that you weren't going to finish high enough."

"You didn't involve me in this, did you?" Aaron looked nervous now.

Wes gave him a guilty grin. "I may have raised our scores ever so slightly – a little bit more so in your case – while lowering everybody else's by a small margin."

Aaron's mouth fell open. "But, why?" he asked. "We're going to be in such huge trouble…. We could go to jail for this!" He started pacing back and forth.

Wes reached out and patted him on the shoulder. "Oh, don't be so dramatic," he said. "I didn't make the changes obvious, and I didn't leave any physical trace either."

"But, why me?" Aaron asked again.

Wes shrugged. "You seem like a fun guy," he said. "I didn't want to be stuck with a bunch of blowhards for the next and-a-half months."

Aaron's bus pulled up to the stop. "But what if they catch us?" he asked.

Wes herded Aaron towards the bus's open door. "They won't," he said. "Besides, cheating shows initiative."

Aaron stepped onto the bus, still in shock and fearing the possible repercussions of Wes's actions.

"You'll thank me later," said Wes as the doors closed behind Aaron and the bus departed, heading back towards Aaron's apartment.

Belford felt more confused than anything else as he watched the bus carrying Aaron drive away down the city blocks – a high-rise hotel on the right, a line of storefronts on the left. None of it was anything like the waking world; there were no horses or wagons, just asphalt and automobiles. Youths in hoodies walked down the street, hands in pockets, listening to music through their earbuds. Men and women in business suits shuffled past in droves, returning to the convention center after their respective lunches.

The old homeless man Wes had paused for was seated against the side of one of the shops across the street from Belford at the mouth of an alleyway. A stack of newspapers and cardboard boxes formed a tiny shelter around him, protecting the man from the elements. As Belford glanced at him, it seemed as if the man were staring back at him from within the boxes. Belford turned away, thinking little of it – after all, Dr. Gerard had appeared to look at him for a moment as well. Belford walked down the street a bit, but a strange feeling in his gut forced him to look back over his shoulder. He was irked to see the man still watching him.

"Hey, you!" Belford shouted. "Can you see me?"

The man jumped spryly to his feet and moved swiftly down the alleyway. He no longer showed any sign of the limp that afflicted him earlier when he first walked by.

Belford sprinted across the street after him. This was clearly no longer part of any actual memory; Aaron was long gone by now – this was something different.

The man shot a look over his shoulder, and upon seeing Belford in pursuit, increased his pace. Belford darted past the man's shelter and a large dumpster overflowing with garbage before the homeless man turned the corner at the end of the alley. Belford quickly closed the distance, but when he rounded the corner, the old man was nowhere to be seen. He found himself standing along a busy street; vehicles speeding past and a throng of people walking by in both directions. Belford scanned the faces of the people on the sidewalk for any sign of the man, but he had vanished entirely.

Belford turned back around, both disappointed and confused. He cried out in surprise as he found the old man standing less than an arm's length away. The man had a plain face; unremarkable and easily forgettable. Although he was covered in filth, his eyes were sharp. They were gray as dawn, but had a meticulous intelligence behind them, evident by the way they were capable of staring right through Belford and out the other side, as if Belford were a figure in the man's dream rather than the other way around. There was a certain malice about them as well, which was especially apparent now that he and Belford were standing face-to-face.

Belford found himself frightened by the old man. The man's face suddenly contorted into a fiery rage as he reached out towards Belford with open palms. Belford let out a gasp as the man's hands collided with his chest – he had been unable to make physical contact with anything in his dream up until now; he passed right through everybody else as if he were made of nothing more than smoke, but for some reason, at the man's touch, he felt himself become solid. The man's shove carried with it quite a bit of force. Belford felt as though the wind had been knocked out of him as he stumbled backwards into the street. The man's face widened into a sneer as Belford looked back at him, dumbstruck.

Belford had just enough time to turn his head towards the oncoming bus before it struck him. Pain shot all throughout his body as he felt the steel of the grill crushing his insides.

Everything went dark.

CHAPTER

25

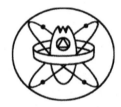

The Fox and the Cradle

Yawning widely, Javic followed Elric and Thorin down a seemingly endless hallway filled with numbered doors on either side. They made their way towards the inn's common room, waiting for Shiara to finish scolding Belford. Javic's need for sleep nearly overwhelmed him as the dull pain behind his eyes grew stronger. The throbbing was becoming more and more unbearable with each passing moment. His head ached as he shook it violently from side to side in an attempt to stave off the drowsiness that was inexorably settling over him. Since being separated from the wagon, the last few days had been grueling, to say the least.

He strained his eyes, attempting to keep them open. To his embarrassment, he nearly tripped over the leg of an old man in pair of faded red trousers who was sitting with his back against the wall of the hallway. Javic stumbled, performing an ungraceful dance around the man's bare feet. The old man was so engrossed in tinkering with a dull brass spyglass – or perhaps it was a kaleidoscope – that he didn't bother to look up at Javic or the others as they passed.

Upon entering the common room, Javic's stomach began to rumble, set off by the mere thought of dinner. He couldn't decide what his body needed more – food or sleep. The hunger pangs helped keep his eyes open as he sat down at the last free table. Javic, Elric, and Thorin were soon joined by Arlin and Mallory. The couple had just finished purchasing a room of their own for the night from the plump innkeeper sitting lackadaisically behind the cashier's counter in the corner of the room.

The innkeeper ran his greasy fingers through his thinning hair, attempting to cover up the bald spot on the top of his head. He picked a morsel of food out of his front teeth before twirling his impressively large mustache around one of his fingertips, giving it a little extra bounce.

The inn, which was called the Shaky Crow according to the wooden placard mounted above the cashier's counter, was very popular. The common room was packed nearly shoulder to shoulder with patrons. More travelers sauntered through the inn's heavy doors in search of a warm bed for the night. The grand festival celebrating the close of the autumn harvest brought many unusual guests to Rasile this evening. Although the crops had been universally poor this season, the Harvest Festival was as good of an excuse as any for farmers and city-folk alike to gather, exchange commerce, and drink excessively. The whole city was in a magnificent stupor of intoxicating vapors and uninhibited behavior.

Festivals tended to attract traveling peddlers, most of which were gypsies; a troublesome group. Javic held no personal biases against the gypsies as a people – he knew they were just trying to get by like everyone else – in fact, he had often looked forward to the arrival of their caravans during festival times back home in Darrenfield. They always filled the town with a wide assortment of goods and services not regularly provided in the marketplace.

It did bother Javic, however, that there always tended to be an upsurge in thievery corresponding with their arrival. The gypsies were more than a community of travelers; each caravan was a family – extended relations, cousins and uncles, nephews and nieces. The young took care of the old. They stuck together with unwavering loyalty and were a tight-lipped bunch if ever Javic had seen one. Despite the obvious ties between the thefts and the gypsies' arrival in town, none of the crimes could ever be traced back to them. There was never more than circumstantial evidence, but the timing was enough for most townsfolk to draw their own definitive conclusions. Every man, woman, and child knew it had been the quick fingers of a gypsy that snatched the fowl from their coop in the middle of the night or stole the shoes right out of their closet while they were off enjoying the festival.

Whenever something went missing, the gypsies were the first to be blamed. Javic had even heard stories of jewelry being stolen right off the wrists of noblemen and women. Despite the gypsies' mischievous reputation, they never committed any crime worse than petty theft as far as Javic was aware. They stole just enough to last them until they reached the next town, ensuring that they would still be welcomed back for the next festival.

Back in Darrenfield, the town would be starting their own harvest festival soon. Elric would always purchase a gift for Javic this time of year while the travelers' exotic commodities were available. He would buy it in secret and keep it sealed up and hidden from Javic for three months, until his birthday finally came around.

When Javic was little, Elric's presents were various unusual toys. His favorite was a mechanical toad capable of jumping great heights if he wound its coil tight enough. It could even spring over Javic's head if he placed it down just right. After playing with the toad for hours on end, the metal crank would start to hurt Javic's tiny fingers. Despite the pain, he never seemed to be capable of putting it away without watching it leap through the air one last time. The toad somehow managed to always land on its feet.

In more recent years, Elric started giving Javic presents that were more suited for the adult he was fast becoming. His bow had been a gift just two years ago. Upon receiving the weapon, he practiced shooting every day for months until he was finally proficient enough to go hunting by himself – a skill Javic was immensely grateful to have cultivated.

On his last birthday, Javic received a very special gift: It was an old photograph of himself, Elric, and his father, Bartan, taken when Javic was a baby. A photographer had come through Darrenfield during the harvest festival before Javic's first birthday. The Elensol men had their portrait taken, posing in front of the old Town Hall back before it was remodeled. The photograph was in black and white and a tad blurry. Though color pictures did exist, the apparatus that processed them was still rare in the north. Despite the low quality of the image, Javic loved the gift – it was the only photo he had of his father. A twinge of regret shot through him as he realized that in their rush to leave the farm, he accidentally left the photograph behind – he would never see it or the farm again.

A troupe of traveling bards was staying at the Shaky Crow tonight as well. They had just finished putting on a performance at the city's amphitheater and had come back to celebrate their good fortune for selling out every seat in the gallery. Drinks in hand, the rest of the common room was celebrating along with them.

For the duration of the festivities, the tavern next door was providing bar service to the inn. Javic wondered what sort of cut the innkeeper was receiving on the sales. The man certainly looked pleased at the moment.

Merriment was plentiful as a few of the bards, half drunk on spirits, began to put on a spontaneous show. After singing a hastily written tribute to the city of Rasile, a particularly imaginative rendition of "The Fox and the Cradle" began to flow through their slurred lips, charming the jovial audience. The performers were rewarded with more alcohol than they could possibly consume, purchased by several generous patrons.

The growing crowd hooted and hollered as a couple of young women brought in another batch of drinks from next door after one especially happy customer ordered everyone present a free round. A barmaid placed a tall glass of mead down in front of Javic. He had never tasted mead before – sweet wines were a staple of the south, as common as hops in the north. He often equated them with nobility, though, due to the fact that the farther north one traveled, the more expensive they became. In Javic's home kingdom, Taris, a single bottle could run upwards of a commoner's weekly salary. In southern Antara and Phandrol, where the weather was unforgivingly hot during the summer – just right for the production of mead – the spirit was said to be more abundant than water. He never quite believed that saying until now. He sniffed the wine first, getting a large whiff of the fermented honey before going in for a sip. The flavor was curious. It started out tangy, but the sweet taste of the honey lingered on his tongue.

Shiara entered the room. She looked pale, as if she had just experienced a fright. Thorin took the glass of mead from Javic's hand and downed it in one gulp. "Thanks," Thorin said as he wiped a trickle of the flaxen-colored honey-wine off of his beard with the back of his hand. His own mead was already long gone.

When Shiara got to the table, she immediately pulled Thorin aside and sent him over to the innkeeper to purchase a key to a second room. Shiara sat down in Thorin's vacant seat as he made his way towards the counter. Shiara's expression was distant as she waited for Thorin to return. If she was surprised to find Arlin and Mallory sitting with them, she did not show it in the least. She remained silent even when the entire rest of the common room burst into song, repeating the chorus of "The Fox and the Cradle" as it came back around.

"When the Fox comes knocking," everyone sang, "she will be turned away—yes, she will be turned away!"

Javic glanced over at Thorin. He was talking to the innkeeper now. The innkeeper shook his head in response to Thorin's question and sent him back empty-handed.

The performing bards continued to play the same riff over and over again on their lutes as members of the audience took turns shouting out what they would do to the fox if they caught her. They attempted to sing their words to the rhythm of the song with varying degrees of success. The rest of the audience rated the attempts with cheers or jeers depending on how creative or explicit the lines became.

"Disgusting song," said Arlin as he took a sip of his own mead.

Javic raised an eyebrow. "How so?" he asked.

"They're not singing about harming an animal, which would be bad enough" he said, "they're singing about Phandolians – the fox is a symbol for Phandrol."

"Oh, like Emily Fox—"

"Exactly," said Arlin. "She was their first queen."

A drunkard stood up to contribute to the tune. "I'd stomp on her head with the heel of my boot—"

Another man interjected: "Then cut out her tongue to make her go mute—"

"And snip off her tail to restring my lute!" finished one of the bards before redirecting the song back into the chorus.

"The hatred runs deep," said Arlin.

"They don't actually think she had a tail, do they?" asked Mallory.

"I wouldn't be surprised if they thought she had scales and horns," said Arlin.

Thorin returned to the table. "There aren't any vacant rooms left," he said.

Mallory turned in her seat to face Thorin. "If you guys need a place to stay, we can set up a few extra cots in our room," she said cheerfully.

Arlin looked up from his glass. "Mallory..." he murmured apprehensively. A poorly masked expression of irritation was clear on his face.

"What? They need somewhere to sleep, and we have space," she said.

Arlin didn't have a suitable retort. He frowned as he buried his nose back into his glass.

"That's very kind of you," said Thorin, "but I'm sure we can find lodging at one of the other inns—"

"No," Shiara interrupted, "we need to stay here." Her tone was overly forceful. "We must speak in private," she added, "right now."

Javic assumed Shiara's behavior was related to the Kara situation. From what he had heard through the door earlier, Belford had already received quite an earful from Shiara for having performed the transformation – perhaps it was their turn to be yelled at for failing to stop Belford. Javic had never been yelled at by Shiara before, that seemed to be Belford's role, but she appeared slightly unhinged – pushed over the edge this time.

Mallory blinked. "Well, okay then," she said. "I guess we can take you to our room now, if you'd like."

Arlin was glaring from behind his glass with a look that clearly displayed his distaste for the situation. Mallory tried to ignore his glower, but a melancholy expression settled onto her face. Her eyes suddenly shifted to Javic. She did not look away as Javic met her gaze. The cloud of sadness quickly lifted.

"Come on," she said, as she stood up and grabbed hold of Javic's arm at the elbow. She pulled him along with her as she exited the common room. Thorin and Shiara followed close behind with Elric and Arlin taking up the rear. As they stepped out into the hallway, Mallory's hand slid down from Javic's elbow to the palm of his hand.

Before Javic realized what he was doing, his fingers interlocked with hers. He glanced over nervously, but she showed no sign of discomfort. Her skin was so soft and warm…. Javic could feel his heart beating faster in his chest. Mallory squeezed onto him even tighter.

If she was trying to make Arlin jealous, it didn't appear to be working. Javic glanced back several times at Arlin during the walk to the room, but his expression never changed. His gaze remained focused ahead, down the hallway, paying no notice to either Mallory or Javic.

Mallory released Javic's hand when they reached the room. He missed her touch already. He stuffed his fingers into his pockets so they wouldn't feel so empty. Mallory opened the door and lit a gas lamp on the wall with a turn of a dial. A quiet hiss escaped the lamp as gas was pumped into the sparked flame. The flickering glow shed a soft-yellow light across the carpeted floor and cast Mallory's shadow long against the far wall of the room. As everyone piled in, Shiara latched the door shut behind them and began to pace the length of the chamber. There was no sitting area, it was a small room, but it did contain two beds and a long table against the far wall.

Javic walked over and sat on the edge of one of the beds. His stomach gave a painful groan. He rubbed his belly over his shirt, trying to ease the discomfort. In addition to the hunger, his drowsiness was approaching a level that would soon be impossible to overcome. Only Shiara's worried face kept him from falling asleep on the spot.

"What's all this about?" asked Elric.

Shiara turned on him instantly. "I think you know very well," she snapped.

Elric was slightly taken aback. He glanced over at Thorin, but if he were seeking support or clarification, he was sorely out of luck. Thorin looked just as confused by Shiara's mysterious accusation.

"Don't play dumb," said Shiara threateningly. "Did you really think you could keep the mark secret from me the entire journey?"

Elric went white.

"That's right," said Shiara, "Belford showed me. I should abandon you all to your own fates right here and now for keeping something this important from me! Do you even know what this could mean for the Ver'konus?"

Elric, though he still looked sheepish, spoke now: "Keep your voice down," he said harshly, "or have you already forgotten where we are?" Elric pointed his index finger straight into Shiara's face. "You should know better than to shout about the resistance, especially in a building full of Kovani nationals." Shiara was clearly surprised by Elric's bravado. "And yes, I do know how important it is that we get Belford to Phandrol. Why else do you think we kept the mark a secret? Revealing it to *anyone* was an unnecessary risk."

Shiara looked hurt. "But I am the one who needs to protect him. If I had known earlier, I would have... been more careful...."

"What mark?" asked Mallory.

Both Shiara and Elric spun around to look at Mallory, who was standing beside Arlin and Thorin, each looking more confused than the last. Javic grimaced; there was no going back now – too much had already been said.

Elric let out a short sigh. "Belford bears the Mark of Kings," he said.

Mallory gasped, throwing her hand over her gaping mouth. Arlin merely narrowed his eyes, uncertain as to whether or not he should believe what he was hearing. He then walked across the room to the opposite corner and took a seat on the floor. Only Thorin seemed unfazed by the news.

"I had my suspicions," he said.

Shiara turned towards Thorin, frowning. "Go retrieve Belford," she said. "He shouldn't be left alone with that

Whune anymore. There is no telling what she might do to him if she reverts back!"

Thorin nodded and exited the room immediately, closing the door behind him.

"That boy is just so stubborn," said Shiara. "He always thinks he knows what's best, but he's still just a child."

Arlin glowered at Shiara from out of the corner of the room. "If he truly does have the mark, then we cannot hope to control him," he said. "The mark is prophesied to bring peace to all of Aragwey, but Garrett and Ethan's feud has brought nothing but strife. How do we know the boy won't make things worse?"

Shiara glared back at Arlin. "Once Belford is with Lord Ethan and Queen Havorie, the balance of power will be tipped in our favor," she said.

"And what if he chooses Garrett's side instead?" Arlin asked. "He could assassinate Lord Ethan the moment we bring him before the man."

Shiara didn't respond, seemingly contemplating the possibility.

"No!" cried Javic, unable to remain silent any longer. "He would never do such a thing! He has saved my life more than once – he would never help *Garrett*." He spat out the name distastefully.

"But how can you know for sure?" asked Arlin. "It could all be part of a ruse. Don't forget the fondness he has exhibited towards the Whune."

Javic stood up clenching his fists at his side. "That's exactly how I know he's on our side," he said passionately. "He won't let her die; he still sees the good in her, and I can see the good in him."

Arlin frowned.

Javic glanced around the room. Elric was smiling at him; he gave his grandson a proud nod. Shiara and Mallory were both looking up at him now as well, as if seeing him for the first time.

"He saved my life too," said Mallory. "When I was freezing to death, he carried me, and he built a fire."

Javic raised an eyebrow at Shiara.

"What?" she asked. Javic continued to stare. "Fine," she said begrudgingly, "I guess he saved me as well, back in Felington when we first met."

Arlin didn't attempt to argue any further.

A bang shook the door as it swung open to reveal Thorin. The usually calm man had a worried expression on his face as he stepped sideways through the threshold carrying Belford in his arms. Belford was unconscious with blood smears down the front of his tunic. It appeared to be pouring from his nose.

"What happened?" Shiara shrieked, a slight glow suddenly illuminating her face. It was as if energy were circling around her. The hairs rose on the back of Javic's arms. Arlin was on his feet in an instant, already drawing his sword as he rushed out into the hallway.

"I don't know," responded Thorin as he swept everything off of the table with the back of his arm and placed Belford down in front of Shiara. "He was like this when I arrived."

Belford's pulse was changing wildly; the veins in his neck bulged as more and more blood was pumped into his head. The leak in his nose appeared to be the only outlet for the pressure.

"Turn him on his side so he doesn't drown," screeched Shiara, her voice full of panic. She put her hands onto his neck and fell into a deep concentration as the glow of the Power intensified around her.

Javic turned towards Thorin, a look of concern heavy on his brow. He couldn't help but remember that Shiara was an admittedly poor healer.

Arlin reappeared in the doorway, his sword still drawn in his hand. "The Whune is gone," he said. Thorin joined Arlin, both men sprinting out the door and down the hallway in a clamor of footsteps. Elric drew his sword as well, preparing to defend the room if required.

Shiara managed to stanch the flow of blood coming from Belford's nose, but he remained unconscious.

Mallory moved past Javic, grabbing a kit of herbal remedies out of Arlin's bag. She opened Belford's tunic and rubbed a vaporous liquid on his bare chest. Belford immediately began to cough and sputter, more blood spurting from his mouth. He tried to sit up, but Mallory and Shiara held him down. He was breathing hard now as he looked around the room with wide eyes. Everyone was staring at him, their facial expressions asking the obvious question: What happened? He attempted to speak, but began to cough up more blood from his lungs. It splattered across the back of his hand and dripped from the corners of his mouth.

"It was a man... in my dream..." he wheezed, still trying to catch his breath. "I know it sounds crazy, but he attacked me – pushed me in front of a bus...." Belford frowned as he looked around the room with nervous eyes. He looked over at Javic. "You've got to believe me," he said. "It wasn't a normal dream."

Javic didn't know what a bus was, but the look of terror on Belford's face was enough to make Javic believe he was sincere.

Shiara remained silent. Despite the skeptical look on her face, she was beginning to realize that seemingly impossible things occurred frequently around the Mark of Kings. She kept any cynical comments to herself.

Thorin and Arlin stepped back through the door, Thorin leading Kara by the arm. She had thick gravy smeared across her face and chunks of meat stuck to her fingers. Her eyes were just as expressionless as ever. She was completely unaware of the tension in the air. Javic wondered where she managed to find a meal at such a late hour.

"Why are you holding her like that?" Belford asked angrily. "Let her go," he said, pulling away from Shiara and Mallory's grasp. He struggled to his feet, putting a hand across his temple as his balance shifted. "She had nothing to do with this."

Kara licked her fingers, drawing a few of the stray meat chunks into her mouth.

Thorin glanced over at Shiara before releasing Kara. Arlin watched with wary eyes as she wandered over towards Belford.

Belford bent down and grabbed a napkin off the floor. He wiped Kara's face, delicately cleaning away the mess from her cheeks and pink lips. He dabbed at the corners of her mouth, dislodging the last few chunks of meat that had nestled there before moving on to her fingers. He held her hand up by the wrist as he folded the dirty part of the napkin in on itself, then began wiping her slender fingers. Even after all the gravy was cleared away, he kept wiping furiously, refusing to look up at all the eyes that watched him, staring at him from out of every corner of the room.

Belford opened his mouth as if to address the room, but continued to stand in silence for a long moment. He kept his eyes down, focusing on Kara's hands which he still had held between his own. Her nails were chipped and dirty, with gravy still caked beneath them.

Without warning, Belford dropped Kara's hands and walked out of the room. He didn't speak a single word to anyone as he exited, not even glancing at Shiara as she pleaded for him to wait.

The door closed behind him with a thud, leaving Shiara speechless. She stood in place for a moment, unable to move.

"Go on," said Thorin, "he's too important to be left alone."

Shiara mumbled in agreement. She shook the hesitation out of her legs and promptly followed after Belford.

CHAPTER

26

A Philosopher's Repose

Outside the Shaky Crow Inn, the party spilled into the streets of Rasile. Drunken figures stumbled about, bumping into one another, leaning against walls to support their unsteady legs. The guards turned a blind eye to the unruly conduct – some were even partaking in the celebration themselves, walking their patrols with drinks in hand. In the distance, a lady broke into cackling laughter as the man she was with slipped between two of the stone steps that bridged from one side of the street to the other at every intersection. He fell face first into the shallow water below, his arms flailing as the iciness sobered him up instantly. Colorful profanities escaped his mouth as he jumped up and sloshed his way over to the side of the road, his arms held stiff at his side.

Belford glanced over his shoulder. Just as he expected, Shiara was making her way out of the inn a short distance behind him. She didn't trust him on his own. She wasn't concerned about him; she only cared about the mark on his arm. He quickened his pace and began taking random turns down alleyways and crossing at intersections whenever he came upon them, hoping to find a crowd large enough to dissolve into. He was sick of the way everybody treated him. Shiara always spoke to him as if he were a child, and whenever she was not patronizing him, she was peering at him out of the corner of her eye like he was some sort of dangerous animal that might turn on her at any moment.

The only thing worse than the apprehension in her eyes was the look of pity that everybody gave him whenever they thought he wasn't paying attention. He had enough problems without their judgmental eyes casting doubt on his ability to heal Kara.

Why won't Shiara give me a break?

If one of them – just one! – would demonstrate a little confidence in me, it would make things a thousand times easier.

It certainly didn't help that he knew their reservations were justified.

What do I know about fixing minds?

His self-doubt weighed on him with enormous pressure.

After turning down a busy street, Belford ducked through the door of a grungy tavern before Shiara had a chance to get him back into her line of sight. The tavern was packed, which was fortunate. He slid in deeper, surrounding himself with the crowd in case Shiara poked her head through the door once she realized she had lost him. He made his way towards the only free table he could see, trying not to bump into anybody in the process. Just as Belford got to the small table, an old man with a pitcher of spirits in his hands stepped up to the opposite side.

"Oh, I'm sorry," said Belford. "Were you sitting here?"

"I was," said the man, "but you may join me if you'd like.

The skin around the man's eyelids sagged, making his expression seem gloomy. He carefully placed the pitcher down on the table. A small tremor ran through his right arm causing him to release the handle prematurely. Fortunately, the pitcher was close enough to the table that it did not spill as it landed. The man grunted and held his shaking limb to his abdomen. He appeared to have been drinking for quite some time already. His eyes were slightly bloodshot and, as Belford observed him now, his whole face seemed to droop under its own weight. Shadows pooled across his forehead, exaggerating his wrinkles and making them look as though they had been painted on his skin by a fine-haired brush rather than etched there over time by years of expression.

Belford glanced around the room once more, but still did not see any other available tables. He sat down opposite the worn-out man. Across the tavern, the door opened. Belford slouched low in his chair, but it wasn't Shiara – just another festival attendee looking for a cheap drink.

"Would you like some?" asked the man, gesturing to the pitcher. Belford hesitated for a moment. The man raised his graying eyebrows in emphasis of the question. "I shouldn't drink it all by myself," he added.

Belford looked up at him. "Sure," he said, "I guess one drink couldn't hurt."

The man smiled. "I'll go get some glasses," he said, rising out of his chair. "I'm Soren, by the way." He held out his hand for Belford to shake.

"My name's Bel—" Belford stopped himself, "I'm Aaron," he revised. He grabbed hold of Soren's hand and shook it firmly.

"Nice to meet you," said Soren. "I'll be right back with those glasses." He began to walk to the bar.

Belford wasn't sure why he said his name was Aaron. That was his name in his dreams, yes, but he felt detached from the person he had seen there. The words Aaron spoke were not Belford's; those were not his actions. He had changed since those events occurred. In his dream, he watched himself in the midst of a temper tantrum, throwing items around his apartment like the child Shiara always treated him as. That boy would have deserved Shiara's condescension. The Aaron he saw existed before he met Claire – before her presence in his life made him want to become a better person. Aaron's problems were laughably insignificant compared to what Belford now faced.

Soren returned to the table with two tall glasses. He sat one down in front of Belford and one in front of himself, filling them both to the brim with the pitcher's tawny liquid. Belford lifted the glass to his nose. It smelled potent, like something one might use to sterilize surgical equipment. Soren took a deep swig, downing an eighth of his glass in an instant.

Belford took a sip, trying his best to send the liquid straight down his throat without it touching his tongue. He still tasted it; acerbic and bitter. When it reached the back of his throat, it burned, causing his esophagus to close up. He felt as though he were attempting to drink gravel. Finally, the liquid went down, but the roughness made him cough as his throat stubbornly tightened up.

"Good, isn't it?" asked Soren, smirking.

Belford narrowed his eyes in response. He looked across the table at Soren before taking a larger gulp of the dark-brown liquor. It wasn't as bad this time; his throat was more acclimatized to the harshness. Both men sat in silence for a moment, staring off into opposite corners of the tavern as they individually worked on drinking their problems away. Belford began to feel the warmth of the alcohol in his abdomen almost immediately: Heat rising in his core as his empty stomach absorbed the caustic brew straight through its lining and into his bloodstream.

"Are you here for the festival?" asked Soren.

Belford shifted slightly in his seat. "No," he said, "just passing through. What about you?" he asked, steering the conversation away from himself.

Soren shook his head. "I'm not celebrating."

Belford took another swig from his glass. Soren seemed to be waiting for Belford to speak again, but he remained silent. Soren began to elaborate anyway.

"I've lived in this city my whole life," he said. "I don't particularly enjoy the crowds the festival brings – the gypsies – too many people, never enough quiet."

Belford nodded absently. His head was buzzing from the effects of the alcohol. He took another large gulp.

"It's usually a quiet city," Soren continued, "a good place to relax and think. When I was a boy, I used to find Rasile dull, but time gradually changes your perspective on things."

Belford let Soren continue to muse, only half listening.

"I never appreciated what I had, but that's always how it is, isn't it? You never realize what a good thing you've got until it's gone." Soren finished off his glass and poured himself another.

Belford wasn't even halfway through his drink and his face was already feeling numb.

"I always used to dream about leaving Rasile," Soren continued, "of moving somewhere else – anywhere else, really – somewhere far away. But then I met my wife, Anika, right here at this tavern, and everything changed after that. You should have seen her," Soren said, smiling. His eyes were beginning to shine in the dim light. "She was so beautiful – never a better woman...."

Belford looked up at Soren's weathered face. The sadness in his eyes suddenly seemed very familiar to Belford: It looked like the same pain Belford felt every day with Claire's absence. Belford knew instantly that Soren's wife must no longer be with him. Soren appeared to have had a lot of practice drinking – perhaps years of slowly drowning himself in alcohol to dull the pain. Belford wondered if this was to be his fate as well – to be alone, reflecting on better times, wallowing in his sorrow until his face began to crease and then crack as he grew older and older and eventually died.

In the end, death would come as a relief.

A bitter reward for all his struggles.

Belford looked into his cup; the alcohol wasn't dulling his pain the way he thought it should. It was only making it harder to contain.

After finishing his first drink and working quickly on his second, Belford found himself unable to stop thinking about Soren's situation. "Why do you stay here now if your wife is no longer with you?" he asked, his speech slurred.

"I'm an old man," said Soren, waving his hand dismissively. His whole body swayed around slowly in a small circle. He was finally beginning to show signs of intoxication as well. "This place is my home," he said.

"This place—this place isn't even... this place is my punishment," said Belford squinting his eyes. "I don't even know. You know? I try to be a nice guy—"

"You're a nice guy, you shouldn't even question that. I can tell you are—"

"I know, it's not that..." Belford interrupted, "it's just that bad things always seem to happen to me. I mean, take Shiara for instance, she's always so mean to me and I don't even know why. She's always saying mean things, and doesn't believe in me, doesn't even give me a chance...."

"I'm sure she cares about you," said Soren. "Maybe she's just afraid to let you in."

"...and then there's Kara. She's broken, and I don't even know if I can fix her—"

"You can't always fix everything—"

"But I have to, it's my fault she's broken, and I'm the only one who can save her. I mean, she's the same as Claire, you know?"

Soren started nodding, causing his upper body to sway even more radically. He didn't seem to mind the fact that he had no idea who Belford was talking about.

"They're both innocent. They didn't deserve this... they didn't deserve *me* – the problems I bring."

"Oh, don't say that," said Soren, frowning.

"I bring nothing but trouble. It's true! They're all better off without me."

"No, no," said Soren, "you can't talk like that! They need you. They might not even know it yet, but they need you."

"How can you be so sure?" asked Belford. He didn't know why he was opening up so much to the old man but it felt like the right thing to do. "I mean, Claire – I don't even know where she is. She might be dead for all I know. Something might have happened to her, and then I forgot about it, along with everything else." Belford put his face in his hands. "All I have are little bits and pieces... I don't even remember how we met, but I know I love her—"

"Love's a beautiful thing—"

"When she touches me, it feels like fire coursing through my veins, growing out of her fingertips and burning through my whole body like... like pulsating heat. Even in my memories, I can still feel it – every touch ripping through me, feeling more real than anything else in the whole world. Like everything else is gray and insignificant, and only the two of us are really there. I mean, she's perfect. She's got to be out there somewhere. If she wasn't, I wouldn't even want to be here anymore. What's the point of going on when you can never be happy?"

Soren looked up somberly. "When Anika died, I didn't want to go on anymore either," he said. His eyes were welling up with tears. "But what else can you do but go on living? I may never love anyone else the way I loved her, but I can't just quit on life. *You* can't just quit on life, because then there would be nobody left who remembers her the way you do."

Belford placed his empty glass down in front of him. Soren was right. It was a horrific thought: If Claire was dead, then all that was left of her was what he held in his head. Who else would mourn her? The world they were from didn't seem to exist – at least not anymore, not here. The thought of her smile made his heart feel like a ball of twine, unraveling, growing from deep down inside of him until it consumed his whole body.

But it was all a sick joke.

It's not enough.

Those are just memories, and what are memories without flesh to make them solid – to make them real?

Every molecule in his body ached at the thought of her, at the idea of never seeing her again. He wanted to touch her skin so much; to smell her hair and run his fingertips up her spine to the nape of her neck; to feel the brush of her soft lips against his and taste the sweet nectar held within; to hear to the sound of her breath, steady throughout the night as she sleeps. He could stay up all night just listening to that sound. If he ever knew for certain that she was gone forever, that they could never be together again, he didn't think his memories would be enough, not nearly enough – not for a lifetime without her.

"What if it's not enough?" Belford asked.

But Soren did not respond.

After a moment, Belford looked back over at the man. Soren's head was down, lying on top of his arms. He was fast asleep, already drooling on his dirty sleeve.

Belford sighed.

Across the tavern, the door opened. Through the blur in his eyes, Belford could just barely identify Shiara's fuzzy form as she made her way towards him. Although he had known his freedom would end eventually, he had hoped it would take her a little longer to find him. He wasn't looking forward to the scolding he would undoubtedly receive. He knew she would see his inebriation as evidence of immaturity, which would only lead to her treating him even worse than before – but for some reason, he was finding it difficult to care about what Shiara would think or do.

He didn't even care about the Mark of Kings anymore. Maybe he would scrape it off with his knife after all. He could probably even do it with the Power; it would be easier than taking a knife to his arm.

I don't care about Ethan and Garrett's feud anyway. I don't owe this world anything. I don't owe anyone anything... anyone except....

Kara's serene face flashed across his mind.

What would she do without me? No one else would look after her the way she requires. No one else would try to fix her.

He wasn't sure if he could fix her, but he was the best chance she had.

He began to wonder about her family; if they were still alive; if they missed her the way he missed Claire – until it hurt all over, tearing apart his insides. She had mentioned having a father back when they first met.

Was he still alive? Was he one of the Whunes we slaughtered in the forest? Maybe he was the one whose face Arlin bludgeoned with his helmet.

Belford began to feel sick again as he thought about the shattered bones and cartilage. A soup of blood and flesh where the Whune's face – a person's face – had once been.

If I ever do manage to fix Kara, what will she do? Where will she go? Will she ever be able to forgive me?

Shiara placed her hand on Belford's shoulder. He expected her to dig her nails into his arm and pull him up, maybe even slap him a few times before dragging him out of the tavern and back to the inn, but she did none of those things. She left her hand on his shoulder for a moment, and gazed down at him – not with anger, not with pity, but with compassion in her dazzling, blue eyes.

"Come on," she said, "let's get you some food and water."

She helped Belford out of his chair and guided him towards the door with an arm around his waist. He leaned against her as she led him back into the street.

How curious, thought Belford, *maybe she really does care about me after all.*

CHAPTER

27

Engines of Darkness

When Javic woke, he found himself greeted by a grand breakfast. Mallory crawled over his legs at the foot of the bed carrying a large lap tray overflowing with crusty rolls layered with mounds of sliced ham. The bite-sized morsels were each adorned with a thin slice of a spicy yellow cheese that smelled both sharp and delectable. The entire dish was slathered with a generous amount of dark gravy, as was the Kovani custom.

Javic could hardly wait to fill his hollow stomach with the rich feast. He was fairly certain he had dreamt about food all night long. He momentarily wondered if the gravy had been poured from the same vat that Kara dipped her fingers into the night before. The likelihood was strong, but even that was not enough to deter his stomach from growling with approval as the savory scent of ham drifted through his flared nostrils. He began to salivate heavily as his hunger pangs grew stronger, grinding away at his stomach lining without mercy. He was to the point where he would have considered eating the gravy directly off of Kara's dirty fingers had there been no other option available to him.

After rubbing the remaining drowsiness out of his eyes, Javic glanced up at Mallory. With a start, he realized she was mostly undressed – clothed only in her slip and a thin cotton camisole that exposed her stomach. The cami's heavy frills and white lacing covered a hidden clasp somewhere between her breasts, below which the shirt hung loose, swinging open slightly as she slid her way across the bed. A strip of caramel-smooth skin flashed out provocatively below the hidden clasp. The gap stretched downward, all the way to her bellybutton.

Javic's cheeks began to redden as Mallory pulled back the covers and slipped in beside him. His eyes lingered over her body for one moment too long. He was certain she caught his stare. He tried to hide his embarrassment by hastily stuffing his face with one of the gravy covered rolls, but as he looked back over at Mallory, her large chocolate eyes seemed to smile at him.

A mischievous little grin.

Javic choked noisily on his bite.

"Are you alright?" Mallory asked, a hint of amusement peaking above her already sing-songy voice.

Javic barely managed a nod as his blush deepened to a bright crimson.

"You've got some gravy on your... never mind, I'll get it." Mallory used her own napkin to clean Javic's cheek. He nearly started choking again.

The door behind Javic creaked open with the soft squeal of worn hinges. Javic's head swung around in a fleeting moment of panic. Arlin was entering, moving at his usual brisk pace. It was the first time Javic had seen Arlin without his armor. His sword, with its gleaming opal-inlayed hilt, was still strapped to his side.

Arlin took no notice of his liege-lady at first, sprawled out as she was, half naked at Javic's side, but when he finally looked over, he began to smile. The man actually smiled! Unlatching the scabbard from his belt, Arlin laid his sword against the wall beside the bed and then began to climb over Javic's feet the same way Mallory had. He positioned himself awkwardly between Javic and Mallory.

"Ooh, I love these," said Arlin, grabbing a roll off the tray.

Javic's heart was racing – he had been fearful of Arlin's reaction. It slowed now and he was left feeling ridiculous. He was no match for Arlin. There would be no competition over Mallory's favor. Arlin didn't see him as a threat – not by any means. The situation probably meant nothing more to Mallory than it did to Arlin. To her, Javic was just an immature boy with a bump on the ridge of his nose.

Belford is the important one – the interesting one – not me. Belford might change the world with his mark.

Javic closed his eyes for a moment as a wave of frustration crashed over him. That was all anyone ever saw in him – a little boy who didn't belong; an outlander in his own skin.

After breakfast, Javic quietly made his way to the stables where Elric and Thorin were readying the tattered wagon for a prompt departure. Belford was already there, napping in the back, with Kara crouched in the corner beside him. Her doe eyes almost made Javic forget about her condition, though she remained eerily distant as always – her eyes unfocused and uninterested to follow as he strolled past the back flap of the wagon. It was as if she were in a trance, her mind floating beyond the confines of her mortal body.

On the other side of the wagon, Shiara stood next to an elderly woman. The lady had straight, silver hair that reached down to her lower back. Her long ruffled skirt was slashed with bright colors – yellows, purples and greens – a style popular amongst gypsy women. She spoke with a hushed urgency.

"I fear the worst for the caravan Ryas Terkona is leading," she said. "The roads are becoming more and more dangerous, especially at night, as I am sure you are aware."

Shiara's face wore a frown. She nodded absently, not really looking at the old woman.

"His caravan should have arrived days ago, and I know he would have sent word ahead if he'd been delayed, even if just for a day."

"When was the last time you heard from him?" asked Shiara, glancing past the woman's shoulder at Javic as he approached.

The woman turned immediately to see where Shiara's gaze had wandered. She scowled at Javic, her pale-gray eyes harsh like a wolf's. Her skin held a natural dark tan, but it was surprisingly unwrinkled, especially considering her age. The entire left side of her face was encrusted with dazzling gems in a spiral design that was reminiscent of a fire sprite. Definitely a gypsy.

"It's alright," Shiara said to the woman, "this is one of the boys I was telling you about – Javic Elensol."

The old gypsy's face immediately softened, the scowl vanishing, replaced by a most pleasant smile, fit for a mother cooing over a young child.

A child is all anyone ever sees in me....

Javic nearly sighed to himself. He wondered what Shiara had told the woman about him.

"This is Illiyna Mek'Verona," Shiara said. "We're going to be riding with her caravan for a few days, until we get to Galdren."

Javic nodded his approval of the plan – there was safety in numbers, or at least the illusion of safety, even if he didn't have much trust for the gypsies. Both women smiled at him, but neither spoke. He suddenly realized, to his embarrassment, they were simply waiting for him to leave so that they could continue their private conversation. Dark bags under Shiara's eyes held a weariness that suggested she hadn't slept at all during the night. Javic thought it best not to test his luck by overstaying his welcome. He respectfully slinked away from the women and took a seat in the back of the wagon alongside Kara and Belford.

After a moment, Javic noticed that Belford was not really asleep like he had originally appeared to be. With one eye slightly open, Belford was squinting up at Javic. He had his ear pressed to the stretched-out canvas of the wagon, and as Javic looked over at him he lifted a finger to his lips. Curious, Javic scooted towards Belford. As he got closer, he realized he could faintly hear Shiara and Illiyna's conversation through the thin fabric. Belford and Javic put their heads together, eavesdropping.

It was Shiara who spoke first. "What news do you bring from the north?"

Illiyna grunted. "Nothing good," she said. "Saldrone is in disarray with King Vouldric's assassination and Kovani soldiers are pressing forward on Taris and Graven. A massive Gravish army has formed to repel them. They hold strong on their eastern border, where Hurspen and Benmoth once stood... burned to the ground...."

"So I've heard."

"...but High King Nemos has remained strangely silent."

"Have you heard any mention of Whunes?" Shiara asked coolly.

Illiyna's voice tensed up, "I have. I prayed they were only rumors, but your inquiry suggests otherwise... oh no, poor Ryas..." her voice faltered. "It's the only explanation... the whole caravan...."

"What rumors have you heard, Illiyna?" Shiara pressed on.

The woman sighed, fear clearly present as she continued, "The Torus desert is expanding... faster than before... faster than natural... whole towns and villages swallowed up in the course of a night. Buildings vanish without a trace, whole populations missing, replaced by nothing more than sand dunes. That's why we're heading south. The rumors speak of trouble in Kovehn. Something is amiss. I've heard word that when the first sands blow in, before a town is consumed, howls can be heard on the wind – dark voices... the cries of the devil.

I know they are only stories, Shiara, but I can't help being reminded of—"

"The Cleansing…" Shiara whispered.

Illiyna's silence confirmed the accuracy of Shiara's assumption. Javic shuddered at the implications of such an analogy. He had heard about how the Cleansing devastated Aragwey when King Garrett first took the throne a century ago. A quarter of the population of Aragwey died within the first three years of war.

"When will the caravan be ready to depart?" asked Shiara.

"Shortly," said Illiyna. "I do not wish to spend one more minute in this blasted kingdom…. Poor, poor Ryas… his father was a great man… a blessing he did not live long enough to see this happen to his family."

It was an ominous start to their travels with the gypsies. Javic and Belford remained silent long after the conversation ended. The whole world was going mad around them – assassinations and wars; armies and monsters. Tensions were building everywhere and the pieces were stacked precariously. Everything was on the brink of crumbling into chaos. The engines of darkness were turning just beyond the veil, the rumblings starting to become audible. There was no use in speculating about the lost caravan. Even if the Whunes were not responsible, the threat of attack from the Goblikan still loomed.

Despite everything, the next few days carried on at a surprisingly normal pace. Rumors of the missing gypsy caravan must have colored the thoughts of the men and women they traveled south with, but Shiara had alleviated their personal safety concerns by being surprisingly open about being Ver'ati. The gypsies' minds were put to ease knowing that they were under the protection of the Arcanum, and Belford was able to continue his training with Shiara whenever the moon was visible in the sky.

Interestingly, something appeared to have put new resolve into Belford – he no longer complained about Shiara's methods of teaching or questioned where her lessons were headed when he did not immediately understand the point of them. Shiara was doing her part to keep the peace as well. She refrained from making antagonizing comments and focused solely on imparting her knowledge of the Power on Belford. She was more cautious with her teachings as well, being careful not to ask anything of Belford that carried even the slightest possibility of killing him if he made a mistake. However, Javic quickly came to realize that almost any use of the Power had at least a small chance of killing the wizard. It must have made planning lessons very difficult for Shiara.

It made sense that she would want to keep Belford and his mark safe for the Ver'konus, but Javic had a sneaking suspicion there was more to Shiara's change in attitude than just politics. She had been looking at Belford differently as of late. Longer gazes – rather than glares – were often directed at Belford when he had his back turned. Shiara perked up slightly whenever Belford was speaking. If Javic was to venture a guess, he would say Shiara was developing feelings for Belford. Belford, on the other hand, was clearly oblivious to all of this. Javic thought it best not to interfere. From what he knew of Shiara's personality, if she wanted Belford to know, she would certainly just tell him.

Shiara wasn't the only one keeping to herself. None of the gypsies wanted anything to do with the newcomers. They acted as if having a young wizard training in their camp was a common occurrence and just went about their daily business as usual. From the few conversations Javic managed to overhear, the gypsies made no talk of the Ver'konus or Whunes. All of the adults, save Illiyna, stayed clear of the little blue wagon whether the moon was up or down. The gypsy children, on the other hand, were enjoying the novelty of the situation.

A pair of fiery-haired siblings by the names of Anya and Gord quickly took a fancy to Belford. Gord was eight years old and Anya was ten. Many of the gypsy children enjoyed watching Shiara's lessons, just as Javic had done, waiting patiently – more or less – to see the miracles of the Power unfold before their eyes. At the end of one session, Anya and Gord didn't leave even after the moon went down.

"Can I become Ver'ati too?" asked Anya after Shiara and Belford completed their session. All the other children had already returned to their coaches to sleep.

Belford was looking at Kara longingly – he had been forbidden by Shiara from trying to fix her mind for the duration of their travels with the gypsies. Belford glanced at the little girl. The question had been directed at him, but Shiara answered Anya before he could respond.

"It's difficult to say," said Shiara. "You must be born with the ability, though the Gift of the Arcanum doesn't usually present itself until later in life, at least after maturity."

"I told you," said Gord, frowning at his sister. "You have to be special – not like us."

Anya's gaze turned towards the ground.

Shiara patted her on the head. "In Phandrol, all children are tested for the Gift. Physicians draw a small sample of blood from each child when they turn thirteen. With that, they can determine whether the correct markers are present to facilitate control over the Power. It's all very scientific. Also, at the entrance to the Queen's Palace in Erotos, there is a beautiful glass orb – an ancient artifact – that when approached by a wizard, will begin to glow with brilliant colors. It reacts more strongly the more powerful the wizard. I've heard that sometimes, when in the presence of a particularly powerful Ver'ati, it may even begin to resonate and hum."

Anya was excited again. "Can I come with you and be tested?" she asked.

"Hmm," said Shiara, "I don't think your parents would like that very much…."

Both Anya and Gord looked up at Shiara with the biggest, most sad eyes Javic had ever seen.

"…but I guess I could take a little bit of your blood with me and have it tested when I get to Erotos," Shiara added.

The next night Shiara created two glass vials out of a little bit
of sand and pricked each of the children's fingers with a
sewing needle. They each squirmed as the needle pierced their
skin, but neither cried out in pain. They put on brave faces as
their blood dripped into the tubes. Shiara sealed the tops of the
vials with the Power so there would be no chance of a spill
during their journey.

Not half an hour later, Anya and Gord's mother appeared at
their wagon. Javic hadn't seen the woman before. She had the
same round face as her children, though her hair was silky
blonde rather than the orange tresses that both Anya and Gord
possessed. She was livid, which was quite obvious before she
even opened her mouth. Her scowl was set so deep it might as
well have been carved from stone. Her eyes held an
unwavering fury that pierced straight through Shiara. The first
words from her mouth were to demand that the vials be handed
over to her. After Shiara complied, the woman smashed them
on the ground under the heel of her boot. Javic did not see
Anya and Gord again after that.

Word traveled fast amongst the gypsies. By the next
morning, none of the other children were allowed anywhere
near their wagon. If not for Illiyna's urgings, Javic had no
doubt they would have been kicked out of the caravan
altogether.

During the day, the procession of coaches rolled on at a slow
pace. Javic periodically walked alongside the wagon to stretch
his legs. He mused over the variety of designs and colors that
decorated the coaches. Flamboyance seemed mandatory
amongst the gypsies. Thorin explained that the intricate murals
on the sides of the coaches were actually family histories, put
on display for longevity. It was a matter of public record as
well as a means for boasting. When different caravans met up,
each family instantly knew the status of every individual within
the visiting group, as well as any notable exploits that had been
achieved since their last encounters with one another.

Outside the gypsy community, the specific meanings of the individual symbols within the murals remained unknown. They did not share their culture with outsiders. Although Javic was unable to decipher most of the symbols, a shadowy black mark that was added to each of the murals since their departure from Rasile had a fairly obvious meaning: It was a memorial to Ryas Terkona's lost caravan. With a bucket of black paint and a brush, each gypsy woman drew the curvy outline of a robed figure within the clutter of their murals; Death embodied.

With the gypsies remaining stubbornly separate from the travelers, Arlin and Elric began spending much of their time together, speaking in hushed conversations. Usually when Javic approached, Arlin was in the middle of sharing military stories with Elric. The fair-haired swordsman always used vague terms, at least when Javic was in earshot, never referring to any specific names or places. It was odd, but then again, most things about Arlin came across that way. He was a very private man.

Mallory excluded herself from Arlin's conversations with Elric by choice. She busied herself helping Belford take care of Kara. Sitting in the back of the wagon, Mallory would talk to Kara for hours, telling stories from her childhood spent growing up along the Gulf of Nerim. Of course, Kara did not speak back, it was unlikely she could even comprehend anything Mallory was saying, but that didn't seem to bother Mallory. Kara stared out the back of the wagon, motionless and unblinking while Mallory went on and on. Javic stayed and listened sometimes, but the stories often made him long for his own lost home. After a while, he began teaching Belford how to play Crowns, a popular tavern dice game, instead.

In the evenings, after the caravan stopped for the night, Javic spent time with Thorin. He offered to help teach Javic how to properly defend himself with a sword. Belford attempted to participate in the exercises at first, but he proved to be dangerously uncoordinated with pretty much every weapon he tried. Everyone, including Belford, thought it best if he focused solely on his Ver'ati training. Arlin and Elric aided Thorin on Javic's sword lessons as well. They each had vastly different styles, favoring different stances in both offense and defense. Fortunately, the composition of the three men's input had a synergistic effect on Javic's training. It would still be months before he progressed beyond a novice, but he was already getting a feel for the basics by the time the Minthune River came into view of the caravan.

Though it was after midday, the opposite bank was still locked in a deep haze, almost entirely invisible at nearly a league away. The Crimson Waters looked like an ocean, wider than Javic had ever imagined it to be. It stretched endlessly in both directions with countless ships floating across its surface – fishing boats mostly; men cast huge nets overboard, letting the steady current draw in their catch. Most of the vessels used sails, but here and there, the smokestack of a steamboat could be seen pumping dark clouds into the sky. The smoke melted into the thick haze along the horizon.

The grandeur of the river was matched only by the sprawling capital city at its shore. A towering palace could be seen rising above the walls – extravagant arches curving high into the mist, built with the Power many centuries ago. Javic could hardly wait to see the massive river gates, fabled to have repelled some of the greatest armies of all time. The city was ancient, and its history extensive; North Galdren had never fallen to siege in all its years. The walled portion of the city was large, but only housed a small fraction of the capital's population. Homes and shops stretched in every direction for leagues beyond the outer wall.

South Galdren, on the opposite bank, was said to be almost equally as impressive – it was built nearly two centuries after North Galdren was already founded, though, so lacked some of the historical presence that seemed to exude out of every stone cornice and ancient ziggurat that decorated the weathered fortress before them.

Javic couldn't see the sister city through the fog. As they got closer to North Galdren, a massive statue of Mast became visible, reaching out of the depths in the middle of the river.

How ironic that an offering to the God of Nature would show such defiance and domination over the natural world.

The deepest and strongest river in all of Aragwey wasn't enough to stop the Antarans from demonstrating their greatness.

As the caravan reached the outskirts of the city, Illiyna Mek'Verona bid Shiara and the rest of Javic's group farewell. The gypsies planned to continue to the west, moving farther upriver before journeying south into the heart of Antara.

Thorin steered the wagon through the bumpy streets of the city sprawl, moving around the clutter of many makeshift homes and buildings. Most of the common-folk and the poor lived outside of the wall. The homes were small and the population extremely dense. Dirty faces peeked out from their tents and huts, huddled together at every corner and overhang, watching as the wagon rolled past. A few struggling fisherman tried to sell overpriced, slightly rotted fish to the passersby. The air reeked of the sour scent.

As they approached the outer wall, they reached a guarded checkpoint and were forced to stop. Elric and Arlin dismounted from their horses and everyone exited the wagon. They waited to the side while a pair of hardened guardsmen performed a routine search of their belongings for any illegal possessions. Permits were required to sell goods within Galdren and everything was documented and taxed. Smugglers were apparently common and well-practiced in these parts, but the guards were equally as crafty. The thickness of the wagon's floorboards were measured and carefully examined for secret compartments, every box of supplies was opened and painstakingly searched, and each saddlebag was stripped of its contents and inspected before anything was allowed to be repacked.

While the search for contraband was underway, Javic idly watched a group of dirt-stained children frolic about, playing in the street near the guard hut. They seemed carefree despite their poverty. He watched as they ran back and forth, bouncing a worn-out leather ball around between them. None of the children appeared to be over the age of twelve. Once again, Javic was reminded of his own childhood. His heart filled with self-pity as he thought about his lack of friends growing up. These children had so much less than he did, from their torn clothing to their ratty hair, but they were happy because they had each other.

How did I manage to estrange myself so thoroughly?

Sometimes he felt like there was something wrong with him.

A few of the smaller children were staring at Javic. He shied away from their glances; their upturned heads and rosy cheeks made him feel more alone than ever.

After the guards finished their search, while everyone was repacking their saddlebags, the children's leather ball rolled over between Shiara's feet. Shiara reached down and picked it up as one of the older children ran over to retrieve it. The boy thanked Shiara as she handed the ball back to him. Before he could return to his friends, Shiara grabbed the child by the nook of the elbow and spun him around again.

"Hey!" she shouted. "What do you think you're doing?"

There was panic in the boy's eyes as Shiara reached under the flap of his vest and took back her own coin purse. Javic hadn't even seen the child's quick fingers take the purse. The boy tugged free of Shiara's grasp with a sharp pull and sprinted deftly down the street. One of the guardsmen who had been conducting the wagon search witnessed the entire exchange and began to chase after the boy. All of the children scattered in different directions and the street was entirely vacant by the time the guard turned the first corner in pursuit.

"Did he get anything?" asked the remaining guardsman.

"No, I don't think so," said Shiara, holding her purse and examining the strap which normally held it to her belt: The band had been severed by a knife.

Javic shivered at the thought of how close the blade must have come to her flesh. How easily the boy could have slid the blade right under her ribcage.

"Sorry 'bout them," said the guard. "Those dock rats been causing lots of problems lately, but they'll get their own, just you wait. Criminals are dealt with harshly here."

Shiara frowned.

"You can enter whenever yer ready." The guard walked back to his post at the checkpoint.

As Javic climbed up into the wagon, he thought about the faces of the children. There was something else behind their eyes, beyond the carefree attitudes they'd been portraying. The children had been watching him carefully, more closely than he observed them. Their dark, hungry eyes could have given away their ruse if he'd been more observant. The ball game was merely a distraction for the gang to carry out their theft.

At first, Javic had envied the street urchins for their comradery, but not anymore. He couldn't imagine having to steal to survive. They appeared so innocent and happy, but nothing was ever exactly as it seemed.

I can't let my attention slip again, not while so much is at stake.

The pieces were going to fall one direction or another. With any luck, Belford and the Mark of Kings would tip the balance in their favor... as long as Belford made it to Phandrol alive. The wheels were already turning beneath the surface, now it was up to Javic to avoid getting caught in the gears.

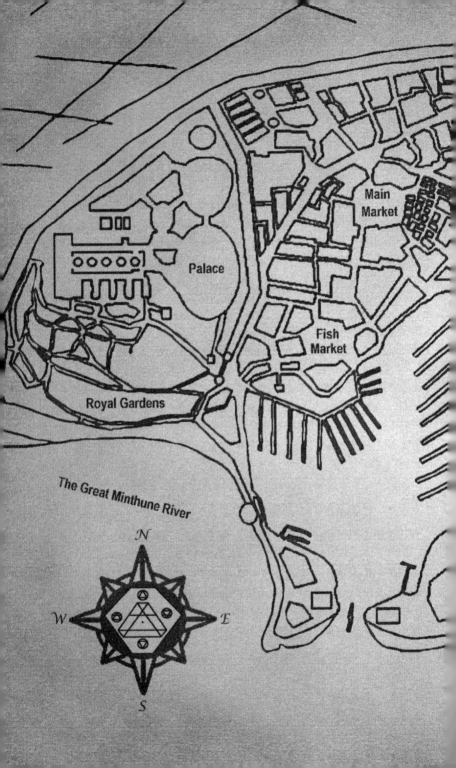

Main Market

Palace

Fish Market

Royal Gardens

The Great Minthune River

N

W   E

S

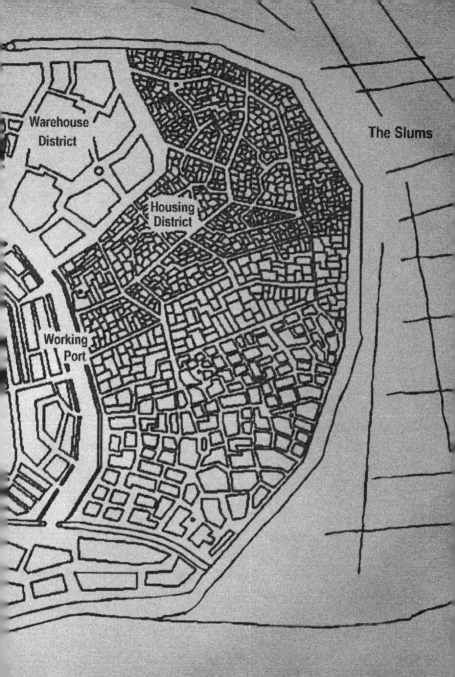

Warehouse
District

The Slums

Housing
District

Working
Port

The City of North Galdren

CHAPTER

28

The Crimson Stalker

The sounds of the docks carried past the fish market to the line of shops where Belford was patiently waiting with Javic for Shiara to return. The clamor of the dockworkers unloading their daily catches from the fishing vessels was strangely relaxing to Belford. The dockhands shouted to one another as they went about their work. The Antarans had peculiar accents. Their words ran together in a drawl that was difficult to understand at times. They spoke quickly with one another, often switching between seemingly random topics of conversation without warning. They used shortened phrases and unfamiliar slang, which only added to Belford's confusion; his mind became exhausted as he tried to piece together what was being said. He hadn't yet attempted to speak with any of the Antarans directly – he was keeping to himself just as Shiara had requested of him – but he did enjoy listening in on their conversations.

The shouts of the dockworkers and the rhythmic thumping of the river water as it slapped against the hulls of the ships in the harbor was joined by a constant chattering of birdcalls, echoing all across the city. The river birds squawked as they dove for fish scraps left by the fishermen, gutters, and packers; the whole city seemed to operate around the preparation and delivery of the river's bounty. The scavenger birds were reminiscent of seagulls, though they had somewhat smaller heads and their feathers were a darker shade than the seagulls Belford remembered. He also noticed some slightly larger pelican-like birds as well. Each one had a narrow band of red running down its back from the base of its neck to the tip of its tail. Belford had never seen either species before.

Javic called them barrelhens and crimson-stalkers, respectively. "Common as horseflies and gravel-hoppers."

Belford wasn't quite sure what a gravel-hopper was, but he didn't bother asking. One of the crimson-stalkers was putting on quite a show, diving into the water to snatch up fish. It promptly snipped them in two with its powerful beak before catching the severed parts, mid-flight, in its flexible throat pouch. After the bird flew off, Belford let his mind wander as he watched Javic pick at a speck of bread between his front teeth, left over from breakfast. They were both leaning against an empty crate outside the only butcher's shop in all of North Galdren's bustling market district.

Shiara was inside the store bartering with the clerk in an attempt to expand their food supplies. Javic and Belford opted to wait outside the narrow shop while Shiara conducted her business. It seemed odd to Belford that there weren't more butchers in the city, considering its massive size, but apparently the demand for red meat was quite small. The locals preferred fish – it was both cheaper and more abundant in these parts.

Belford's stomach turned uneasy at the slightest thought of seafood. The smell, the taste, the texture – it all revolted him. It didn't really have any redeeming factors as far as he was concerned. Luckily for him, fish spoiled faster than beef, or else Shiara probably would have insisted on purchasing the less expensive option and he would have been forced to go hungry.

Belford learned early in their journey that it was best to avoid complaining while in Shiara's presence. It made everything go much smoother when he kept his opinions to himself. Their truce had made his life considerably more pleasant since his drunken night in Rasile, but even so, Shiara still snapped at him every now and then when she was in a bad mood. She was short with everybody, though, so he tried not to take it personally.

Today, Shiara was in a particularly foul mood, carried over from yesterday's debacle with her coin purse. After the incident at the gates, Shiara discovered that the child-pickpocket somehow managed to swap out all of her money with rocks. Belford was impressed with how quickly the boy had made the switch. Shiara was less amused. No one suspected anything was missing until Shiara went to pay for their rooms with a mound of river rocks. The bout of cursing that escaped her lips was quite colorful, even by her standards.

Apparently, the term "conch-blowing fisheater" was offensive enough to the Antarans to warrant Shiara's removal from the hotel. The owner refused to let her back through the door even after she begrudgingly offered an apology. Their whole party was forced to find accommodations elsewhere for the night. Shiara pouted silently to herself as Elric paid the room fees at a less appealing inn down the street. She was clearly embarrassed to have to take Elric's charity, but there was nothing else to do – Elric was the only one in the group with more than a handful of coins left.

Belford suggested refilling their coffers with the Power, but Shiara informed him that transmuting gold or any other form of currency broke several Arcanum laws – a matter which Shiara took very seriously. Belford made a mental note to never mention having created the golden butterfly pendant that Kara still wore around her neck. With Arlin and Mallory's money exhausted, and Shiara's funds stolen, Elric's stash was all they had to restock their supplies and hire a cheap vessel for their continued travels. Finding an inexpensive ship large enough to carry their wagon and horses downriver was going to be quite the challenge.

That morning, Elric divvied out his remaining coins so that Shiara and Arlin could gather supplies while he and Thorin looked into charting a vessel. Mallory stayed at the inn to look after Kara. Belford would have rather stayed behind as well, but Shiara insisted on keeping him within arm's reach. It seemed she had taken it upon herself to be his personal bodyguard. While it was annoying, he supposed it was just part of the burden of the Mark of Kings. He was important, after all – he was finally coming to terms with that idea. Fortunately, he managed to convince Javic to tag along on Shiara's errands as well, so he wasn't left entirely alone with her while she was in such an irritable state.

It had taken quite a bit of coaxing to convince Javic to leave Mallory and Kara behind. At first, Belford was confused by Javic's resistance, but soon he realized what was motivating him: Javic was hoping to spend some time alone with Mallory. It was as clear as day once he recognized it; Javic kept making fleeting glances towards Mallory, always finding one excuse or another to be near her. Mallory had been acting slightly different around Javic lately as well. She was almost flirty, though that was a little too strong of a word. There definitely was something going on, though.

When Arlin was present, Mallory gave her attention to him. They acted like a couple, though Belford had never heard anything official on the subject. Arlin would often ignore Mallory entirely, though, turning away from her advances, or simply not noticing them at all; it was no wonder she was seeking attention elsewhere. When Arlin was absent, there was more than a hint of playfulness in Mallory's demeanor towards Javic. Belford was doing Javic a favor by dragging him away from Mallory, even if he didn't realize it yet. Mallory was trouble.

Outside the butcher's shop, the air held a sweet aroma. The shop door was propped open and the lingering scent of honey-glaze drifted out to entice the nostrils of potential customers walking by. It was an excellent advertisement for the shop, as the scent overpowered the unpleasant fishy stink that surrounded most of the market. As Belford inhaled a deep breath full of the savory scent, Javic tapped him lightly with the back of his hand. Belford glanced over to see what he wanted.

"I'm telling you," said Javic, "there really is nothing going on between me and Mallory."

"Mmhmm," said Belford, rolling his eyes. It didn't matter how many times Javic denied it, he was clearly smitten. It was written all over his face every time he looked at her.

"I mean it!" he insisted. "It wouldn't be proper. It's too soon for me to be liking anybody else…."

Belford's smirk faded immediately. He'd forgotten about the missing girl back in Darrenfield, taken shortly before he first appeared. Javic had only mentioned Salvine's name a couple times since then, but Belford never doubted that she had meant the world to him. Her absence had been a heavy cloud over Javic's head since before the start of their journey. It only took Belford a moment to put the pieces together now. Salvine had probably been turned into a Whune, just like Kara.

He immediately felt terrible for teasing Javic about Mallory. "I'm sorry," he said. "I won't bring it up again." Still, he knew Javic was developing feelings for Mallory, even if Javic didn't want to admit it to himself. Given Javic's loss, having new feelings was an exceptionally positive thing – it meant his heart had not been entirely destroyed; he was already starting to mend. It was more than Belford could say for himself.

Javic nudged him again. "Look at that boy," he said, pointing down the street past a man with a handcart stacked with crates. Javic was gesturing towards a young street urchin dressed in a filthy vest, walking past the display stand for the bakery on the opposite side of the cobblestone intersection.

The boy quietly snatched a loaf of bread from the stand and hid it under his vest. He thought nobody was looking, and he would have been correct if it hadn't been for Belford and Javic. The boy continued on his way nonchalantly. Nobody around him lifted an eye; it was as if he were invisible.

"That's the boy that stole from Shiara," said Javic.

Belford squinted his eyes as he tried to remember what the boy from yesterday looked like, but he had only seen him briefly and wasn't paying much attention at the time. The street urchin turned out of sight down an alleyway before Belford could get a better look.

"Are you sure?" Belford asked.

"Of course I am," said Javic. "Let's follow him."

Belford looked over his shoulder briefly at the butcher's shop. Shiara would likely be a while, but he knew she wouldn't approve of them wandering off.

Javic was already heading towards the narrow alley after the boy. "You coming?" he asked. "He'll get away if we don't hurry."

Belford sighed to himself.

Shiara probably won't even notice we're gone.

He ran after Javic. Together they moved down the alleyway, weaving through a clutter of empty crates that were stacked along the sides of the buildings. When they emerged, they were on another busy market street.

The thief was close; still walking.

"Let's hang back a bit," said Javic. "We can confront him when he turns down another alley."

Belford was nervous; the moon was down. There wasn't much he could do without the Power. The boy was young, but he was quick, and based on the severed strap of Shiara's coin purse, he had a hidden blade somewhere on him that he wasn't afraid to use. They weren't completely unprotected, though – Javic had his training sword attached to his hip. Even so,

Belford always felt vulnerable when he couldn't reach the Power.

They followed behind at a comfortable distance, watching as the boy bumped shoulders with passersby, stealing wallets and jewelry. He was impressively efficient. He even slipped his hand into the open veil of a sedan chair and swiped a wealthy woman's gemmed handbag right out from between her feet. Belford noticed another child on the other side of the street, a young girl with long brown hair, walking parallel with the boy. She was watching the boy just as intently as Javic and Belford were.

The boy gestured for the girl and she came across to him immediately. The sedan woman's purse must have been valuable enough that the boy decided to hand it off in case he was caught. They stepped into the entrance of an alleyway and swiftly transferred all the stolen valuables into the girl's pack. The boy tore the loaf of bread he had stolen from the bakery in two, giving the smaller portion to the girl and then they parted ways just as quickly as they had come together.

Javic and Belford continued to follow the boy as he returned to stealing. He would approach a person in a crowd and extract the contents of their pockets with only a passing graze. Belford began to notice how the boy was choosing his targets: People carrying valuables often had their trousers riding low or their coats hanging tight from significant weight in their pockets. Coin purses were most common amongst such individuals. Sometimes the young girl would distract the boy's victims first by striking up conversations or begging for money – doing anything she could to put their minds elsewhere as the boy bumped past them, snatching everything he could get his quick fingers on.

The girl stopped an older man with mid-length graying hair. The man appeared to be in a hurry, but the girl blocked his path and started talking to him. He had a downtrodden look about him, wearing a tattered, old jacket and a pair of faded red, dirty trousers. Sure enough, they were riding low, just like the others had been.   There was something different about this man, though.   He stood with his back to Belford, but even so, something about him seemed oddly familiar.

The boy bumped into the man, slipping a stout metal cylinder out of the man's pocket and concealing it again within his own vest.   The cylinder was made of dull brass and appeared to be a simple collapsible telescope.

Belford began to tense up, though he wasn't sure why.   He had a strange feeling – a nervous tingling between his shoulder blades.

He knew the man somehow... he had seen him before but couldn't quite place when or where.

The man quickly evaded the girl, still trying to strike up a conversation with him.   He continued on his way, never providing Belford with more than a view of his back.   He hadn't noticed the brief intrusion to his pocket.

As soon as the man escaped, the girl ran over to the boy to see what he had taken.   The boy looked irritated – brass held little value, and telescopes must have been quite common this close to the water.   The boy handed it to her, giving a quick shrug as they went separate ways.

Javic continued to follow the boy, but Belford's eyes were stuck on the strangely familiar man.   As if aware of his thoughts, the man stopped midstride and reached his hands into his trousers.   He patted his coat and pants on both sides, checking all his pockets before spinning around.   The man's face was round and plain; none of his features stood out apart from his intense gray eyes, and even those would have been easily forgettable if Belford hadn't already had their image burned into his memory.

The old homeless man from my dream....

Belford was certain it was him.   The man who tried to kill him and nearly succeeded – he was here, now, in the waking world!   He looked exactly as Belford remembered him, all the way down to his faded red trousers.

How is this possible?

Belford began to panic. His knees went weak as the man scanned his head across the crowd. Belford shrank back. The man didn't notice him, but immediately honed in on the boy who stole his spyglass.

The boy was walking away at a steady, brisk pace, and Javic was exactly a dozen steps back. The man never took his eyes off the thief – he was stalking the boy with a bloodthirsty stare fit for a leopard on the prowl. He moved quickly and with purpose. The crowd sensed his mood, forming an empty space around him as he passed through. There were no noticeable weapons at his side, but Belford still had an urgent feeling; the man was dangerous – he just knew it. He needed to stop Javic before he attempted to corner the boy. Moving as quickly as he could through the crowd without drawing attention to himself, Belford prayed the man wouldn't turn around and see him.

As the thief crossed the street and turned down another alleyway, Javic stopped at the corner and looked back to see if Belford was keeping up. This would have been their opportunity to confront the boy without causing a scene. As soon as Javic looked over at him, Belford began to wave his hands frantically back and forth. He hoped it would be enough to make Javic wait. The man from Belford's dream brushed past Javic without a glance and disappeared down the alleyway after the boy.

"What's wrong?" asked Javic when Belford caught up.

Belford almost didn't want to tell him. He knew it would sound absurd. He was more than a little shaken by the idea himself. "That man that just passed... he's the one from my dream where I almost died...." Belford's voice was timid. He hardly sounded like himself as his throat shook. He couldn't tell what Javic was thinking.

To Belford's horror, Javic, with a concerned and slightly confused look still on his face, drew his sword and rushed down the alley after the man.

"No, don't!" Belford tried to say, but his voice escaped as barely a whisper. Javic had no idea what he was getting into. Belford had no choice but to follow.

Javic remained ahead of Belford, slinking quickly back and forth, staying hidden behind stacks of crates as he pressed forward. Belford wished he could access the Power, but it was still at least an hour before moonrise. He felt so utterly useless. Ahead, Belford could see both the boy and his stalker moving through the shadows of the buildings.

The boy stopped walking; finally sensing that something was amiss. He turned around and saw the old man closing on him. With panic in his eyes, the boy spun back away to flee, but it was as if something gripped him invisibly from the inside; he remained rooted where he stood. Belford didn't understand why the boy wasn't running. The man was only a few steps away now, holding his hand out as if waiting for the boy to return his property. Belford crouched down beside Javic, behind the last stack of crates between the old man and themselves.

Belford had a profile view of the man now; it was unnerving to see him give the boy the same malevolent expression he had shown Belford the moment before pushing him in front of the bus in his dream. The man's eyes seemed to drill through the boy's head. The look of terror in the child's eyes was unmistakable, but his face otherwise remained strangely blank. It wasn't fear that was holding his legs in place – the man had control over the boy's body, forcing his limbs rigid.

How is he doing that?

It doesn't make any sense. The moon is down!

Maintaining his intense stare, the man gave a quick flick of his wrist and the boy's left arm jerked backwards behind him with a sickening crunch.

Belford had to put his own hand over his mouth to stop from gasping. He felt like he was going to be sick.

The image of the crimson-stalker slicing fish in half earlier that day forced its way back into Belford's mind. The surgical precision of the man's mental strike was chilling – a clean break, sending the boy's arm twisting unnaturally behind his body.

Javic shifted uncomfortably at his side. Belford put an arm in front of him in case he was thinking of running out from their hiding place to attack the old man. Javic's face was sheepish white and he too appeared to be on the verge of throwing up.

Belford mouthed the words: "He'll kill us."

Javic nodded slightly, but Belford could tell it was only with great restraint that Javic managed to stay still as Belford lowered his arm back to his side.

Belford tried to reach the Power even though he already knew what the result would be. His continued training with Shiara taught him how to sense when a connection to the Power was possible. When the moon was up, he could feel a certain affinity towards the world around him; it was almost a spiritual state of mind – he could sense that he was only a small part of a greater existence, with every molecule connected by a common thread. He was tiny and yet infinite; insignificant, but capable of anything his imagination could conjure.

He could not feel that connection now.

Reaching out to it was like trying to walk on water.

The boy's suffering caused a strong emotional response in Belford, which would have been more than enough to reach the heightened state of awareness that using the Power required, but the ability was simply absent. Without the moon, there was nothing to stand on and his feet fell right through the threshold no matter how many times he tried to cling to it, or how hard he concentrated.

The child never cried out.

His face did not change, though dozens of tiny droplets of sweat began to form all over his forehead and cheeks. The man flicked his wrist the other way, and the boy's right arm did the same as his left, snapping in several places as it twisted behind him into a human pretzel. His bones protruded from his skin. A thick pool of crimson blood began to form at the boy's feet. His eyes rolled into his head. More blood oozed from his nostrils. The man clenched his hand into a fist now and the boy collapsed to the ground.

The pool of blood expanded to consume the man's shoes, causing his feet to make a disgusting sticky noise as he lifted them away from the stone and stepped casually over to the boy's fallen body. He bent down low and began to search the boy's vest and through his many pockets. He tossed aside the half loaf of bread, a short blade, a couple of wallets, and a silver pocket watch. He checked the time on the watch before putting it aside with the rest of the boy's meager possessions. The man remained crouched for a long moment as he thoroughly searched every piece of the boy's clothing, but the brass spyglass was not there, having already been transferred to the girl. He made an annoyed guttural noise from deep in his throat.

Belford could feel his heart pounding in his chest. It was becoming increasingly difficult for him to stay silent as the pressure built. He felt as if he weren't getting enough oxygen, but he didn't dare breathe any deeper for fear that it would be audible and the man would notice. Panic was rising inside him, making him think irrationally

I have to run away – I need get out of here... he's going to find me and kill me!

Before the urge to run could entirely overwhelm Belford, the young thief sputtered, miraculously still alive despite the blood loss and his mangled limbs, folded neatly beneath him.

Belford held his breath.

With a flourish of his wrist, a small straight edge razor appeared in the terrible man's right hand. With a single slash across the boy's throat, he ended his life.

The man dragged the razor sideways over the boy's shirt when he was finished, wiping the blood away before folding the blade back into its wooden handle. He slipped the razor up his sleeve before standing and slowly cracking his knuckles, one at a time. He proceeded calmly to the end of the alleyway and out of sight.

How could he do that to a child? He didn't speak a single word – never even asked him to return the spyglass!

Belford's head was spinning; nothing made any sense.

How did he use the Power with the moon down?

His throat stung as bile tore at his esophagus. He was vomiting, though he wasn't sure if it was from fear or disgust. His stomach didn't feel any easier afterwards, but Javic helped him to his feet.

"How...? Why...?" Belford tried to speak, but no other words would come out.

"I think I remember him from Rasile; he was there – not just in your dream. I almost stepped on him in the hallway, but he just kept playing with some device in his hands...."

"A spyglass?" asked Belford.

"I don't remember what it was," said Javic. "Regardless, we have to tell the guards what he's done. Someone has to stop him...."

Belford's legs were still weak as he and Javic stumbled after the old man. Even though Belford was terrified, he knew he had to keep a cool head. They had to follow the man; had to keep him in sight... they couldn't just let him get away with this, it was too terrible. Although Belford still couldn't reach the Power, he thought perhaps if enough guards cornered the man... *they can overwhelm him... can't they?*

There was no telling the extent of the man's abilities. From everything Shiara had told him, what he just witnessed was impossible. Without the moon, Ver'ati were just regular men and women. This man was something else entirely. He had walked Belford's dream, and demonstrated unbridled power – a crimson-stalker, deadly and without mercy. Belford didn't know what to think; he just kept following Javic.

As they exited the alleyway and crossed the street, they found themselves against a short stone wall with a hedge growing along its opposite side. Javic quickly climbed onto the barrier and helped Belford up behind him. Through a thin spot in the hedge, they could see a huge garden filled with cherry blossom trees. There were banks of colorful flowers and a pathway of leafy hedges extending far into the distance. The old man was in the garden. They only saw him for a brief moment before he ran behind one of the taller hedges.

"Wait…" said Javic before Belford could leap through the hedge after the man. "These are the Royal Gardens!"

Sure enough, Belford could see the massive towers and striking arches of the ancient palace rising above the treetops.

"We can't go in there," said Javic. "It's restricted to royalty. We would be arrested, or worse…." Javic's voice trailed off as he shifted his head towards the sound of footsteps approaching from behind.

Belford turned to see who was coming towards them. Relief washed over him as he realized that it was a guardsman, dressed in a blue tunic with the royal crest – a red falcon – stitched across his right breast. The guard was whistling to himself, his eyes cast downward as he stepped carefully over a rough section of cobblestone. He appeared to be patrolling, though he hadn't yet noticed Javic and Belford standing on top of the wall.

"Guard!" shouted Belford. "Over here!" He waved to the guardsman as he hopped down from the wall. Javic climbed down behind him, though he seemed a touch apprehensive, shifting his weight back and forth as the guardsman approached.

"What're you two doin' up there?" the guard asked, suspicion clear in his voice. His hand was stiff on the hilt of his sword.

"There was a murder," said Belford. He tried to speak calmly, though it was difficult to do so. "An old man used the Power to kill a boy and then he ran into the gardens."

The guardsman studied Belford carefully. "Impossible," he said, "the moon's down."

Javic took a few tiny steps back as the guard turned his gaze on him. "He isn't lying," said Javic, "the boy's body is just down that alleyway." Javic pointed over the guardsman's shoulder, but the man did not turn to look, instead his eyes focused sharply on the sword at Javic's side.

Belford could tell the guardsman didn't believe a word they were saying. The man continued to stare in silence, searching for any hint of insincerity on their faces.

There isn't time for this, the words screamed across Belford's mind, *the killer is getting away!*

From the palace, a bell began to ring, a frantic pinging that was soon joined by other chimes as an alarm was raised. In moments, all across the city, bells were being struck at every watchman's post. The guard wrinkled his forehead as his eyes grew wide. Scraping steel sounded as he unsheathed his blade. He pointed it towards Belford's throat, his arm shaking slightly.

"Yer coming with me—" he began to say, but Javic swung his sword, still sheathed, with devastating quickness, clipping the side of the guardsman's head. It struck him in the temple and he fell hard to the ground, landing with a thud.

Belford jumped back in surprise as the guard crumpled between his feet, unconscious. "What did you do!?" he exclaimed.

"Let's go!" said Javic as he began to sprint back down the long alleyway where the boy had been murdered.

The whole city rumbled and shook as the chorus of bells echoed through the streets. Belford's lungs burned as he tried to keep up with Javic. His heels ached as they slapped the ground with every step. Ahead, Javic slowed down when he reached the location where the boy's life was ended.

The young girl who had been the boy's accomplice sat with the boy's head resting in her lap. She was facing away, but turned her head towards them as they drew near, visibly startled. The clamor of the bells along with the sound of her crying had masked their footsteps.

"Don't be frightened, we won't hurt you," said Javic, bending over and resting his hands on his knees, catching his breath.

The front of the girl's tattered dress was smeared with blood from holding the boy's head tightly against her chest.

"We saw the man who did this," Javic continued, "gray hair, red trousers, scruffy jacket... you two took something from him."

The girl's eyes were puffy from her tears. Her hair fell in front of her face as she carefully placed the boy's head back down on the ground. She pushed her hair back behind her ears as she stood up, smearing blood across her cheeks in the process.

"It's not even worth anything," she said, her tiny voice barely audible over the bells. She reached her hand into her bag and pulled out the brass spyglass. "The blasted thing doesn't even work...." She stared at it intently for a moment as she turned it over in her hands. More tears began to stream down her cheeks as she dropped to her knees. She let the spyglass fall from her fingertips, grabbing hold of the hem of her dress instead. She began frantically trying to wipe the blood off her hands on the front of her dress, but there was still quite a bit under her fingernails that she couldn't remove with her hands shaking as badly as they were.

The brass cylinder rolled slowly across the ground, stopping at Belford's feet. He bent over and picked it up, being careful to avoid touching the bloody handprint left behind by the girl on its dull surface. It appeared to be an ordinary old telescope, but if that's all it was, he couldn't understand why the man had gone to such extreme lengths trying to get it back. Belford held the lens to his eye and extended the adjustable tube back and forth, but he saw only darkness. Nothing came into focus. There was no cap on the end, but when he turned it around to see what was blocking the sight, he heard a sound from inside. Something was tumbling around in the tube. Perhaps it truly was broken – a piece that had come loose, stopping the light from reaching the viewing lens.

While Javic was trying his best to console the girl, Belford wrapped the spyglass with a handkerchief and put it in his pocket. There had to be more to the object than what he'd observed. Why else would the man have been willing to kill for it? He would examine it thoroughly later when he got the chance.

The bells ceased ringing gradually, the city returning to its normal, quiet state, but it only lasted for a moment before a shrill whistle began to sound from down at the end of the alleyway where they had left the guardsman unconscious.

Without a word, the girl leapt to her feet and ran off at full speed.

"We better go find Shiara," said Javic as he watched the girl sprint away. "The guards will be looking for us."

Belford nodded. He took one last glance at the boy's mangled corpse. He had been avoiding looking directly at it until now. He still couldn't comprehend how someone could do something so senseless. He understood why the Whunes killed – they were more animal than human – but there had been no reason for the old man to murder the boy. He struck so casually, so calmly.

It was the surgical efficiency of the kill that frightened Belford the most. The boy's arms were twisted behind his back in what first appeared to be nothing more than an act of torture. As Belford observed the body now, he realized that the position in which the boy had fallen helped the man search his pockets more efficiently. He really was like one of those crimson-stalkers, quickly snatching up its prey without remorse before flying off in search of another kill.

CHAPTER

29

The Rosa Marsa

Turning right, then left, the stone walls whizzed past Belford in a gray blur. He bounded down the alleyway after Javic. They emerged into the street, backtracking their way to the butcher's shop.

Why couldn't I have just listened to Shiara?

She told him to stay outside the butcher's shop and sit tight. In that, he had clearly failed. For some reason, trouble always seemed to find him. Perhaps that was part of the curse of the Mark of Kings... he had been blaming a lot on the mark recently. The only thing he knew for certain was that the nightmare of a man had invaded his dreams – it couldn't be a coincidence. Javic claimed to have seen him in Rasile that same night, and now he was here.

He must be following me. Everything always leads back to the mark.

He was changing the lives of everyone around him with every little decision he made. He couldn't get the image of the boy's twisted body out of his head. All that blood pooling on the cobblestone. The thought was enough to make his stomach turn again.

And that poor little girl....

It was so tragic and wrong.

No one deserves such brutality.

The act was as close to pure evil as Belford could imagine. First Wilgoblikan, and now this *Crimson Stalker*.... In his mind, he gave the man the same name as the river birds – both were animals capable of merciless killings.

As if having one psychopath running around wasn't bad enough.

He couldn't decide who was worse: Wilgoblikan, turning children into vicious monsters, or the Crimson Stalker, killing them outright without a hint of remorse.

The streets of North Galdren were in a panic. Guardsmen rushed throughout the city whilst the civilians gathered in large clusters to gossip, waiting for any kind of official word regarding the cause of the alarm. Rumors began to arise and spread in the absence of answers.

"It was a call to arms," said a man dressed in a peacoat-like jacket as Belford ran past. "I heard it started over at the palace." But no one, not even the guards, appeared to know what the emergency actually was. Nevertheless, the guardsmen were preparing to quell any civil unrest before it could begin.

Ahead, Belford spotted Shiara standing amidst a growing crowd in the center of the market. She was looking back and forth with a hopeless expression on her face. As soon as she saw Javic and Belford approaching, she put her hands firmly on her hips and her frown deepened into a deathly glower. Once Belford came within reach, Shiara grabbed hold of his ear and pinched the cartilage painfully between her fingertips. Belford gritted his teeth.

"How am I supposed to protect you if you keep running off?" Shiara screamed at him. "I've been worried sick! Can't you see that there's something serious going on here?"

Shouts in the distance caught Belford's attention. Someone was yelling, but it was too faint to understand their words. Shiara let go of Belford's ear and faced the noise as well. Everyone grew silent as an official crier came into view, rushing around a corner and down the street from the direction of the palace. His tabard, displaying the bright-red falcon of the royal crest, flapped wildly as he jogged closer. He stopped suddenly, shaped his hands into a cone over his mouth, and began shouting his message again. "The king is dead! The king is dead! King Lodrin has been murdered!" Shiara's eyes grew wide. "The assassin is still loose; return to your homes immediately while a search is conducted! I repeat, return home immediately!"

Belford could hardly believe his ears. *It's just one thing after another!*

He shared a glance with Javic. The Crimson Stalker was headed towards the palace – it could hardly be coincidence.

Shiara put her anger for Belford and Javic aside as concern over the crier's message settled on her. "King Garrett," she spat. "This must be his doing: First King Vouldric, and now Lodrin – at this rate, all of Aragwey will be in ruins by the time we reach Phandrol...." She shook her head in disgust, causing her earrings to flail wildly. "There's no telling how long we will be stuck here now. They'll lock down the whole city until the assassin's captured—"

"There they are!" came a shout.

Belford turned around quickly as he recognized the voice.

"We should run," said Javic.

Fifty paces off and closing fast, the guardsman Javic knocked unconscious at the garden wall was sprinting towards them, his sword unsheathed. Four more guardsmen were at his flanks, also ready to fight.

"What have you boys gotten yourselves into?" Shiara asked, her face drooping in exasperation.

"Halt!" yelled another guard from behind them, already blocking their escape.

"Stay behind me," said Shiara.

All six guards closed in fast, surrounding them with weapons drawn. They were stuck in a corner. Belford bumped the wall behind him with his shoulder blades as he backed up – there was no escape. He doubted very much that there was anything they could say to talk their way out of this one. Javic had assaulted a royal guardsman and resisted arrest. Both he and Shiara would certainly be considered accomplices, equally guilty.

There was already a massive yellow and green bruise forming in a diagonal stripe across the side of the guardsman's head where Javic had landed his blow. The welt ended at the guard's right eye, forcing him to squint slightly from the swelling.   "You are all under arrest for suspicion of assassination," he said with a smirk.

Assassination!

Belford couldn't believe the absurdity. They never even entered the palace gardens. The guard was clearly upset over Javic hitting him in the face and this was his way of getting back at them. Whenever Belford thought things were as bad as they could get.... This was just his luck. Their innocence should be easy to prove – they had never entered the palace so there couldn't possibly be any evidence against them – but once they discovered the Mark of Kings on his arm, there would be even less appealing questions to answer. There was no telling what their reaction to the mark might be; fear did unpredictable things to people. They might even see it as proof of him being the assassin. That would certainly lead to a swift execution.

Shiara stood in front of Javic and Belford with her arms spread wide, forming a human shield. The moon still down, and Shiara was just as helpless as Belford, but her back remained stiff and her stance unyielding. She wasn't backing down, despite the insurmountable odds. Belford didn't understand how she could remain so fearless.

As the guards moved closer, something strange began to happen. An odd shimmer formed in the air, like heat rising off asphalt in the distance, but it was contained to the area directly in front of Shiara. It was barely noticeable at first. Belford thought he might be seeing things, but the shimmer increased in turbulence and one of Shiara's teardrop-shaped earrings began to glow with a kernel of orange light as the air wavered. The ripples flowed inwards to the firestone gem like iron filings lining up under the influence of a magnet. Belford felt a tingle all over his body as his hairs were drawn to the static energy as well. A chill settled over the air.

As soon as the guardsmen realized that something was amiss – that the Power was being used – three of them sprang forward to attack Shiara, but it was already too late. Once they entered the ripples, their skin immediately went pale, as if all of the blood had drained from their bodies. Their limbs flopped to their sides like rubber sheets as the guards fell to the ground.

Screams sounded in the street as the once-curious onlookers began to fear for their lives. The guardsman that Javic originally assaulted, along with the other two remaining guards, all recoiled as their companions fell. They turned to flee with varying degrees of quickness; one of them even dropped his sword to the ground to lighten his load as he hurried away.

"The moon's down... how did you—" Belford began to ask the obvious question.

"No time for that," Shiara interrupted. "We have to find the others and get out of here!"

The three collapsed guards were still breathing, but were very much incapacitated. They actually looked peaceful, as if they'd simply fallen into a deep sleep rather than being zapped by whatever Shiara had done to the air around them. Shiara grabbed the sack of provisions from the butcher's shop off the ground and began moving as quickly as she could with the heavy bag slung over her shoulder. They started in the direction of the rundown inn. It was only three blocks over, but with the news of King Lodrin's death spreading quickly, the streets were nearly deserted of all the usual traffic. They stopped in the mouth of an alleyway as a group of guardsmen ran by.

"Get back," said Shiara, "don't let them see you; I can't drain anyone else until the gem cools down." Shiara's right earring was still glowing with a dazzling orange hue.

Belford had so many questions....

He watched nervously from around the corner as the guardsmen quickly climbed the steps of a nearby building. It was the hotel that Shiara got them all kicked out of the day before. A guard with a red band around the left sleeve of his uniform was carrying a wooden case with him. He set it down on the top step of the hotel's entranceway and unlatched the lid. Inside were dozens of syringes and a couple of beakers filled with a clear solution. The man began to distribute the needles amongst the guardsmen.

"They're testing for Ver'ati!" Shiara exclaimed, placing a hand over her mouth. "I've seen these field kits before in Phandrol, but I had no idea the Antarans had gotten ahold of any...." She stepped into the street as the guards disappeared into the building. "Quickly now. No time to waste."

They ran across the street and down yet another alleyway. A second crier was there, shouting the same message as the first. The people in the street began hastily dispersing as they were ordered to return to their homes and remain indoors.

When their inn came into sight, they found Arlin returning at the same time. News of the assassination had interrupted his shopping, but he still managed to purchase most of their needed supplies. Mallory and Kara were waiting in the room when they arrived. Details of the emergency had not yet reached them. Shiara filled Mallory in on what was happening while everyone else gathered their bags.

"It's only a matter of time before they search this building," said Shiara. "We'll be detained, and they'll find the Mark of Kings...." She spoke mostly to herself, attempting to sort out the problem. Belford listened intently, but she did not go on to say what she thought would happen to him if his mark was discovered.

"Clearly we must leave," said Arlin, "but if the gates are shut, how can we escape the city?"

"That will be easier once the moon rises," said Shiara, "though I fear the guards will find us long before then if we stay here." Shiara frowned, contemplating their next move.

The door's latch clicked as someone on the outside pushed a key into the lock. Everyone apart from Kara turned towards the door apprehensively. Arlin and Javic both silently drew their swords, preparing to defend the room.

Kara whimpered slightly at the sight of the blades. She quickly curled herself up in the corner beside the bed. The poor girl was still terrified by the sight of weapons.

The door opened, revealing Elric, to everyone's relief. His chest was heaving in and out from a hard run. Arlin and Javic relaxed their stances and sheathed their weapons again.

Belford crouched next to Kara, doing his best to comfort her. He reached over to stroke her hair, but she flinched at his touch, withdrawing farther into the corner.

I wish I knew how to fix you....

"Have you heard what happened?" asked Elric, barely pausing to catch his breath.

Shiara nodded. "King Lodrin's dead."

Elric grunted in affirmation. "We found a ship," he said. "The captain is an Antaran man named Artimus Gupree. Thorin should nearly be finished loading the horses and wagon as we speak."

Shiara's eyes lit up. "We just may escape this wretched city after all," she said with a devilish grin.

Elric didn't look as optimistic. "The harbor gates have already been sealed shut," he said. "The guards are searching for a Ver'ati assassin...."

Shiara waved it off as if it were of no concern. "Let's focus on one problem at a time," she said.

As soon as Belford was able to get Kara back to her feet, everyone gathered their bags and set out towards the docks. If Shiara had a plan, she wasn't sharing it with anyone. There weren't many options remaining; escaping on foot was clearly out of the question – if they somehow managed to break through the checkpoints at the gates they would be run down almost immediately by the cavalry. The walls were built to keep invaders out, but they worked equally well at trapping them inside right now. Until the moon came up, evasion was their only choice.

With Elric leading the way, they joined the last of the civilians passing through the industrial district. By now, long lines were forming at each of the city's exits. People with homes outside the walls had to wait for their turn to leave. The guards were surely testing everyone who passed through to see if they were Ver'ati. Some of the wealthier individuals had homes within the walls, along the eastern side of the harbor. Although it was not the optimal route to the docks, they moved with this more affluent crowd.

They were able to remain inconspicuous for a while, but the farther they walked, the wealthier the households became. They began to stand out as the crowd thinned. Their clothes simply did not match the standard expected amongst the rich. At this point, many of the people in the street were held aloft in fancy sedan chairs, supported by teams of straining servants. The masters remained hidden, their pale faces veiled from the sun by drapes of delicate silk. Elric veered to the right, heading straight towards the working port where the larger vessels were moored. A few guardsmen watched curiously from a nearby way station, but none moved to interfere.

Elric was moving too quickly for Kara. She stumbled over her own feet as Belford dragged her along at the fast pace. Mallory latched onto Kara's other arm to help steady her. The three of them moved in tandem, stepping speedily up to the smooth stone pilings that marked the entrance to the wharf. Once their feet were on the narrow boards of the dock, they were forced to squeeze even closer together. Belford moved under Kara's armpit, practically lifting her off her feet as he hoisted her scrawny arm over his shoulders. Mallory did the same on the opposite side, lifting Kara between them so they could increase the speed of their shuffle.

Ahead, Belford could see Thorin standing next to the steamboat he and Elric chartered for their journey. The vessel had two massive waterwheels, one on each side of the ship, and a sizeable smokestack protruding aft and center between the turbines. Their weathered, blue wagon was already strapped to the stern deck and the last of the packhorses was being led down into the bulkhead by a boy in a striped shirt as Belford approached.

The ship was roughly half the size of most of the other trading vessels moored in the harbor, but it still wasn't small by any means. "The Rosa Marsa" was painted across her hull, barely legible beneath a thick layer of rust. Her captain was a round man, his skin rough and wrinkled from exposure. Streaks of gray ran through his salt-colored hair and a day's worth of stubble was drawn across his prominent chin. His waistcoat and trousers were made of velvet and he wore a black satin sash tied tight around his ample middle. He was seated on a wooden crate on the dock beside his vessel, legs dangling beneath him.

He idly twirled a dull silver coin across his fingertips. It bounced with ease over each digit, though he paid it little mind. He was focused instead on the tobacco pipe buried deep in his mouth. Puffs of smoke rose up, dancing in wisps around the red plume of his captain's hat. He clenched the pipe tight in his teeth when he noticed Shiara barreling down on him.

Quickly slipping the coin into his coat pocket, he hopped down from the crate as she came to a stop directly in front of him. He removed the hat from his head with his left hand, a bald spot revealed top and center as he flourished the cap around in a showy gesture. He finished the move by placing the hat firmly to his chest, greeting Shiara with a deep bow.

"Captain Gupree?" Shiara inquired.

"Please, call me Arti, it's short for Artimus," said the captain, a thin smile on his lips, "or Bundles, that's what my mates call me – whichever you prefer."

"We need to depart immediately, Captain Gupree, ready your vessel," said Shiara.

"Now wait just a moment, can't you see the harbor gates are closed? We won't be headed nowhere until the port is reopened...."

"I'm afraid I must insist," said Shiara.

Thorin, Elric, and Arlin began untying the mooring lines from the dock and throwing them onto the deck of the steamer. Javic and Mallory stepped aboard at the stern of the vessel. Mallory turned around to aid Belford in guiding Kara across the gap. As soon as she was clear, Belford hopped on behind her.

"I don't think you understand me," said Captain Bundles. "The gates are closed; there ain't nowhere to go! There's no way out of the harbor."

"Don't you worry about that," said Shiara.

Captain Bundles puffed out his cheeks. He had a desperate frown on his face. He looked over at Thorin pleadingly, his eyebrows raised, as if expecting him to explain to Shiara the impracticality of her request, but Thorin merely tossed the last of the mooring lines onto the bow of the Rosa Marsa and gestured for the captain to step aboard.

"We will still pay you of course – this isn't a hijacking," said Shiara.

"You could've fooled me—"

"How does quadruple your normal rate sound?"

The captain's eyes widened slightly, though he otherwise maintained a straight face. "Well, I s'pose if the gates were open, we could depart in five minutes or so, just as soon as my first mate returns."

Shiara glanced up the dock. The pair of guardsmen that had been watching them from the way station were sprinting towards the Rosa Marsa now, moving as fast as their feet would carry them. "There's no time," said Shiara, "we need to go now."

"But my first mate…" said Captain Bundles as Shiara ushered him onboard. Shiara, Elric and Arlin all hopped on behind him. Thorin was last, giving the vessel a hard push off from the dock as he jumped onto the stern.

The two guardsmen on the dock watched helplessly as the steamer drifted out of reach just in time. They shouted for Captain Bundles to return, but Shiara pointed towards the closed harbor gates. "Just go that way," she said.

Bundles was clearly torn between the two. The lines on his face deepened as he stood motionless at the helm.

"We don't have all day," said Shiara.

"Was it you who killed our king?" he asked, lowering his arms stubbornly to his side.

"Of course not," said Shiara. "There's really no time for this…."

The boy in the striped shirt who led the pack horses below deck came back up now. "Papa?" he questioned the captain with a worried look on his face. Belford could see the family resemblance now that the boy was closer. He had the same strong chin as his father, but his eyes were softer and set slightly narrower. The boy did not have the ample build that the captain commanded; he was skinny, barely into adolescence.

Captain Bundles didn't respond to his son. He continued to stare at Shiara expectantly.

Shiara threw her hands in the air. "Fine!" she exclaimed. "We had nothing to do with the death of your king, but there are Ver'ati among us who will be unjustly prosecuted if we delay any longer. We also have vital... *information*... that must reach Erotos." Though her tongue was sharp, this was still as close to pleading as Belford had ever seen Shiara.

The captain looked her over for a moment longer. He studied her face. Although Shiara looked as if she might start pulling out her own hair, Captain Bundles turned back to his son and nodded calmly. "Tell 'um to start the wheels," he said.

The boy still looked worried, but moved without delay, ducking down through the hatch. He shouted to some unseen crewmen below as he disappeared.

It was no surprise that a riverboat trader such as Captain Bundles didn't like to take sides when it came to politics. The waterways skirted nations, surely making travel dangerous enough without adding military pressures to the list of perils. The Minthune River was nicknamed the Crimson Waters for a reason; according to Elric, much blood had been spilt on her shores. Captain Bundles probably wanted nothing to do with the war, least of all with the Ver'konus. Unfortunately for him, Shiara just recruited him. Knowingly or not, he would be aiding the Ver'konus today.

A low rumble emanated from deep in the belly of the ship and the two great wheels suddenly sprang to life, slowly turning, edging the ship forward. They were barely moving, meandering about slightly as the Rosa Marsa putted along the fairway towards the closed harbor gates. There were more guardsmen on the docks now, engrossed in commandeering a vessel to mount a pursuit. A bell tolled at the nearby way station.

"It takes 'er awhile to warm up," said Captain Bundles, his face tensed with a nervous pinch.

Shiara's eyes were closed, her fists clenched together against her chest, almost as if in prayer. Belford recognized the concentration in her face; she was attempting to reach the Power. The moon was still down, but as the time to moonrise drew nearer, Belford could feel a subtle hint of the exhilaration that always seemed to consume his body whenever the Power was in reach. It was growing inside him now, getting stronger with each passing moment. The moon would rise shortly. He could already feel its influence.

Wielding the Power was like breathing in fire. He could extend the energy outwards and control the world around him, change anything he pleased. It gave him such a rush – made him feel whole again. When the Power was nearly in reach, he could feel a hollow version of that exhilarating sensation. It came at him like a vivid memory calling back reality – just like the simple thought of Claire's touch could summon up a ghostly tingle of fingers caressing his side – so close, yet so far away. When he closed his eyes, he could almost believe it was real.

Arrows struck the water around the steamer, splashing in uneven intervals. The sound stood apart from the consistent churn of the waterwheels, now picking up speed as they labored onwards. Everyone took cover as a few arrows crashed against the side of the steamer. Captain Bundles ducked down behind his wheel as one of the arrows hit too close for comfort. The ship was made of steel, so the arrows bounced off, but they clanged loudly against the side, echoing throughout the vessel like a tin can caught in a hail storm.

A sudden fiery blaze in the distance caught Belford's attention. A towering fortification near the harbor gates had flames leaping from its crown. At first, Belford thought the flames signaled yet another emergency for the guardsmen to deal with, but he quickly realized what it actually was: The guardsmen had ignited a large tar-covered rock in the sling of a trebuchet catapult located at the top of the tower.

The trebuchet fired, hurling the flaming stone towards them. Belford held his breath as it soared through the mist-filled sky. The projectile fell short, landing with a huge splash and an loud hiss as the flames extinguished in the harbor. Minor swells rose in a circular formation, spreading outwards from the point of impact. The Rosa Marsa rocked slightly, front to back, as she cut through the waves.

"That was a warning shot," said Captain Bundles. "The next one won't miss."

Behind them, the newly commandeered vessel was quickly gaining. The guardsmen onboard continued to fire arrow after arrow from the bow of the vessel. The shots were becoming increasingly accurate as the distance between the two ships diminished.

Shiara put her hand on Belford's shoulder. "I need to ask something of you," she said.

For the first time that Belford could recall, Shiara had a genuinely frightened expression on her face. Shiara tended to fret a lot, but in this moment, she looked more vulnerable than ever. She was like a child, exposed and defenseless. To Belford, Shiara had always been the strong one – her willpower was unrelenting – and yet here she stood, with her hand visibly shaking on his shoulder. It was unnerving to see her in such a state.

"You are stronger than me," she said, her eyes wide. "I need you to go out onto the bow and stop the trebuchet from sinking us."

Belford reached for the Power, but it was still beyond his grasp. Panic surged in his chest. "I can't," he said. Shiara's anxiety was rubbing off on him. "The moon's still down...."

"It will come up any moment now," she said, "and when it does, I need you to be in position."

"But the arrows—"

"I will handle the arrows as soon as I am able," she said. "But the trebuchet stones are too large for me to control at the speed they will be moving. Trust me, I wish it weren't the case, but...."

Belford stood hesitant for a moment, his heart racing. He eyed the walkway he would need to traverse in order to get to the bow. Arrows were raining down along its length. The front of the ship would hardly be any safer.

"Your strength is our only chance," said Shiara.

As Belford turned to look back at her, he realized he was still holding Kara's hand. He'd been gripping it tightly ever since coming aboard. Kara's blank expression saddened him every time he saw it. It reminded him of what she'd lost – what she would never regain… unless he helped her.

"I will go," he said, "but you have to promise me something first." Belford took Kara's hand and placed it in between Shiara's fingers. "If something happens to me, and you get out of here alive, you have to promise me you won't give up on Kara." Belford felt moisture forming in his eyes, but he didn't wipe it away. "Promise me!" he said. "I know she can be fixed. There has to be a way!"

Shiara stared at him for a moment. Tears were welling up in her eyes. Suddenly, she leaned forward and embraced Belford in a tight hug. "Alright," she said quietly. "I promise."

Belford stroked his hand through Shiara's silky hair as she continued to squeeze him.

Before pulling away, she kissed him gently on the cheek. "For luck," she said. "You can do this. Keep your head low."

Belford didn't waste another moment. He slipped out from behind the safety of the hull and moved as quickly as he could down the side of the steamer towards the bow. He stayed low, pushing onwards with pure adrenaline as arrows struck dangerously close all around him. The waterwheel provided cover for a moment, but then he was out the other side and back under fire. As soon as Belford reached the bow, he dropped down, pressing his chest against the deck as more arrows whizzed overhead.

The guards in the trebuchet tower were finished loading a second projectile into their sling. Belford watched with alarm as they ignited the tar and carefully adjusted the rock's intended trajectory through a series of cranks. "Come on," Belford whispered to himself. "I *need* the Power." He said it over and over again as he searched for the connection he had grown so accustom to.

The trebuchet lurched forward.

Its sling whipped over its top like a scorpion's tail.

Belford watched in horror as the rock soared through the air, descending towards him in an arc.

His awareness spiked. He could feel the moon even before he could see it – a bright beacon of beautiful silver icing peaking up above the distant hills. It was only a sliver, but it was enough. He grasped desperately at the energy. It zapped through his lungs with a surge that couldn't have come a moment too soon. He had no trouble attaining the emotional state that the Power required of him – that part of him had been held at the ready ever since stepping out into the barrage of arrows. The trebuchet stone was nearly upon the Rosa Marsa. He only had seconds to figure out how to stop it from colliding with the vessel. If he failed, there would be no second chance. No one would survive.

Belford drew inspiration from his dreams. He willed an energy shield into existence. He pulled water from the harbor and converted it into the polymer bonding layer the dome would need in order to maintain its form.

The air gleamed with a sharp distortion as Belford conjured a massive amount of energy from the oxygen, the ship, the harbor, and everything else in between – there was no time to discriminate. The heat was even drawn out of his breath as the dome hungered for life. He had never tried this process on such a large scale before. He wasn't sure if it would even work. The glow of his creation hung in the air as the projectile smashed down on top of it.

The dome bent inward. The mighty force of the impact rattled Belford's teeth. The invisible structure absorbed the strike, transferring the stone's kinetic energy across its surface. At the base of the dome, the thin edge of the shield sliced deep into the wooden deck forming a perfectly circular groove around Belford's position. The Rosa Marsa lurched downward under the sudden pressure, sending a swell of white water crashing over the bow. The spray rained down on top of the dome, marking its position clearly as the stone continued to bear against it like a hammer on the head of a nail.

The outside world appeared distorted from within the bubble. The dome warped the light that passed through it, twisting everything that lay beyond with increasing severity as the transparent wall compressed downward towards Belford. The buoyancy of the vessel brought the steamer back up just as the dome sprang into its original shape. A hollow thud sounded as the rock bounced off nearly as quickly as it approached. It shot away like a bowling ball off a trampoline. A small residual flame remained on the dome's surface where the projectile made contact. The rock splashed harmlessly into the harbor.

Although the dome was still intact, Belford quickly realized how difficult it was to feed energy into such a large shield. It constantly hungered for more, faster than he could locate it in the environment. Chunks of ice formed in the harbor where the heat was drained from the water so thoroughly that the molecules could no longer maintain their liquid state. Belford released the dome, allowing the polymer compound to collapse onto the deck of the ship. He was immediately enveloped by the clear, gel-like goo.

Shiara let out a warning cry from the stern; the guards' vessel was upon them. Their arrows were now deathly accurate. Shiara was having a difficult time stopping them from striking any of the passengers. The guardsmen's vessel was inching towards the starboard side of the Rosa Marsa and several men were preparing to jump onto the stern of the steamer.

Thinking quickly, Belford looked down at the water around the enemy ship and focused on drawing energy directly out of the harbor. A swarm of buzzing electrons formed in the air above the two ships. As the process unfolded, the water began to freeze, the molecules coming to a standstill. The ice expanded, pushing the ships farther apart and forcing the guardsmen to abort their boarding attempt. Both ships lurched sideways as their hulls collided with the ice sheet. The jarring motion was accompanied by a high-pitched grinding sound as the ice scraped against the metal underbellies of both vessels.

Belford was knocked over momentarily by the impact. He put his arms out, trying to steady himself, but slipped in a pile of the polymer goo that was still slathered across the deck. Despite the fall, he kept his concentration, drawing even more energy out of the water and into the sky. He could feel every hair on his body fighting against gravity, pointing straight up towards the immense cloud of invisible energy above his head. The only thing stopping the negatively charged swarm from crashing back down on top of him with deadly consequence was his extreme concentration. He continued to freeze the water until the guards' ship collided head-on with the ice and ground to a halt. With that problem taken care of, he turned his attention back towards the trebuchet tower.

The sling was already loaded with a third projectile. The guards were in the process of adjusting the trajectory for their next shot. By now, his fear was gone; the exhilaration of the Power had fully taken hold. He felt strong now – more aware – like he could do anything he wanted.

The guards should be afraid of me!

Suddenly, Belford felt a flash of rage rising inside him. The guards had tried to kill him – they tried to kill his friends.

I won't allow those bastards to make another attempt!

Without fully realizing what he was doing, he lashed out, using the energy from the cloud. It shot out with his anger, streaming in a massive bolt of blue lightning straight into the wooden frame of the trebuchet tower. The lightning cracked as the air around the bolt became superheated. The roar was deafening. Belford was disoriented; his ears rang painfully. He was blinded by the flash. For a moment, all he could feel was his heartbeat – his uneven breaths shuddering in and out.

The energy did just as he intended – what he wanted it to do in his moment of fury – but the magnitude of the strike surprised him. He hadn't intended on using the energy as a weapon when he set out to gather it. The attack had been a spontaneous impulse. He hadn't thought it through in the slightest; it just leapt out from somewhere deep inside of him. A dark place he didn't care to revisit. He used to think he could control everything when he used the Power, but that wasn't really true. When his emotions ruled him, they took over. He wasn't in control of himself. Instinct and passion overrode his conscious mind. He couldn't trust himself in such a state. He acted without any regard for consequence. He could lose himself entirely and do something terrible – something he would forever regret. He couldn't shake the thought that it was possible he already had.

Did I just murder those guardsmen?

His sight was the first sense to return, albeit partially obscured where the bolt was still seared onto his retinas. Black smoke was rising out of the tower. Belford couldn't see any of the guards that had been lining the railings. His mouth grew dry and a lump formed in his throat. His stomach twisted into a knot. They had angered him, but he knew they were only doing their jobs. Those men had just been following orders after the assassination of their king. He couldn't blame them for mounting a pursuit.

He prodded his ear with his index finger, urging his hearing to return. Steadily, the ringing began to subside. He could hear shouts coming from within the tower fortification. Someone was still alive up there, at least. The guards were trying to put out the fire, but the flames spread quickly to the barrels of tar that were stacked up alongside the catapult's base. The blaze intensified. The guardsmen were soon forced to abandon the tower entirely. The trebuchet was a complete loss.

Belford clung to the hope that his lightning strike hadn't killed anyone. With no evidence to prove one way or the other, he chose to believe that he was not a murderer. He didn't think he could live with himself if the opposite were true.

Just to the left of the burning tower stood the harbor gates, reaching more than quadruple the height of the steamer. The gates were attached at either side of a tall central. They were so immense that it was a wonder they could be moved at all.

Shiara rushed to join Belford on the bow while he stared at the daunting obstacle. She had an air of smugness about her that Belford could only interpret as pride. "Next time, try not to deafen us all," she said. "It's quite echoey inside there."

Belford attempted a smile, but his heart wasn't in it. He couldn't be so careless with the Power in the future. He pushed his concerns away – he would have to worry about that later. They weren't out of danger yet. "How are we supposed to get through that?" he asked, pointing at the imposing barrier of the harbor gates, dead ahead of them.

The corners of Shiara's mouth tightened as she returned to her usual serious demeanor. "The fabled Gates of Galdren," she said. "No one's ever broken in through them, though I doubt anyone's ever tried to break out before." She pursed her lips for a moment. "That central pillar is the key," she said. "It's a miracle of engineering, really – it uses the current of the river to turn hidden turbines that allow the gates to rotate in a full circle around it like a waterwheel. Our only chance is to destroy the gears that hold it in place...." Shiara's voice trailed off. The gates had started to revolve open on their own. "Merciful Mast!" she exclaimed. "Someone must be looking out for us after all!"

A building adjacent to the gates was in flames, smoke pouring out of every crack. It didn't make sense; it was on the opposite side of the water from the flaming trebuchet tower – the fire could not have spread across the harbor.

"That building must have housed the gates' control room," said Shiara. "I knew it was one of these old buildings, but I'd no idea which one!"

In Belford's experience, there was no such thing as a fortunate coincidence. For a second, Belford thought he saw someone staring out at him from one of second-story windows of the burning building, but then they were gone. It could have been the smoke playing tricks on his eyes, but he couldn't shake the feeling that perhaps it was the man from his nightmare.

Maybe my Crimson Stalker isn't through with me just yet.

The flames licked at the harbor air like a thousand snake tongues searching for the taste of prey on the wind. The fire roared with intense heat, consuming every ounce of fuel within its reach. It hollowed out the building from the bottom up. Belford remained uneasy as the Rosa Marsa made its way through the open gates towards freedom.

CHAPTER

30

The Lifting Fog

The Rosa Marsa skirted through the harbor opening. The fabled gates spun slowly in an endless circle at the mercy of the current. Ahead, the towering statue of Mast rose out of the center of the channel. Javic's face remained hot even after the inferno at the gate control building was long behind them. He felt strange – the excitement of the escape had overwhelmed him – his whole body was jittery. He had been about to tell Shiara his idea on how they could open the gates when a thick curtain of dark smoke began to rise out of the control building. Javic turned to watch the gates in anticipation; the moment he saw the smoke, he knew what would happen next.

When Javic was younger, he had been keenly interested in stories of ancient battles. He read fixedly about the Gates of Galdren in a book his grandfather got for him during one of the harvest festivals. *Rokan of Destavia and Other Stories*, it was called. He read and reread the pages within its bindings so many times that he practically committed the words to memory. The tales provided a much needed escape when the other children of Darrenfield were being particularly cruel. With the knowledge he gleaned from the historical stories, he knew how the gates worked, and he knew their one weakness: A crank in the control building could lock or release the turbines to rotate the gates. A high intensity fire could easily damage or destroy the precisely calibrated machinery, allowing the gates to open. There was no backup system.

Rokan of Destavia was an ancient conqueror of much literary fame. Stories of his life were amongst the most popular within the historical genre. While many of his biographies exaggerated his feats and adventures, the story of his fall held more or less constant across every rendition of its retelling.

Javic had read many stories about the man. They were always pleasantly exciting. Rokan never backed down from a fight and always took what he wanted. He was both cunning and ruthless. Being a skilled military tactician, he took city after city for his home kingdom, Destavia, in an extremely successful nine-year campaign. Rokan had sought to exploit the control building's weakness during his assault on the Gates of Galdren nearly six hundred years ago. Ultimately, he was defeated at the gates, though not at the fault of his tactics. It was a betrayal within his ranks that brought him down. Destavia fell shortly after Rokan's death; without Rokan's leadership, Destavia's armies were outmatched by the combined military strength of Graven and Antara. The territories of the once great kingdom were carved up between the victors. Now, since the Cleansing, Kovehn held most of that land.

Javic knew the history of the Gates of Galdren well, and so had quickly recognized the significance of the nondescript building sitting just within the mouth of the harbor. As soon as he saw the building, he knew what needed to be done: Shiara or Belford would have to concentrate on creating a fire. It would have to be powerful enough to work its way into the control room, located two stories beneath the building in an underground complex.

The thrill of figuring out how they could escape the city made Javic's heart flutter; he was excited by the thought of being the useful one in the group for a change – maybe people would write stories about him one day; the boy who finished what Rokan started – but before he could tell Shiara his plan, someone else enacted his idea so precisely and efficiency that it sparked a torrent of jealousy within Javic.

That was my plan! I was supposed to save the day!

Shiara and Belford looked at one another in bewilderment as the gates opened and the Crimson Waters beckoned the Rosa Marsa forward. Javic's hopes were dashed. This had been his one chance to prove to everybody that he wasn't just some kid, some farmer – some outlander.

I was supposed to be the hero!

He wanted so badly to follow in the footsteps of his mother and father – to have his actions truly matter – but somebody out there had stolen the moment from him.

"I think it was *him*," Belford said quietly to Javic as soon as he was back from the bow, "the *Crimson Stalker*."

Javic assumed Belford was referring to the mysterious man who murdered the poor boy in the alleyway. Calling him the Crimson Stalker felt too respectful for Javic's taste – crimson-stalkers were majestic birds. Yes, they were hunters, but they only ate fish. The man they had seen was a disgusting monster.

Only a pile of filth would slay a defenseless child.

He certainly didn't like the idea that such a terrible man might have been responsible for helping them escape. It seemed unlikely, though. Javic couldn't think of a single reason for the man to want to help them get away.

"That there was a mighty fine job," Captain Bundles said to Shiara. "I've never seen nothin' like it." The captain was apprehensive of Belford, passing his complement through Shiara instead.

After what Belford had done, Javic could hardly blame the captain. Belford's abilities were extraordinarily impressive, beyond anything Javic had ever even read about. And to think, Javic had imagined himself capable of similar renown and greatness just moments before. It was laughable, really.

Shiara was peering behind the steamer through the fog. "No one appears to be pursuing us," she said. "I guess they finally wised up – realized we'd sink them." Shiara smiled at Belford. She moved in closer and started ruffling his disgusting, goo-covered hair.

Belford hunched his shoulders, ducking away from the playful attack. Shiara let out a joyous chuckle.

From below deck, an argument erupted. There was shouting, but Javic couldn't make out the words over the clamor of the waterwheels. The captain's son popped his head up through the bulkhead. The shouting continued below. "Where's Weni?" he asked his father, a look of concern present on his face.

Captain Bundles grimaced. "That's my first mate," he explained to Shiara before turning towards his son. "She's left behind I'm 'fraid. Nothin' I could do about it."

Captain Bundles' son glanced back below deck for a moment. "Garcenus won't be happy," he said, mirroring his father's pensive frown.

"I s'pose not," said the captain, "but there's no going back now."

The boy glanced briefly at the passengers before quickly vanishing back below deck. Captain Bundles was left shaking his head. "Garcenus and Weni," he began, "they... well... they have a *thing* for each other."

Shiara nodded in understanding.

"I'm never gunna hear the end of it," he said with a sigh.

With the giant statue of Mast barely behind them and North Galdren already becoming hazy at the edge of the mist, the Rosa Marsa steadily crept onwards down the vast channel. The dense fog left nothing to help gauge the steamer's speed. The ship appeared almost to stand still in the whiteness as it drifted on, concealed in its own private world. Only the constant hum of the engines and the pattering of the waterwheels reminded Javic that they were still underway.

Shiara took a seat at the end of the stern, looking out at the water behind them. Javic joined her. The river was a murky sheet of gray. It reflected Javic's face back up at him when he looked down upon its sheen, though the choppy undercurrent formed eddies that distorted his appearance. Javic and Shiara watched the seemingly endless wake of the Rosa Marsa stretch out behind them until it was swallowed by the fog.

Belford walked over and placed a hand on Shiara's shoulder. Turning around, she chewed on her lower lip as Belford recounted the entire story of their run in with the man he insisted on calling the Crimson Stalker. Shiara listened without interrupting until the point where Belford removed the handkerchief-wrapped spyglass from his pocket.

"Be careful with that!" she said. "You've no idea what it might do!"

Belford let Shiara take the object from his hands. She picked it up delicately using only her fingertips. She folded back the handkerchief with finesse, as if the spyglass might crumble under the slightest pressure. The bloody palm-print of the little girl stamped around the center of the cylinder in the dead boy's blood was only partially dry. Much of it had rubbed off onto the handkerchief while in Belford's pocket, but without a proper cleaning, there would always be a trace of the evil it had witnessed on its dull surface. Javic could smell the iron of the blood in the air.

Shiara avoided touching the spyglass with her skin, handling it only with the handkerchief as she held it up to her eyes. She examined the outside for a long moment before finally picking it up with her fingers and looking through the lens. She frowned, then looked into it from the opposite side. Something rattled within the tube. Shiara tried twisting the lens off to get at whatever was inside, but the lens was sturdy and would not come loose. She put it back down on the handkerchief, her interest quickly waning.

"Seems like just an ordinary telescope," she said.

"But then why was he after it?" asked Belford.

Shiara shrugged. "You never actually heard the man say what he was looking for, did you? Maybe the boy stole something else from him as well and you just didn't notice."

Belford looked over to Javic for support, but Javic had nothing to say. It certainly was possible that they had missed something. The man had been crouched over the boy's body for quite some time and they hadn't exactly had the best vantage point for seeing what he was doing.

"Well, even if this is just a broken spyglass, none of that explains how he used the Power without the moon," Belford said, "or how *you* stopped those guards from attacking us." Belford's tone was starting to become accusatory.

Shiara didn't respond well to accusations. She narrowed her eyes at Belford. "No one can use the Power without the moon. Certain objects, however…." Shiara began to fumble around with her right earring. She removed it and held it in the palm of her hand. The gem was still glowing slightly, though it was much dimmer than when Shiara first incapacitated the guards. "This is a Power Artifact," she said. "It is capable of channeling a specific task, and it can do so no matter the position of the moon." As Shiara turned the firestone in her hands, it gleamed as if struck by sunlight, though no rays were descending through the fog.

Belford's eyes grew wide with wonder.

"What does it do?" asked Javic.

Shiara sat back farther in her seat so that they could both get a better view. "This one draws energy from the environment," she said. "It once belonged to a pair, though its sister was lost to the ages." Shiara reached up with her left hand and removed her other earring. "This one's a fake," she said. "I just wear it so I don't look odd." The replica earring was dull in comparison. "It is said that the original was capable of harnessing the energy gathered by my Artifact's gem in some manner, though exactly what it did remains a mystery, forgotten in time as well."

"So the Crimson Stalker was using Artifacts?" asked Belford.

Shiara put her earrings back on. "He must have been," she said, "though they are extremely rare. The Arcanum controls most of the known Power Artifacts. Ver'ati can submit requisitions when assigned important or dangerous missions, and the Archives will check them out to us, that is, if the request is approved by the council. That's how I got this one. And before you ask, because I can see what you are thinking, the council would never approve a mission to assassinate King Lodrin."

"I wasn't thinking that," said Belford, "but I was curious about what other Artifacts are capable of doing."

Shiara laughed. "Oh, loads of things. The Archives researches known Artifacts and tracks their histories, but many things are still unknown about them, for instance, no one knows how they were originally created, or when. Objects imbued with the powers of Mast... there is much myth and legend surrounding them, as you can imagine. The Archives have to weed through such nonsense on a daily basis. Power Artifacts are ranked right up there with Echoes when it comes to unexplained phenomenon. Many Artifacts don't even have any known uses at all. The only reason we know they are Artifacts in the first place is because there are a few known detector Artifacts like the Erotos palace orbs which glow when in the presence of any object that can wield the Power."

"So that's what you thought this spyglass might be?" asked Javic.

"I suspected as much, yes, but there is no way of telling for sure without access to a detector. Some Artifacts have obvious functions, but most do not. If it does have a connection to the Power, it could do anything, or nothing."

"What should I do with it for now?" asked Belford, tucking the spyglass back into the handkerchief and returning it to his pocket.

"Just be cautious," said Shiara. "Some Artifacts respond only to the touch of a wizard, while others can be manipulated by common men who don't have the Gift of the Arcanum at all. This object didn't do anything when I touched it, but that's not to say it's impossible for it to channel under the right circumstances – that is, if it indeed turns out to be an Artifact at all."

The fog was beginning to thin by the time they finished their conversation. The banks on either side of the vast river were flat and barren. Only grass-weed could grow in the coarse, sandy dirt carried by the Minthune's current from the Arid Hills far to the west. Night was quickly approaching when Captain Bundles invited everybody below deck for a much needed supper.

Javic saw the man, Garcenus, for the first time as he came up to take over the helm. Garcenus was no older than Belford, though his skin was rough and dry from the salty air. He had a black scruffy beard and a dark complexion that matched his eyes. He glowered at the captain and the passengers – a scowl that could put Shiara's own to shame. Garcenus directed the brunt of it towards Captain Bundles; the captain did his best to ignore the look.

"I daresay he ain't takin' any of this very well," said Captain Bundles. He apologized for his deckhand's rudeness once everyone was below deck, then began a quick tour of the ship's facilities, leading them through the narrow hallways of the vessel.

The cargo area was behind them, down a short hallway. It took up the entire back portion of the steamer. Javic could see Olli and Amit tied up alongside the other horses through the open doorway. The quarters were tight, but the horses would have to make due. The group moved forward, passing through the crew's living quarters before entering the mess hall.

A woman cursed loudly from within the adjoining galley as the steamer rocked with unexpected sharpness. Dangling pots and pans banged together with the series of rolling bumps. A petite woman in her late thirties stormed out of the galley with red sauce splattered down the front of her aproned blouse. The sauce drizzled down onto her pants and shoes, causing her to leave behind a trail of red shoeprints as she approached.

An image of the Crimson Stalker walking through the boy's blood in the alleyway flashed across Javic's mind. The sour expression on Belford's face indicated that he was likely picturing the same thing. Javic did his best to shake the imagery as he focused back on the furious woman.

She was carrying a now mostly empty pot in her left hand. In her right, she held a wooden stirring spoon, raised up like a weapon, as if she were about to strike somebody with it. She had blonde hair, cut short for a woman. She moved her bangs out of her eyes with her forearm as she marched up to Captain Bundles and pointed the spoon directly in his face.

"You know he did that on purpose," the woman said angrily, an Antaran accent clear on her tongue. "How can you let him pilot? He'll sink us by dawn!" She was short, only coming to the captain's shoulders, but she had an opposing stature for her size, not that unlike Shiara's.

"Coriva, these here are our passengers," said Captain Bundles, gesturing to the procession of people in the hallway behind him. "And this is Coriva Lethos," he said over his shoulder.

A glob of sauce dripped from the lady's wooden spoon onto the ground as she eyed the group for a moment with an unchanging expression. Kara sniffed the air; she looked as if she might lunge at Coriva to eat the sauce right off her apron, but Belford was quick to hold her back. Coriva didn't seem to notice, instead turning her attention back towards the captain. "What're you gunna do about Garcenus?" she asked.

"Nothin' I can do," said Captain Bundles. "Ain't no one else to keep 'er afloat while I'm sleeping 'less you want to give 'er a shot."

"If I did that, there wouldn't be anybody left to cook you dinner," she said, flicking her wrist slightly, launching another dollop of sauce off her spoon and onto the floor. Coriva turned around and walked back to the galley, leaving a second trail of sauce overtop the first one as she retraced her steps.

"She's a sweet lady," said Captain Bundles, "just stressful circumstances is all."

Forward on the ship, beyond the mess, the passenger quarters took up most of the remaining deck space. Captain Bundles let the travelers figure out their own sleeping arrangements while Coriva began to cook another batch of sauce for their meal. Captain Bundles went down to the engine room for a moment while everyone began to settle in.

Belford sat with Kara. He was tinkering with her mind again – Javic could tell. Kara had beads of sweat forming at her temples, though she hadn't yet started to scream like the first time Belford tried to fix her. The intensity on Belford's face matched Kara's expression, though her face appeared to be contorted from pain rather than concentration. Kara began to make a noise. It started out as a whine, but grew into a high-pitched whimper. Everyone stopped what they were doing and looked at Belford. Kara quieted down as soon as Belford ceased his invisible actions.

Belford let out a disgruntled sigh. "The key is in the pain, I think," he said, turning around to face the onlookers. "It shows she's still capable of feeling, at least. I just wish I knew what Wilgoblikan..." Belford cut himself off mid-sentence, his voice freezing up as his eyes grew wide. He glanced at Elric for a moment with a worried expression.

Elric's face turned slightly red and the fingers of his right hand immediately began caressing the ring on the chain around his neck – Javic's father's wedding band.

"Wilgoblikan..." said Javic, confused. He stared blankly towards Belford as he tried to comprehend what was going on. "Who... what... you know the Goblikan's name?"

Belford bit his lower lip and continued to stare wide-eyed across the room, but neither he nor Elric met Javic's gaze.

"I..." said Elric. "There's something I should tell you." Elric's eyes remained downcast as he began to squeeze Bartan's wedding band tightly in his fist. After a moment, he put a hand on Javic's shoulder and led him to the edge of one of the cots.

As Javic sat down, he had a sense of dread rising within him, though he wasn't really sure why. It was an uneasy feeling in his stomach – like he was about to float away. Everybody else cleared the room. Belford cast a sad glance towards Javic as he exited and closed the door behind him. The pressure in his chest made Javic feel like he was holding his breath.

"The Whune pursuing us..." Elric began, "there's no easy way to say...." Elric was having difficulty speaking. "Wilgoblikan... he killed your parents...."

The room began to spin around Javic's head. He felt simultaneously hot and cold, like there was fire pouring through his ears and mixing with his frozen brain. He felt a lump forming in his throat, as if he had swallowed a rock. All of his thoughts were jumbled in his head and none of them were making any sense.

The captain of the guard in Felington fighting valiantly one moment, his skin crumbling away under its own weight in the next, flattened into a pile of ash.

The flames bursting forth beneath the trees on the road south of Bronam while Javic clung to the branches above; his broken arm mangled at his side; nearly smothered by the smoke but not daring to make a sound as the man roared from down below.

The darkness of the dank cave as the lone Whune threw itself towards him and Mallory; having to crawl on hands and knees over the slimy cave rocks; clawing at the moss with fingernails as the Whune gnashed its teeth against his ankles; he was too slow as the Whune smashed him against the rough wall; Mallory screaming his name, sheer terror in her voice as he lost consciousness.

His parents' faces; only a vague reconstruction in his mind, formed from extrapolations of his own reflection; so hazy now; so unfocused in his thoughts; he wasn't even sure anymore what they had looked like.

Salvine… oh, sweet Salvine, I can *picture her face….*

She was just another victim in a long line, torn from his life by that monster.

Wilgoblikan; the dark wizard; the beast that took her away; took his whole family away; the man who made him grow up without the touch of his mother; the pride of his father; the laughter of his grandfather – all lost so many years ago; so many dark days where a warm lap to cry on and caring arms to hold him would have made all the difference.

He wouldn't have grown up on a farm; he would have lived in a city; trained to be a soldier like his father; gone on grand adventures; marveled at the powers of his mother; learned how to talk to women; how to not be so ashamed of himself all the time – so shy; so afraid of rejection. Without his parents to raise him, he had turned out weak; afraid; pathetic; a failure; a disappointment to their memory.

Wilgoblikan – Wilgoblikan had taken everything from him. He would kill Wilgoblikan; he would slay the beast that had destroyed so many lives and tainted so many more.

"I'm sorry I kept this from you until now," said Elric, "but I hope you understand why…."

Javic stood up and pushed past Elric. He hardly even heard his grandfather's words. Elric had hidden the truth from him, and that angered him, but even that was minuscule compared to the hatred he felt for Wilgoblikan. Putting a name to the face helped focus his animosity. There was nothing that could change his mind now. He would not rest until the monster that murdered his parents was dead. He would see justice enacted, no matter how long it took, no matter the price. He would avenge the loved ones that were taken from him, even if doing so was his last act on earth.

Elric called to Javic once more, but he dashed out of the room and down the narrow hallway. His feet were moving under their own control, he barely noticed them at all. His mind was searing now – the fire had won the battle of hot versus cold – he could think of nothing but revenge. His feet carried him through the mess hall and crew quarters and over to Olli where his bow and quiver were still tied to his saddlebag. He took the weapon with him as he went up to the top deck of the steamer. Garcenus watched in silence as Javic made his way along the thin walkway on the side of the Rosa Marsa and onto the bow. Javic looked ahead in the darkness, beyond the spotlight that Captain Bundles' son was using to illuminate the ship's course, beyond the glow cast down from the moon. He did not know exactly what he was looking for, or how he would know it once he found it, but he crouched down and just watched as the waves rolled by in front of him.

Wilgoblikan was out there somewhere, and if he came at them again, Javic would see him coming, and this time he would be ready. Wilgoblikan was going to die.

There was no other way.

CHAPTER

31

The Graveyard

The desert wasteland stretched endlessly in every direction. Rolling dunes danced in the heat of the sun, forming a shimmer in the distance. The mirage taunted Wilgoblikan with thoughts of water. It had been three days since he entered the unforgiving Torus Desert, and nearly twelve hours since his canteen ran dry.

The procession of Whunes behind him trudged diligently through the sand with a slow but steady pace. They were having more difficulty than Wilgoblikan – their immense weight caused them to sink deep into the dunes with each step they took. They would never quit, of course, but that did not mean there weren't limits to how much their bodies could take. Just like horses, they could be marched to death if Wilgoblikan wasn't mindful.

Normally, he would have used the Power to transform some of the endless sand that plagued these lands into a much needed watering hole, but the Power did not work within the Torus Desert. Not for a century had any wizard been able to reach the Power here. It was the Arcanum's doing – back during the battle that ended the Cleansing. The Arcanum used a legendary Power Artifact known as the Orb of Parphim to defeat a grand Goblikan army on these grounds. The Goblikans would have enjoyed a full victory over Aragwey if not for the orb's devastating blast. To everyone's surprise, the orb's light did more than just destroy all who gazed upon it – the energy it released wrecked the land itself, forming the desert and turning the region into a dead-zone for the Power.

Nothing could grow here anymore. The rich soil and forests all crumbled into sand within the first decade. Now there was nothing left but dunes. The land was dead.

This was the domain of the Goblikans now.

The trek through the desert was taking longer than Wilgoblikan had anticipated. He had to be close to his destination now – the Graveyard. It was difficult to tell exactly how far he had come. With no permanent landmarks to gauge his travels, he was relying on his compass alone to maintain the necessary heading – due northeast from Bronam. The decision to take this path had not been an easy one, but ultimately it was the only viable option that remained if he was to have any hope of completing his mission.

After receiving word from one of his Whunes that his target was holed up in a cave in the forest northwest of Rasile, he searched the area for two long days before realizing that the boy must have escaped his net. His search was thorough; the boy should not have gotten away. The Whune who discovered the boy's whereabouts must have been delayed in delivering the information to Wilgoblikan – a fact which had been glaringly left out of its report. Such a blunder was the only explanation that made sense.

Now, Wilgoblikan realized that Whunes were not the brightest creatures – he had gifted them with brawn, not brains – but even the stupidest of Whunes should have known to mention that it had wandered through the forest for over a day before finally returning to its master.

Since entering the desert, the offending Whune had been acting strange – Wilgoblikan couldn't quite put his finger on it. The Whune's movement was a little jumpier than the rest of its brethren. It had a tendency to hang back from the other Whunes as well, almost as if it were frightened.

A cowardly Whune....

He could hardly imagine such a thing.

He supposed he had no one to blame but himself. He must have screwed up with this one's transformation somewhere along the way. He made a mental note to go back into its head if its behavior did not improve by the time they left the dead-zone.

With so much time wasted searching for the boy, little chance remained of catching him on the open road. Even so, Wilgoblikan hadn't yet given up hope that he would be able to find and kill his target before it was too late – he knew exactly where the boy was headed after all, and so there was still one last chance to head him off.

As Wilgoblikan crested another dune, the fingertips of a giant, buried statue reached through the shimmering mirage in the distance.

The Graveyard. Finally.

No doubt the other Goblikans already knew he was upon them. No one got within ten leagues of the Graveyard without the Sentinels spying them.

As he drew nearer, more half-buried monuments became visible, protruding out from the dunes. A grand city had once thrived here, back before the Orb of Parphim unleashed its unholy light. Eversted, it had been called. This was ground-zero for the orb's blast. Only buried ruins remained. The Goblikans now called this place the Graveyard.

The giant head of the statue whose hand signaled Wilgoblikan's arrival became visible just above the surface of the sand. Unsurprisingly, there was a cluster of Sentinels perched atop the statue's brow. Even at this distance, their yellow eyes glowed brilliantly beneath their head wrappings. They sat crouched like spiders, awaiting prey.

Wilgoblikan didn't much care for the Sentinels. The mummy-like wrappings around their faces kept the sand out of their decaying flesh, but also hid the vertical divide of their jaw. It wasn't the way they could unhinge their heads to form a gaping maw that disturbed Wilgoblikan, nor was it the terrible screech they sounded in order to announce his presence to the nearby Goblikans stationed at the Pit. Wilgoblikan hated the Sentinels because they did not respect his authority. He was one of King Garrett's chosen ones – elite amongst the Goblikans – but they knew he could not use the Power here, so they did not fear him.

Three gangly Sentinels of the dozen or so positioned upon the statue's brow descended from their perch and began an all-out sprint across the sand towards Wilgoblikan's procession.

It was not a welcoming party.

Although they moved upright while walking, they ran on all fours, hunched over with their long legs and slender arms galloping together in unison. They kicked up a cloud of dust behind them as they moved between the dunes, their limbs rolling fluidly beneath them like elk fleeing a wildfire. Nothing could move through the sand quite like the Sentinels.

Wilgoblikan's Whunes grew apprehensive behind him. The few amongst them who were with him the last time he journeyed through the dead-zone still had scars from the Sentinels' harassment. Although the Sentinels were themselves Whunes, they had little in common with Wilgoblikan's creations. They enjoyed jabbing at his ilk with their long narrow fingers. Their claws, sharp as spear tips, always drew blood.

The approaching Sentinels moved against his Whunes, using their superior speed to separate several of his unfortunate herd apart from the rest of the procession. The devilish Sentinels proceeded to circle the Whunes, striking randomly at their haunches, all the while cackling infuriatingly like hyenas from their vertical maws.

Despite not fearing Wilgoblikan, the Sentinels were not senseless enough to jab at him directly. Even so, Wilgoblikan's glower darkened further with every grunt his Whunes made behind him. He could not heal their wounds while the desert masked his connection to the Power. Whunes were just as susceptible to infection as any natural born creature, so there was a good chance he would lose more than a few to the Sentinels' attacks. He needed his Whunes in good health for the mission ahead.

He continued through the Graveyard until a sharp cry from one Whune brought his attention back around again. A hamstring had been severed by a well-placed poke. The Whune was down – useless to Wilgoblikan now. The loss enraged him. He lashed out the only way he could.

Kill them! Fight back! He sent the mental command to his Whunes, allowing them to strike against the jeering Sentinels. The Sentinels hopped away with ease from the dehydrated Whunes' flailing attempts at retaliation. The Sentinels hooted and cackled even louder as they danced just out of reach of the swinging axes. It was all just a big game to them. The simpleminded buffoons were jeopardizing his mission.

Wilgoblikan sighed. He wished he could torture whatever dastardly excuse for a Goblikan had spawned the meddlesome shits. There was a good chance their creator was already dead, though. When a Whune's master died, the enslaved became free to make their own decisions. It would certainly explain why these three Sentinels in particular were so unruly.

His Whunes were tiring themselves out trying to catch the evasive troublemakers. He reined them back in, giving up on teaching the Sentinels a lesson. He ordered the procession to march on, leaving behind the downed Whune. As soon as the other Whunes stepped clear, the Sentinels swarmed over the injured creature, answering its cries with more cackling laughter. They stabbed at it mercilessly, putting out its eyes before turning their focus towards its midsection. They gouged it repeatedly, digging for vital organs. Distracted by the kill, the Sentinels stopped following Wilgoblikan's procession long enough for them to reach the Pit without further harassment.

The Pit was a massive excavation site nestled in the center of the Graveyard. Wilgoblikan stepped up to the wide opening and looked in. An updraft made him squint slightly as he searched for the bottom. It was obscured in shadow by the low angle of the sun. Fortification walls held the desert back, but occasional storms still brought down substantial clouds of sand. A never-ending line of Whunes marched up the spiraling pathway that circled the wall of the Pit, working like ants as they carried buckets of the encroaching sand back to the surface.

For several decades, the Goblikans had overseen the formation of the Pit. The secret undertaking had exposed a significant portion of the derelict city of Eversted, now converted into a Goblikan stronghold, but they did not stop there – uncovering the city was not their goal. They continued going down, burrowing deeper and deeper as the years transpired. Explosives were used to blast through the bedrock once iron tools became ineffective on the dense stone. Without the Power, it was an arduous task. Many Whunes had given their lives working the Pit, and many more to the vast tunnels that came next.

"You've come too late to join the Saldrone raiding party."

Wilgoblikan spun to face the voice. An old Pit warden stood behind him. The half-senile Goblikan watched him with a glazed-over expression. He was shirtless. His skin looked like old leather, toasted by the sun. The updraft coming from the Pit blew the tip of his tangled, white beard around the side of his head.

"Though, I suppose you can still catch them if you hurry. They took the West Tunnel early this morning."

"I'm not here for that," said Wilgoblikan.

The warden scratched his beard, pulling it back around to the front of his face. "Are you sure?" he asked. "I don't remember there being any other departures scheduled for today."

"I'm not on the schedule," said Wilgoblikan. "I require access to the South Tunnel. How soon can a train be readied?"

The warden stared at him blankly. "No one ever goes south," he said.

"Well, I am. Can you ready a train?"

"Are you sure? I don't remember a south train departure on the schedule." The warden's pale-blue eyes were starting to bulge slightly.

Wilgoblikan let out a slow exhale. "Look, I already told you, I'm not on the schedule." He was tempted to have one of his Whunes throw the warden off the ledge, but he restrained himself.

"Are you here to join the Saldrone raiding party? I'm afraid they've already departed this morning."

Completely sun-crazy....

The other Goblikans were probably watching him, laughing at having sent the old warden to do their job. Being stationed in the dead-zone was a punishment. Without the Power, the desert was terribly boring. Only particularly special morons were saddled with the task of watching a hole in the ground.

If Wilgoblikan failed to kill his target, there was a fair chance he would end up reassigned here. He doubted his sanity would last long in a place like this.

"Just ready a train for the South Tunnel," ordered Wilgoblikan. He turned his back to the old warden and began the long spiral hike into the Pit to the secret tunnels below.

"South?" the old warden said behind him. "No one goes south!"

Wilgoblikan hastened his steps, lest the urge to watch the warden fly should overwhelm him.

Hopeless

Dinner aboard the Rosa Marsa was awkwardly silent. Captain Bundles and his son, Eben, joined the passengers as they ate, but none of the other crewmembers were present for the meal. Between everyone carefully avoiding talking about what just transpired between Elric and Javic, and the inedible fish stew sloshing around in the pot at the center of the table, Belford would have rather been almost anywhere else in the world.

Javic was still out on the bow. No words from Shiara or Mallory had managed to bring him back inside. Once it was obvious that he intended to remain up there for a while, Mallory brought him a blanket and a serving of stew. Belford had not yet attempted to speak with him; he probably didn't want to see Belford right now anyway. Javic would come back in when he was ready, Belford figured. Until then, there was nothing anyone could do but wait – Javic would keep watch into the darkness.

While most of the passengers picked gingerly at the stew set in front of them by Coriva, neither Belford nor Elric touched their bowls. Belford simply wasn't hungry enough to eat seafood, but Elric's troubles were deeper. He sat with his eyes half closed and downcast – a motionless stare into the thick, fishy broth below. Everyone else slowly consumed the stew, Kara somewhat more ravenously than the rest. She was making quite the mess, ignoring the spoon set out before her. Eben gawked at her throughout most of the meal as she scooped up handfuls of stew with her slender fingers.

Belford couldn't help but blame himself for the mood of the room.

Why couldn't I have just kept my stupid mouth shut?

With his slipup, he'd forced a terrible secret out of Elric. Not all of Elric's skeletons had been exposed yet, though, so Belford was still stuck in the middle of everything. Elric hadn't told Javic the part about Wilgoblikan being his great uncle and killing his grandmother. Considering Javic's reaction to the first part of the news, Belford wasn't surprised Elric hadn't mentioned the rest. There was only so much a person could take in all at once. He just hoped Javic would be alright – he couldn't imagine how difficult it must be to finally put a face to the pain of losing his parents. Javic didn't need to know that Wilgoblikan was family as well. Belford couldn't remember anything about his own family... perhaps that was for the best. Missing Claire was bad enough without memories of his parents and childhood tugging at his heartstrings as well.

After dinner, Elric walked with Belford while he led Kara back to her cabin.

"I am going to tell him the rest," Elric said, "eventually."

Belford waved his hand through the air. "It's really none of my business."

"I just don't want you to think.... I'm not going to make you keep any more secrets."

Belford's shoulders slumped. "I really am sorry about all that," he said. "I screwed up."

Elric shook his head. "No, no, it's not your fault. I knew the truth couldn't stay hidden forever. I should have told him myself, much earlier."

Belford opened the door to Kara's cabin and she walked inside with little prompting. He directed her to the bed and had her lay down. She wouldn't sleep, but Belford tried to get her off her feet as often as possible.

"Let me watch over her tonight," said Elric. "I don't have anything better to do."

"Are you sure?" Belford asked.

Elric nodded. "I wouldn't be getting much rest tonight anyway."

Belford accepted the offer. He used his free time to wander the ship. He listened to the sounds of the river slapping against the side of the hull, and the waterwheels pattering away, propelling the Rosa Marsa downstream through the darkness. The sounds were relaxing; a white noise that could easily lull a man to sleep, but Belford was far from tired. It had been an eventful day, and after everything with the Crimson Stalker, Belford was more than a little fearful that the nightmare of a man would appear in his dreams again.

From the stern, Belford watched the moonlight dancing on the water – it was a beautiful sight, but not nearly pretty enough to take his mind off his worries. He sat reflecting on Claire, Kara, the Crimson Stalker, and Wilgoblikan and the Whunes for a long while until he grew cold. A brisk breeze was picking up and it was becoming chilly on the open stern deck. Belford stepped back down the stairs into the body of the steamer as he started to shiver. His body was protesting his decision to skip dinner by refusing to heat itself.

As he glanced over at the horses, tied up in the cargo area, he heard lively voices coming from the deck below. Following the sounds of laughter, Belford made his way down the steps that led into the bilge. The walkway was tight, but ahead he could see an orange glow coming from the steam furnace that provided pressure for the waterwheels. The flickering flames lit the walkway well. A wet heat filled the air – it was repressive to the lungs, but quite welcome after sitting in the cold for so long.

Belford stepped through the bulkhead into the engine room. Two men, copper-skinned and shirtless, stood before him with shovels in their hands, scattering coals over the flames within the wide-open furnace at the heart of the ship. They had their backs to Belford and hadn't yet noticed him. Both men's biceps and shoulders were bulging from their labors. The man on the left had a slightly darker complexion and stouter appearance than the one on the right. The taller man began to speak in a language that Belford could not understand. "*Erestan bri netri vec serivo*, Garcenus *tren ceserivo* Bundles," he said. Both men laughed.

"Hello," said Belford.

The men ceased their laughter and turned towards him at once. They had similar facial features; matching bumps on the ridges of their noses, like Javic's, and narrow jawlines. The taller man quickly shut the metal hatch of the furnace, cutting the amount of heat radiating into the already sweltering engine room.

"Oh, you the young Ver'ati," said the shorter man as he wiped soot and sweat off of his forehead with a rag procured from his back pocket.

"Sorry if I'm bothering you," said Belford. "I was just walking by and I heard your voices...."

"Is no problem," said the taller man. "You like *prestina*?" The man gave a pained expression as Belford stared back blankly. "This, this!" he said, opening the furnace again and using a wide scooper to remove a bready, pancake-like dough from a flat stone inside.

They're using the steam furnace as an oven!

"You must eat." The man placed the bread on a plate and handed it to Belford.

"I am Mikel Naffeim," said the shorter man, "this is Ader."

The taller man pounded his fist to his chest. "We are brothers."

Belford took a bite of Ader's offering. It was bland and slightly undercooked, but the heat warmed his belly. "I'm Belford," he said, his mouth still full of the prestina bread.

The brothers laughed again as if Belford had said something funny. Mikel pulled up a stool for Belford to sit on as Ader ladled out another batch of chunky batter from a bucket next to the furnace. It sizzled and steamed in the intense heat as he poured it onto the flat cooking rock.

It took more than a few minutes to get used to the way the brothers spoke, but soon Belford was chatting with them about all sorts of things. He learned that the language they were speaking when he first walked up was an ancient Aragwian dialect that had all but been replaced in Aragwey by John Graven over a thousand years ago – they referred to him as the Rainbringer. The language was still commonly spoken in the Eastern Territories, where Ader and Mikel were born and had lived until recently. The Eastern Territories were across a narrow sea, beyond the city of Odenbar on Kovehn's eastern border. It was a harsh region – mostly desert with a spattering of unincorporated villages and townships – but Ader and Mikel Naffeim spoke of it fondly.

The brothers were actually fraternal twins, a sign of good fortune amongst their people. They made it very clear that they were not identical twins, as that would have meant darkness had split them in two. Identical twins were called *curdender*, the soulless – walking death; doppelgangers – and were killed at birth. When Ader and Mikel were first born, they had appeared almost identical and had nearly been mistaken for curdender. Mikel pointed out the tiny skin tag on his shoulder that had saved both of their lives. Belford shivered at the thought.

Three years ago, Captain Bundles piloted the Rosa Marsa to the Eastern Territories, to the tiny village of Karzshupe, Ader and Mikel's home town. Growing up, the Naffeim brothers had always been far too adventurous, constantly getting into trouble for one thing or another. Both had nearly died several times as children, but fortune had always somehow landed in their favor and they had survived to become adults despite the ominous predictions of their *Fayhadjur* – their village's mystical healer. The prospect of excitement was too tempting to pass up when Captain Bundles offered the brothers positions amongst the Rosa Marsa's crew, and the rest was history. They chose adventure over a life in their homeland. Belford wished he had the same luxury; there was no choice but to go where the Mark of Kings led him.

After talking for what felt like hours, Belford bid the brothers farewell and headed back upstairs to rest in his cabin. He found Thorin still awake, sitting at one of the tables in the mess hall with a drink in his hand.

"Long day," said Belford.

Thorin gave a gruff chuckle. "I'd invite you to have a drink with me, but Shiara says you can't hold your liquor."

Belford pursed his lips to one side.

"She actually came through here looking for you not too long ago," said Thorin. "She's back in her room now – should still be awake."

"She say what she wanted?" Belford asked.

Thorin shrugged. He returned to his drink as Belford continued through the mess and down the hallway towards the passenger cabins. Belford nodded to Elric, still sitting at the end of the hall in front of Kara's room, before stepping through a short side passage that led to Shiara's cabin. The door was already ajar when he arrived. He could see lamp light escaping through the crack. He knocked softly with the back of his hand. There was no response. He knocked harder. The door opened under the force.

As it swung inwards, Belford's eyes immediately fell across Shiara. She was standing in front of a tall mirror, completely nude! Her back was to him, but her breasts were fully visible in her reflection – larger than he expected, round and perky, with light-brown nipples, which she immediately covered up with her arm.

Belford stumbled backwards into the hall.

I'm dead! Shiara is literally going to kill me!

His heart was racing from the shock as he braced himself against the wall beside the open cabin door. There was no running from this.

"I'm so sorry!" he said. "The door wasn't latched!"

Shiara stepped out into the hallway a moment later with a robe drawn around her body. Belford expected her to be furious, but her expression was far from it. A light-pink blush settled over her cheeks. Belford's face burned with his own embarrassment.

"Get a good look there?" she asked.

Belford gritted his teeth.

Shiara's blush deepened slightly. She glanced down the hallway, making sure they were still alone. "Get in here," she said, grabbing the front of Belford's shirt and pulling him into the cabin. She closed the door behind them.

"Thorin said you were looking for me?" He didn't know what else to say. He couldn't get the image of her breasts out of his mind.

Shiara walked over and sat down on the edge of the bed. She nodded towards her side, prompting Belford to join her. "Earlier, yes," she said. "I was going to start preparing you on what to expect once we reach Erotos, but that can wait now."

Belford sat down on the bed and stared at his feet. He couldn't even look at her.

"You know, you don't have to be so shy with me," said Shiara.

Belford looked up, confused. Her eyes, unblinking, stared back at him with an intense gaze. Suddenly, she reached out and placed her hand firmly on his leg. She held it still for a moment, but then her fingers began to slowly caress their way up his thigh.

Belford squirmed away. "I can't..." he said.

"Can't?" repeated Shiara, raising an eyebrow. "Your face wouldn't be so red right now if you didn't see me as your teacher." She slid her robe off her shoulders, exposing her breasts once more. "I never wanted to be your teacher."

Belford's heart was beating out of his chest. *What is happening!?*

Shiara scooted closer to him. "There's nothing wrong with wanting to look. Nothing wrong with touching, either. Life's too short not to have a little fun."

"But you hardly even tolerate me," he said. "If it wasn't for my mark, you wouldn't want anything to do with me!"

Shiara clasped his wrist and pulled his hand to her, placing it on her left breast. Her nipple tickled his palm as she moved him against her.

Belford realized his mouth was hanging open. His trousers tightened.

Shiara smirked slightly as she reached for his other hand.

This is cheating. I love Claire!

He pulled away again, standing up this time and backing away until he was pressed against the door. "I said I can't! There's someone else," he said.

Shiara sat silently for a moment, her eyes glistening in the flickering lamp light. "I thought you didn't have any memories."

"I don't remember much," said Belford, "but I know I love her."

Shiara promptly pulled her robe back over her shoulders and wrapped it around herself tightly. Her playful smirk had entirely faded, replaced by her usual serious demeanor. She hadn't blinked in quite some time. She did so now – the moisture in her eyes gathering on her lashes.

Belford felt terrible.

"Where is she?" Shiara asked, a dull expression falling over her.

Belford shook his head. "I don't know," he said quietly. "I don't even know if she's alive. I don't really have any specific memories – mostly just emotions – how she makes me feel. I've had dreams, but I don't know what's real and what's made up. Sometimes a sensation will set off a memory, though – like a smell, or a taste – if it's similar enough to something I've experienced before."

Shiara nodded, her eyes becoming unfocused. "So you don't even remember how you first met?" She looked back up at him. "Your first kiss?"

Belford shook his head.

"That's really sad."

A slight chuckle forced its way out of him. "Tell me about it," he said.

Shiara stood up from the bed. She cinched her robe tighter as she walked up to Belford with a curious expression on her face. She moved in really close, not stopping until their faces were only a few inches apart.

Belford narrowed his eyes slightly.

"I've got an idea," she said. "Something to help you remember." Shiara was looking at him strangely again. "Close your eyes." She put her hands on his shoulders.

"What are you doing?" Belford asked.

"Just do it," she said. "Trust me."

Belford did as he was told, squeezing his eyes shut tightly.

"Not like that," said Shiara. "Just shut your eyes gently, like a normal person."

Belford laughed, shaking his head as he relaxed his eyelids.

"Good," said Shiara. "Now picture her standing in front of you. Forget the room around you. Try to imagine every little thing about her, until you can almost feel her presence."

He focused on his task. He imagined Claire's face, lightly freckled skin, emerald eyes, auburn hair, the way her smile formed little wrinkles on the sides of her nose. He simultaneously knew everything and nothing about her. He could smell the sweet mixture of apricot and vanilla from the moisturizer lining her skin; feel the soft caress of her fingers between his own. He knew his heart beat faster when she was around, that his lips would quiver just thinking about her kiss. He knew that without her, he was empty.

Lips brushed against his own, slightly parted – a soft kiss, not aggressive – moving slowly, tempting him to reciprocate.

An image flashed through his mind, him and Claire standing together in a park at night, streetlamps lighting a narrow pathway.

His eyes shot open.

Shiara's kissing me!

He drew back.

"Keep them closed," she ordered.

Belford frowned.

"Was it working?"

He thought back to the flash he'd just seen. It was new – something he hadn't remembered before. He'd seen the park in his early dreams, but not at night with just him and Claire. Shiara's idea was working, though he couldn't shake the feeling that she was just trying to take advantage of him. His craving to remember anything he could about Claire outweighed his trepidation.

He closed his eyes again, albeit hesitantly. He felt her warm breath on his lips before they touched. He tried to forget that it was Shiara, focusing solely on his memories of Claire. Her tongue grazed his bottom lip ever so gently.

The image of Claire in the park returned. He was grasping the back of her head with his hand – cupping the nape of her neck as they kissed passionately. His body was a torrent of sparks – tiny fireworks shooting off all over the place.

Other images began to flash across his mind, crashing upon him:

Claire baking banana bread at Christmas; spitting up cherry soda all over their board game after her little brother, Aiden, told a joke.

Camping by the lake one summer evening; eating snow cones to cool off in the sun.

The jasmine bushes that grew outside her window, filling her room with their heavy fragrance every spring and summer until the white petals blew through the air and covered the ground like a fine blanket of snow.

Waiting outside her house in Dublin while her mother filled a huge twenty-person, above-ground swimming pool; climbing the ladder and hopping into the chilly hose water; the giant orca whale floaty; Aiden wearing his water-wings. They never wanted the day to end.

Shiara pulled back from the kiss.

Belford bit his lower lip as he replayed all the new memories over and over again in his mind.

"You're lucky to have a friend like me," said Shiara. She tapped his cheek twice with the palm of her hand. "Now get out of here. I need some sleep."

Belford's head was spinning from the elation of learning more about Claire. He turned around, almost falling over in his lightheadedness. He stepped out into the hallway. Shiara shut the door behind him without a word.

Despite the excitement of recovering the new memories, Belford had a pinch in his gut – guilt from allowing the kiss to continue. His intentions had been pure, but it still felt wrong. He hoped things wouldn't be uncomfortable between him and Shiara now. The heat returned to his face as he thought about her breasts once more.

It's hopeless. Things are definitely going to be weird....

"Belford?" Shiara was speaking to him through the closed door.

"Still here," he responded.

"No more peeping."

Breaking the Veil

With his mind racing, Belford stumbled back to his cabin. The rocking of the ship didn't help his already unsteady feet. He bumped into the side of the hallway as the Rosa Marsa made a fairly sharp turn – Garcenus was still at the wheel, making unnecessary, harsh movements to annoy everyone as he piloted the night shift. The lightheaded elation that came with remembering more details about Claire made him feel nearly invincible. He hoped it would lead to even more memories resurfacing. He needed to know what had happened to her if he was to have any hope of getting her back.

Indigestion gurgled inside him. Belford winced as he brought his hand to his stomach. He couldn't tell if the rumble was a symptom of guilt from kissing Shiara, or just the undercooked prestina bread the Naffeim brothers gave him earlier disagreeing with his digestive track.

Remembering Claire is worth any pain.

He just wished he could have avoided hurting Shiara's feelings. He wasn't looking forward to the awkwardness of their future interactions either. She had opened up to Belford, literally, and there was no coming back from something like that – not after having her breast cupped in his hand. Shiara seemed to take the rejection in stride, but Belford had a feeling it hurt her more than she was letting on.

When he opened his cabin door, he was a little surprised to see Javic already asleep in one of the cots. They'd decided to bunk together before the truth about Wilgoblikan came out, but Belford had half expected him to stay out on the bow all night. Javic's presence was a very good sign. He hoped that any rift the secrets had formed between them would be just as fleeting as his stint on the bow.

Belford sat on his cot and removed the brass spyglass from his pocket. He had found himself thinking about the device often since Shiara told him about Power Artifacts. He hadn't yet had an opportunity to fully inspect it. The spyglass intrigued him – it would make a good distraction from his upset stomach. He knew the spyglass was significant – the Crimson Stalker had been after it, no matter what Shiara or Javic believed.

He looked through the lens, but just like before, all he saw was blackness. Whatever was inside was still rolling around as he panned the sight back and forth. It clinked against the sides of the tube as he twisted the eyepiece. Just as he was lowering the spyglass, a flash of color struck his vision. It only lasted a fraction of a second, but he was certain it had not been his imagination. The color flickered from out of the darkness like a reflective surface in the distance. He lifted the lens back to his face and tried to find it again, but there was nothing there. He scanned across the room searching for the source of the light.

The object inside the tube bounced up by itself; too hard for how slowly he had been moving the spyglass. After a moment of holding the device steady, the loose object jumped up again, locking into place against the inner side of the front lens. The pieces became one, like two magnets snapping together. A hint of color glinted against Belford's pupil. It was fuzzy and unfocused, only appearing when he aimed the spyglass just right. He lowered the tube again and found he had been pointing it directly at Javic's sleeping head.

Belford was apprehensive to do anything more at first. Shiara's words of caution against playing with the potential Artifact bounced around his head, but eventually curiosity got the better of him. He put the spyglass to his eye and held it loosely between his fingers. He thought about Javic and the sight drew towards him all on its own, as if nudged by a ghostly hand. Soon it was aimed directly at Javic's head again. The unfocused light pierced through the darkness. As he twisted the eyepiece, the colors grew stronger and he suddenly felt a sharp tug behind his eyes. A strange sense of weightlessness enveloped him and he felt as if he were falling through the looking glass.

It was sickening at first, but soon the sense of nausea faded. When he opened his eyes, the spyglass was gone and he found himself standing within a narrow stone passageway. The rocking of the Rosa Marsa was absent as well, replaced by an unusual lightness in his feet. Belford reached a hand in front of him, touching the passageway wall. The stone felt warm. It pulsated under his fingertips as if it were alive. He swung his head from side to side; everything blurred – his senses dulled. Everything about the place felt false; his body was rejecting it.

The passageway continued in both directions as far as he could see. There appeared to be an ambient light emanating from the walls. Everything was illuminated despite the lack of an obvious light source. Belford started walking down the passage, but he knew instinctively that the task was pointless; he wasn't getting anywhere, the passageway continued endlessly. He reached his hand out again, touching the stone wall, but this time pushed as hard as he could. The wall gave way, crumbling into a cloud of dust.

As the air cleared, he found himself looking upon a royal court – a huge open hall with long tables set, as if for a banquet. A golden throne sat at the head of the main table and there were hundreds of chairs, all fancily upholstered, positioned across the floor. There were no people in the hall, but the tables were laid out with dishes of all kinds; a grand feast.

Platter upon platter of food: Roasted bird, golden brown and glistening with fats, bodies too large to match any creature Belford could imagine; jugs of wine, blood red, ready to be poured from ornate spouts into the many gilded goblets placed around the long tables; towering soufflés, impractically tall, each adorned with a tiny pastry, twisted to resemble the conical point of a spire – all staggered around massive centerpieces – huge bouquets of orchids and chrysanthemums; lilies and violets; silver dishes, finely engraved; and gem-encrusted candelabras holding dozens of thin candlesticks.

Extravagant chandeliers, interwoven like bird nests, dangled overhead, though everything was still lit with an unnaturally even glow, as if illuminated from within. Patterned tapestries decorated the walls, and the far end of the hall was open to the outside. Belford made his way to the opening. A stone balcony with low railings overlooked a sprawling city of dark towers, each with matching spires, narrow like the stalagmite teeth of a cave. The ground, many stories below, appeared to be burning; a blanket of flames that consumed everything around the towers. Although the sky was cloudless, there were no stars, no sun, no moon, just a blank palette of charcoal.

Belford heard a loud noise behind him – a clash of steel echoed out from an enclosed spiral staircase that twisted upwards at the start of the balcony. More crashes sounded, and Belford could hear grunting now as well. Through the opening, he could only see the first few steps before they curved out of sight. An animalistic shout was coupled with a thud as someone tumbled down the stairs. Belford watched as a man dressed in all black fell around the corner and down the last few steps. He landed with a groan, sprawled out on his stomach. The sword that had been in his hand scraped across the floor, coming to a rest a few paces away, out of the man's reach. Javic swooped down the steps after the fallen man, a pristine silver blade gleaming like a mirror in his hands. Javic kicked the fallen man's sword even farther away and pointed his own blade down towards the back of his neck.

Javic sent a wide-eyed grin towards Belford. "You made it!" he said. "I thought you were trapped with the others!"

The man on the floor lifted his head for the first time and Belford recognized him immediately. It was Wilgoblikan, though he was frail and broken compared to Belford's memory of him.

"Get up!" Javic ordered, kicking Wilgoblikan in the ribs as he struggled to climb to his feet. "Take his sword," Javic said to Belford, "in case he tries anything sneaky."

Belford did as he was told; the blade felt surprisingly light in his grip, as if it were made of plastic. Javic prodded at Wilgoblikan's back with the tip of his sword, gouging him as he urged him towards the edge of the balcony.

"You deserve worse than a thousand deaths," said Javic. His voice was cold and emotionless, but his lip curled up in a sneer as he jabbed Wilgoblikan again and again with his blade – drawing blood, but not killing him.

Wilgoblikan's face stretched into a fearful grimace; he was gray and pathetic, but Javic showed no mercy as he herded him to the knee-high railing.

"Turn around!" shouted Javic.

Wilgoblikan hissed quietly at Javic, but he did as he was instructed, turning in place. Without another word, Javic thrust his sword into Wilgoblikan's chest, looking him in the eyes as he did so. The blade stayed in Wilgoblikan as he crumpled backwards, falling silently over the railing.

Belford was sickened; no matter what Wilgoblikan had done, it was still difficult to watch him die in such a gruesome manner. Even worse was seeing Javic's face contorted by his hatred. Javic stood looking over the balcony, watching as Wilgoblikan plummeted towards the fires below.

Belford felt his feet lift off the ground. His vision elongated, stretching into a tunnel. He drifted farther and farther away until Javic and the balcony were only specks of light in the distance. Everything faded to darkness.

Belford suddenly became aware of a pain in his leg. He shifted and his arm dropped, lowering the spyglass away from his face. He had been leaning on his leg with his elbow. He sat up and looked around. He was back in his cabin aboard the Rosa Marsa. It had all been a dream... Javic's dream. He eyed Javic, still fast asleep beside him. Javic twitched slightly, kicking the covers off one of his legs.

Belford immediately put the spyglass up to his eye again. As he looked around, he began to notice other points of light in the otherwise dark field of vision of the spyglass. There were two auras emanating through the wall, coming from the adjacent cabin where Arlin and Mallory were surely asleep by now. He thought about Mallory and the sight drew to the right; thinking about Arlin shifted it towards the left point of light.

Across the way and down the side passage was another aura. It belonged to Shiara. Thinking about her drew the spyglass her way. *No more peeping,* the words repeated in his head. He didn't dare visit Shiara's dream.

He thought about Thorin, but nothing happened, the spyglass just remained where he already had it positioned. Belford realized after a moment that he could hear Thorin walking down the hallway, in the process of retiring to his cabin for the night. The spyglass could only find somebody if they were asleep; no points of light appeared for Thorin through the eyepiece.

After hearing Thorin's door shut, Belford stepped out into the hallway. Elric was still sitting against the wall by Kara's room, but he'd fallen asleep on his watch. Belford could see the flickering aura of Elric's dream through the spyglass. What drew Belford nearer, though, was the light coming from inside

Kara's cabin. The aura was dimmer than the others, but just like the rest, it shimmered and flashed like a beam of sunlight shining through a dusty room.

Belford silently crept into Kara's cabin, being careful not to wake Elric as he passed. Kara stirred as Belford stepped inside. The room was dark, but Belford could tell that Kara was sitting upright on the edge of her bed. It was puzzling. She was clearly awake and watching him from across the room, but her aura was still present when looking at her through the spyglass.

Sitting down next to Kara, Belford aimed the spyglass directly at her head. She stared back at him with silent disinterest. He turned the end of the spyglass to focus on the aura, but unlike Javic's dream, he was not immediately pulled in. What he saw through the spyglass was a shimmering, black velvet wall – a dark veil where the window to her mind should have been. It was dense, like looking into an endless, star-filled sky. Belford wanted to go in; he needed to see into her mind to figure out how to fix her. He twisted the spyglass's eyepiece back and forth, causing the veil to shift between fuzzy and clear. Each time, the aura wavered slightly. Like striking a piece of steel with a hammer, it shook with each blow.

Kara seemed to sense that something was happening. She began to grow uneasy as Belford attempted to focus on her dream. She whimpered as he beat against the veil. Cracks were starting to form. The veil was undulating now, rolling like ripples across a rubber sheet. Belford was clawing his way in, tearing away the lining Wilgoblikan had placed there to keep him out. As the cracks spread, Belford felt the uncomfortable tug behind his eyes. It felt more violent this time, though that could have been his imagination. His body began to tingle all over as he floated into darkness once again.

The first thing he became aware of was the heat. It stung his skin as if he were standing too close to the blazing furnace aboard the Rosa Marsa. Screams surrounded him – pained shrieks and wails, twisted moans and sobs, begging for mercy.

When Belford opened his eyes, he knew his location immediately: The city of Bronam, where he and Kara first met, stretched out before him. He was standing in the street, looking towards the inner wall that encompassed the Duke of Bronam's unfinished palace. Its golden dome was cracked and huge slabs of roofing, along with much of the scaffolding surrounding the dome, now lay in collapsed piles of rubble around the base of the structure. The whole city was in flames. The scent of seared human flesh bit at Belford's nostrils with an overwhelming stench.

At the palace gate, a crowd of terrified people pushed against the iron fixture. It flexed, but did not open. The duke and a number of city guards were locked away inside the walls while the city burned around them. The people in the crowd had no escape from the flames.

The air whipped into a swirling firestorm as Wilgoblikan and his army of Whunes flooded in through the outer gates. No one could stop them as they tore through the streets, searching for Belford and the Mark of Kings. But he had already left that morning in the little blue wagon, bound for Rasile. He watched now, struck with horror by the sheer violence and ferocity with which Wilgoblikan lashed out.

Kara was trapped.

Belford saw her at once as Wilgoblikan approached.

She was stuck under a fallen beam just within the entrance of the hotel where she and Belford first met. She cried for help, reaching towards Belford with outstretched arms. There was no chance of escape, her legs were pinned and Wilgoblikan was nearly upon her. When the dark wizard noticed her, he had one of his Whunes grab hold of her arms and wrench her free. She howled in agony as her shoulders dislocated and her legs snapped under the weight of the beam. Her limbs twisted beneath her as one of the Whunes threw Kara down at Wilgoblikan's feet.

"Ah, a fine specimen," Wilgoblikan said, caressing the side of her face with an outstretched finger. "You will do very well – young enough to survive the transformation, anyway."

The Whunes carried more people out of the hotel. Wilgoblikan let his creations dismember most of them after a brief search to make sure none of them were Belford. The beasts discarded the limbless torsos to the side of the building when they were finished playing with them. The adolescents and young adults were left intact as Wilgoblikan began to transform them one by one to join his hideous army.

This wasn't just a dream – it was a memory, playing on repeat in Kara's mind. She was trapped here, in the worst moment of her life, fighting to survive, but failing every time as Wilgoblikan stripped her of her humanity and freedom and desecrated her body. She was powerless to stop Wilgoblikan as he selected her like a piece of meat – something to be used and forgotten. There was glee in Wilgoblikan's eyes. He was even more twisted than the Whunes he created.

Belford needed to free Kara. He had to stop Wilgoblikan right here if Kara was to have any hope of regaining her capacities. Just like the stone passageway in Javic's dream, Kara's nightmare was endless. Belford knew that he had the power to break the loop, just like he had pushed through the stone wall. Memory or not, this was still a dream.

Belford was the one in control now.

He reached behind him and pulled a sword out of the nothingness. The Whunes ignored him as he walked straight up to Wilgoblikan and thrust his blade into the dark wizard's back. Wilgoblikan dropped to his knees as Belford laid his hands on Kara's legs. The bones mended themselves instantly, just as surely as if he'd used the Power on them. He was using the power of thought, and that was all it took.

"Come on," said Belford as he helped Kara to her feet. She was panting with exhaustion, barely conscious as Belford attempted to pull her back through the veil with him.

Wilgoblikan reached towards Belford – the tormentor was still alive, a manic grin on his lips.

Belford was floating now, above the ground, pulling back towards the edges of the dream.

Wilgoblikan laughed, flames springing up all around him. He wrapped his fingers around Belford's ankle, trying to drag him back down.

The touch burned Belford's skin with an intense, physical pain. His flesh bubbled beneath Wilgoblikan's hand, but he refused to let go of Kara. He kicked with all his might until he managed to break free of Wilgoblikan's grasp.

The dream faded away.

Belford could still feel the pain in his leg as he lowered the spyglass from his eye. A ghostly, red impression lingered on his ankle.

Kara lay in her cot, completely still. Belford dropped the spyglass to the ground and rushed to her side. She was weak, barely breathing, her eyes mostly closed. She looked at him as he crouched beside her. She was actually looking at him this time, rather than staring through him the way she had since her transformation at the cave.

She was trying to speak.

Belford could see her lips quivering, but it was proving difficult for her. He lowered his ear to her face so that she could whisper to him.

"…thank you…" she murmured before brushing her lips lightly against his cheek. Her breathing became irregular as her chest began to spasm. Each breath was a struggle.

"No!" Belford cried out. "I fixed you! You're better now!"

Kara's body went limp; her heart giving out as her lungs made their final tremors. Belford scooped her frail frame into his arms as her chest collapsed one final time. Her last breath escaped as a wheeze.

This isn't right! She's supposed to be healed! I did it!

The room grew ice cold as Belford drew all the heat energy into a bolt of electricity. He zapped it straight down into

Kara's heart, leaving singe marks behind on her snowy-white gown.

She did not come back.

He tried again and again, each bolt sending out a deafening crack until he ran out of energy to draw on.

Kara remained still.

He began to compress her chest with his hands, trying to pump life back into her heart without the Power. Her body shook under the force of his thrusts. He didn't give up, even as his fingers grew numb from the cold he'd created.

"Belford!" a voice cried from behind him. "She's gone. It's over." Shiara was standing in the doorway.

Belford fell to his knees on the floorboards beside Kara's body and began to cry. The tears poured out of him like never before. His chest shook as he gasped for air.

I was supposed to save her.

It was my task – my fault that she needed saving. She was so young... so innocent... still a child. Her whole life was ahead of her... not like this.

They had come so far and he'd finally figured out how to free her mind from Wilgoblikan's evils, and yet she died anyway. He had failed, but Kara paid the ultimate price.

He didn't know how long he stayed there.

Eventually his tears ran out, but his body continued to go through the motions. Belford couldn't even remember her last name, though he knew she'd told him when she first introduced herself in Bronam.

It's not fair... it's not fair....

The words repeated in his head. She had died among strangers, all because she'd gotten tangled in his mess.

Someone lifted him up, probably Thorin, though his eyes were swollen shut so he couldn't really be certain. His body felt almost comatose as he was carried back to his cabin and laid upon his cot.

It's not fair... I was supposed to save her....

CHAPTER

34

The Crimson Waters

Overnight, the algae in the river blossomed, turning the Great Minthune blood red. Javic tried to imagine how the sight might look from above – the river was like a winding vein, pumping life across Aragwey. Mast's beating heart.

The blossoming occurred annually, usually towards the end of summer, lasting for about a week. The water would then return to its normal, murky-brown hue. The blossoming was how the Minthune earned its moniker, the Crimson Waters. The algae spawned in the Arid Hills to the west before being carried down the length of the Minthune by its current. No fish were to be caught or eaten during this time according to Antaran law. The dccree was typically followed universally outside of Antara's borders as well.

The fish ate the algae, causing their scales to turn pink. Most believed their flesh to be poisonous for human consumption until the river returned to its normal state and the crimson faded from their scales. It was a time of national fasting, especially for those living along the river's influence and throughout much of Antara where the fishing industry was so crucial for feeding the population. The crimson-stalkers had free reign of the river during this time, stuffing as many fish down their gullets as they could manage, just in time for nesting season.

Legend had it that the waters first turned red following the death of John Graven on her shores, then repeated annually to commiserate his passing, but that was just superstition. Many great battles had been fought along the Minthune River. It marked a natural border in the land. Some siege or skirmish took place between Phandrol and Kovehn almost every day with the increased military tensions of Garrett and Lord Ethan. Whenever one of these conflicts coincided with the blooming algae, rumors would spread and the battle would acquire national notoriety.

The blossoming always reminded Aragwians of a great loss. This year, the warm weather persisted longer than usual and so the metamorphosis was delayed through autumn, all the way to the eve of winter. The delay would mean a smaller crimson-stalker population next year, as their nesting season had come and gone the month prior, before the fishing ban could result in an influx of fish that usually fed their babies.

No great battles took place before this year's bloom, but most Antarans would likely see the assassination of King Lodrin as the cause of the display. Aboard the Rosa Marsa, it was the loss of Kara that was felt most heavily.

Captain Bundles ordered the Rosa Marsa to a full stop for the duration of Kara's funeral. Her body was taken ashore, placed upon a pyre of kindling, and lit aflame, as was Kovani custom. One more victim of Wilgoblikan's wicked ways; it only fueled Javic to see the murderer destroyed.

No one besides Belford had known Kara before her transformation into a Whune, but even so, her presence was missed by all. Mallory was particularly stricken by her death.

After hearing of Kara's passing, Mallory locked herself away in her cabin and did not emerge again until after the ceremony. She had spent much time caring for Kara like a mother to a child. Kara had been an infant in her eyes.

By now, each of the travelers had partaken in looking after Kara at one point or another – whether by leading her around, keeping an eye on her in the night, bringing her food, cleaning up after her messes, or tending to her self-injuries of which she was greatly prone. Shiara warned Belford that Kara's recovery was unlikely at best, but even so, everybody recognized that Belford was no ordinary wizard. Belford had been so determined to heal Kara that Javic took it for granted that he would succeed – after all, Belford possessed the Mark of Kings, anything seemed possible.

At the ceremony, Javic met a pair of brothers named Mikel and Ader Naffeim. They were outlanders from the Eastern Territories – the same area his mother, Kali, was born. They had never heard of her – he asked – but they were able to tell him a little bit about life in the savage regions. He'd read stories before, but nothing could compare to the firsthand knowledge that the brothers were able to offer. Both brothers were fluent in the ancient tongue, which fascinated Javic as well. Ader recited a prayer for Kara. The words sounded beautiful even though Javic couldn't understand them: "*Fortano umpendium eliqueth. Evenroth cortonus bri denderum.*"

After Ader was finished, Mikel translated the prayer into Aragwian so everyone could fully appreciate its meaning. "Find peace in the next life," he said. "Death claims all souls."

Although Mallory had not taken the news of Kara's passing well, Javic was most worried about Belford. He'd started to tell Shiara about his experience with the brass spyglass, but wasn't able to get many of the details out before breaking down again.

"I fixed her," he whispered, "she was better... she was better."

During the funeral, Belford remained aboard the Rosa Marsa. He sat by himself, legs dangling over the side of the steamer, watching from the distance. He was holding the golden butterfly necklace in his hands – Kara's only possession from before she was a Whune – he looked to be contemplating whether or not to cast it into the water.

Once everyone was finished silently paying their respects at the pyre, Javic approached Shiara on their walk back to the steamer. "I don't understand," he said. "Why did she die? Belford freed her mind, and her body was already healed."

"I cannot say with absolute certainty," said Shiara. "But I believe it was her mind being freed that allowed her body to finally give way."

Javic furrowed his eyebrows. "So, Belford shouldn't have released her mind?"

"On the contrary," said Shiara. "She was trapped in a hell. Being a Whune was keeping her from death, but it was also keeping her from living. He did a good thing by releasing her from that suffering, even if he can't see it yet."

The mood remained somber aboard the Rosa Marsa as they continued east along the Crimson Waters. Whether they were in Kovehn or Phandrol was impossible to say. The border between the two kingdoms drifted in and out like the tide. Several Phandolian ships as well as one Kovani vessel approached them over the next week, all checking Captain Bundles' papers and documents of intent.

As a foreign trading vessel, the Rosa Marsa was allowed to remain neutral to the Kovehn-Phandrol conflict as long as certain guidelines were followed. The specific terms for what constituted neutrality were among the points of contention between the two kingdoms, though. Captain Bundles had several different drafts of his paperwork written up and ready to present, depending on which kingdom the prying official hailed from. Everything checked out each time, so the Rosa Marsa was able to continue with little delay.

Eventually, the steamer reached the Etto River, a tributary to the Great Minthune. The two rivers mixed together, diluting the red current into a rusty brown which resembled the degradation on the Rosa Marsa's hull. Captain Bundles ordered full ahead to the waterwheels as they turned south, fighting their way upstream against the clear waters of the Etto and into the heart of Phandrol.

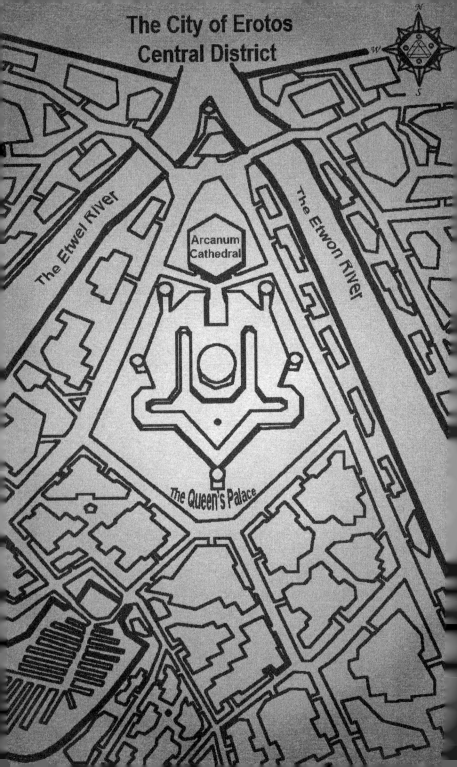

The City of Erotos
Central District

Arcanum
Cathedral

The Etwel River

The Etwon River

The Queen's Palace

CHAPTER

35

The Glowing City

During their final days aboard the Rosa Marsa, Belford rarely spoke. He ate his meals alone in his cabin, only venturing out if Javic was already occupying the space during meal time. He slept throughout the day, and wrote fervently in a dream journal he'd started to keep during his waking hours. Despite sharing the cabin with Javic, the two saw little of each other.

Javic found himself absorbed by thoughts of his parents most of the time. They'd been married in Erotos, and would have known the capital city well. He wondered how often his parents had traveled through these waters and looked out on the same sights he was seeing now. Unlike the Minthune River, the Etto had many small towns and villages along its shores. War drove people away from the Crimson Waters, but the Etto thrived under the protection of the Phandolian military.

Javic came up from below deck to watch as they made their final approach to Erotos. Belford, despite his reclusiveness, was already up top, sitting beside Shiara. Javic joined them, peering out in silence as the massive city crawled into view. The capital was in three parts. The center portion sat upon a thin strip of land at a fork in the river – the west branch was called Etwel and the east branch Etwon, but most people simply referred to them both at once as the Rivers Etto. They flowed through the capital, dividing it into three sections.

Javic had read that Erotos was built with the Power, but it wasn't until now that he truly appreciated what that meant. A mass of seamless stone – black, like obsidian – jutted out from the water, producing a steep overhang where the two rivers met. Its shape resembled the hull of an enormous ship, curving upwards to tower above the Rosa Marsa. As they got closer, they were cast in shadow beneath its glossy sheen. The imposing wall was littered with battlements – massive cannons that could fire projectiles half a league down river according to modest estimate. The Kovani military had never advanced close enough to test the full capabilities of the city's defenses, the exact number and nature of which was a tightly kept secret amongst the Phandolian military.

Once alongside the battlement wall, Javic could see a pointed obelisk piercing the sky at its top. Its dark surface was engraved with strange symbols that glinted with a golden finish in the afternoon sunlight. Javic stared up in awe. He had never seen anything remotely like it before.

"What's with those symbols?" he asked. "What do they mean?"

Shiara followed his gaze up to the obelisk. "No one knows," she said. "It's some ancient language – remnants of a lost society. Archeologists found the obelisk along with several other relics buried beneath the city a few decades back. Each piece is marked with similar carvings, but no one has been able to decipher any of the writing."

"They're called hieroglyphics," said Belford. "Probably the story of some long-dead pharaoh."

Shiara turned in surprise – it was strange to hear Belford speak since Kara's death. Javic could see the curiosity biting behind Shiara's eyes, but she didn't speak. She knew better than to question Belford about how he knew the things he knew.

Belford didn't elaborate. He stared out across the city, soaking in the sights.

Javic let his eyes wander as well. Erotos was impressive all around. Every structure flowed together, as if carved from a single block of magnificent black stone; every building, every tower, every lamppost, all grown from the earth and attached together on the level of individual molecules. There were no weak points in the fortifications.

Arching bridges, taller than any ship capable of navigating this far up the channel, soared above both the Etwel and Etwon, connecting the three segments of the capital. The section between the two rivers was known as the Central District, or the Old City – centuries of history packed densely into the city center – housing the Queen's Palace and the Cathedral of the Arcanum. The rest of the capital was much newer, built in the thirty-five years since the founding of the Ver'konus. From the deck of the Rosa Marsa, Javic couldn't distinguish any significant difference between the old and new architecture – the Ver'ati Builders who expanded the city were careful to stay consistent with the old styles. Javic wondered how different Erotos looked now compared to when his parents lived here. Through his grandfather's stories, he almost felt like he knew the city already.

Another significant change since the arrival of Lord Ethan was the addition of luminescent bulbs in place of the old torches that once resided in the lampposts across the city's extensive promenades. The bulbs emitted a steady light similar to the orbs that Belford created with the Power, only these lights lasted indefinitely, shining brilliantly day and night.

Erotos was often called the Glowing City because of this. Its aura could be seen from many leagues away, especially during the darkest hours of the night.

It was said that only Lord Ethan knew how the bulbs truly worked. There were those outside of Phandrol who'd attempted to recreate the lights, but even when they duplicated the bulbs exactly, none would glow. The mystery left more than a few royals in the court of Graven jealous of Phandrol's grandeur. Their scholars remained stumped after years of trying to recreate the miracle.

Several of the men involved in the failed attempts later collaborated to write a book about their struggles. Its release was considered a great embarrassment to Graven, leading to the executions of its authors for crimes against the state. The book was banned in Graven, but Javic managed to procure a copy a few years back from a peddler passing through Darrenfield. It was an interesting read with a poignant cautionary tale: Never embarrass the kings of Graven.

The Rosa Marsa traveled up the Etwel, the western branch of the Rivers Etto, and under its bridge. The massive Cathedral of the Arcanum stood on their left beside the Queen's Palace, the grounds of which covered nearly half of the central city. It put the palace in North Galdren to shame. Before their escape from the Antaran capital's harbor aboard the Rosa Marsa, Javic had been impressed by North Galdren's many narrow spiral towers.

Although the towers of the Queen's Palace here in Erotos did not reach quite as high as the ones in North Galdren, they were more aesthetically pleasing and better protected by the city walls. No one ever got to enjoy the view from atop the towers in North Galdren – Javic had heard they were built purely to show off, requiring far too many steps to reach their pinnacles. The stairs simply ended at a ceiling with no effort taken to build a viewing room. Here in Erotos, every tower supported such a room, and were still high enough to look across an extensive portion of the countryside. It was rumored that

Queen Havorie Elveres had taken to spending much of her time contemplating her rule from atop the towers.

She could be looking upon us even now.

Captain Bundles steered the Rosa Marsa into a man-made harbor, dug into the central city, south of the Queen's Palace. Officials greeted them in the harbor, helping them secure the Rosa Marsa by catching and tying the mooring lines thrown to them by Garcenus and Eben. Everyone waited on the stern deck as the officials boarded the steamer. Men dressed in cream-colored shirts with white sashes overtop their uniforms questioned Captain Bundles briefly while checking his paperwork once again. The officials moved on to the passengers next. Shiara stepped forward to speak on the group's behalf. Once they learned that she was Ver'ati, they took her aside and spoke to her privately for a few minutes before disembarking, their queries satisfied. Everyone was free to go about their own business.

"What's going to happen now?" asked Belford.

Shiara looked over at him. "It's just as we suspected," she said. "Thorin and I must report to the head of Ver'konus operations, Guther Aldune, immediately."

Thorin's face soured at the mention of Aldune – the man who had attempted to drown him in a fountain after refusing to promote him to officer status.

"Despite our rocky history, he has Lord Ethan's ear," Shiara said. "If we show him the Mark of Kings, he will grant us an audience with Lord Ethan. After that, it's in his hands."

Rather than sitting around on the Rosa Marsa, Javic opted to join Shiara, Thorin, and Belford as they made their way to the east city where Guther Aldune's office was located within the Ver'ati training academy. At the top of the wharf, men with peddled taxi carts were lined up, offering rides to anyone coming from the harbor. Shiara hired the nearest driver, handing him a silver mark as they all piled into the back of his cart.

As they rode through the city, Javic couldn't help but notice an abundance of people standing around doing nothing at all. Every building had a doorman, sometimes two, as well as a greeter, and there were multiple stable boys at every stable, many of which were not even boys at all – their graying hair peeking out from under their caps.

Their taxi took them past a building that had young women peering out from each of its second and third story windows – dozens of them, all done up in makeup and smiling at the men passing below on the sidewalk. Javic glanced at one of the women as she sent an exaggerated eyelash flutter his way. She twirled her hair between her fingers and gave a little wink before promptly pulling down her blouse to expose her breasts.

Javic's face grew hot, simmering in a dark blush as she jiggled them for his enjoyment. Despite his embarrassment, he didn't blink until Shiara placed her fingers over his eyes. He smiled to himself – the image was already fully engrained in his mind. Shiara gave a disapproving growl from deep in her throat. She didn't remove her hand from his face until the brothel was far behind them.

The greatest city on Earth!

When she removed her hand, they were passing an excavated pit beside a mountain of piled dirt and rubble. An endless supply of workers labored with shovels and other digging tools, hollowing out the ground and adding to the massive pile. Others transported loads of the dirt, sometimes as little as by the bucketful, away from the excavation site. They formed a line, hauling each load off into the distance in a slow procession.

Javic didn't understand – Erotos was supposed to be the most magical city in the world. There were more Ver'ati here than anywhere else. A single wizard could have done all the work that these hundreds of men had clearly labored at for weeks on end, and it would only have taken a few hours, if not less, to do so.

"Why doesn't someone just use the Power to do that?" Javic asked.

Shiara laughed. "That's a complicated question," she said. "The government employs workers because the people need money to pay the taxes on their homes within the city, but the taxes were only levied to force the population into needing jobs..." she waved her hand through the air, dismissing the circular logic. "You see, in Phandrol, especially here in Erotos, there are so many Ver'ati that the standard of living is quite high. A trained Ver'ati can make anything they need or want with the Power, so all goods became very cheap after the reformation of the Arcanum, and that meant nobody needed to work to fulfill their basic needs."

"But isn't that a good thing?" asked Javic. "Without work there would be more time for people to do whatever else they want. Why does the government need taxes when the Power makes the whole concept of money obsolete?"

"Ah, but that's not really true: There are other uses for money than just goods. Ver'ati cannot use the Power to bring you tea in the morning, or replace the luminescent bulbs in the lampposts when they burn out, or run a tavern, or bring you your dinner after it's prepared, or grow produce and raise cattle for slaughter – food made with the Power is often tasteless and downright inedible if you ask me. The Power cannot take your coat, or massage your back, or trim your hair – well technically it could, but Ver'ati have better things to do than stand around cutting everyone's hair.

"The point is, after the Arcanum brought Ver'ati to the city, no one had any reason to work, which caused a labor shortage in the service industry. So the government put heavy taxes on everyone living within the city limits to force them to work, but there's not enough jobs to go around in the service industry, so the crown has to offer employment, like at the site we just passed, to ensure the unemployment rate doesn't spiral out of control, causing people to lose their homes."

Javic was beginning to understand: If the government taxed the population, it could force people to work service jobs, but with not enough jobs to go around, the government had to provide a means to make a living, no matter how inefficient the task. Suddenly, the extra doormen, stable boys, greeters, and taxi peddlers made sense – it was just a means for people to keep their homes within the Glowing City.

"I guess that explains all the prostitutes," said Belford.

"Actually," said Thorin, "unlike some of those other service jobs, Ver'ati really do have ways of making sex better."

Shiara grimaced deeply.

Javic felt his cheeks flush once more.

"There are Ver'ati prostitutes?" asked Belford, surprised.

Thorin grinned. "Not exactly. But Ver'ati tend to deal in other forms of payment rather than just simple currency. Lots of secrets and *favors*," he said, laughing.

Shiara smacked them both on the backs of their heads.

Javic gave a grim chuckle. Shiara shifted her glare towards him.

Their taxi driver took them past the Queen's Palace. Javic stared up at the towers as they went by. The closer they got to them, the taller they appeared. The Arcanum's ancient cathedral was next. It had a domed structure similar to the Duke of Bronam's Palace, but was considerably more impressive. It rose up with the same black stone as the rest of the city, but was joined by huge stained-glass windows interwoven into the frame of the building. The depictions in the window decorations were varied, but high and center, Javic recognized the shield crest of the now extinct Vestori – an offshoot of the Arcanum, destroyed by King Garrett during the Cleansing nearly a century ago. Every word of his grandfather's elaborate stories really was true, the evidence unfolding before his eyes. The history within the cathedral's walls could rival any structure in Aragwey. He hoped he would have a chance to visit later.

Over the Etwon Bridge, the Ver'ati training academy was the main attraction. It was a military base, training facility, and university rolled into one. Right now, the streets were almost entirely empty, but the moon was still down. Javic could only imagine what went on after moonrise. He envisioned classes full of young Ver'ati in training, all standing in rows, launching rocks into the Etto River, having competitions to see who could send them the farthest, or perhaps they would create and destroy intricate objects or even whole buildings to hone their techniques, as if molding miniatures out of clay.

The possibilities were endless.

Javic's mother trained here. She walked these very grounds, learning how to use her abilities. He had been told that she was strong with the Power – one of the strongest in fact – but that hadn't saved her life, not from Wilgoblikan. Javic realized he was clenching his fists. He eased his grip and tried to put the dark thoughts aside.

The taxi stopped in front of a tall building. It was square in shape and plain compared to the other, more ornate buildings which surrounded it. Shiara led the way to its entrance. A doorman held the double doors open for them, bowing respectfully as they entered. Inside, a receptionist wearing a military uniform greeted them before they even had a chance to step through the doorway. His uniform was formal – deep blue in color with golden buttons running up to a tight collar. Two yellow stripes decorated the front of each of his shoulders, signifying his rank. He wore a white sash across his chest, identical to the ones worn by the officials at the marina.

"I have an urgent matter to discuss with Guther Aldune," said Shiara, approaching the man's station.

The receptionist blinked several times. "Audience with General Aldune is by appointment only," he said.

A gleam in Shiara's eyes suggested she had been hoping for a little resistance. "Listen, Cadet," she berated him, "you have no idea who I am, but let me assure you that bringing me to Guther will be the most important thing you ever do in your pathetic, little life!" She practically shouted the last part at him.

Thorin handed the receptionist a piece of paper containing their official orders, issued to them by one of the agents at the docks. The receptionist said nothing, merely glancing back over his shoulder at them awkwardly as he wandered off to notify the general.

"He shouldn't have *needed* the paper," Shiara said to Thorin, irritation in her voice.

The receptionist returned shortly, still looking slightly confused as he directed them around a corner to their left and down a long hallway to the general's office. The walls were lined with painted portraits of various men in uniform, most middle-aged and steel-eyed. Their frowns seemed to follow the party as they continued down the walkway. When they reached the lacquered, wooden door at the end, Shiara grabbed hold of the handle and entered without knocking.

Inside the office, the general stood by a stone-mantle fireplace, his back to the door. He was a thick man – not heavyset, but large, with wide shoulders and biceps to rival Thorin's, each nearly the size of a honey melon. His hair was cut short like Belford's, and his uniform was pressed with a neat crease that ran the length of his sleeves. Thorin was the last one through the door. He closed it behind him.

Aldune still did not turn around even after it latched shut. He began to speak in a gruff voice. "When Eldin described the obnoxious woman who so rudely demanded my attention, I knew it could be none other than you, Shiara Nighfield," he said. "Though I must admit, I am curious about the company you are keeping."

Shiara scowled as the general turned to face her.

He kept his hands together behind his back as he strolled to his desk. He took a seat in the only chair in the room. "To what do I owe the pleasure?" he asked, glancing at Javic and Belford in turn. Aldune ignored Thorin's presence altogether. Both men's faces were emotionless.

Shiara smirked at the general. "You are about to grant us an immediate audience with Lord Ethan," she said.

"Oh?" Aldune sounded amused.

"Indeed," said Shiara.

"And why should I do that?" he asked, placing his elbows on his desk and interlocking his fingers.

Shiara touched Belford on the shoulder. "Because we have discovered another Mark of Kings," she said smugly, staring into the general's face without blinking.

He squinted slightly back at her, tensing at the words. "What is this nonsense?" he demanded, standing up from his seat.

"Exactly as I've told you," said Shiara. She gestured towards Belford. "This young man here has the Mark of Kings, and I assure you it is legitimate. His abilities with the Power are unprecedented." Shiara stepped aside as Belford began to roll up his sleeve.

"I don't know what you're playing at, but..." Aldune trailed off as Belford exposed the mark on his bicep. The general's mouth hung open for a moment as he stared. He moved around his desk and touched the bump under Belford's skin at the center of the mark. "Remarkable...." Aldune shook his head in disbelief. He took a moment to compose himself before speaking again. "This boy will get an audience with Lord Ethan, *after* I am through with him," he said. "The rest of you will wait here for my return."

It was Shiara's turn to frown now.

Aldune pulled Belford's sleeve back down for him with a sharp yank, and then grabbed hold of his arm tightly. "You have quite a bit of explaining to do," he said as he led Belford from the room and back down the long hallway.

Belford turned one last wide-eyed glance towards Shiara as he was whisked out of sight.

"Pray to Mast..." Shiara said softly.

Thorin frowned, staring at the floor tiles.

From what Javic knew of Guther Aldune, he was not a man with whom Belford should be left alone, but Shiara and Thorin were only cogs in the Phandolian military machine, and as such, had no choice but to do exactly as they were ordered.

Javic, on the other hand, had no such qualms with disobedience. He glanced at Shiara and Thorin once more, trapped in their reluctance. "What's going to happen to him?" he asked.

Shiara shook her head. "I don't know," she said. "If Aldune perceives Belford as a threat…" Shiara trailed off, the shame of her inability to help was clear on her face.

Javic had heard enough. He left Shiara and Thorin behind, sprinting down the hallway after Belford and the general. He owed that much to his friend; Belford deserved an audience with Lord Ethan, not just some watery grave if Guther Aldune decided he hadn't answered his questions to his liking.

CHAPTER

36

The Underground

When Javic rounded the corner of the receptionist's desk, he immediately knew something was very wrong. Guther Aldune and Belford were standing by the entrance, but neither the doorman nor the receptionist was anywhere to be seen. The general was pushing hard against the door with his shoulder, but it seemed to have been locked from the outside.

"What's going on? Eldin!" shouted Aldune. "Where has that boy run off to...? I'll have his stripes for this!"

A streak of blood was smeared across the patterned floor tiles beside the receptionist's desk. Aldune bashed against the door's steel plating with his fist and forearm once more, rattling it to its hinges, but it remained solid.

A faint scent of decay and bile drifted into Javic's nostrils. *Whunes!* They'd been here – there was no mistaking it. *But how did they get into the city undetected?* It didn't make any sense.

"General Aldune…" Javic said tentatively. The general spun around, a look of surprise on his face.

"You! What are you doing here?" he spat.

Javic pointed at the smear of blood on the ground. It led over to a stairwell, going down to the basement. "Wilgoblikan is here," Javic said. "I can feel it…."

Aldune unsheathed a small belt knife. "Get out of my way," he ordered Javic as he pulled Belford along with him towards the stairwell.

"What are you doing?" Belford demanded. "Let me go!"

Aldune ignored Belford's struggles. "We're getting out of here through the Underground," he said. Belford continued to fight against the general's motion, punching him in the arm repeatedly. Aldune spun him around and put him in a chokehold.

"Stop it!" cried Javic, but there was nothing he could do. All his weapons were on the Rosa Marsa. Attempting to stop Guther Aldune was like trying to roll a boulder uphill with nothing but his bare hands.

Aldune held his blade out threateningly until Javic stepped aside and let him continue towards the stairwell. Belford stopped struggling as he lost consciousness in the general's headlock. The large man simply lifted him under one arm and proceeded down the steps.

"The Whunes are down there!" Javic said desperately. "They'll kill you!" But the general did not listen. With no time to spare, Javic shouted for Shiara and Thorin, warning them about the Whunes. He hoped his voice had managed to carry all the way down the long hallway to Aldune's office, but there was no way to be certain they had heard. He followed after the general, skipping steps as he made his way into the basement. He was barely able to keep up as he raced down one passageway then the next, weaving through the expansive corridors of the Erotos Underground.

The tunnels supposedly connected every building in the city, routing sewer and water lines, and even dipped beneath the

Rivers Etto to connect the three sections of the capital. Running through the corridors now, there appeared to be more city beneath the ground than above it. Lit by the same shining bulbs that gave the Glowing City its nickname, the tunnels should have been brightly illuminated, but many of the bulbs were burnt out and had not yet been replaced despite the extensive work crews employed by the crown. Some of the sections Aldune carried Belford through were as dark as the cave where Javic last encountered Wilgoblikan's minions. The thought alone made Javic's skin crawl.

They're down here, somewhere....

Despite the dim light, everything suddenly became clearer in Javic's eyes. His vision sharpened, piercing through the darkness. He had an anxious feeling in his stomach – butterflies dancing around in his belly. The stench of the Whunes intensified, forcing Javic to breathe through his mouth to stop from feeling like he was going to be sick.

"They're here for Belford, and you're bringing him right to them!" Javic cried out to the general, his hands shaking in nervous anticipation.

Aldune stopped running and took a deep breath of air into his lungs. "The moon has risen," he said. "The Power flows through my veins – it will protect me." The general's voice boomed. He put his belt knife away and readjusted Belford under his left arm as he flexed his fingers.

The general charged forward, entering a large cavern that looked to have been part of a natural cave system prior to the formation of the tunnels. The ground was uneven here, and the dripping ceiling far above was made of regular rock rather than the reinforced black stone that formed the rest of the Underground. A lone bulb dangled from a long cord – it flickered sporadically while swinging back and forth along a draft blowing through the passageway – it was all that lit the wide cavern. Shadows shifted across the walls from the swinging light as Aldune ran through the darkness without hesitation and bounded down several flights of stairs, carved into the bedrock. As they hurried deeper into the tunnel system, the air grew damp. The drippy ceiling maintained a steady trickle in places, forming wide puddles that occasionally covered the entire width of the tunnel floor. The sound of rushing water grew stronger the farther they progressed. The Etwon River flowed through the earth overhead.

They were several stories underground now. Passing beneath the river into the Old City, the passages grew narrower and more labyrinth like. They were approaching what must have been the subbasement of the Queen's Palace, though after several more turns, Javic completely lost his sense of direction. Aldune slowed as well, studying each divergence in the tunnel carefully before choosing his path. One fork in the corridor ahead caused the general to come to a complete halt as he tried to determine which tunnel to take. Javic stopped beside him, his footsteps continuing to echo down the corridor for a moment even after he was still. When the sounds finally faded, Javic realized he could still hear something moving in the darkness.

"I hear them," said Javic.

Aldune raised an eyebrow. "Good ears," he said. "I can barely hear them myself, even with the Power heightening my senses."

"Which passage are they in?" asked Javic.

Aldune shook his head. "Too many echoes," he said, "they could be anywhere."

The footsteps were growing louder. Whichever way the sound was coming from, there was definitely more than one pair of feet coming their way.

Belford began to stir under Aldune's arm, but did not regain consciousness.

"Here they come," said Aldune. "Stay behind me." The general placed Belford on the ground against the damp passageway wall and then used the Power to merge several shimmering puddles of moisture into a huge sphere.

Several grunts sounded from ahead as the Whunes drew near. Javic saw their shadows stretched long against the far walls before the Whunes themselves appeared around the bends in the corridor. They came from both branches of the passageway. Javic was fairly certain he could hear footsteps closing in from behind as well. They were completely surrounded.

Aldune sprang into action, getting low in a solid stance as he willed the ball of water into a thick wall, blocking off the left passageway. The water froze with a snap, clouding over as the general drained all of the energy out of the particles. The Whunes in the left corridor smashed their bodies against the ice, but it held surprisingly well. Javic could only make out their silhouettes through the frozen wall as they chipped away at it with their claws and axes. Aldune turned his attention towards the other passage.

Down the open corridor, the Whunes increased their speed as their bloodlust overtook them. Aldune used the remaining moisture from the tunnel to form sharp icicle spikes which he launched at the oncoming Whunes with a flick of his finger. The spikes penetrated through several rows of the creatures before stopping. The beasts collapsed into a pile, forcing the rest to climb over their dead bodies before coming any closer.

With Aldune's supply of water exhausted, he changed his stance, holding his hands in front of him and curling his fingers as if they were claws. He squeezed the air with his right hand and the closest Whune in the line, still traversing its dead brethren, suddenly dropped its axe to the ground and began digging at the sides of its own skull. It howled sharply as it ripped bits of flesh from its temples. The creature's eyes froze like glass marbles, turning pale as they frosted over. It collapsed to the ground, dead, deepening the barricade of bodies.

The ice wall blocking the left corridor was beginning to crack under the pressure of the Whunes lined up behind it. Aldune swung his hand towards the ice and it exploded at the Whunes, killing several that were nearest the front and knocking the rest back momentarily.

The general used the lull in their advance to unsheathe his belt knife again. As soon as the first Whune reached him, he shoved his blade through its neck and wrenched upwards, splitting its jaw clean in two. The monster's tongue flapped about as it fell to its knees. Aldune stabbed it in the top of the head, killing it. The next Whune received similar treatment as Aldune slashed its vital organs with his dagger. The general pushed the Whunes back again with a burst of kinetic energy, staggering their advance and putting a chill on the surrounding air as the heat energy was metabolized into force. There were only a few living Whunes left in the passageway.

As the next creature approached Aldune, it stopped short, several paces beyond the reach of the general's blade. The monster staggered back on its own for a second before falling against the side of the tunnel. Aldune cocked his head in confusion. Javic heard laughter coming from behind him. He spun around just in time to see Wilgoblikan gesturing towards the immobilized Whune. The creature shrieked as its skin bubbled with boils that then ignited into flames, exploding with a force great enough to blast chunks out of the black stone of the tunnel wall. Both Javic and Aldune were sent flying towards Wilgoblikan.

Bits of rubble struck Javic hard in the side of the face as he smashed against the ground. His cheek stung as if splashed with boiling oil. He felt like he'd been kicked in the chest by a horse. Pain filled his lungs; he was certain a few of his ribs were broken.

Aldune was closer to the blast than Javic. He lay crumpled on his back, his face torn up in a mesh of blood, almost unrecognizable.

Wilgoblikan walked over to Belford and crouched down beside him. He peeled back the sleeve of his jacket, confirming the mark on his arm.

Aldune remained motionless. He had fought well, but there was no defending against Wilgoblikan's vicious attack. The few remaining Whunes stood obediently at Wilgoblikan's side like trained dogs.

Though Javic's ears were still ringing from the explosion, he could hear a voice inside his head. It was a female voice, his mother's voice – how he imagined her voice to sound anyway – and she was crying in pain. Wilgoblikan was torturing her; pressing her for information until the stress of the torment caused her body to give out, killing her. He then tossed her aside – lifeless; useless to him – and moved on to do the same to Javic's father.

Javic's heart filled with rage. Salvine's cries joined those of his parents within his mind, tearing like nails against his insides. The kind girl had brought nothing but compassion and love to all those around her until Wilgoblikan desecrated her body and mind, destroying everything that made her human.

Though still dazed, he felt a surge inside of him. It filled him from his fingertips to his toes. His breath caught in his lungs as his entire body tensed under the pressure of the energy.

Exhilarating waves of emotion flowed over him – his anger towards Wilgoblikan; his fear of death; of losing more people that he loved; of never truly getting to live at all; his shame of being useless and defenseless; of having everything taken away from him.

He was like a conduit – a lightning rod being struck again and again in a storm. His emotions piled on, becoming too much to bear. And then they burst out of him.

The Whunes, still waiting for Wilgoblikan's orders, turned to ash one by one. Javic couldn't believe his good fortune as they disintegrated in front of him. He looked around, searching for his savior – for who was rescuing him from Wilgoblikan – but Belford was still unconscious, Shiara was not there, nor was Thorin, and Guther Aldune was still heaped over, burned and broken from Wilgoblikan's attack.

There was no one there to save him.

It was only Javic.

He wished for the Whunes to die – had wanted it with every fiber of his being – then his emotions welled up and each one turned to dust, Combusted, evaporated from existence.

He was a wizard....

He was a wizard! Just like his mother and grandmother before him! He knew it true, just as surely as he knew the pain in his heart, placed upon him by Wilgoblikan. He wanted to cry with relief.

Suddenly he knew he wasn't just an outlander, a farmer, a weak, useless victim – he was a wizard, capable of great miracles, with a greater destiny than he ever could have imagined. He was just like Belford – maybe not destined to be a king, but he was special; he was somebody. All that remained in his way was Wilgoblikan: The man responsible for so much pain in Javic's life; so much suffering. He was face-to-face with the monster he had vowed to destroy.

The plumes of dust exploded outwards from the Whunes into the narrow corridor, surprising Wilgoblikan. He dropped Belford's arm and turned to face Javic.

With the Whunes gone, there was nothing else standing between Javic and his revenge. This was his moment – the moment that would make everything better, that would right all the wrongs – the moment that Wilgoblikan would finally pay for his crimes.

Javic directed everything he had at him; all of his intentions and emotions; all the energy he could muster into a deadly blast. He would rip Wilgoblikan into billions of tiny particles and watch him blow away into the darkness once and for all.

He felt it true, and so it would be true; it needed to be true. And yet, the moment stretched by, and there Wilgoblikan stood, staring right back at him, alive and well with his dark eyes locked onto Javic's. And that infuriating grin!

"You try to destroy *me* from the inside out?" Wilgoblikan sneered. "You stupid Ver'ati."

Javic didn't understand what went wrong. He'd focused the same intentions towards Wilgoblikan that had obliterated the Whunes before him. The dark wizard should have been nothing more than a puff of dust; flakes of used carbon crumbling away.

"Don't you know anything?" Wilgoblikan laughed openly at Javic's confusion. "Did you really think I would just let you Combust me?" he asked. "Such a vicious skill for one so young." Despite his mocking, Wilgoblikan looked mildly impressed at Javic's attempt. The dark wizard flicked his wrist at Javic.

Javic felt a sharp tug in his chest, like his whole body was trying to expand in every direction at once, but he was able to suppress it after only a moment of discomfort.

"We are both connected to the Power," Wilgoblikan said while walking towards Javic. "We command its currents – it does not control us." Wilgoblikan passed Guther Aldune – apparently still alive, sputtering as he choked on his own blood. "If you want to kill a wizard, you have to be a little more creative than that."

Javic's throat began to burn. Wilgoblikan was staring at him intently. Javic coughed desperately, spitting up globs of vile slime that suddenly coated his lungs. The substance replenished inside of him faster than he could spit it up. Dense gobs of black snot, thick as molasses, came pouring from his mouth, but it wasn't enough. Panic flooded his mind as he began to suffocate.

"You see, I cannot affect you directly, but it is simple to fill your lungs with fluid." Wilgoblikan lowered his hand, allowing Javic to cough up the remaining sludge. He was toying with him.

"You killed my parents!" Javic stammered between gasps of air as he closed his fist around a chunk of rock that had exploded from the wall earlier.

Wilgoblikan turned his head slightly, amused. "I've killed many people," he said.

"My name is—" Javic started.

Wilgoblikan flicked his wrist again and Javic's tongue instantly dried out. "I really don't have time for your life story," he said. "I have someone important to kill, and you've already wasted enough of my time. Say goodbye now... oh, I forgot, you can't." Wilgoblikan laughed to himself again as he picked up Guther Aldune's knife off the ground. He then stomped down hard on the back of Javic's hand, forcing him to let go of the rock. The dark wizard raised the knife to Javic's exposed neck.

Staring into Wilgoblikan's face, Javic's heart burned with regret.

This is it. The last face I will ever see.

It was the last face Salvine had seen. The last image to float through her mind before it was taken from her. For his parents as well. Just a wrinkled old man with creases around his bloodshot eyes. Gray stubble sprouting out from his chin.

Wilgoblikan curled back his lips, exposing his gritted teeth as the blade of his knife spontaneously melted in his outstretched hand. The metal turned red and flowed down his fingers before he could use it to slash Javic's throat. He cried out as it dripped across his digits, stripping his skin away.

A bolt of lightning struck Wilgoblikan square in the back, knocking the dark wizard down in front of Javic. The crack of the electricity was deafening as it echoed throughout the tunnel. Wilgoblikan was only down for a moment before he began to rise to his knees. Javic wasted no time: He grabbed the rock back off the ground and swung it as hard as he could against Wilgoblikan's temple. The dark wizard fell face first into a smoldering pile on the ground.

"Close one," said Belford, brushing powder from the Combusted Whunes off his face as he stood up. He walked over to Guther Aldune first, turning him on his side so that he could cough up the considerable amount of blood pooling in his lungs, then went over to help Javic to his feet.

The smell of burnt flesh simmered in the air.

Belford wrinkled his nose. "Is he dead?" he asked.

Javic poked Wilgoblikan with his foot. The dark wizard's leg twitched. "Not yet," said Javic. He raised the rock once more, adjusting his grip slightly so he wouldn't smash his own fingers when he forced it back down on Wilgoblikan's head, but the stone was knocked from his hand by the Power before he could finish the deed. Javic glared at Belford. "Why'd you do that?" he asked, but Belford had a confused look on his face as well.

Guther Aldune grunted as he rose to his hands and knees. He spit up some more blood as well as a whole tooth. "Don't do that," he said as he climbed unsteadily to his feet.

More footsteps echoed through the tunnel from the direction they had come. Javic clutched his side as pain from his ribs shot down his leg. Belford and Aldune prepared themselves for another fight, but around the corner came Shiara and Thorin, as well as several men dressed in black uniforms. All the men, as far as Javic could tell, were Ver'ati – none of them had any conventional weapons at their sides, their sleeves wide at the wrists, freeing their hands for gesturing.

"Praise Mast, you're safe!" Shiara said upon seeing Javic and Belford.

"We have to get you guys out of here now," said Thorin, eying Wilgoblikan, the pile of Whune corpses, and the ample amount of gray powder lying on the floor of the tunnel. "There are more Whunes around still, hiding in ambush all over the Underground."

"Lieutenant Canbel," said Aldune, addressing one of the men in uniform, "go find the doc and bring back some inhibitor, quickly." There were several deep gashes on the general's face, still oozing blood, but he ignored them.

The lieutenant nodded and left briskly, taking another Ver'ati with him as backup.

"You need Amelioration, sir," said another soldier who was inspecting Guther Aldune's wounds. He was a scrawny man, both small in stature and build, only a little older than Belford.

He had black hair, cut short and combed forward into bangs coming down to the top rim of his corrective eyeglasses. He didn't wait for Aldune to respond before lifting his hands to the general's face. A pure, white light shone out from his fingertip as he traced it across the general's cuts. Aldune's skin closed up as the light passed over it, but left behind an ugly, pink scar.

Aldune clenched his teeth as his skin fused back together. Beads of sweat formed on his forehead. After only a few moments, he had about as much as he could take. He shoved the young Ver'ati's arm away. "Captain Grine," he said through his teeth, "never use the Power on me again without asking for permission."

Belford placed his hand on Javic's shoulder. "Are you alright?" he asked.

Javic shook his head. "We need to kill him," he said, focusing again on Wilgoblikan's frail body.

"You will do nothing of the sort," said Aldune, prodding the jagged side of his broken tooth with his tongue. "When Canbel returns with the inhibitor, we won't have to worry about him channeling anymore. There's no telling what secrets we could pry from his mind." Aldune eyed Wilgoblikan greedily.

"I meant physically," Belford said to Javic. "Are you alright physically? I can heal you."

Javic wanted to scream at Aldune, or just smash a rock against Wilgoblikan's head before anyone could stop him, but he knew the thought was futile. He had failed – Wilgoblikan was alive, and there was nothing he could do about it. He felt just as weak and useless as ever – wizard or not, he couldn't avenge Salvine or his parents. His heart sank with disappointment. He couldn't do anything. Instead, Javic just lifted his shirt so Belford could see the massive bruise forming below his broken ribs. The pain was nothing compared to the frustration and regret whirling inside him.

"Ouch," said Belford as he examined Javic's injury, "that must have hurt. I think I can cinch that right up though, no problem."

Javic looked away as Belford used the Power to set his bones. The sounds of several ribs snapping back into place was sickening. The pain was sharp as they shifted, but as soon as they were aligned properly again, they felt completely normal. The young Ver'ati who had healed Aldune, Captain Grine, watched Belford's method with a confused scowl on his face.

"How did you do that?" the captain asked. "That's not to protocol."

"We really do have to get you out of here," said Shiara, glancing nervously back and forth down the passageway.

Guther Aldune cleared his throat. "Yes, yes, I suppose so," he said, his gaze still directed at Wilgoblikan. "Captain Grine, escort these folks out of the Underground, and take that one to Lord Ethan at once," he said, gesturing at Belford. "I'll wait here for Canbel to return so we can take the Goblikan into custody. And once you're finished, send back reinforcements; we've got quite a bit of tunnel to clear, and I'd like to have this situation under control before Queen Havorie learns of the breach."

"Yes, sir," said Captain Grine, still staring curiously at Belford.

Shiara kept looking at Javic as Captain Grine led them through the twisting tunnels. Her eyes flashed as light from one of the luminescent bulbs reflected off of them. She fluttered her eyelids, but never stopped watching Javic as they walked.

"You know," said Shiara, "Wilgoblikan is a Whune, and just like any other, he was Compelled to do the things he has done."

Javic frowned; he knew where this was headed.

"A Whune cannot resist the will of its master," she said. "It's best that things happened this way. He will be tamed and the information he provides the Ver'konus will undoubtedly save lives. You don't want his death on your conscience anyway. Killing changes a person."

Javic wasn't so sure.

He wanted nothing more than for Wilgoblikan to be dead. Preferably by his own hands.

He knew killing Wilgoblikan wouldn't make up for the deaths of his parents, or for the horrors that had befallen Salvine, but he thought that it would at least bring some closure.

Wilgoblikan didn't even know who Javic was.

The monster didn't care what he'd done to Javic, or to anyone else for that matter. There was no justice in the world as long as men like Wilgoblikan were allowed to go on living without having to answer for their crimes. Javic's cheek still stung where the explosion had seared bits of his flesh. He tried to give Shiara a reassuring expression, as if everything were alright, but his heart just wasn't in it.

CHAPTER

37

Harbingers of Death

Captain Grine continued asking Belford questions about Amelioration: How he managed to mend Javic's bones without being able to see them; how much force did he exude to set the ribs without damaging them further; in what manner did he divide the required energy within Javic's body between creation of new tissue and removal of the old – it was all starting to really annoy Belford. He had come to Erotos seeking answers about himself and his past, but all he had received so far was a bombardment of questions and maltreatment from that buffoon of a general, Guther Aldune. Belford's confidence that Lord Ethan would be able to help him was quickly fading.

"When you formed the new marrow, how did you stop the excess irradiative particles from damaging his organs?" asked Captain Grine.

Belford ignored the question at first, but when Captain Grine continued to stare at him expectantly, Belford fired back with a question of his own. "If you're so into healing, why do you wear glasses? Surely there's got to be someone around here who could fix your vision with the Power."

Captain Grine's jaw tightened for a moment. "Amelioration is dangerous," he said. "One wrong move and I'd be blind forever, or worse, a schism could form inside me. It starts with the sweats, then comes the vomiting, then you're dead."

"It's like a miniature Echo," Thorin added.

Belford shot him a dirty look.

Grine nodded. "You start the crack and then your body literally splits itself apart from the inside; nothing anyone can do to help you."

Belford sighed to himself. "I drew the extra energy out of Javic," he said, answering the captain's original question. "I just separated the high energy particles and combined them with low energy ones from the air until they all balanced out and decayed in the visual spectrum."

Captain Grine stared at him blankly.

"I made it glow pretty colors…" Belford said, running his hand through his hair in annoyance as he over-simplified his explanation.

"No, I get it," said Captain Grine. "I just would never have thought of doing that – quite a lot to hold straight in your mind all at once."

They came to a ladder and began to climb its dirty metal rungs up to street level. Thorin pushed aside the cover so they could get out. When they emerged, they found themselves across the street from the Queen's Palace. Men and women in horse-drawn carriages, and a number of peddled taxi carts, mostly empty, filled the main drag. A few pedestrians on the sidewalk stopped to watch as Thorin climbed out of the Underground, followed quickly by Javic and Belford, still trailing gray dust with every step. Shiara and Captain Grine exited last.

Captain Grine struggled to replace the heavy cover. It scraped across the stone unpleasantly before locking into place. Belford bid Javic, Shiara and Thorin farewell and followed Captain Grine across the street past a guarded checkpoint. The palace guards, each wearing the royal crest – a blue fox with golden trim – on their dark tabards saluted the captain as he hurried by.

"Channeling isn't allowed within the palace," Captain Grine warned as they entered the anteroom.

The high-arched ceiling reminded Belford of a cathedral. Two rows of elaborately carved stone columns formed a walkway, along which more guardsmen were posted every few paces. Captain Grine marched straight ahead without pause to the next chamber.

Before Belford even reached the door, he could hear a high-pitched hum coming from within the room. It sounded as if someone were swirling their finger around the rim of a crystal glass, only much, much louder. Inside the small chamber, several more guards were present, all of which had worried expressions on their faces. They looked back and forth between Captain Grine and Belford.

"The *Charisms* are going mad!" exclaimed one of the guards, cautiously eying the altar at the center of the chamber.

A soft, yellow light shone from within an open wooden box at the top of the altar. The case rattled violently, looking almost ready to tear itself loose from its base. Belford could feel the vibrations under his feet as they transferred up through the marble floor tiles. The guardsman directed Captain Grine and Belford to approach the altar one at a time. They were to place their hands on either side of the glowing case.

Captain Grine went first. The light coming from the box grew slightly brighter as he got closer to the altar. He stood there for a moment as one of the guards inspected whatever was inside the box. It didn't take long, then they let him continue on into the palace.

Belford went next. With every step he took towards to the altar, the vibrations grew stronger. The light began to strobe – colorful sparks shot out like fireflies into the night sky. As he touched the sides of the altar, the palms of his hands tingled under the intense vibrations. The hum changed pitch, raising to a higher note and becoming noticeably louder.

Belford looked down into the felt-lined box: Three crystal orbs sat in a row, each strapped down by a leather harness. The orb on the left was clear and still, but the other two glowed actively. The middle orb was producing the majority of the light as well as the whirring vibrations. It was like a tiny golden sun, shining and spitting out charged flares. The orb on the right had a purple spiral twisting through its core, but it was far less dramatic than the middle orb. The purple was nearly lost in the brilliant yellow shine.

"What are these?" asked Belford.

The guardsman inspecting the orbs had a look of nervous excitement on his face. "I've never seen anything like it…" he said. "You must be even stronger than Lord Ethan!"

The other guardsmen all approached the altar now, staring down in awe at the display below.

"These are the *Charisms* – ancient Power Artifacts," said the eldest guard. "The first one detects any channeling nearby, the second shows your strength in the Power, and the third glows in the presence of any foreign Artifacts. And by the looks of it, you have an Artifact on you right now," he said, tapping lightly upon the third orb. It clinked under his nail. "You'll have to turn it over before proceeding any farther into the palace."

Belford had almost forgotten about the brass spyglass, still wrapped in the handkerchief inside his shirt pocket. He pulled it out and handed it over to the guardsman.

Good riddance.

He was glad to be through with the cursed thing. It had brought him nothing but misery and pain. The guardsman took it from his hands and secured it inside a heavy steel chest at the side of the room, being careful to touch it as briefly as possible.

All of the guardsmen continued gawking at him as he exited the chamber and rejoined Captain Grine.

"I knew there was something special about you," said Captain Grine. There was an added shine in his eyes now as he looked upon Belford. "Come on, this way," he said, continuing his brisk pace down the hallway. "I rang ahead to Lord Ethan, and we don't want to keep him waiting. His quarters are in the East Wing."

"Rang ahead?" asked Belford.

"Ah, yes," said the captain, "another one of Lord Ethan's miracles," he stopped momentarily at the next junction in the hallway and pointed to a thin metallic box framed on the wall. "Just push one of the buttons and you can transport your voice to any of the other communication depots in the palace."

The primitive intercom system was the most advanced piece of technology Belford had seen in Aragwey thus far. Add a display screen and a camera for video communication and it would have looked exactly like the call box outside his old apartment building from his dream. If Ethan really was responsible for creating such a device, maybe he would have the answers Belford sought.

The palace was extensive. It had clearly been built prior to the addition of the electric light bulbs to the city. Exposed black stone walls were lined with wiring from the lighting and communication systems, and though the area was sufficiently lit, every room and hallway had at least one window overlooking the palace grounds or the central courtyard so that natural light could permeate. Fancily engraved wooden trim had been put in place throughout much of the hallway to conceal the extensive wiring, but it was still a work in progress.

Captain Grine's legs were moving so fast that Belford could barely keep up with him. "Come on, now," said the captain, "we're almost there."

In the final stretch of hallway, they passed several of the palace staff – one carrying a silver tray stacked high with dirty plates; another with a basket of linens. The maids stepped to the side of the hallway and bowed as Belford and the captain passed. The door to Ethan's quarters stood open. Belford could see a sparsely decorated sitting room containing a short table and several leather chairs. Captain Grine stopped at the threshold and knocked firmly on the frame.

A young lady wearing a green, cotton-twill bodice, laced tightly across her chest, walked over to greet them. Her brown hair was tied back in a loose ponytail under a thin bonnet which framed her face in the same pale green as her dress.

"Hello, Vera," said Captain Grine with a smile. He dropped his shoulders and stood up slightly taller than before.

"Sharith Grine," said the woman, her dark, oval eyes giving away nothing of her emotions. "His Lordship isn't well today," she said, turning towards Belford, "but he still wishes to speak with you privately." Vera stepped aside, allowing Belford to enter alone.

Captain Grine remained at the door as Vera led Belford through the sitting room and up to a set of wide double doors which led to a bedroom. There was an uncomfortable hush over the room, only broken by the raspy breathing of Lord Ethan, obscured from sight by a draped canopy, dangling between the bedposts.

Vera did not enter the bedchamber. She closed the doors behind Belford, leaving him alone with the lord. Belford stepped around the side of the bed and lifted the drapery.

Lying before him was an ancient-looking man. White, wispy hair, matted from resting on his pillow; the skin on his arms and hands almost translucent, every vein bulging visibly as his heart struggled to pump blood to his extremities; his beard merely a puff of gray, unkempt and thin. His eyes, in contrast, were dazzling-blue sapphires in the sea of white wrinkles that formed the rest of his face.

Belford hadn't known what to expect from Lord Ethan, but this certainly was not how he'd imagined him – frail and about one cough away from a coffin, lying under a mound of blankets that could just as easily become his burial mound.

"Aaron Levy," said Ethan, staring Belford dead in the eyes.

Belford pulled back slightly, surprised to hear his true name spoken aloud.

"It's been so long... I never thought I would see you again," Ethan continued. "Please, sit." He reached his hand over and patted the arm of a chair facing his bedside. "You seem confused," he said as Belford sat himself awkwardly in the seat. "Have your memories not returned yet?"

"Only bits and pieces," said Belford, frowning at Ethan's amused expression. "How do you know me?"

Lord Ethan smiled weakly. "I must look quite different since the last time we saw each other," he said. "I wasn't such an old man back then. So much has changed, though you don't appear to have aged a day."

"I don't understand," said Belford.

"If any of your memories have returned at all, you must realize by now that you're not from this place, that this is not our time," said Ethan.

Belford rolled up the sleeve of his shirt, exposing his mark. "I came here because of the Mark of Kings," he said, "because people said you could help me learn the truth about who I am."

"You really don't remember..." said Ethan. "I'm not even sure where to begin." Ethan studied Belford's face for a long moment. "We were the first," he finally said.

Belford looked at Ethan quizzically.

"We were the first people to use the Power," he elaborated. "The mark was just our fool-hearted way of celebrating the curse upon humanity that we represented. We were harbingers of death – we just didn't know it yet." Ethan had a look of nostalgia in his distant eyes. "The time we came from... it couldn't handle our abilities. Nothing remains of it now – only the little things that live on in our heads."

A shiver ran up Belford's spine.

"We were part of a project," Ethan said. "We were meant to fix the world... to be heroes..." he shook his head in disgust. "The scientists created a *virus* – though not really a virus in the classical definition, it acted as a virus in the way it spread – like a virus to the world itself. It replicated once released, implanting itself into the very fabric that makes up the world, quickly altering and converting all matter. Where a virus can only replicate inside of living cells, this technology replicated into every atom.

"Like tiny markers, computer chips, it imbedded itself into the nuclei that make up rocks, water, air... even people. On Earth, everything was affected. Only the vacuum of space could stop its outward expansion. Alone, it did nothing, but with guidance from an extremely powerful computer, we were able to impose our will upon anything, manipulating its very atoms."

"The Power..." said Belford.

"Exactly," said Ethan. "It's no more magic than electricity or magnets. The scientists altered our DNA so that we could communicate with the computer, doing our bidding on a whim. It was supposed to be a gift for all mankind, but not everyone saw it that way. We were supposed to end hunger and poverty, create homes for the homeless, provide the world with infinite energy, infinite wealth – everything the world lacked and more. The power of creation at our fingertips; the power of God.... We were so naïve; idealists trying to make the perfect world... it all seemed so close, so possible given the boundless resources at our disposal... then the war started...."

Visions of arcs of fire descending through the sky leapt across Belford's mind – the city by the park vaporizing right before him; the eyes of the dead staring up at him, judging him, blaming him for not stopping the massacre. His dreams had shown him the truth, though he had so desperately wished them to be nothing more than nightmares.

"You know, you just might be better off without those memories," said Ethan. "I wish I could forget some of the things I saw. Enjoy the bliss of ignorance while it lasts."

It was too late for ignorance – it had always been too late for that. He felt the weight of the world's destruction on his chest from the moment he opened his eyes in Belford Quarry. His body knew the touch of the dead, dragging him down, even before he could recall a single memory. The blood of the innocent stained his hands.

His mind jumped to Claire.

Did I leave her behind in that burning world? Is she just a number among the dead, long forgotten to the bowels of history?

"Claire…?" Belford couldn't even form the question that was searing at the front of his mind.

Ethan frowned. "I do not know what has become of her," he said.

Belford instantly felt as if his heart had been ripped from his chest. He finally knew his past, but still felt emptier than ever – completely lost without Claire.

"She was with us when the computer memorize our bodies, but she may have come back thousands of years ago, even before John Graven, and just lived out a quiet life, or she might still be locked away somewhere in the memory banks of the computer just like you were until recently."

Belford saw a glimmer of hope and latched onto it: "If she's still in the computer, can't we go to it and take her out?"

Ethan's eyes shimmered with the presence of a sympathetic tear. "I'm afraid it's not that simple," he said. "I've no idea why any of us returned when we did… it wasn't supposed to be this way, we were all supposed to come out together, but something went wrong. The computer must be breaking down and expelling us randomly… but we cannot simply go to it and fix it or demand it release our friends and loved ones."

"Why not?" Belford demanded stubbornly.

"Because the computer isn't within our influence… it's not somewhere we can go…."

Belford wasn't hearing any of it. He didn't care how far away it was, or how deep it was buried, or whatever else stood in his way. If going to the computer gave him a chance at bringing back Claire, he would find a way. "We have the

Power," said Belford, "we can do it! Everything is possible now!"

Ethan shook his head violently from side to side. "No, no, no, it is *not*!" he shouted.

Belford was surprised by Ethan's change in tone.

"The computer is on the moon – there, I've said it – it's on the moon and you can't just go to the moon, it's too difficult, too far away and there is no Power on the moon. You would need a ship and computers of your own with intricate programs to calculate your trajectory, sophisticated hardware that *doesn't exist* anymore, and I don't know how to build a computer from scratch. Do you? You can't create what you don't know... all the power in the world to an ignorant man and all he creates are rocks! Nothing! Useless! So stupid! You can't reverse time – what's gone is gone is gone is *gone*!"

It was the ravings of a madman. Belford's heart fluttered with apprehension.

Ethan thrashed his arms around violently. "I've tried to change the past!" he shouted. "But time is a constant – one way! So much is impossible – can't be fixed. Michelle! Michelle! Why are you gone!? What have you done to her? Where is my Michelle!?"

Ethan was screaming now and kicking his legs like a child amidst a tantrum. He swung his arms at Belford, knocking the ceramic lamp from his nightstand. Belford jumped to his feet as it shattered on the ground. The double doors burst open and Vera rushed in with Captain Grine. Belford's heart was racing now. Vera pushed Belford out of the way as she ran to Ethan's side. She quickly grabbed a syringe from a kit attached to her hip. Captain Grine held Ethan down as best as he could. Ethan continued to thrash around as Vera injected the clear liquid directly into his neck.

"Michelle! Michelle!" Ethan shouted out some more. He was already beginning to slow down; his eyelids drooped under the weight of the sedative. "Michelle?" he asked, looking up into Vera's face with a brief look of pained confusion before losing consciousness.

Belford was left standing in the corner of the room, his hands shaking. He didn't know what had just happened – what he did to set off Ethan's episode.

Can I really believe the things this old man said?

It would mean that they were responsible for the destruction of their world…. That was quite a heavy burden.

Maybe he's just going senile, Belford thought wistfully.

Given the grim nature of Ethan's tale, Belford hoped his words were nothing more than a delusion-fueled rant. Unfortunately, Belford could not disprove a single thing Ethan had told him – everything seemed to line up with what little he could remember about his past.

Vera and Captain Grine both released Ethan and looked over at Belford.

If the computer was on the moon, then there really was no way of reaching it. If Claire was even still inside of it, there was no telling if she would return in fifty years or a thousand.

"What happened?" asked Captain Grine.

"I told you he wasn't well today," said Vera. "I wouldn't have let you see him, except that he was so insistent on speaking with you."

"Who's Michelle?" Belford asked.

Vera sighed. "She was his wife, but King Garrett had her killed many years ago."

It made a little more sense now, but it didn't make Belford feel any better. Ethan had lost somebody too; he had wanted to make everything right, and had fallen short, just like Belford. It took everything Belford had to stop himself from wanting to crawl into a hole and die. Ethan had thought Belford was gone forever, yet here he was, seeing him again for the first time since the end of the world. That was the only thing keeping Belford going.

Though he did not yet remember having met him before, Ethan had confirmed that, given enough time, his memories would return. The Mark of Kings had appeared more recently in the past one hundred years than ever before, though no one knew exactly why. Perhaps the trend would continue.

There was still a chance that he would see Claire again in his lifetime, and though every moment without her was hardly worth being called a moment at all, he had no choice but to keep going. Even if he only got to see her once more, even just for a day or an hour when he was eighty years old and succumbing to weakness, it would make it all worthwhile.

As much as it pained him, he would continue.

CHAPTER

38

Cog in the Machine

A dense crowd gathered outside the palace, stretching from the courtyard entrance all the way back through the street to the walls of the ancient Arcanum Cathedral. The entire population of Erotos seemed to have turned out for General Aldune's announcement, in which he would reveal the existence of Belford and his Mark of Kings to the world.

Queen Havorie Elveres emerged from the palace entrance to introduce Aldune. As soon as she appeared, the crowd cheered for her with the kind of proud sincerity that can only come from deep-rooted patriotism. Havorie was an unusually young queen, having taken the throne when she was just four years old following her mother's death. Lord Ethan stopped the other houses of Erotos from usurping her power at the time. Now eighteen, she had already managed to expand upon her late mother's legacy and rallied the spirits of an entire kingdom behind her despite her youth. Some even compared her to the great Emily Fox. Her crown was all but consumed by her flaxen hair, leaving only the gems visible, floating atop her golden curls. She wore a regal, blue dress, embroidered along the hem and conservatively cut.

Javic found her beauty breathtaking. He had never seen anyone command so much attention with such seemingly little effort. He couldn't help but stare up at her, along with the rest of the city. He was seated up front near the podium due to Belford being the guest of honor. Queen Havorie carried herself with great poise and spoke eloquently, much beyond her years.

After the queen's introduction, General Aldune made his announcement as quickly as possible before withdrawing, at which point Belford stepped out in front of the crowd. The city erupted into a hysteric celebration. The roar of the crowd grew so loud that Belford could hardly be heard during his brief speech. He managed a sheepish grin as he revealed his mark for all to see. The sound of the crowd did not diminish even after Belford retreated into the palace. The celebrations continued nonstop into the night. Several Ver'ati even set off colorful explosions in the sky while people danced and cheered. It was all anyone could talk about for several days afterwards.

With Lord Ethan's health in decline, the arrival of a second mark in the Glowing City breathed new life into the Ver'konus. What brief concerns had surfaced after Wilgoblikan's attack within the Underground were quickly swept aside. A war march was underway almost at once, being led by none other than General Aldune. He was bringing a third battalion of Phandolian troops to the Crimson Waters' edge, readying for a strike across the border into Kovani territory. The general was in charge of leading the Phandolian military and the Ver'konus for as long as Lord Ethan remained indisposed. With the lord's recovery becoming increasingly unlikely, Aldune was turning into a more permanent figurehead.

As the celebrations died down, word of Antara's King Lodrin being assassinated finally spread to the people of Erotos. Rumor had it that a demon woman with wings of fire had literally ripped the king apart in his study along with every guard and servant on duty at the time of the attack. Supposedly, she had melted the harbor gates with her eyes; an unstoppable assassin of King Garrett's creation.

Javic now realized that it was he who started the pivotal fire that released the Gates of Galdren, not the Crimson Stalker. He was a wizard – he'd managed to tap into a part of himself that he hadn't known existed, and it saved them during their moment of greatest need.

Shiara cringed every time anyone spoke of the demon woman – a new type of Whune, some said, the offspring of harpies and the soulless *curdender* in the Torus Desert – they were all just twisted accounts of Shiara using her firestone earring Artifact fused together with the rest of the events of that day. Other stories were even more ridiculous. None spoke of the old man Belford and Javic knew to be truly responsible for the king's death. The Crimson Stalker had simply vanished like a ghost into the night.

Javic, to Elric's great disapproval, was now to remain within Erotos indefinitely to undergo Ver'ati training at the academy. During Javic's enlightening encounter with Wilgoblikan, he had assumed Guther Aldune to be unconscious or otherwise too distracted by choking on his own blood to notice that Javic used the Power to disintegrate the remaining Whunes, but apparently the general had seen everything.

"An untrained wizard is a danger to himself and everyone around him," Guther Aldune said to Javic after emerging from the Underground. "That sort of power left unharnessed is an affront to Mast herself."

By law, even though Javic was not a Phandolian citizen, he was still required to enlist at the academy. He could wield the Power, therefore the Ver'konus claimed him as one of their own. They had a strict policy – he either joined them, or became an enemy of the state.

Javic didn't really mind joining the academy. He was glad to be pursuing his destiny, even if that meant being yet another cog in the Phandolian military machine. He was following in his mother's footsteps – he hoped she would have been proud. The best part, though, was that Belford would be joining the academy right alongside him.

Unsurprisingly, the Ver'konus wanted to keep a close eye on Belford's development. He was to be their leader one day; a prodigy of wisdom and Power, like Lord Ethan before him.

There was little for Javic to do but gather his things from the Rosa Marsa and report to the registrar's office at the academy. He returned to the steamer after his talk with Guther Aldune and was immediately greeted by his grandfather.

A nervous pinch formed in Javic's throat as he began to recount his frightening encounter with Wilgoblikan. Elric's posture tensed as soon as Javic mentioned smelling the Whunes inside the academy. By the time he got to Wilgoblikan's appearance, Elric became pale and needed to take a seat.

Javic wasn't sure how to tell the next part. Mallory and Arlin joined Elric on the bench on the stern of the Rosa Marsa. All three were listening intently to Javic's story. "The Whunes all turned to dust," he said, "and I was the only one there...." Everyone continued to stare at him, not comprehending what he was saying.

"So who saved you?" asked Arlin. "Surely Wilgoblikan didn't destroy them himself."

"Belford woke up?" asked Elric. "Or General Aldune did it?"

Mallory had a curious expression on her face. Javic could see the wheels spinning in her mind, piecing together the only possible answer that remained.

"It was me," he said. "I can use the Power. I'm a wizard." Javic locked his eyes on Mallory as he spoke, too afraid to watch his grandfather's reaction.

Mallory's eyelashes fluttered quickly several times as her cheeks flushed a light shade of pink. She broke away from Javic's gaze.

She's blushing?

Javic felt heat rising in his own cheeks at the realization.

No one spoke. The awkward silence stretched on for what felt like an eternity.

Finally, Javic looked over at his grandfather. Elric had tears in his eyes.

"I never would have brought you here if I'd known you inherited your mother's abilities," said Elric.

Javic gazed out onto the still waters of the harbor. "I tried to kill him – Wilgoblikan – but I failed," he said. "They took him away for interrogation."

Elric nodded silently.

Mallory and Arlin stepped off the Rosa Marsa onto the dock, giving Javic a moment alone with his grandfather.

"The political currents here could tear a man apart," Elric warned. "It's more dangerous than you know – I went through it with your parents."

Javic hugged his grandfather. "Don't worry," he said, "I'll be careful."

Elric tugged on the ring attached to his necklace harder than usual, wincing in pain as the chain dug into the back of his neck. He let his fingers drop, and the ring slipped back beneath his shirt. "You'll do great things one day," Elric said. "But you don't have to do them here. We can go somewhere else – somewhere they won't tie strings to you. If you're anything like your mother and grandmother, your strength has only just begun to show and they will try to use you for their own purposes if you stay."

Javic shook his head. "They will teach me how to control my abilities. I can't leave until I know what I'm capable of – what I can become. Where else can I learn that?"

Elric remained silent.

"Shiara and Thorin are staying as well," said Javic. "They'll help me and Belford, I know it." Javic had never seen his grandfather look so defeated in his entire life, not even when their farm was destroyed.

"Once you join the academy, I won't be allowed to see you again for a long time," said Elric. "You must promise me you won't forget who you are – what you stand for. They will try to turn you into one of their dogs. They will make you feel obligated to their cause, willing to sacrifice yourself for reasons that serve their purposes. If you let them, they will control you as surely as any Compelled Whune. Always be mindful of to whom your actions truly serve. Remember who you are."

Javic gave his grandfather one last hug before retrieving his solitary sack of belongings from below deck. It was all that remained from the farm. Olli had carried it for him on her saddle the whole way from Darrenfield. He wished he could bring her with him to the academy, but that wasn't practical. Elric was going to have to care for her now. Javic already missed them both as he disembarked from the Rosa Marsa. Elric was not leaving the city, but until Javic's training progressed beyond the apprenticeship stage, Javic was not permitted to have any visitors or leave the grounds of the academy. Elric would have to find lodging somewhere within the city and wait for him to complete his training.

On the dock, Arlin and Mallory wished him good luck. Mallory gave him an extra-long hug before he departed once and for all. It was still awkward for Javic to have Mallory pressed up against him with Arlin standing right there at their side, but he ignored the discomfort as much as he could and focused instead on the knowledge that Mallory truly appreciated him and would miss him while he was away. He had craved acceptance and friendship like that his entire life. Although he knew he and Mallory would never be anything more than friends, it still felt good knowing that she cared about him.

The sky was completely clear, stretching overhead like an unfilled canvas, deep blue in the crisp evening air as Javic set out towards the academy. He had no idea what his future held, but one thing was certain: Whatever happened, his adventures would definitely be far more exciting than anything Harvey McGrutto or any of the other Darrenfield children would ever get to experience. He just wished Salvine could have been here to experience it with him. He was in the greatest city in the world, surrounded by royalty and history and hundreds of Ver'ati, of which he would soon be joining the ranks. At this moment, he couldn't imagine being anywhere else.

Directly in front of him, the southernmost palace tower reached into the heavens. Javic traced his eyes up the length of the sleek construct, rising from the earth like an obelisk. Just above its highest point, the moon hung in the impenetrable, blue beyond, completely full, just like the night Belford appeared in his life for the first time. It was hard to believe that only a month had passed since then; so much had changed. He wasn't a farmer anymore – a lonely boy too ashamed and embarrassed of himself to reach outside his comfort zone. He had been friendless because his peers shunned him for being different, and he believed every word they spoke. He was different, yes, but now he realized that it was his differences that made him great.

Perhaps Salvine had seen that in him – he would never know for sure. He could only hope there was someone else out there who would love him for who he was – love him without compromise. He just needed to open himself up to the experience.

CHAPTER

39

Playing with Fire

Deep beneath the streets of Erotos, the Calvenite cage shook violently as the beast strained against its confinement. Doctor Hilven Crane stood opposite General Aldune, a smoke stick poking out from between the doctor's lips as he oversaw the transfer of the Whune back to his laboratory. A group of technicians carefully positioned a dolly underneath the base of the cage and began to wheel it slowly down the narrow, winding corridor. Try as it might, Doctor Crane had no fear of the creature breaking free. The bars of the cage were made of Calvenite, the same impervious material that formed every building in the Glowing City. Calvenite was created with the Power, and only the Power could so much as scratch its surface.

"How many does that make?" asked General Aldune, picking mindlessly at the scabs on his cheek. The long, pink scars left over from his encounter with the captured Goblikan were infected – most likely from his picking – his flesh beginning to fester beneath the crusty ridges of the lacerations.

Doctor Crane took another puff off his smoke stick before answering the general. "Seven live ones, so far," he said, "not counting the Goblikan of course."

"Of course," said Aldune. "That one should make quite an interesting subject. It's a pity I have a war march to attend to. I would very much have liked to lead that interrogation myself."

The doctor smiled, though it did not extend to his eyes. He was already mentally planning all of the experiments he wanted to conduct on the Whunes. He had never had a chance to study a live specimen before – they were difficult to catch, always fighting to the death. There was still so much that the Ver'konus did not understand about the Whunes. The thought of being the first to discover exactly what makes them tick was quite an intriguing prospect for Doctor Crane. He took a final drag off his smoke stick before flicking it to the tunnel floor and squashing the smoldering butt with the heel of his boot.

"You know those things will kill you," said Aldune, scratching hard at his scabs.

"How do you suppose they got in?" Doctor Crane asked, ignoring the general's comment.

Aldune shook his head. "Haven't found the breach yet. We probably never will, either. These tunnels stretch for leagues, at least half of them unmapped. A real rat's nest."

Screams from down the corridor brought Doctor Crane's Ver'ati senses to a sharpened point. Aldune was racing towards the panicked cries before the doctor even had a chance to gather his bearings. It was the technicians around a bend in the corridor, just out of sight. Doctor Crane chased after General Aldune, staying right on his heels as they rushed to aid the alarmed men.

They rounded the corner. The caged Whune was still locked away, but the unlucky procession had happened upon a second Whune. The technicians were not Ver'ati – they had no means of protecting themselves. The free Whune swiped them with its razor-sharp claws fully extended. The men screamed, throwing themselves backwards in an attempt to escape. One poor fool hurled himself against the side of the cage, where the captured Whune wasted no time at reaching between the bars and eviscerating him where he stood.

Aldune launched his own attack before anyone else became a casualty. Using the Power, he ripped the iron spokes out of one of the dolly's wheels and sent them soaring towards the free Whune. It was a direct hit. The force of the impacts drove the spikes all the way through the charging monster's limbs, knocking it back against the wall of the tunnel. It was speared in place, as if crucified. Aldune quickly bent the portions of the rods that were still protruding from the front of the beast into hooks so that the Whune could not pull its body all the way through and off the other side. The creature pulled forward anyway, only stopping once the hooks blocked its advance.

"That makes eight for you," said Aldune.

The Whune roared, sending phlegm rocketing out of its mouth as Aldune approached.

"Feisty one," said the general. He took a pair of brass knuckles out of his pocket and slid them over the fingers of his right hand.

Doctor Crane saw to the mangled technicians as Aldune began to beat the Whune in the side of the head with his fist, attempting to knock it unconscious. The technician that fell against the cage was already dead, but the rest had only suffered superficial wounds. They were still breathing anyway. Crane took another smoke stick out of his pocket and lit it with the Power – a short flame floated just above the tip of his index finger. He took several puffs before starting the process of mending several long gashes that were running diagonally across the forearm and abdomen of one of the injured technicians.

The pinned Whune grew silent as Aldune pounded it into submission. When Doctor Crane was finished with the technicians, he walked over to inspect his new specimen. It was quite a beauty – tall and lanky for a Whune, but still equally as terrifying as the rest. Its unconscious body slumped against the iron wheel spokes as a pool of thick, dark blood expanded around its feet.

A flash of silver around one of its wrists caught Doctor Crane's attention. It was a bracelet, tight against its flesh. Tarisian silver – the quality was too fine to be anything less. It gleamed white like the full moon as it reflected the harsh glow of the tunnel's bulbs. There was a charm attached to the chain, fashioned in the shape of a flying dove.

"Hello there, little bird," said the Doctor, caressing the edge of the fine charm with his fingertip. "You're a long way from home now, aren't you?"

* * *

Wake up! Wake up, you idiot!
The presence in her head was screaming at her. Her battered face pulsated with warm blood.

Her back ached as the cold metal bars of the narrow cage pressed against her, drawing all the warmth from her pummeled body.

The pain from her injuries did not bother her directly, but it took its toll on her strength. She hardly had enough energy to open her eyelids, but once she did, she found the darkness of the surrounding chamber to be all encompassing. She was still underground.

Where are we? What is this place?
She ignored the voice, focusing instead on stretching her limbs as much as possible, getting a feel for the edges of her confinement. Her hands and feet tingled as blood began slowly flowing back into them. She still had gaping holes in her wrists and ankles from the attack by that Ver'ati during her last

lucid memory. As sensation returned to her limbs, she could feel the sticky wetness of her own blood soaking through several gauze packed bandages, placed over the impalement sites. She would have bled out without them.

Why didn't they let us die?

She pressed firmly against the bars of her tiny cage, testing their strength. The bars flexed slightly, but remained solid.

Beyond a closed door, a light came on. It shone through the gap beneath the door, illuminating a thin patch of tiled flooring. Her eyes quickly adjusted to the minimal light. There were eight other cages surrounding her, placed in a semicircle around a metal table which was fitted with a number of thick leather restraints. She was not the only Whune present. Each of the surrounding enclosures was occupied by her brethren. Some were unconscious, lying at the base of their cages in heaps, while others, like her, glanced around curiously.

A pair of yellow eyes flashed in the darkness from out of an adjacent cage.

It was her master! Wilgoblikan was trapped alongside the rest of them.

She focused to communicate with Wilgoblikan with her mind. She could feel his presence, but something was wrong: Although he was right beside her, he felt faint, as if they were leagues apart.

"Muuuarp!" she groaned, vocalizing her frustration.

Wilgoblikan locked his gaze upon her.

She could still intuitively sense his direction without looking, but she could no longer hear his mental commands. It was as if a fog had fallen across their connection.

Wilgoblikan's cage was significantly smaller than hers — barely the size of his body. He was forced to stand upright. He continued to stare at her.

She strained to hear his will, but was met only with silence. The annoying presence in her head took the opportunity to fill the void.

He did this to us. I hope he burns for his crimes.

Wilgoblikan's eyes suddenly shifted towards the doorway on the opposite side of the room. Footsteps were drawing near. The lock clicked outside and the door shifted, sliding sideways as it opened. It clanged as it bounced along its track.

Light from the hall poured in, flooding her vision. The silhouette in the doorway hit a switch on the wall, illuminating the entire chamber with an even more intense glow. The brightness made her head spin, compounding the wooziness she was already experiencing from her blood loss. She squeezed her eyes shut as a dull ache in her head grew into a blaze of flickering stars, blanketing her vision in sparks.

The door to the chamber scraped shut. Footsteps approached her cage. By the time she managed to open her eyes again, the man was already at the cage beside hers.

"Hello," he said. He was speaking to her master. "My name is Doctor Hilven Crane."

Wilgoblikan eyed the doctor with a deathly glare.

Doctor Crane drew a smoke stick from his pocket and lit it with a flame that sprang up from his fingertip. He inhaled deeply from its end. "Not feeling chatty?" he asked, a cloud of smoke escaping with his words. He took another drag, leaned in close to Wilgoblikan's cage, and blew out directly in his face.

Wilgoblikan didn't react, not even blinking as the smoke swirled around him.

Doctor Crane narrowed his eyes. With the smoke stick between his fingers, he reached through the bars and pressed the burning end hard against Wilgoblikan's forehead.

Her master shook in place, letting out a pained squeal as his flesh sizzled. His cage was too tight for him to withdraw. There was nothing he could do to escape the burning.

The Whunes all howled at once. She joined the chorus, rattling her cage as the ruckus grew to an impressive volume. She expected the presence in her head to gloat, but it held its thoughts to itself for the moment.

A loud clang stole her attention.

One of the other Whunes had managed to topple its cage over during the violent fervor. The cage remained intact. The Whune was now awkwardly stuck on its belly. She ceased her own shaking to avoid a similar fate.

Doctor Crane ignored the clamor, only removing the smoke stick from Wilgoblikan's forehead once it was entirely snuffed out. He tossed it aside. "You'll talk," he said. "Everyone does, sooner or later."

He walked across the chamber to a cabinet, eying the overturned cage as he passed. He retrieved a filled syringe from a drawer before approaching the fallen Whune, still thrashing around, even on its belly. He righted the cage, making a simple hand gesture to direct a burst of kinetic energy in a precise blast. Once vertical, one more blast slid the cage back so it was pressed squarely against the wall of the chamber. It would not fall again so easily. The process tossed the Whune about like a rag doll.

"You may have noticed that you can no longer reach the Power," Doctor Crane said to Wilgoblikan. He eyed the tip of his needle as he pressed lightly on its plunger, clearing the syringe of any air that might have been caught in the tube. "That is because you have been injected with inhibitor. You are just a powerless old man now."

The Whune in the righted cage growled at the doctor through gritted teeth. Crane quickly jabbed the syringe between the bars and pricked it on the thigh. The doctor quickly pulled his hand back, but before he could withdraw entirely, the Whune slashed downward at him with its claws extended. A moment later, the Whune collapsed to the bottom of its cage, the sedative already taking effect.

Doctor Crane frowned. The back of his hand trickled with a thin trail of blood. He wasted no time healing the scratch with the Power – his skin glowed with a bright, white light as it fused back together. After that, he unlocked the cage and directed another blast of energy to propel the unconscious

Whune across the floor to the metal table at the center of the chamber. He lowered the table to the floor with a foot pedal and strapped the Whune in place before cranking it back up to waist height.

The Whune's tongue flopped out of its mouth as it breathed heavily under the sedation. Doctor Crane stepped around and placed his hands on either side of its motionless head. He stared down his hooked nose at the hapless creature. Intense concentration burned in his eyes. He was using the Power inside its head. The Whune's body shook momentarily in an uncontrolled spasm, yet it remained unconscious as the doctor worked.

"You will see I can be very persuasive," Crane said to Wilgoblikan.

The Whune's tremors intensified.

I don't think he intends to fix us at all. We need to get out of here....

For once, she agreed with the voice. Unfortunately, there was little she could do from behind the bars. Even if she could escape her cage, her master was Powerless – there would be no escaping the city.

The Whune on the table stopped shaking. Doctor Crane glanced up, blinking several times before throwing another glance over to Wilgoblikan. Her master was leaning against the back of his cage with his eyes closed, ignoring the doctor entirely.

Doctor Crane went back to the cabinet. This time he retrieved an apron from a hook on the inside of the main door. He looped it over his head before tying the strings into a bow behind his back. He opened one of the cabinet's drawers and ran his fingertips across several gleaming instruments before settling on a pair of heavy pliers. Tool in hand, he returned to the table, where he immediately clamped the pliers down on one of the unconscious Whune's claws.

"I don't expect this to make you talk, Goblikan," said the doctor, "but perhaps you will understand that there's no length I will not go to in order to extract the information I need."

Wilgoblikan still wasn't watching.

Doctor Crane wrenched sideways with a forceful grunt, tearing the claw free from the Whune's finger in one swift jerk. He discarded it into a tin. It clinked as it bounced against the bottom of the tray. He moved on to the next finger. The Whune woke up before Crane was halfway through maiming its digits.

The Whune's agonizing screams pierced the chamber.

Wilgoblikan opened his eyes now – a hint of concern set on his face.

Whunes were not supposed to experience pain. This was Doctor Crane's doing.

Whatever he'd manipulated inside the Whune's head was forcing it to feel. Every bit of the excruciating torment was playing out across its twisted face. It writhed in its restraints, thrashing pathetically. The unforgiving straps held tight.

She realized the voice in her head had grown completely silent. She could feel a chill of dread coming from the portion of her brain where the presence resided. All of the other Whunes had quieted down now as well. They all watched tensely as Doctor Crane mutilated his patient's hands.

The doctor pulled a small device out from his coat pocket and pressed a button before speaking into its end. "Doctor Crane, trial one, subject number..." he glanced over at the empty cage, "subject number three," he finished. "I have already managed to isolate the altered pain sensors and have repaired the subject's nerve endings. For safety, I have removed its claws and the distal tips of its fingers." He clicked another button on the device before placing it back into his pocket. He looked at Wilgoblikan once again. "Don't worry," he said, "your turn will come soon enough."

The restrained Whune was sweating profusely, its skin glowing in a slimy sheen. It breathed with an uneven rasp as its eyes wandered wildly across the chamber before rolling up into its trembling head.

Doctor Crane walked back to the Whune's head and placed his hands along its temples once again. "As for you, my friend," he said to the Whune, "you'll tell me exactly what makes you tick, without saying a word."

Her gut fluttered uncomfortably. The uneasy feeling slithered like an eel in her belly, making her intestines contract. She'd truly failed her master this time. The doctor would be the death of them all, and there was absolutely nothing she could do to stop him.

Mast help us....

CHAPTER

40

Secrets and Lies

The water spouts of Candeer Fountain splashed down noisily behind Belford into the fountain's circular basin. Mist from the splashes filled the air as he scanned his eyes across a group of students in the distance, emerging from the examination hall. He didn't recognize any of them, but that didn't mean they wouldn't recognize him. He had become an overnight celebrity the moment his mark was revealed to the city. He turned away before any of the students looked his direction. The academy was in full session, the moon just above the eastern horizon.

Shiara, Thorin, and Javic were supposed to be meeting him here, but they were all late. Belford hoped his letters hadn't been intercepted. After his unpleasant experience with General Aldune almost getting him killed in the Underground, Belford didn't have much trust for the Ver'konus. Aldune was the leader of the academy, and second-in-command of the

Ver'konus, behind Lord Ethan. Captain Grine and Lieutenant Canbel, appointed by Aldune, followed Belford everywhere he went. It wouldn't surprise him if they were reading his private correspondences as well. They lived with him, attended classes with him, and if it wasn't for Belford sneaking out the window of their apartment, they would be with him right now. Since his meeting with Lord Ethan, Belford literally hadn't had a moment to himself.

His disheartening conversation with Ethan unfortunately left him with more questions than answers. He hoped Ethan would be able to tell him more about his past – about who he was. Instead, the meeting only confused him even more.

He was more alone than ever. No one else in Erotos could tell him about the past. To the Phandolians, the obelisk covered in hieroglyphics at the tip of the Old City was a mystery – an ancient curiosity uncovered from beneath their feet – but to Belford it meant so much more.

The pharaonic civilization was ancient even to the people of Aaron's time. The obelisk was the first sign that any remnants of the past still existed. In some ways, it was comforting to know that not everything was erased over the millennia that had passed since he was memorized by the computer, but in other ways, it was entirely devastating. There was no longer any doubt.

Everyone I knew is dead and gone. There's no going back.

He still had Elric's old map of Aragwey in his pocket. He had spent many hours staring at its unfamiliar contours. Glancing at it now, he could distinguish the outline of northeast Africa. Everything else had changed since his time. Mountain ranges filled regions that were once flat deserts. The weather here was anything but dry now. The people of Aragwey were an ethnic mixing of Middle Eastern and European, blended over a multitude of generations.

Many elements of Aragwian culture were familiar to Belford, however – for one, everyone still spoke English – which seemed peculiar at first, especially considering how many years had passed since he was locked away inside the computer. Before Ethan confirmed the truth about their origin, the cultural similarities had been comforting. Home had felt like it was still within reach. The mystery of the similarities had resolved itself, though, once Belford realized that John Graven and the other returnees were also from his time. They were responsible for instating English, now known as Aragwian, as the official language of the nation. The cultural shift was a reflection of their influence over these lands. It wasn't that elements of Belford's time still existed, rather, the returnees had desperately fought to bring back the home they had lost – Aragwey was a reflection of a place long forgotten by the passage of time.

Ethan said they'd been stored inside a computer, which meant Belford's body was made up of a bunch of quarry rocks that had been resequenced into organic material.

Am I still me? Am I even a person?

He was beginning to remember who he was, but he was no longer certain of *what* he was. From what he understood, he was basically a copy of Aaron Levy, someone who died long ago – a perfect computer reproduction.

If my memories are recreations, are they still real? Are my emotions even valid?

He felt so utterly alone. Only Lord Ethan and King Garrett could relate to his situation, and he couldn't exactly have a heart-to-heart with either of them.

I may have the same genetics and the same memories as the original Aaron, but is that all it takes to make a person?

Do I have a soul?

"When the moon first shines its light, meet me where the endless rain isn't the only test…" Shiara's voice made Belford jump. "Could you have been any more cryptic?"

Belford spun around. Shiara was dressed in black Ver'ati robes with her hood drawn over her head. He hardly recognized her in the official Arcanum garb. "New robes?" he asked.

"Old ones," she said, "from storage."

Belford nodded. "The test part of the clue is because of the exam hall," he said.

"I got it. Why all the secrecy?"

Belford waited until a pair of passing students moved out of earshot. "I have a lot to say... I'd rather wait for Thorin and Javic to arrive before starting."

Shiara glanced around briefly as well. "Thorin isn't coming," she said. "Aldune cut him new orders working at the docks. It's a job typically given to non-wizards." Shiara shook her head in disgust.

Belford found Shiara's blue eyes under her hood. "What about you?" he asked. "Are you being punished as well?"

Shiara stared back at him with hesitation. "I... no. General Aldune hates Thorin more than me. I was actually commended by the Ver'konus for bringing you in," she said. "I've been promoted to major."

Belford clasped her around the shoulder with his right arm. 'That's great news! Congratulations!"

Shiara smiled, a rosy blush growing in her cheeks as she stared down at her feet.

Belford released her from the half hug. Things had never quite returned to normal after their kiss aboard the Rosa Marsa.

"Don't worry about Thorin," he said. "They're grooming me to take over this place. I won't let Aldune punish him forever."

"Thank you," said Shiara, still staring at her feet. "That would mean a lot to him."

As awkward as things had become between Shiara and Belford, he was actually starting to think he preferred this Shiara over the old one. He didn't get yelled at anymore. She seemed to have become kinder overall. She glanced up, finally meeting his eyes again. Suddenly she frowned and punched his arm.

"Ouch!" Belford rubbed his bicep. "What was that for?"

"It's been weeks," said Shiara. "You should have written sooner. No one's allowed to contact you, so everyone's been writing to me, trying to find out how you've been doing."

"Sorry," said Belford. "I didn't know anyone cared."

Shiara put her hands on her hips. "Well, we do."

"I'll try to do better," he promised. He reached out and playfully pulled Shiara's hood down over her face.

She swung at him wildly, batting his hands away before readjusting her robe.

Belford gave her a wide grin. She glared back, but he could tell her irritation was mostly feigned.

Approaching from the south side of campus, Javic arrived at the fountain. He increased his pace as he saw Belford and Shiara at the fountain's edge.

Belford ruffled Javic's hair as soon as he came within reach. "How are you doing?" he asked. "Training going well?"

Javic nodded absently. "I miss you guys. Unfortunately I can't stay long. Class starts soon."

"Alright," said Belford, "I guess I'll jump right into it then." He rubbed his hands together, the serious nature of their meeting falling over him like a shadow. "Do either of you know anything about the computer on the moon?"

Shiara and Javic both stared at him blankly.

"Didn't think so," said Belford. "Well… according to Lord Ethan, the Power isn't magic at all. It's science. There's an ancient computer system on the moon. People with the Power are able to mentally connect to it, then the computer sends signals back down to earth to control matter for us."

Shiara and Javic shared a brief glance.

"I was inside the computer," continued Belford. "Or more accurately, the computer memorized a blueprint of me and stored me in its memory banks a long time ago. All of the people throughout history who've had the Mark of Kings came from the same time – when the computer was first built – to escape an apocalypse. There was a war that destroyed the whole world."

"What's a blueprint?" asked Javic. "And what's a computer?"

Belford sighed.

"Lord Ethan told you all of this?" asked Shiara. "It sounds pretty far-fetched. He is getting pretty old. Are you sure he knew what he was saying?"

"Ethan is a bit senile," admitted Belford, "but I've seen what he described in my dreams. I'm sure at least most of what he said is true – the technology... the war.... I know I'm not from this time." He looked at Javic, whose eyebrows were arched up in a vastly confused expression.

I must sound insane right now.

Belford hadn't realized how difficult it would be to explain himself to the people of this time.

"A blueprint is a schematic as to how something is built," he said. "The computer stored instructions for how to recreate me. And a computer is..." he wasn't really sure how to describe that concept. "Well, it's like... an electric device that uses numbers to calculate and store information."

"Electric device?" asked Shiara.

Belford made a wide sweeping gesture with his hands. "Electricity... energy, like lightening. It's what's powering the light bulbs across the city."

Shiara and Javic still looked confused.

"So... like magic?" Javic asked.

Belford made a slow blink. "Let's just move passed this," he said. "There is a reason I asked you both here. You guys are the only ones I can trust. Do either of you know how Wilgoblikan found me so fast when I first appeared in Darrenfield?"

They both remained silent. Javic began scratching his arm.

"Somehow he knew when and where the computer was going to place me – he was at the farm in less than a day."

"I have no idea," said Shiara. "Until now, I just assumed he was already pursuing you before you lost your memory, but if those were really your first moments in Aragwey, he must have had some method of determining your arrival."

"My thoughts exactly," said Belford. "I need to find out how he did it. I need to question Wilgoblikan, but no one seems to know anything about him – where he's being held, who's responsible for interrogating him…. Aldune's ignoring all of my messages."

"Why does it matter?" asked Javic. "Who cares how that monster found you?"

Belford glanced down at his feet. A wave of sadness hit him as he thought of Claire. If it wasn't for her, he could simply ignore his past and be all the happier for it.

Surprisingly, Shiara answered Javic for him. "He wasn't the only one trapped inside the… *computer* thing," she said. "He's looking for a girl."

Belford lifted up his head and glanced over at her. *How perceptive,* he thought. He was a little surprised she managed to piece together the truth with so few details. Their eyes met briefly. Shiara gave a sympathetic smile.

"Questioning Wilgoblikan won't do you much good," she said. "Whunes are incapable of knowingly betraying their masters. He probably wouldn't be able to tell you anything more than lies, even if he wanted to help."

"I still have to try," he said.

Shiara nodded understandingly.

"With Aldune ignoring me, though, I don't even know where to start," said Belford. "I asked Captain Grine and he said he would look into it for me, but it's been three days now and he just keeps changing the subject whenever I bring up Wilgoblikan."

"You can't trust any of them," said Javic. "The Ver'konus doesn't have your best interest at heart. They only want to keep us in line. Just before joining the academy, Grandfather told me to be careful – he said they would try to use me for their own purposes. We're coming into this at the bottom level, with no real idea of what the Ver'konus intends to do with us or how much they are willing to sacrifice to attain their goals."

"That is a very dangerous line of thinking," warned Shiara, her expression darkening. Her hood cast a shadow across her face. "You are both members of the Ver'konus now," she said. "You simply can't question its integrity without very serious repercussions. It's insubordinate. And you, Belford, if you can muster up some patience and do as you're told, you could be running this place sooner than you think."

Belford shook his head. "Who says I want to run this place? Do I look like a military leader? I don't want to wage wars… send people to die."

Shiara bobbed her head slightly, making her firestone earrings swing in circles. "It does take a strong spine," she said. "Still, even though Aldune is a complete fisheater, it's not really the Ver'konus you should be worrying about. If King Garrett gets his way, we'll all wind up dead or enslaved."

"Just because one side is evil doesn't make the other side good," said Javic.

"There's no such thing as *good* in the real world," Shiara spat back. "There's always going to be shades of gray. You're being an idealistic fool!"

Lord Ethan's words repeated in Belford's mind:
We were so naïve; idealists trying to make the perfect world. Then the war started….

"My Grandfather used to be in the Ver'konus too," said Javic. "He wouldn't have warned me against them without good cause."

"*Them* and *us*. We're all just pieces in a bigger picture. If you want to change things around here, you have to put in the time to earn rank!" Shiara gestured sharply with open palms to emphasize her words, her irritation showing. "With the Mark of Kings, Belford can rise through the ranks quickly and then, if he so desires, he can start changing the way things are done around here." She turned towards Belford. "If you're not willing to do that, you really don't have any right to complain."

Belford chewed on his lip. The old, angry Shiara was back. She wasn't quite yelling at him, but her voice was painfully harsh.

"It's not about complaining," Javic said defensively. "It's about trust. You saw how General Aldune took Belford into the Underground despite my warning that the Whunes were down there. Who's to say any one of us won't end up dead in our sleep if we don't fit his plans?"

"Belford's too valuable, for one," said Shiara. "And nobody is going to pay any attention to you, Javic. You're just an initiate. Command couldn't care less about what you do once you finish your proficiency exam. If you're so against following the Ver'konus, you can leave the academy after passing your test."

"Stop it!" Belford said forcefully. "Both of you!"

Shiara and Javic both turned towards him at once.

"You're both right. Trust the Ver'konus – don't trust the Ver'konus. Either way, they are already controlling our lives. They don't care about any of us – we're just fodder to be used as they see fit. I, for one, wouldn't trust the Ver'konus even if they made me the leader of the whole damned organization. A military is bigger than any one man."

Shiara scowled deeply. She opened her mouth, about to interrupt.

Belford raised his hand to stop her. "I'm going to follow orders and do as I'm told," he said, trying to avert Shiara's concerns. "But my first priority is getting Claire back. I'm going to do whatever it takes, with or without you."

Shiara let out a sigh. "You make me sound like such a heartless bitch," she said. "Of course I'll do whatever I can to help you find out what happened to her. I just don't want to see anyone get court marshaled in the process. You have to go about things the right way around here or you'll just make things harder for yourself."

Belford smiled. "Isn't that what I have you for?"

Sharia narrowed her eyes.

"To help me get through things the right way – not to make my life harder," he clarified.

"I'm with you too," said Javic. "I've already come this far. I'll stick around and do whatever I can to help push you to the top."

Belford's heart swelled with gratitude. Shiara and Javic were both looking at him expectantly, waiting for him to give them some direction.

I'm not alone in this after all.

It was a nice thought. Figuring out how to get Claire back was a daunting task, but having his friends support him made it feel a little less impossible.

"First, we need to find Wilgoblikan," he said. "Someone around here has him, and I have some questions that need answering."

Continue reading for a special preview of:

Ashen Sky

Book Two of:

The Arcadian Complex

Paul James Keyes

CHAPTER

1

Reborn

The earth shuddered in Erotos as another tremor raked through the palace's foundation. It came as a dull vibration, not unlike the massive Machina of old, though most knowledge of those grand devices had been lost to the bowels of history – few references remained, even within the ancient Archives of the Arcanum deep beneath the grand cathedral just north of the palace.

The walls of the royal chamber groaned in distaste as the Echo, too wide to pinpoint its exact origin, threatened to rattle every door from its hinges and sent each of the richly colored tapestries that lined Queen Havorie's bedchamber swaying back and forth in vaunting ripples of cloth. The draperies, now centuries old, were still as vivid as the days they were first woven. Their threads were tempered to outlast countless generations of inhabitants by careful workings of the Power.

461

Havorie woke as the tremors grew stronger. She sat up in bed, pushing the down-filled blanket off her upper body. A flash of light drew her attention to her left wrist. She pulled up the sleeve of her frilly nightgown, exposing the golden clasp of the device that was cinched around her arm like a wristwatch. Its function had nothing to do with the time of day. It was a Power Artifact – similar to the trio of Charisms that guarded the palace's entrance hall with their abilities to detect the presence of the Power. The device had a crystal face that was positioned on the inside of her forearm. She held it up to get a better look at its glowing dials.

The Detector – as Havorie called it – was her personal version of the Charisms. One hand detected individuals in the process of channeling, another determined one's strength in the Power, and a third identified the presence of other Power Artifacts in the vicinity, just like the three Charisms. The dials would glow and point in the direction of whichever property they were honed to detect, similar to a compass finding north. There was a fourth hand on the Detector, but it did nothing, or at least had done nothing for as long as Havorie could recall, but three out of four working dials wasn't bad considering the age of the relic.

All of the known Artifacts had histories longer than Aragwey, their origin as much of a mystery to their keepers as the Power itself. They outdated even the oldest records kept by the Arcanum historians, which meant they existed well before John Graven, the first Ver'ati, walked the lands a thousand years ago. Havorie discovered the Detector, along with a number of other interesting trinkets, among her mother's possessions a few years after her passing.

It hadn't taken long for Havorie to figure out how the three working dials operated. The Power was as common in Erotos as honey mead. One of the three working dials was always glowing at least faintly. The hand that sensed one's strength in the Power had been pointing towards Aaron Levy, the odd man with the Mark of Kings on his arm, ever since his arrival in Erotos a little over one month ago.

Havorie met him briefly on the day he revealed his mark to the world. The dial rapidly spun in circles as soon as she was within twenty paces of him. The Detector glowed so intensely that she was forced to slide it up her arm and fold back her sleeve, doubling the layers covering it to conceal the illumination from the public during her introduction speech. Farther away, as she was now, the dial remained fixated in his direction, but the glow was diminished.

That young man is the most powerful Ver'ati in the city, she mused. Before his arrival, the Detector had always pointed towards Lord Ethan. That was not the only hand glowing tonight, however. The dial that detected active channeling was shining with bright pulses of light. Someone nearby was using the Power. Only a massive display could bring such brilliant flashes to the dial. It was forbidden to channel within the palace – someone was clearly breaking the law. All that energy flowing through the halls was most certainly the cause of the tremors.

Through the window, Havorie could see that the Echo stretched far beyond the palace grounds. All across Erotos, buildings swayed with the motion of the earth. Within the harbor directly south of the palace, a segment of the dock had broken loose and several ships had capsized and caught fire. Smoke from the flames covered the harbor like a thick fog. First responder Ver'ati were doing their best to squelch the flames, but the fire was spreading too quickly for them to handle without reinforcements.

What an utter mess....

"Step back from the window, my queen."

The stern voice of Damian Sarvo, her head of security, caught her by surprise. She would recognized it anywhere – always gruff and emotionless. Damian had watched over her for her entire life and over her mother for half of hers before that as well. She quickly hid the Detector under the sleeve of her gown before turning around. Damian was poised in the doorway of the chamber. His steps were always eerily silent.

"The glass could shatter from all the rumbling," he said. "Best if you return to bed and wait out the Echo."

Havorie frowned, but did as she was told, walking back to the bedside. Damian approached as well, drawing the canopy around the edge of the bed so that Havorie would be fully enclosed as she slept.

A butterfly, trapped in a net.

With the Detector fluctuating so brightly, Havorie had to place her hand over top of it so Damian wouldn't notice its shine. Power Artifacts were quite rare, even in Erotos, and tightly controlled by the Arcanum. If anyone learned she had several in her possession, they would most certainly be taken away. Havorie was queen, but she was still young, only eighteen years old. She was still treated like the heiress – a fragile ornament that must be kept locked away to ensure her survival into queendom…. No one seemed to care that she had already arrived.

It had been fourteen years since her mother's passing, Mast guide her soul, but everyone still acted like Havorie was the poor, four-year-old girl she had been when she first took the throne. Her duties had increased since that time, of course, but in the last few years, little had changed. She occasionally met with officials who had traveled across Aragwey to visit her court, but through the urging of her aids, every decision had already been made for her. She had daily coaching lessons on the conditions of her kingdom as well as continued classes on etiquette and public speaking from Lord Resoldo Byron, her steward, but ultimately she was little more than a figurehead.

Lord Ethan, despite his deteriorated state, headed the military, and all real decisions went through him and his men – the worst of which was that despicable general, Guther Aldune. Havorie was glad General Aldune was out of the city leading a war march along the Minthune River, as it meant she no longer had to tolerate him during her weekly briefings with the

Ver'konus. Lieutenant General Cale Fisman had taken over in his absence. At least he treated her with some respect, even though he too was versed in hiding the truth.

"Try to get some rest," said Damian after Havorie was once again under the covers. He silently exited the room, shutting the door behind him.

If it wasn't for the threat of losing her Detector, Havorie would have told Damian about the illegal channeling. Lives could easily be lost if the shaking got worse. Whoever was abusing the Power this recklessly needed to be stopped before it was too late.

With a sharp clink, a diagonal crack formed across the bedchamber window.

Havorie frowned. She couldn't tell the guards what she knew without explaining how she knew it, but she couldn't just allow this to continue either.

She slipped out of bed once more. She positioned one of her pillows perpendicularly beneath her covers so that its silhouette resembled her sleeping body. Stepping gingerly over to her dresser cabinet, she retrieved another one of her late mother's Power Artifacts from its perch. It was hidden atop a ledge inside the central cabinet drawer.

She peeked out her chamber door – Damian had begun his rounds. He would be back shortly. Now was her chance. She checked the pulsing dial. It was pointing east, towards Lord Ethan's wing of the palace. With her heart racing, she stepped briskly down the corridor, using the shaking as cover to move from room to room without notice. Damian's warning about the glass had not gone ignored. Havorie skirted the hallway along the wall opposite the windows. The maids and servants had paused in their duties when the vibrations first struck a low rumble in the panes of glass that faced the inner sanctums. They took cover away from the windows and the luminescent bulbs that Lord Ethan invented several decades ago. Until the shaking stopped, they would huddle in dark rooms beside walls they knew would not crumble, no matter how violent the tremors became.

Like the rest of the city, the palace was indestructible, built with Calvenite, an unnatural stone developed by Ver'ati Builders many centuries ago. The obsidian-colored material gleamed in the light – a modified version of slate; only the Power could mar its dark façade. Under pressure from the tremors, the walls would flex, but they would never crumble, no matter the strain.

Though tremors had been a common occurrence in the capital for as long as Havorie could remember, their frequency seemed to have increased significantly in recent memory. With the Power being summoned hundreds of times a day within the city's vicinity, it was a wonder they didn't occur more often. The quakes were usually among the easiest Echoes to manage, but Havorie had never experienced any this violent before.

Within an Echo, the properties of matter could fluctuate in countless ways once a vortex began to form; random, invisible undulations turning stone into liquid or drawing energy into uncontainable lightning storms. Loose objects could find their mass reduced to nothing and float away in defiance of the laws of physics, breaking rules even the most powerful Ver'ati could never hope to challenge. At times, whole sectors of the city had to be shut down until particularly offending Echoes had time to dissipate. It was not uncommon to hear of deaths during such occasions, but the Ver'konus did their best to obscure the truth when it came to matters of the Power.

While pausing to catch her breath, Havorie risked a glance out of one of the rattling windows. The garden atriums were well lit, even now as the night air cooled the eaves, drawing the heat up and out into the cloudless sky. Towering lamps illuminated the gardens in splotches of light that shifted with shadows as mostly bare branches wavered like spindly fingers in the crisp breeze. The air had a bite to it, leaving a light frost on the few leaves that still lingered within the brush. Winter was fast approaching – the days becoming shorter.

Havorie barely managed to keep her footing as the ground lurched violently to the side. She threw herself into the nearest room as the rumbling momentarily grew stronger. She had to wait until the shaking diminished enough for her to continue deeper into the east wing.

Chancing only a fleeting look out of her hiding place to check that no one was following, Havorie couldn't help but smile to herself. The corridor was still completely vacant. She had half expected to see Damian barreling after her, hand on his hilt, always ready for a fight. Little escaped him – he was the head of palace security and captain of the royal guard for a reason. Though her ruse had not yet been discovered, she knew her absence would not go unnoticed for much longer. It was only a matter of time before Damian or one of the other palace guards found her snooping out of bounds.

She inspected the Detector once more. The light was growing brighter as she closed the distance to the source of its attraction. The pulses were like a living heartbeat – invisible currents of energy flowing everywhere around her. The Detector picked up the subtle charges in the air.

"My queen?" came a confused voice from behind her in the dark.

Havorie jumped at the words. Spinning around, she breathed a sigh of relief as the light from the corridor lit the face of a young maid, no older than Havorie herself. She did not recognize the girl, which was fortunate. Many of her own maids would have turned her over to Damian on the spot. If the unfamiliarity went both ways, perhaps the girl could be intimidated into leaving her be.

There was a chance that the east wing maids were not fully briefed on her "voluntary" captivity. She had been all but a prisoner in her own home ever since the Whunes infiltrated the Underground. Havorie had to admit that King Garrett's slave beasts getting so close was a truly frightening reminder of his vast reach, but the lapse in security had been addressed. The only lingering result was that she now had to be sequestered away to keep her "safe" from the dangers of life. In reality, she knew it was just an excuse to minimize her rule.

Havorie couldn't help but think things would have been different had she developed the Gift of the Arcanum like her mother. The queen of Phandrol being Ver'ati was considered a good omen, and Havorie's mother, Nestra, had been a very good omen indeed. She brought a light to the people of Phandrol that Havorie could only aspire to. Havorie's subjects rained praise upon her. They rallied around her, cheered her every spoken word, but it was mostly just wishful thinking – the last stranglehold of hope lingering after her mother's unexpected demise. Queen Nestra's death was still mourned heavily, which was all the more reason for them to hold Havorie up in her place, apparently. They wanted to love her, needed to perhaps, simply because of the hope for peace and justice her mother had represented.

Havorie felt the disappointment in the air – saw it on the faces of every official she met with. She could never quite lived up to their expectations. Her blood tested negative for the gene that controls the Power. It skipped over her. She was just a regular person, where her mother had been barely one step short of Mast herself. Queen Nestra Elveres had been a kind leader – decisive, elegant, beautiful; she commanded the people and the military with grace. She gave Lord Ethan his title and allowed him to form the Ver'konus in her name, and the light shone brighter on the people of Phandrol for it. She was steadfast against King Garrett's threats and the military hordes of Kovehn – they had not been allowed to step one foot across the Crimson Waters during her reign.

The same could not be said for Havorie. The Whunes crawled through the Underground. Even though it had been a month now since the attack, and every last Whune had been purged from the sewers, people were still scared to go out at night. The streets of her own capital were unsafe! Havorie could hardly fault her subjects for their fear.

She stared at the young maid. The girl's brown hair gathered beneath a cream-colored bonnet before running behind her ears in two short braids. She had a look of fear in her eyes, though Havorie couldn't tell if it was from the increased intensity of the earthquake or if the girl was simply shocked to see her queen sprinting through the hallways dressed only in a nightgown. No one could blame her if it was the latter. Havorie glanced around the room – it was one of the many linen closets that serviced the guest rooms along this corridor – she could think of no plausible excuse for her presence in such a place.

"What is your name, girl?" Havorie asked the maid, being sure to speak in the most stately, regal tone she could muster. Lord Byron would have been proud – old Resoldo had spent countless hours trying to mold her into a proper queen during their daily lessons together, starting back before she even knew how to walk. He probably thought it all landed on deaf ears.

"Ervia. Ervia Sindel... my queen," said the maid, her voice escaping as a squeak. "Pardon me, but what... is that?" Her eyes were locked on the amber glow of the Detector, its light pulsating under the thin lace of Havorie's sleeve. A pile of folded linens toppled over in the corner of the room as the intensity of the quake grew stronger.

Havorie swept a lock of flaxen hair out of her eyes as it dangled into view. The fluffed out nest of hair that was usually styled into dense curls by Madam Jusair, her personal maid, was beginning to fall flat at this hour. Ervia was staring back at Havorie questioningly. She had to say something....

"Ervia," Havorie said, trying to construct a better excuse than simply speaking the truth outright, but nothing came to mind. "I can't have you telling anyone that you've seen me," she said simply. Ervia waited for her to continue, but Havorie realized she wouldn't believe a word of her explanation until she witnessed the reading on the Detector firsthand.

Havorie pulled up the sleeve of her nightgown, fully exposing the glowing Artifact on her wrist. She held it up to Ervia so the young maid could get a look at what had drawn Havorie from her chambers at such a late hour. "It's like the Charisms," she explained. "Someone is channeling a vast amount of Power within the east wing."

"But that's forbidden within the palace," said Ervia, frowning.

Havorie nodded. "I'm on my way to investigate.... Are you with me?" Ervia had a nervous look on her face again, but Havorie couldn't resist smiling. It was clear from Ervia's expression that she didn't want to go against her queen.

Just as Havorie expected, Ervia smiled meekly back at her. Most people had no idea of the diminished state of the queen's authority and would never risk openly antagonizing her. Together, they went into the hallway as the intensity of the tremors finally waned. Havorie ran as fast as her legs would carry her. She was more than a little surprised to see Ervia keeping up as they rounded the corner, entering Lord Ethan's residence within the palace. Ethan's study and personal chambers were one floor down, leaving the floor Havorie and Ervia were on open for use mostly by the wait staff.

Havorie glanced at the Detector. The channeling was directly ahead now. There were a few rooms to pick from. The doors were all closed – any one of them could be concealing the source of the dial's attraction.

"Not that one," Ervia whispered. "Cherry and Silvia were still tidying up in there when the shaking started."

Havorie pointed questioningly at the next room over. Ervia shrugged. There was only one way to find out.... Havorie turned the knob delicately. The clicking sound it made was too soft to be heard over the rumble of the quake. The door opened inward. Havorie pushed on it slightly and peered through the crack. It was too dark to see anything. She gave up on caution and pushed the door fully open, letting the hallway light fill in the shadows. She hit a switch on the wall just to the right of the door and several luminescent bulbs flickered on overhead, lighting the empty meeting hall in its entirety. They were directly above Lord Ethan's quarters now.

Checking the Detector again, Havorie watched as the dial began spinning in circles. She was too close to the channeling to get any further information from the device.

We must be directly above the culprit.

Havorie reached into a pocket in her nightgown and pulled out what appeared to be a rolled up scroll with ornately engraved silver end caps – the Power Artifact she retrieved from her dresser. Havorie crouched to the floor and pulled the scroll open. Where one would expect to see canvas, a thin film of translucent material reflected the luminescent bulbs overhead. As she pressed the see-through sheet to the floor of the meeting hall, a curious thing began to happen along the film. The tile beneath shimmered and began to disappear. It was as if the floor had turned to glass. Looking into the translucent material allowed Havorie to peer directly into Lord Ethan's bedroom as if through a window. Her view was blocked slightly, so she slid the scroll across the tile to a location with a better vantage point. The tile had not actually been altered at all.

Havorie glanced up at Ervia. The girl was dumbfounded, her jaw held partially askew. It must have been a strange sight for a commoner, even in the capital of magic. Havorie smiled faintly. "You can't tell anyone about this either," she said.

Peering through the floor, she could see Lord Ethan lying motionless in his bed, his thin, white hair matted to his brow by perspiration. Doctor Hilven Crane – head physician and Ameliorator of the Ver'konus – and Lieutenant General Cale Fisman – acting commander – along with several other men Havorie did not recognize, all stood over Lord Ethan. He was strapped to his bed.

At first, it appeared that Ethan was entirely doused with a thick layer of sweat, reflecting the room's lights off his skin, but after a moment, Havorie realized that it was his skin itself that was glowing with shimmering, white light and not a reflection at all. The men standing over him were drawing on the Power, and together they were doing something to Lord Ethan's body.

Ethan suddenly convulsed, his chest ratcheting up despite his restraints. Havorie could clearly see he was screaming in pain, but no sounds carried through the floor or her little window. Calvenite could deaden even the harshest screams.

"What are they doing to him?" asked Ervia, her complexion becoming ashen as she sat beside Havorie, watching intently through the window.

Before Havorie could answer, Ethan stopped convulsing, but the lull lasted only a moment before something even more horrifying started happening. Ethan's skin, along with his clothes, seemed to be melting off his body. His wispy hair fell away as his scalp drooped off and something black began poking through. His entire body was turning into gray goo, his skin shearing off in piles on the bed. Ervia stifled a scream as Ethan's fingernails detached and fell away from his hands. Havorie felt like she was going to be sick. She gagged slightly, covering her mouth with her hand as she watched his pink insides bubble to the surface. They were spilling out all over.

They were killing him and there was nothing she could do but watch....

Without warning, a face emerged from the mound of sticky flesh that was once Ethan's old face. The new mouth gasped for air and eyelids shot open, revealing new eyes which Havorie could only describe as sparkling, blue gems. They appeared to stare straight at her, though there was no way anyone below could have known she was watching.

She suddenly realized that she was actually witnessing a new layer of skin forming beneath the old. Ethan was shedding his old body like a cocoon. The black fibers poking through his old scalp was a full head of new hair. His new skin was smooth and unblemished; youthful and vibrant. He was rosy pink like a newborn baby. Despite having been around Ver'ati her entire life, Ethan's transformation was by far the strangest thing Havorie had ever witnessed.

As the men standing around Lord Ethan lowered their hands, the glow vanished from Ethan's skin and, simultaneously, the earth stopped trembling. Their concentrated use of the Power had caused mayhem all across the city.

Havorie's heart fluttered mercilessly as she took in Ethan's naked form. Doctor Crane stepped up to Ethan's side and released the restraints holding his arms and legs in place, allowing him to rise up from his bed. The remainder of his old skin slopped onto the floor as he took his first steps around the room. He appeared to be only twenty-five years old now, fresh muscles bulging in his arms and shoulders. He was perfectly healthy, in the prime of his youth – handsome didn't even begin to describe him! Havorie could feel her cheeks warming as she spied down on him. She dared not glance over at Ervia, though she knew the girl was watching her now with a curious smile on her lips.

"There you are!" said a voice from the hallway, making both girls jump in surprise.

Havorie had been so engrossed in watching Ethan as he twisted and flexed his new body that she hadn't even heard the door open. She immediately pulled the scroll off the floor, causing the little window to vanish as soon as it was lifted.

Havorie hoped the blush had faded from her face; she wanted to giggle just thinking about how silly she had been, spying on Lord Ethan like that, though she wished she could get one more glimpse of his chiseled body....

"I see you've made a new friend," said Damian, stepping forward, allowing his large frame to fill the doorway. "It's perfectly alright if you want to see more of her. In fact, I think it is good for a young lady such as yourself to have friends, but I can't have you running away like this again, especially not during a quake."

"I'm sorry, Damian," said Havorie, playing on his assumptions. "I just didn't think I would be allowed to be friends with a maid."

"Nonsense," said Damian.   His stubble-covered chin wrinkled slightly as if Havorie had insulted him. "You are queen and may choose your own company. Let's just make next time an official visit."

"Alright," said Havorie as she stood up from the floor.

She slid the scroll back into her pocket, being sure to call no notice to it as she followed Damian out through the doorway. He stayed a pace in front of her, his watchful eyes always searching meticulously for hidden threats, even here within the safety of the palace.

"See you tomorrow, Ervia!" she said cheerfully. She shot the girl one last meaningful glance before she stepped out of sight entirely. She hoped it would be enough to keep her silent about what she had seen, at least for the time being.

About the Author:

 **Paul Keyes** was born and raised in Washington State between the beautiful waterways of the Puget Sound and the always majestic Cascade Mountains. Fascinated by the political and social workings of the world, he obtained degrees in both creative writing and economics from the University of Washington. In his spare time, he is an experienced pianist and composer, which has helped him bring a heightened sense of rhythm and emotional resonance to his written passages. Over the years, he has traveled everywhere from China to the Mediterranean, soaking in the many diverse cultures and histories. Throughout it all, there is no place he would rather be than back home, drifting on a boat somewhere between the San Juan Islands and his home port of Edmonds.

You can follow Paul on Twitter **@PaulJKeyes**, visit his website, **ArcadianComplex.com**, or like the series at **Facebook.com/ArcadianComplex** to become an honorary Arcadian!

CPSIA information can be obtained
at www.ICGtesting.com
Printed in the USA
FSOW04n0529240815
10082FS